FEAST DAY OF FOOLS

FEAST DAY OF FOOLS

JAMES LEE BURKE

WHEELER
WINDSOR
PARAGON

This Large Print edition is published by Thorndike Press, Waterville, Maine USA and by AudioGo Ltd, Bath, England.
Copyright © 2011 by James Lee Burke.
The moral right of the author has been asserted.
Wheeler Publishing, a part of Gale, Cengage Learning.

Wheeler Publishing Large Print Hardcover.
The text of this Large Print edition is unabridged.
Other aspects of the book may vary from the original edition.
Set in 16 pt. Plantin.

LIBRARY OF CONGRESS CATALOGING-IN-PUBLICATION DATA

Burke, James Lee, 1936–
    Feast day of fools / by James Lee Burke.
      p. cm.
    ISBN-13: 978-1-4104-4214-7 (hardcover)
    ISBN-10: 1-4104-4214-4 (hardcover)
    1. Texas—Fiction. 2. Large type books. I. Title.
PS3552.U723F43 2011b
813'.54—dc23   2011033664

BRITISH LIBRARY CATALOGUING-IN-PUBLICATION DATA AVAILABLE
Published in the U.S. in 2011 by arrangement with Simon & Schuster, Inc.
Published in the U.K. in 2012 by arrangement with The Orion Publishing Group Ltd.
U.K. Hardcover: 978 1 445 87325 1 (Windsor Large Print)
U.K. Softcover: 978 1 445 87326 8 (Paragon Large Print)

Printed in the United States of America
1 2 3 4 5 6 7 15 14 13 12 11

For Dora, Mike, and Alicia Liu

The wild beasts will honor me, the jackals and the ostriches, for I give water in the wilderness, rivers in the desert, to give drink to my chosen people.

— Isaiah 43:20

CHAPTER ONE

Some people said Danny Boy Lorca's visions came from the mescal that had fried his brains, or the horse-quirt whippings he took around the ears when he served time on Sugar Land Farm, or the fact he'd been a middleweight club fighter through a string of dust-blown sinkholes where the locals were given a chance to beat up what was called a tomato can, a fighter who leaked blood every place he was hit, in this case a rumdum Indian who ate his pain and never flinched when his opponents broke their hands on his face.

Danny Boy's black hair was cut in bangs and fitted his head like a helmet. His physique was as square as a door, his clothes always smelling of smoke from the outdoor fires he cooked his food on, his complexion as dark and coarsened by the sun and wind as the skin on a shrunken head. In summer, he wore long-sleeve cotton work shirts buttoned at the throat and wrists to keep the heat out, and in winter, a canvas coat and an Australian flop hat tied down over his ears with a scarf. He fought his hangovers in a sweat lodge, bathed in ice water, planted by the moon, cast demons out of his body into sand paintings that he flung at the sky, prayed in a loincloth on a mesa in the midst of electric storms, and sometimes experienced either seizures or trances during which he spoke a language that was neither Apache nor Navajo, although he claimed it was both.

Sometimes he slept in the county jail. Other nights he slept behind the saloon or in the stucco house where he lived on the cusp of a wide alluvial floodplain bordered on the southern horizon by purple mountains that in the late-afternoon warp of heat seemed to take on the ragged irregularity of sharks' teeth.

The sheriff who allowed Danny Boy to sleep at the jail was an elderly six-feet-five widower by the name of Hackberry Holland, whose bad back and chiseled profile and Stetson hat and thumb-buster .45 revolver and history as a drunk and a whoremonger were the sum total of his political cachet, if not his life. To most people in the area, Danny Boy was an object of pity and ridicule and contempt. His solipsistic behavior and his barroom harangues were certainly characteristic of a wet brain, they said. But Sheriff Holland, who had been a prisoner of war for

10

almost three years in a place in North Korea called No Name Valley, wasn't so sure. The sheriff had arrived at an age when he no longer speculated on the validity of a madman's visions or, in general, the foibles of human behavior. Instead, Hackberry Holland's greatest fear was his fellow man's propensity to act collectively, in militaristic lockstep, under the banner of God and country. Mobs did not rush across town to do good deeds, and in Hackberry's view, there was no more odious taint on any social or political endeavor than universal approval. To Hackberry, Danny Boy's alcoholic madness was a respite from a far greater form of delusion.

It was late on a Wednesday night in April when Danny Boy walked out into the desert with an empty duffel bag and an army-surplus entrenching tool, the sky as black as soot, the southern horizon pulsing with electricity that resembled gold wires, the softness of the ground crumbling under his cowboy boots, as though he were treading across the baked shell of an enormous riparian environment that had been layered and beveled and smoothed with a sculptor's knife. At the base of a mesa, he folded the entrenching tool into the shape of a hoe and knelt down and began digging in the ground, scraping through the remains of fossilized leaves and fish and birds that others said were millions of years old. In the distance, an igneous flash spread silently through the clouds, flaring in great yellow pools, lighting the desert floor and the cactus and mesquite and the greenery that was trying to bloom along a riverbed that never held water except during the monsoon season. Just before the light died, Danny Boy saw six men advancing across the plain toward him, like figures caught inside the chemical mix of a half-developed photograph, their torsos slung with rifles.

He scraped harder in the dirt, trenching a circle around what appeared to be two tapered soft-nosed rocks protruding from the incline below the mesa. Then his e-tool broke through an armadillo's burrow. He inverted the handle and stuck it down the hole and wedged the earth upward until the burrow split across the top and he could work his hand deep into the hole, up to the elbow, and feel the shapes of the clustered objects that were as pointed and hard as calcified dugs.

The night air was dense with an undefined feral odor, like cougar scat and a sun-bleached carcass and burnt animal hair and water that had gone stagnant in a sandy drainage traced with the crawl lines of reptiles. The wind blew between the hills in the south, and he felt its coolness and the dampness of the rain mist on his face. He saw the leaves on the mesquite ripple like green lace, the mesas and buttes shimmering whitely against the clouds, then disappearing into the darkness again. He smelled the piñon and juniper and the scent of delicate flowers that bloomed only at night and whose petals dropped off and clung to the rocks at sunrise like translucent pieces of colored rice paper. He stared at the southern horizon but saw no sign of the six men carrying rifles. He wiped his mouth on his sleeve and went back to work, scooping out a big hole around the stonelike objects that were welded together as tightly as concrete.

The first shot was a tiny *pop,* like a wet firecracker exploding. He stared into the fine mist swirling through the hills. Then the lightning flared again, and he saw the armed men stenciled against the horizon and the silhouettes of two other figures who had broken from cover and were running toward the north, toward Danny Boy, toward a place that should have been safe from the criminality and violence that he believed was threading its way out of Mexico into his life.

He lifted the nest of stony egg-shaped artifacts from the earth and slid them into the duffel bag and pulled the cord tight through the brass eyelets at the top. He headed back toward his house, staying close to the bottom of the mesa, avoiding the tracks he had made earlier, which he knew the armed men would eventually see and follow. Then a bolt of lightning exploded on top of

13

the mesa, lighting the floodplain and the willows along the dry streambed and the arroyos and crevices and caves in the hillsides as brightly as the sun.

He plunged down a ravine, holding the duffel bag and e-tool at his sides for balance. He crouched behind a rock, hunching against it, his face turned toward the ground so it would not reflect light. He heard someone running past him in the darkness, someone whose breath was not only labored but desperate and used up and driven by fear rather than a need for oxygen.

When he thought that perhaps his wait was over, that the pursuers of the fleeing man had given up and gone away, allowing him to return to his house with the treasure he had dug out of the desert floor, he heard a sound he knew only too well. It was the pleading lament of someone who had no hope, not unlike that of an animal caught in a steel trap or a new inmate, a fish, just off the bus at Sugar Land Pen, going into his first night of lockdown with four or five mainline cons waiting for him in the shower room.

The pursuers had dragged the second fleeing man from behind a tangle of deadwood and tumbleweed that had wedged in a collapsed corral that dog-food contractors had once used to pen mustangs. The fugitive was barefoot and blood-streaked and terrified, his shirt hanging in rags on the pencil lines that were his ribs, a manacle on one wrist, a brief length of cable swinging loosely from it.

"*¿Dónde está?*" a voice said.

"*No sé.*"

"What you mean you don't know? *Tú sabes.*"

"*No, hombre. No sé nada.*"

"*¿Para dónde se fue?*"

"He didn't tell me where he went."

"*¿Es la verdad?*"

"*Claro que sí.*"

"You don't know if you speak Spanish or English, you've sold out to so many people. You are a very bad policeman."

"*No, señor.*"

"*Estás mintiendo, chico. Pobrecito.*"

"*Tengo familia, señor. Por favor. Soy un obrero, como usted.* I'm just like you, a worker. I got to take care of my family. Hear me, man. I know people who can make you rich."

For the next fifteen minutes, Danny Boy Lorca tried to shut out the sounds that came from the mouth of the man who wore the manacle and length of severed cable on one wrist. He tried to shrink himself inside his own skin, to squeeze all light and sensation and awareness from his mind, to become a black dot that could drift away on the wind and re-form later as a shadow that would eventually become flesh and blood again.

Maybe one day he would forget the fear that caused him to stop being who he was; maybe he would meet the man he chose not to help and be forgiven by him and hence become capable of forgiving himself. When all those things happened, he might even forget what his fellow human beings were capable of doing.

When the screams of the tormented man finally softened and died and were swallowed by the wind, Danny Boy raised his head above a rock and gazed down the incline where the tangle of tumbleweed and deadwood partially obscured the handiwork of the armed men. The wind was laced with grit and rain that looked like splinters of glass. When lightning rippled across the sky, Danny Boy saw the armed men in detail.

Five of them could have been pulled at random from any jail across the border. But it was the leader who made a cold vapor wrap itself around Danny Boy's heart. He was taller than the others and stood out for many reasons; in fact, the incongruities in his appearance only added to the darkness of his persona. His body was not stitched with scars or chained with Gothic-letter and swastika and death's-head tats. Nor was his head shaved into a bullet or his mouth surrounded by a circle of carefully trimmed beard. Nor did he wear lizard-skin boots that were plated on the heels and tips. His running shoes looked fresh out of the box; his navy blue sweatpants had a red stripe down each leg, similar to a design a nineteenth-century Mexican cavalry officer might wear. His skin was clean, his chest flat, the nipples no bigger than dimes, his shoulders wide, his arms like pipe stems, his pubic hair showing just above the white cord that held up his pants. An inverted M16 was cross-strapped across his bare back; a canteen hung at his side from a web belt, and a hatchet and a long thin knife of the kind that was used to dress wild game. The man leaned over and speared something with the tip of the knife and lifted it in the air, examining it against the lights flashing in the clouds. He cinched the object with a lanyard and tied it to his belt, letting it drip down his leg.

Then Danny Boy saw the leader freeze, as though he had just smelled an invasive odor on the wind. He turned toward Danny Boy's hiding place and stared up the incline. *"¿Quién está en la oscuridad?"* he said.

Danny Boy shrank down onto the ground, the rocks cutting into his knees and the heels of his hands.

"You see something up there?" one of the other men said.

But the leader did not speak, in either Spanish or English.

"It's just the wind. There's nothing out

here. The wind plays tricks," the first man said.

"*¿Ahora para dónde vamos?*" another man said.

The leader waited a long time to answer. "*¿Dónde vive La Magdalena?*" he asked.

"Don't fuck with that woman, Krill. Bad luck, man."

But the leader, whose nickname was Krill, did not reply. A moment that could have been a thousand years passed; then Danny Boy heard the six men begin walking back down through the riverbed toward the distant mountains from which they had come, their tracks cracking the clay and braiding together in long serpentine lines. After they were out of sight, Danny Boy stood up and looked down at their bloody handiwork, scattered across the ground in pieces, glimmering in the rain.

Pam Tibbs was Hackberry's chief deputy. Her mahogany-colored hair was sunburned white at the tips, and it hung on her cheeks in the indifferent way it might have on a teenage girl. She wore wide-ass jeans and half-topped boots and a polished gun belt and a khaki shirt with an American flag sewn on one sleeve. Her moods were mercurial, her words often confrontational. Her potential for violence seldom registered on her adversaries until things happened that should not have happened. When she was angry, she sucked in her cheeks, accentuating a mole by her mouth, turning her lips into a button. Men often thought she was trying to be cute. They were mistaken.

At noon she was drinking a cup of coffee at her office window when she saw Danny Boy Lorca stumbling down the street toward the department, bent at the torso as though waging war against invisible forces, a piece of newspaper matting against his chest before it flapped loose and scudded across the intersection. When Danny Boy tripped on the curb and fell hard on one knee, then fell again when he tried to pick himself up, Pam Tibbs set down her coffee cup and went outside, the wind blowing lines in her hair. She bent down, her breasts hanging heavy against her shirt, and lifted him to his feet and walked him inside.

"I messed myself. I got to get in the shower," he said.

"You know where it is," she said.

"They killed a man."

She didn't seem to hear what he had said. She glanced at the cast-iron spiral of steps that led upstairs to the jail. "Can you make it by yourself?"

"I ain't drunk. I was this morning, but I ain't now. The guy in charge, I remember his name." Danny Boy closed his eyes and opened them again. "I think I do."

"I'll be upstairs in a minute and open the cell."

"I hid all the time they was doing it."

"Say again."

"I hid behind a big rock. Maybe for fifteen minutes. He was screaming all the while."

She nodded, her expression neutral. Danny Boy's eyes were scorched with hangover, his mouth white at the corners with dried mucus, his breath dense and sedimentary, like a load of fruit that had been dumped down a stone well. He waited, although she didn't know for what. Was it absolution? "Don't slip on the steps," she said.

She tapped on Hackberry's door but opened it without waiting for him to answer. He was on the phone, his eyes drifting to hers. "Thanks for the alert, Ethan. We'll get back to you if we hear anything," he said into the receiver. He hung up and seemed to think about the conversation he'd just had, his gaze not actually taking her in. "What's up?" he said.

"Danny Boy Lorca just came in drunk. He says he saw a man killed."

"Where?"

"I didn't get that far. He's in the shower."

Hackberry scratched at his cheek. Outside, the American flag was snapping on its pole against a gray sky, the fabric washed so thin that the light showed through the threads. "That was Ethan Riser at the FBI. They're

20

looking for a federal employee who might have been grabbed by some Mexican drug mules and taken to a prison across the border. An informant said the federal employee could have gotten loose and headed for home."

"I've heard Danny Boy has been digging up dinosaur eggs south of his property."

"I didn't know there were any around here," Hackberry said.

"If they're out there, he'd be the guy to find them."

"How's that?" he said, although he wasn't really listening.

"A guy who believes he can see the navel of the world from his back window? He says all power comes out of this hole in the ground. Down inside the hole is another world. That's where the rain and the corn gods live. Compared to a belief system like that, hunting for dinosaur eggs seems like bland stuff."

"That's interesting."

She waited, as though examining his words. "Try this: He says the killing took fifteen minutes to transpire. He says he heard it all. You think this might be the guy the feds are looking for?"

Hackberry bounced his knuckles lightly up and down on the desk blotter and stood up, straightening his back, trying to hide the pain that crept into his face, his outline massive against the window. "Bring your recorder and a pot of coffee, will you?" he said.

The report Danny Boy gave of the murder he had witnessed was not one that lent itself to credulity. "You were drinking before you went digging for dinosaur eggs?" Hackberry said.

"No, sir, I hadn't had a drop in two days."

"Two days?" Hackberry said.

"Yes, sir, every bit of it. I got eighty-sixed. I didn't have no more money, anyway."

"Well, you must have seen what you saw," Hackberry said. "Want to take a ride?"

Danny Boy didn't answer. He was sitting on the iron bunk of his cell, wearing lace-up boots without socks and clean jailhouse jeans and a denim shirt, his hair wet from his shower and his skin as dark as smoke. His hands were folded in his lap, his shoulders slumped.

"What's the problem?" Hackberry said.

"I'm ashamed of what I done."

"Not helping this guy out?"

"Yes, sir. They was talking about La Magdalena."

"Who?"

"A holy woman."

"Don't feel so down about this, partner. They would have killed you, too. If they had, you wouldn't be helping us in the investigation, would you?" Hackberry said.

Danny Boy's eyes were focused on a spot

22

ten inches in front of him. "You didn't see it."

"No, I didn't," Hackberry replied. He started to say something about his own experience in No Name Valley many years ago but thought better of it. "Let's get this behind us, partner."

Pam Tibbs drove the three of them down the main street of the town in the department's Jeep Cherokee, the traffic light over the intersection bouncing on its cable in the wind. The newer buildings on the street were constructed of cinder blocks; some of the older ones were built out of fieldstones that had been cemented together and sheathed with plaster or stucco that had fallen off in chunks, leaving patterns that resembled a contagious skin disease. Pam followed a winding two-lane state highway southward through hills that looked like big brown ant piles or a sepia-tinted photograph taken on the surface of Mars. Then she drove across Danny Boy's property, past his stucco house and his barn that was plated from the bottom to the eaves with hubcaps, onto the geological fault that bled into Old Mexico and a strip of terrain that always seemed to ring with distant bugles echoing off the hills. For Hackberry Holland, these were not the horns blowing along the road to Roncevaux.

Pam shifted down and kept the Jeep on the high ground above the riverbed that Danny had walked the previous night, the hard-packed gravel vibrating through the frame. "There," Danny said, pointing.

"Under the buzzards?" Hackberry said.

"Yes, sir."

"Where are your dinosaur eggs?"

"At the house."

"You sure those aren't rocks?" Hackberry said, his eyes crinkling at the corners.

But his attempt to relieve Danny Boy of depression and fear was to no avail. The guilt and sorrow Danny Boy had taken with him from the previous night would probably come aborning in his dreams for many years, and all the beer in all the beer joints in Texas would not make one dent in it, Hackberry thought. "Get upwind from it," he said to Pam.

She crossed a slough chained with red pools and layered with clusters of black butterflies sucking moisture from the sand, their wings shuddering as though they were ingesting toxin. She parked on the incline, above the collapsed rails of the corral that had been used by a one-eyed man who killed and sold mustangs for dog food. When Hackberry stepped out on the passenger side, his eyes roved over the tangles of tumbleweed and bleached wood and the remains of the man whose death may have been the most merci-ful moment in his life. "You ever see anything like this?" Pam said, her words clotting in her throat.

"Not exactly. Maybe close, but not exactly," Hackberry replied.

"What are we dealing with?" she said.

"Call the coroner's office, then get Felix and R.C. down here. I want photos of this from every angle. String as much tape as you can around the crime scene. Make sure nobody disturbs those tracks going south."

She went to the Jeep and made the calls, then walked back down the incline, pulling on a pair of latex gloves, her upper arms ridging with muscle. Danny Boy remained in the vehicle, his head lowered. "What did he say the leader's name was? Krill?" she said to Hackberry.

"I think that was it."

"I've heard that before. It's Spanish?"

"It's a shrimplike creature that whales eat."

"Funny name for a killer with an M16 strapped on his back." When he didn't answer, she looked at him. "You okay, boss?"

He nodded at the slope above where the victim had died.

"Jesus Christ," she said.

"He was scalped, too."

Then the wind changed, and a sickening gray odor blew into their faces. It was like fish roe that had dried on warm stone and the putrescence of offal and the liquid wastes poured from a bucket into a ditch behind a brothel on a Saturday night, and it made Pam Tibbs hold her wrist to her mouth and walk back up the incline, fighting to hold back the bilious surge in her stomach.

Hackberry stepped back from the site and repositioned himself so he was upwind again. But that did not change the nature of the scene or its significance. Often he wondered, as an anthropologist might, what the historical environment of the human race actually was. It wasn't a subdivision of sprinkled lawns and three-bedroom houses inside of which the television set had become the cool fire of modern man. Could it be a vast sun-baked plain broken by mesas and parched riverbeds where the simian and the mud-slathered and the unredeemed hunted one another with sharpened sticks, where the only mercy meted out was the kind that came as a result of satiation and exhaustion?

The compulsion to kill was in the gene pool, he thought. Those who denied it were the same ones who killed through proxy. Every professional executioner, every professional soldier, knew that one of his chief duties was to protect those he served from knowledge about themselves. Or at least those were the perceptions that governed Hackberry's judgments about societal behavior, even though he shared them with no one.

He looked to the south. Dust or rain had smudged out the mountains, and the plain seemed to stretch endlessly into the distance, the way a snowfield could extend itself into the bottom of a blue winter sky, dipping over the edge of the earth into nothingness. Hackberry found himself swallowing, a nameless fear clutching at his viscera.

The coroner was Darl Wingate, an enigmatic single man who had been a forensic pathologist with the United States Army and CID before he retired back to the place of his birth. He was laconic, with sunken cheeks and a pencil mustache, and he often had liquor on his breath by ten A.M. He also had degrees from Johns Hopkins and Stanford. No one had ever been quite sure why he chose to spend his twilight years in a desolate place on the edge of the Great American Desert. It was certainly not because he was filled with compassion for the poor and the oppressed, although he was not a callous man. Hackberry believed that Darl Wingate was simply a pragmatist who saw no separation or difference between the various categories of the human family. In Darl's mind, they all belonged to one long daisy chain: They were creatures who came out of the womb's darkness and briefly saw light before their mouths were stopped with dust and their eyes sealed six feet down. As a consequence of his beliefs, he remained a witness and not a participant.

Darl placed a breath mint on his tongue

and put on latex gloves and a surgeon's mask before he approached the remains of the dead man. The day had grown warmer, the sky more gray, like the color of greasewood smoke, and gnats were rising from the sand.

"What do you think?" Hackberry asked.

"About what?" Darl said.

"What you're looking at," Hackberry replied, trying to repress his impatience.

"The fingers scattered up on the slope went one at a time. The toes were next. My guess is he died from shock. He was probably dead when he was scalped and taken apart, but I can't say for sure."

"You ever work one like this?"

"On a couple of backstreets in Bangkok. The guy who did it was a church missionary."

"So the human race is rotten?"

"Say again?" Darl said.

"You're not giving me a lot of help."

"What else can I provide you with?"

"Anything of specific value. I don't need the history of man's inhumanity to man."

"From the appearance of the victim — his nails, his emaciated condition, the infection on his manacled wrist, the scabs on his knees, and the lice eggs in the remnant of his hair — I'd say he was held prisoner in primitive and abusive conditions for at least several weeks. The scarring on his face and neck suggests smallpox, which tells me he's probably

Mexican, not American. What doesn't fit is his dental care."

"I don't follow you."

"It's first-rate."

"How would you explain the discrepancy?"

"My guess is he came from humble origins but did something good with his life," Darl said.

"Successful criminals don't see dentists?"

"Only when the pain makes it imperative. The rest of the time they're getting laid or huffing flake up their nose. I think this guy took care of himself. So far, I see no tattoos, no signs of intravenous use, no scars on his hands. I think we might be looking at the remains of a cop."

"Not bad."

"What happened here says more about the killer than the victim," Darl said.

"Pardon?"

"Whatever information he had, he shouted it to the heavens early on. But his tormentor took it to the finish line anyway. You got any idea what he wanted?"

"You ever hear of somebody called La Magdalena?" Hackberry asked.

Darl nodded. "Superstitious wets call her that."

"Darl, would you please just spit it out?"

The coroner screwed a cigarette into his cigarette holder and put it between his teeth. "Sometimes they call her *la china.* Her real name is Anton Ling. She's Indo-Chinese or French-Chinese. She looks like an actress in a Graham Greene film. Ring any bells?"

Hackberry blinked.

"Yeah, that one," Darl said. He lit his cigarette and breathed a stream of smoke into the air. "I remember something you once said. It was 'Wars of enormous importance are fought in places nobody cares about.' "

"Meaning?"

"Deal me out of this one," Darl said. "It stinks from the jump. I think you're going to be splashing through pig flop up to your ankles."

CHAPTER TWO

Six hours later, Pam Tibbs and Hackberry Holland drove down a long dirt track, twenty miles southwest of the county seat, to a paintless gingerbread house that had a wide gallery with a swing on it and baskets of petunias and impatiens hung from the eaves. The landscape looked particularly strange in the sunset, like terrain that might have been used in a 1940s movie, hard-packed and rolling and biscuit-colored and notched with ravines, marbled by thunderheads and the reddening of the sky and dissected by lines of cedar fence posts that had no wire on them.

Lightning rods flanged each end of the house's roof, and a windmill in back was ginning furiously, pumping a jet of water into an aluminum tank where three spavined horses were drinking. A white-over brick wall surrounded the house a hundred feet out, like the walls at the Alamo, the top festooned with razor wire and spiked with broken glass. The wood gates on three of the walls had been removed and pulled apart and the planks used to frame up two big vegetable gardens humped with compost, creating the effect of a legionnaire's outpost whose defense system had been rendered worthless.

"What's the deal with this place?" Pam asked.

"Miss Anton bought the house from a secessionist who took over the courthouse about twenty years ago. After she moved in, I think the Rangers were sorry they locked up the secessionist."

"Miss?" Pam said.

Hackberry was sitting in the passenger seat, his Stetson over his eyes. "It's a courtesy," he said.

They parked the Jeep outside the wall, and got out and studied the southern horizon through a pair of binoculars. "Take a look at this," she said.

Hackberry rolled a folder filled with eight-by-ten photos into a cone and stuck it in the side pocket of his trousers, then focused the binoculars on a rocky flume rimmed by mesquite and scrub oak and willow trees. The sky above the hills looked like green gas, the air glistening with heat and humidity, the shell of an automobile half buried in the bleached-out earth, the metal wind-polished as bright as foil. But the contemporary story of this particular place was written across the bottom of the flume. It was layered with moldy clothes, scraps of plastic tarp, tennis shoes split at the seams, smeared toilet paper, spoiled food, empty water bottles, discarded sanitary napkins, and plastic diapers slathered with feces. A circle of turkey buzzards floated just above the hills, the edges of their wings feathering in the wind.

"She used to be part of that Underground Railroad or whatever?" Pam said.

"Up in Kansas, I think," Hackberry said. "But I wouldn't put it in the past tense."

"You call the feds yet?"

"I haven't gotten to it."

He could feel her staring at the side of his face.

"If I can make a suggestion —" she began.

"Don't," he said.

"You were a lawyer for the ACLU. That name has the status of whale shit around here. Why add to your problems?"

"Can you stop using that language on the job? I think both you and Maydeen have an incurable speech defect."

He had stepped into it again, allying his dispatcher Maydeen Stoltz with Pam; they were undefeatable when they joined forces against him, to the extent that he sometimes had to lock his office door and pretend he was gone from the building.

"You don't know how to cover your ass," Pam said. "So others have to do it for you. Ask anybody in the department. Your constituency might tell you they love Jesus, but the truth is, they want you to grease the bad guys and not bother them with details."

"I can't believe I'm the sheriff of this county and I have to listen to this. And I mean listen to it every day."

"That's the problem. Your heart is too big. You need to be more assertive. Ask Maydeen." Pam took the binoculars from his hand and replaced them in the leather case and dropped the case on the driver's seat. "I say too much?"

"No, why would you possibly think that?" he replied.

But Pam's hands were on her hips, and she was obviously thinking about something else. "This woman is supposed to perform miracles? She's Our Lady of Lourdes out on the plains?"

"No," he said. "No, I mean I don't know. I can't keep up with your conversation. I can't track your thoughts, Pam. You're impossible to talk with."

"What you're not hearing is that other people know your weak spot. Don't let this Chinese broad jerk you around. Too many people around here already hate your guts. Wake up. You're kind to the wrong people."

"I don't see it that way. Not at all."

"That's exactly what I'm talking about."

Hackberry fitted on his Stetson and widened his eyes, letting the moment pass, his face tight in the wind. "When we talk with this lady, we remember who we are. We treat people with respect, particularly when they've paid their share of dues."

"People with causes have a way of letting others do their time on the cross. Tell me I'm full of shit. I double-dare you."

Hackberry felt as if someone had set a small nail between his eyes and slowly tapped it into his head with a tack hammer.

It was hard to estimate the age of the Asian woman who came to the door. She had a compact figure, and wore dark glasses and a white dress with black ribbon threaded through the top of the bodice, and looked no older than a woman in her early forties. But Darl Wingate, the coroner, had told Hackberry that she had lived through Japanese incendiary raids and the massacre of Chinese civilians by Japanese troops, and perhaps had worked for Claire Chennault's Civil Air Transport. The latter had overtones Hackberry didn't want to think about.

He removed his hat when he stepped inside and let his eyes adjust to the poorly lit interior of her home. The furniture looked second-hand, the couch and chairs covered with cheap fabric, the rugs threadbare, an ancient glass wall case stuffed with books probably bought at yard sales. "We're looking for a man who may have been an intended victim in a homicide, Ms. Ling," he said.

35

"Why do you think he's here?" she asked.

Through the back window he could see a stucco cottage by a slat-wall barn, alongside a flat-roofed, oblong building that once could have been a bunkhouse. "Because you live in the middle of an unofficial international highway?" he said.

"What's this man's name?" she asked.

"We don't know. The FBI does, but we don't," he answered.

"I see. Well, I don't think he's here."

"He might have a manacle on one wrist, but we can't be sure of that. I suspect he's terrified and desperate," Hackberry said. "The man he may have been manacled to was tortured to death by six men carrying rifles. They probably came out of Mexico."

"If this man is desperate, why wouldn't he come to you?" the Asian woman said.

"My guess is he doesn't trust the authorities."

"But he would trust me?"

"We're not with ICE or the Border Patrol, ma'am," Pam said.

"I gathered that from your uniform and your badge."

"The point is, we're not worried about somebody feeding or sheltering wets," Pam said. "They've been with us a long time."

"Yes, they have, haven't they?"

Pam seemed to think about the implication of the statement, plainly wondering if the barb was intentional or imaginary. "I was admiring your side room there. Is that a statue of the Virgin Mary in front of all those burning candles?"

"Yes, it is."

"It doesn't weep blood, does it?" Pam asked.

"Ms. Ling, if you don't feel you can confide in us, talk with the FBI. The man we're looking for barely escaped a terrible fate," Hackberry said.

If his suggestion had any viability at all, it did not show in the Asian woman's face. "I'll keep in mind what you've said," she replied.

Pam Tibbs's arms were folded on her chest. She gave Hackberry a look, waiting for him to speak, the fingers of her right hand opening and closing, her breath audible.

Hackberry took the manila folder from his side pocket and removed the sheaf of eight-by-ten photos. "These were taken today at a crime scene no more than a half hour from your house. What you see here was done by men who have no parameters, Miss Anton. We have a witness who indicates the victim gave up the name La Magdalena before he died. We think the torture death of the victim was conducted by a man called Krill. That's why we're here now. We don't want these men to hurt you or anyone to whom you may have given shelter. Have you heard of a man named Krill?"

Her eyes held on his. They were dark, unblinking, perhaps containing memories or knowledge she seldom shared with others. "Yes," she replied. "Three or four years ago, there was a coyote by that name. He robbed the people who paid him to take them across. Some say he raped the women."

"Where is he now?"

"He disappeared."

"Do you know how he came by his name?"

"He was a machine-gunner somewhere in Central America. His nickname came from the food of the whale. He ate the 'krill' in large numbers."

It was silent in the room. Hackberry glanced through the door of the side room, which must have served as a chapel of some kind. Perhaps thirty or forty candles were burning in red and blue and purple vessels, the light of the flames flickering on the base of the statue. "You Catholic, Miss Anton?" he said.

"That depends on whom you talk to."

"Expecting some visitors tonight?" When she didn't reply, he said, "Can we look out back?"

"Why do you ask me? You'll do it whether I like it or not."

"No, that's not correct," Pam replied. "We don't have a search warrant. We'll do it with your permission, or we can get a warrant and come back."

"Do whatever you wish."

"Excuse me, ma'am, but what if we just leave you alone here?" Pam said. "Would you prefer that? Then you can deal with Mr. Krill and his friends on your own."

"We'll wander out back, if you don't mind," Hackberry said, placing a business card on the coffee table. Then he smiled. "Is it true you worked for Civil Air Transport, Claire Chennault's old airline?"

"I did."

"It's an honor to meet you."

Minutes later, outside in the wind, Pam Tibbs's throat was still bladed with color, her back stiff with anger. " 'An honor to meet you'?" she said. "What the hell is that? She's a horse's ass."

"Look at it from her point of view."

"She doesn't have one."

"She stands up for people who have no power. Why not give the devil her due?"

Pam went inside the stucco cottage, then came back out, letting the screen slam behind her. "Check it out. There's a mattress in there soaked in blood, and bandages are scattered all over the floor. The blood is still sticky. I bet that guy was here while we were talking in the house. What was that stuff about Claire Chennault's airline?"

"It was a CIA front that became Air America. They supplied the Laotian resistance and flew in and out of the Golden

Triangle."

"They transported opium?"

Hackberry removed his hat and knocked a dent out of the crown and put it back on. He felt old in the way people feel old when they have more knowledge of the world than they need. In the south the sky was blackening in the sunset, and dust was rising off the hills. "I think it's fixing to blow," he said.

Krill squatted on the edge of the butte and looked out at the desert and at the red sun cooling on the horizon. The sky had turned green when the wind drove the rain from the west, and dust devils were spinning across the landscape below, the air blooming with a smell that was like wet flowers and chalk. He had washed his body with a rag and canteen water, and now his skin felt cool in the breeze and the layer of warm air that had risen from the desert and broken apart in the evening sky. His eyes were a milky blue, his expression composed, his skin dusky and dry and smooth and clean inside his wind-puffed shirt. As often happened in these solitary moments, Krill thought about a village in a country far to the south, its perimeter sealed by jungle, a dead volcano in the distance. Across the road from the house where he had lived, three children played in a dirt yard in front of the clinic that had been constructed by East Germans and burned by the army. In

Krill's reverie, the children turned to look at him, their faces lighting with recognition. Then their faces disappeared, as though airbrushed from his life.

"What we gonna do now, *jefe?*" Negrito said, squatting down next to him. He wore a greasy leather flop hat pushed back on his head, his hair curling like flames from under it.

Because Negrito was of mixed blood and his first language was bastardized English, he believed he and Krill were brothers in arms. But Krill neither liked nor trusted Negrito, whose facial features resembled those of an orange baboon that had fallen into a tub of bleach.

Krill continued to gaze at the desert and the way the light pooled in the clouds even though the sun had already set.

"Don't believe that stuff about La Magdalena. She ain't got no power, man," Negrito said. "You know what they say about *puta* from over there. It's sideways. That's the only difference."

Krill's expression never changed, as though Negrito's words were confetti falling on a flat stone. Out of the corner of his eye, he could see Negrito leaning forward, dangerously close to the edge of the bluff, trying to earn his attention.

"Why's this guy so important?" Negrito asked. "He got a lot of dope hid someplace?"

41

"See down there below?" Krill said. "That's a coyote den. See in that creek bed? Those are cougar tracks. The cougar has to kill fifty fawns to feed just one kitten. Except there aren't fifty fawns around here. That means the coyote's pups have to die instead."

Negrito's eyes went back and forth as he tried to puzzle through Krill's statement. In the fading spark of sun on the horizon, his face was as rosy as a drunkard's, his jutting forehead knurled, his mouth ringed with whiskers. "I'll get it out of her. You say the word, *jefe.* She'll be asking for knee pads," he said.

Krill stared into Negrito's face. "I'm not your chief. I'm nobody's chief. You follow me or you don't follow me."

Negrito brushed one hand on top of the other, the horned edges of his palms rasping like sandpaper, his gaze avoiding Krill's. He rocked on his heels, the points of his cowboy boots inches from the edge of the bluff. "You need a woman. It ain't natural to be out here long without a woman. We all need a woman. Maybe we ought to go back to Durango for a while."

Krill stood up and looked at the other men, all of whom were cooking pieces of jackrabbits they had killed and dressed and speared on sticks above a fire they had built inside a circle of stones. He picked up his rifle and put it across his shoulders and draped his arms over either end of it, creating a silhouette like that of a crucified man. "In the morning," he said.

"We get out of here in the morning?" Negrito said. "Maybe to Durango?"

"You heard me, *hombre*."

"Where you going now?"

"You'll hear one shot. It'll be for the cougar. You hear more than one shot, that means I found some real pissed-off gringos out there."

"Because of what we done to that cop?"

"He worked for the DEA."

"Man, you didn't tell us that."

"You still want to go after La Magdalena?"

Negrito's eyes contained no emotion, as though they were prosthetic and had been inserted into his face by an indifferent thumb. He stared emptily at the desert, his eyelids fluttering when a cloud of bats lifted from a cave opening down below. Then he looked into the darkness, perhaps considering options, entertaining thoughts he hid by rubbing his forehead, shielding his eyes.

"You think too much, Negrito," Krill said. "When a man thinks too much, he's tempted to go beyond his limitations."

Negrito stood up and took off his hat. "Watch this," he said. He flipped his hat in the air, then scooted under it, catching it squarely on his head, his face splitting into an ape's grin. He wobbled slightly, his arms straight out for balance, rocks spilling from under his boots over the edge of the bluff. "*Chingado,* that scared me. Don't worry, *jefe.* I'll always back you up. I don't care about no pissed-off gringos or Chinese *puta* that thinks her shit don't stink, either. You're my *jefe* whether you like it or not. I love you, *hermano.*"

Hackberry Holland had come to believe that age was a separate country you did not try to explain to younger people, primarily because they had already made up their minds about it and any lessons you had learned from your life were not the kind many people were interested in hearing about. If age brought gifts, he didn't know what they were. It had brought him neither wisdom nor peace of mind. His level of desire was the same, the lust of his youth glowing hot among the ashes each morning he woke. He could say with a degree of satisfaction that he didn't suffer fools and drove from his company anyone who tried to waste his time, but otherwise his dreams and his waking day were defined by the same values and frame of reference that came with his birthright. If age had marked a change in him, it lay in his acceptance that loneliness and an abiding sense of loss were the only companions some people would ever have.

The most influential event in Hackberry's life had been his marriage to Rie Velasquez, a labor organizer for the United Farm Workers of America. When she died of uterine cancer, Hackberry had sold his ranch on the Guadalupe River and moved down to the border, leaving behind all memory of the idyllic life they'd shared, ridding himself of the things she had touched that made him so lonely he wanted to drink again, embracing the aridity of a parched land and its prehistoric ambience and its violent sunsets, the way a Bedouin enters the emptiness of the desert and is subsumed and made insignificant by it. Then bit by bit the horse farm he bought became a hologram, a place that fused past and present and re-created his childhood and adolescence and his life with Rie and their twin sons in one shimmering, timeless vision. It was a place where a man could see his beginning and his end, an island that was governed by reason and stewardship and the natural ebb and flow of the seasons, a place where a man no longer had to fear death.

He had two good wells on his land, and a four-stall barn and two railed pastures where he grazed his quarter horses and registered Missouri foxtrotters. He was also the unofficial owner of three dogs, a one-eyed cat, and two raccoons, none of whom had names but whom he fed outside the barn every morning and night.

His house was painted battleship gray and had a wide gallery and a breezy screened porch in back and a rock garden and a deep-green lawn he watered with soak hoses and flower beds planted with roses he entered each summer in the competition at the county fair. A china-berry tree grew in his backyard, and a slender palm tree grew at the base of the hill behind the house. He built a brooder house on the side of the barn, and his chickens laid eggs all over the property, under his tractor and in his tack room. On each of his horse tanks he had constructed small ladders out of chicken wire that he wrapped over the lip of the tank, so small creatures that fell into the water could find their way out again. In one way or another, every day that he spent on his ranch became part of an ongoing benediction.

The two gun cases in his office held a Henry repeater, an 1873 Winchester, a .45–70 trapdoor of the kind the Seventh Cavalry carried into the Little Big Horn, an '03 Springfield, a German Luger, a nine-millimeter Beretta, a Ruger Buntline .22 Magnum, and the converted .44 Navy Colt his grandfather, Old Hack, had carried the morning he knocked John Wesley Hardin from his saddle and kicked him cross-eyed and nailed him down with chains in a wagon bed before transporting him to the Cuero jail.

Hackberry loved the place he lived, and he loved waking inside its soft radiance in the morning, and he loved following his grand-

46

father's admonition to feed his animals before he fed himself. He loved the smell of his roses inside the coolness of the dawn and the smell of well water bursting into the horse tank when he released the chain on the windmill. He loved the warm odor of grass on the breath of his horses and the vinegary smell of their coats, and the powdery green cloud of hay particles that rose around him when he pulled a bale apart and scattered it on the concrete pad in the barn.

All of these things were part of the Texas in which he had grown up, and they were unsoiled by political charlatans and avaricious corporations and neocolonial wars being waged under the banner of God. He did not tell others about the bugles blowing in the hills, less out of fear that they would suspect him of experiencing auditory delusions than out of his own conviction that the bugles were real and that from the time of Cortés to the present, a martial and savage spirit had ruled these hills and it was no coincidence that a sunset in this fine place looked like the electrified blood of Christ.

Early on the morning after he and Pam Tibbs had interviewed the Asian woman known by the Mexicans as La Magdalena, Hackberry looked out his bathroom window and saw Ethan Riser park his government motor-pool car by the front gate and walk up the flagstones to the front entrance, holding

47

two Styrofoam containers on top of each other, pausing briefly to admire the flowers in the bed. Hackberry rinsed the shaving cream off his face and stepped out on the veranda. "This can't wait till eight o'clock?" he said.

"It could. Or maybe I could come back another day, when you're not tied up with something important, like shaving," Riser said.

"I have to feed my animals."

"I'll help you."

Ethan Riser's hair was as white as cotton and had all the symmetry of meringue. His nose and cheeks were threaded with tiny blue and red capillaries, and his stomach and hips protruded over the narrow hand-tooled western belt he wore with a conventional business suit and tie. He had been with the FBI almost forty years.

"Fix some coffee while I'm down at the barn," Hackberry said.

Twenty minutes later, he returned to the house through the back door and washed his hands in the kitchen sink.

"You got a reason for always making it hard?" Riser said.

"None I can think of."

"Why didn't you call me about the homicide south of that Indian's property?"

"It's not a federal case. It's not y'all's damn business, either."

48

"You're wrong about that, my friend. The victim was a DEA informant."

"It's still our case. Stay out of it."

"Beg your pardon?"

"I've been on a need-to-know basis with y'all before. I always had the feeling I was a hangnail."

"The informant's name was Hector Lopez. He was a dirty cop from Mexico City who worked both sides of the fence. Our people weren't entirely comfortable with him. Lopez and a physician once tortured a DEA agent to death."

"I remember that case. The physician went down for it. Why not the dirty cop?"

"That's the way it is. I'm sharing this with you because we can help each other."

The microwave made a dinging sound. Ethan Riser took out the two Styrofoam containers and opened them on the breakfast table. They contained scrambled eggs and hash browns and sausage patties smothered with milk gravy. He took the coffeepot off the stove and set cups and silverware on the table. Hackberry watched him. "Does everything meet the standard here? My house tidy enough, that sort of thing?" he said.

"We talked to Danny Boy Lorca already," Riser said. "He gave us the name of this guy Krill. Have any idea who he is?"

Hackberry hung his hat on the back of his chair and sat down to eat. "Nothing real specific other than the fact he's a killer."

"We think he takes hostages and sells them," Riser said. "The guy we want is the guy who was on the other end of the cable locked on the dead man's wrist. We think he's the federal employee we've been looking for."

"What kind of federal employee is he?"

Riser went silent. Hackberry put down his fork and knife. "Tell you what, Ethan," he said. "This is my home. People can be rude whenever and wherever they want. But not in my kitchen and not at my table."

"He's a Quaker who should have been screened out of the job he was assigned to. It's the government's fault."

"I guess Jefferson should have gotten rid of Benjamin Franklin at first opportunity."

"Franklin was a Quaker?" When Hackberry didn't answer, Riser said, "Your flowers are lovely. I told you my father was a botanist, didn't I? He grew every kind of flower mentioned in Shakespeare's plays."

Hackberry got up from the table and poured his breakfast into the trash can and wiped his hands on a piece of paper towel. "I'm running late. Can you let yourself out?" he said.

"I've tried to put you in the loop."

"Is that what y'all call snake oil?" Hackberry said.

Through her windshield Pam Tibbs saw the

oversize pickup on a winding stretch of isolated two-lane road that was spiderwebbed with heat cracks and broken so badly in places that it was hardly passable. The road went nowhere and had little utilitarian value. The sedimentary formations protruding in layers from the hillsides had been spray-painted by high school kids, and the areas under the mesas where the kids parked their cars at night were often littered with beer cans and used condoms. The road dipped over a rise and ended at the entrance to a cattle ranch that had gone out of business with the importation of Argentine beef in the 1960s.

Through the cruiser's windshield, Pam saw the pickup weave off the road, skidding gravel down a wash. Then the driver overcorrected and continued haphazardly down the center-line, ignoring the possibility of another vehicle coming around a bend, as though he were studying a map or texting on a cell phone or steering with his knees. Pam switched on her light bar and closed the distance between her cruiser and the truck. Through the pickup's back window, she saw the driver's eyes lock on hers in the rearview mirror.

When the driver pulled to the shoulder, Pam parked behind him and got out on the asphalt, slipping her baton into the ring on her belt. The truck was brand-new, its hand-buffed waxed yellow finish as smooth and glowing as warm butter, a single star-spangled patriotic sticker glued on the bumper. The driver opened his door and started to get out.

"Stay in your vehicle, sir," Pam said.

The driver drew his leg back inside the truck and closed the door, snugging it tight. Pam could see his face in the outside mirror, his eyes studying her. She heard his glove compartment drop open.

Pam unsnapped the strap on her .357 Magnum. "Put your hands on the steering wheel, sir. Do not touch anything in your glove box." She moved forward but at an angle, away from the driver's window, her palm and thumb cupped over the grips of her holstered revolver. "Did you hear me? You put your hands where I can see them."

"I was getting my registration," the driver said.

"Do not turn away from me. Keep your hands on the wheel."

His hair was gold and cut short, his sideburns long, his eyes a liquid green. She moved closer to the cab. "What are you doing out here?" she asked.

"Taking a drive. Looking through my binoculars."

"Turn off your engine and step out of your vehicle."

"That's what I was trying to do when you told me to get back inside. Which is it?"

"You need to do what I say, sir."

"It's Reverend, if you want to be formal."

"You will step out of the vehicle and do it now, sir," she said.

"I have a pistol on the seat. I use it for rabbits. I'm no threat to you."

She pulled her revolver from its holster and aimed it with both hands at his face. "Put your right hand behind your head, open the door, and get down on the ground."

"Have you heard of the Cowboy Chapel? Don't point that at me." He looked straight into the muzzle of her gun. "I respect the law. You're not going to threaten me with a firearm. My name is Reverend Cody Daniels. Ask anybody."

She jerked the door open with one hand and stepped back. "Down on the ground."

"I will not do that. I will not tolerate your abuse, either. I did nothing to deserve this."

She was holding her .357 with both hands again, the checkered grips biting into her palms. "This is your last chance to avoid a very bad experience, sir."

"Do not call me 'sir.' You're deliberately being disrespectful in order to provoke me. I know your kind, missy."

She was gripping the pistol so tightly, she could feel the barrel tremble. Her temples were pounding, her scalp tight, her eyes stinging with perspiration. She stared at the driver in the silence. The skin around his mouth was bloodless, his gaze iniquitous, dissecting her face, dropping to her throat and her breasts rising and falling inside her shirt. When she didn't move or speak, his eyes seemed to sweep the entirety of her person, noting the loops of sweat under her arms, a lock of her hair stuck on her damp forehead, the width of her hips, the way her stomach strained against her gun belt and the button on her jeans, the fact that her upper arms were as thick as a man's. She saw a smile wrinkle at the corner of his mouth. "You seem a mite unsettled, missy," he said. "Maybe you should be in another line of work."

"Thank you for saying that," she replied. She pulled her can of Mace from her belt and sprayed it in his face and jerked him out of the cab, then sprayed him again. He flailed his arms blindly, his eyes streaming tears, then he slapped at her hands as a child might, as though he were being violated. She threw him against the side of the truck, kicking his feet apart, stiff-arming him in the back of the neck, the tensions of his body coursing like an electric current through her palm.

When he continued to struggle, she slipped her baton from the ring on her belt and whipped it behind his calves. He dropped straight to his knees, as though his tendons had been cut, his mouth open wide, a cry breaking from his throat.

She pushed him facedown on the ground and cuffed his wrists behind him. His left cheek was printed with gravel, his mouth quivering with shock. He wrenched up his head so he could see her. "No hot coal will redeem your tongue, woman. You're a curse on the race. A pox on you and all your kind," he said.

She called in her location. "I've got a lulu here. Ask Hack to pull all the reports we have on somebody who was shooting at illegals," she said.

CHAPTER THREE

Hackberry Holland sat behind his desk and listened to Pam Tibbs's account of the arrest. Outside the window, the American flag was straightening and popping in the wind, the chain rattling on the pole. "What's our minister friend doing now?" he asked.

"Yelling for his phone call," she replied. "How do you read that stuff about a hot coal on my tongue?"

"It's from Isaiah in the Old Testament. Isaiah believed he was a man of unclean lips who dwelled in an unclean land. But an angel placed a burning coal on his tongue and removed his iniquity."

"I'm iniquitous for not letting him kill himself and others in an auto accident?"

"The sheriff in Jim Hogg told me about this guy a couple of months ago. Cody Daniels was a suspect in the bombing of an abortion clinic on the East Coast. He might not have done it himself, but he was at least one of the cheerleaders. He roams around the country and tends to headquarter in places where there's not much money for law enforcement. I didn't know he was here."

She waited for him to continue, but he didn't. "You think he could be the guy taking potshots at the illegals coming across the border?" she said.

"Him or a hundred others like him." Hackberry took off his reading glasses and rubbed his eyes. "Did he threaten you in a specific way?"

"On the way in, he told me I was going to hell."

"Did he say he was going to put you there or see you there?"

"No."

"Did he touch the gun on the seat?"

"Not that I saw."

"Did he make a threatening gesture of any kind?"

"He refused to get out of the vehicle while telling me he was armed."

"He told R.C. you hit him in the head after you cuffed him."

"He fell down against the cruiser. What are you trying to say, Hack?"

"We don't need a lawsuit."

"I don't know if I'm more pissed off by this nutcase or what I'm hearing now."

"It's the kind of lawsuit that could cost us fifty thousand dollars in order to be right."

Hackberry looked up at her in the silence.

Pam's eyes were brown, with a reddish tint, and they became charged with light when she was either angry or hurt. She hooked her thumbs in her gun belt and fixed her attention outside the window, her cheeks spotted with color.

"I'm proud of the way you handled it," he said. "You did all the right things. Let's see if our man likes his accommodations."

Hackberry and Pam Tibbs climbed the steel spiral steps in the rear of the building and walked down a corridor of barred cells, past the old drunk tank, to a barred holding unit that contained nothing but a wood bench and a commode with no seat. The man who had identified himself as Reverend Cody Daniels was standing at the window, silhouetted against a sky that had turned yellow with dust.

"I understand you were potting jackrabbits from your pickup truck," Hackberry said.

"I did no such thing," Cody Daniels replied. "It's not against the law, anyway, is it?"

"So you were cruising down the road surveilling the countryside through your binoculars for no particular reason?" Hackberry said.

"What I was looking for is the illegal immigrants and drug transporters who come through here every night."

"You're not trying to steal my job, are you?"

"I go where I've a mind to. When I got up

this morning, this was still a free country."

"You bet. But you gave my chief deputy a hard time because she made a simple procedural request of you."

"Check the video camera in your squad car. Truth will out, Sheriff."

"It's broken."

"Pretty much like everything in this town. Mighty convenient, if you ask me."

"What are you doing in my county?"

"Your county?"

"You'd better believe it."

"I'm doing the Lord's work."

"I heard about your activities on the East Coast. We don't have any abortion clinics here, Reverend, but that doesn't mean we'll put up with your ilk."

Cody Daniels approached the bars and rested one hand on the cast-iron plate that formed an apron on the bottom of the food slot. The veins in his wrists were green and as thick as night crawlers, his knuckles pronounced, the back of each finger scarred where a tattoo had been removed. He held Hackberry's gaze. "I have the ability to see into people's thoughts," he said. "Right now you got more problems than your department can handle. That's why you select the likes of me as the target of your wrath. People like me are easy. We pay our taxes and obey the law and try to do what's right. How many drug dealers do you have locked up here?"

"There's a kernel of truth in what you say, Reverend, but I'd like to get this issue out of the way so you can go back to your job and we can go back to ours."

"I think the real problem is you got a romantic relationship going with this woman here."

"Deputy Tibbs, would you get the reverend's possessions envelope out of the locker, please?"

Pam gave Hackberry a look but didn't move.

"I think Reverend Daniels is a reasonable man and is willing to put this behind him," Hackberry said. "I think he'll be more mindful of his driving habits and the next time out not object to the requests of a well-meaning deputy sheriff. Is that a fair statement, Reverend?"

"I'm not given to making promises, particularly when I'm not the source of the problem," Cody Daniels said.

Hackberry drummed his fingers on the apron of the food slot. "Deputy Tibbs, would you get the paperwork started on Reverend Daniels's release?" he said.

"Yes, sir," she replied.

Cody Daniels's eyes followed her down the corridor, his gaze slipping down her back to her wide-ass jeans and the thickness of her thighs. "I guess it's each to his own," he said.

"Pardon?" Hackberry said.

"No offense meant, but I think I'd rather belly up to a spool of barbed wire. That's kind of coarse, but you get the picture."

"I hope you'll accept this in the right spirit, Reverend. If you ever sass one of my deputies or speak disrespectfully of Chief Deputy Tibbs again, I'm going to hunt around in that pile of scrap wood behind the jail until I find a long two-by-four, one with sixteen-penny nails sticking out of it, then I'm going to kick it so far up your ass you'll be spitting splinters. Get the picture? Have a nice day. And stay the hell out of my sight."

Anton Ling heard the man in the yard before she saw him. He had released the chain on the windmill and cupped water out of the spout, drinking it from his hand, while the blades spun and clattered above his head. He was gaunt and wore a short-sleeve shirt with no buttons; his hair hung on his shoulders and looked like it had been barbered with a knife.

"*¿Qué quieres?*" she said.

"*Comida,*" the man replied.

He was wearing tennis shoes. In the moonlight she could see his ribs stenciled against his sides, his trousers flattening in the wind against his legs. She stepped out on the back porch. The shadows of the windmill's blades were spinning on his face. "You didn't come out of Mexico," she said.

61

"How do you know?" he replied in English.

"The patrols are out. They would have stopped you if you came out of the south."

"I hid in the hills during the day. I have no food."

"What is your name?"

"Antonio."

"You are a worker?"

"Only for myself. I am a hunter. Will you feed me?"

She went into her kitchen and put a wedge of cheese and three tortillas on a paper plate, then covered them with chili and beans that she ladled out of a pot that was still warm on the stove. When she went back outside, the visitor was squatted in the middle of the dirt lot, staring at the moon and the lines of cedar posts with no wire. He took the paper plate from her hand and ignored the plastic spoon and instead removed a metal spoon from his back pocket and began eating. A knife in a long thin scabbard protruded at an angle from his belt. "You are very kind, *señora.*"

"Where did you learn English?"

"My father was a British sailor."

"What do you hunt, Antonio?"

"In this case, a man."

"Has this man harmed you?"

"No, he has done nothing to me."

"Then why do you hunt him?"

"He's a valuable man, and I am poor."

"You'll not find him here."

He stopped eating and pointed at the side of his head with his spoon. "You're very intelligent. People say you have supernatural gifts. But maybe they just don't understand that you are simply much more intelligent than they are."

"The man you are looking for was here, but he's gone now. He will not be back. You must leave him alone."

"Your property is a puzzle. It has fences all over it, but they hold nothing in and nothing out."

"This was a great cattle ranch at one time."

"Now it is a place where the wind lives, one that has no beginning and no end. It's a place like you, *china.* You come from the other side of the earth to do work no one understands. You don't have national frontiers."

"Don't speak familiarly of people you know nothing about."

The man who called himself Antonio lifted the paper plate and pushed the beans and chili and cheese and pieces of tortilla into his mouth. He dropped the empty plate in the dirt and wiped his lips and chin on a bandanna and stood up and washed his spoon in the horse tank and slipped it into his back pocket. "They say you can do the same things a priest can, except you have more power."

"I have none."

"I had three children. They died without baptism." He looked toward the west and the heat lightning pulsing in the sky just above the hills. "Sometimes I think their souls are out there, outside their bodies, lost in the darkness, not knowing where they're supposed to go. You think that's what happens after we're dead? We don't know where to go until someone tells us?"

"How did your children die?"

"They were killed by a helicopter in front of the clinic where they were playing."

"I'm sorry for your loss."

"You can baptize them, *china*."

"Do not call me that."

"It wasn't their fault they weren't baptized. They call you La Magdalena. You can reach back in time before they were dead and baptize them."

"You should talk to a priest. He will tell you the same thing I do. Your children committed no offense against God. You mustn't worry about them."

"I can't see a priest."

"Why not?"

"I killed one. I think he was French, maybe a Jesuit. I'm not sure. We were told he was a Communist. I machine-gunned him."

Her eyes left his face. She remained motionless inside the pattern of shadow and light created by the moon. "Whom do you work for?" she asked.

"Myself."

"No, you don't. You're paid by others. They

64

use you."

"*Conejo,* you are much woman."

"You will not speak to me like that."

"You didn't let me finish. You are much woman, but you've lied to me. You've given Communion to the people who come here, just like a priest. But you turn me away."

"I think you're a tormented man. But you won't find peace until you give up your violent ways. You tortured and killed the man down south of us, didn't you? You're the one called Krill."

His eyes held hers. They were pale blue, the pupils like cinders. In silhouette, with his long knife-cut hair and torso shaped like an inverted pyramid, he resembled a creature from an earlier time, a warrior suckled in an outworn creed. "The man I killed in the south did very cruel things to my brother. He had a chance to redeem himself by being brave. But he was a coward to the end."

"Others are with you, aren't they? Out there in the hills."

"Others follow me. They are not with me. They can come and go as they wish. Given the chance, some of them would eat me like dogs."

"When you were a coyote, you raped the women who paid you to take them across?"

"A man has needs, *china.* But it wasn't rape. I was invited to their beds."

"Because they had no water to drink or

65

food to eat? Do not come here again, even if you're badly hurt or starving."

The man watched the heat lightning, his hair lying as black as ink on his shoulders. "I can hear my children talking inside the trees," he said. "You have to baptize them, *señora*. It doesn't matter if you want to or not."

"Be gone."

He raised a cautionary finger in the air, the shadow of the windmill blades slicing across his face and body. "Do not treat me with contempt, Magdalena. Think about my request. I'll be back."

Three days later, on Saturday, Hackberry rose at dawn and fixed coffee in a tin pot and made a sandwich out of two slices of sourdough bread and a deboned pork chop he took from the icebox. Then he carried the pot and sandwich and tin cup down to the barn and the railed pasture where he kept his two Missouri foxtrotters, a chestnut and a palomino named Missy's Playboy and Love That Santa Fe. He spread their hay on the concrete pad that ran through the center of the barn, and then he sat down in a wood chair from the tack room and ate his sandwich and drank his coffee while he watched his horses eat. Then he walked out to their tank and filled it to the rim from a frost-proof spigot, using his bare hand to skim bugs and dust and bits of hay from the surface. The water had come from a deep well on his property and was like ice on his fingers and wrist, and he wondered if the coldness hidden under the baked hardpan wasn't a reminder of the event waiting for him just beyond the edge of his vision — an unexpected softening of the light, an autumnal smell of gas pooled in the trees, a bugle echoing off stone in the hills.

No, I will not think about that today, he told himself. The sunrise was pink in the east, the sky blue. His quarter horses were grazing in his south pasture, the irrigated grass riffling in the breeze, and he could see a doe with three yearlings among a grove of shade trees at the bottom of his property. The world was a grand place, a cathedral in its own right, he thought. How had Robert Frost put it? What place could be better suited for love? Hackberry couldn't remember the line.

He slipped a halter on each of the foxtrotters and wormed them by holding their head up with the lead while he worked the disposable syringe into the corner of their mouth and squirted the ivermectin over their tongue and down their throat. Both of them were still colts and liked to provoke him by mashing down on the syringe, holding on until he had to drop the lead and use both hands to pry the flattened plastic cylinder loose from their teeth.

Just when he thought he was done, the

chestnut, Missy's Playboy, grabbed his straw hat and threw it on the branch of a tree, then thundered down the pasture, trailing the lead between his legs, kicking at the air with his hind feet. Hackberry did not hear the woman come up behind him. "I let myself in the gate. I hope you don't mind," she said.

She was wearing khakis and sandals and a white shirt with flowers on it and a white baseball cap with a purple bill. When he didn't answer, she looked around her, uncertain. "You have a beautiful place."

"What can I do for you, Miss Anton?"

"Two nights ago a man came to my house. He said his name was Antonio. But I think he's the man called Krill."

"What did this fellow want?"

"He said he was a hunter. He said he was hunting a man for pay. I told him the man he was looking for had been at my house, but he had gone and wouldn't be there again."

"Why did you wait to report this?"

There was a beat. "I'm not sure."

"You thought you would be violating a confidence?"

"This man is deeply troubled. In part, I think he came to me for help. Why are you shaking your head?"

"Don't be disingenuous about these guys. You know what the conversion rate is on death row? Try a hundred percent. Turn them loose and see what happens."

68

"You believe the state has the right to kill people?"

"No."

"Why not?"

"Who cares?"

"Sheriff, I came here as an act of conscience. This man probably won't harm me, but eventually, he'll kill others. So I had to come here."

"You don't think he'll hurt you? Why should you get an exemption?"

"Three of his children were killed by a helicopter gunship. He believes their spirits will wander until they're baptized. He thinks somehow I can baptize them retroactively. He says he can't take his problem to a priest because he murdered a French Jesuit."

"I think you're dealing with someone who's morally insane, Miss Anton. I think it's both naive and dangerous to pretend otherwise. Who's he working for?"

"I asked him that. He wouldn't say."

"Who's the guy you gave refuge to?"

"A man of peace. A man who became involved in a military program that kills innocent people."

"Has the FBI interviewed you?"

"No."

"When they do, I suggest you give them a better answer than the one you just gave me. You were in the employ of Air America in Indochina, Miss Anton. People who have a lot of guilt have a way of showing up under one flag or another."

She took a Ziploc bag from her pocket. In it was a dirty paper plate. "Antonio ate from this. I suspect it will be of some help to you."

"Why are both the FBI and Krill after the same man?"

"Ask them. Before I go, I need to straighten out something. My work has nothing to do with guilt. We live in a country that has created a huge serving class of illegals who work for low pay at jobs Americans won't do. We get along very well with these people during prosperous times. But as soon as the economy goes down, they're treated like dirt. You're obviously an intelligent and educated man. Why don't you act like it?"

She turned and began walking back toward the gate. Then she stopped and faced him again. For some reason, her baseball cap and her tight-fitting flowered shirt made her look younger and smaller than she was. "One other thing, sir," she said. "Why do you look at me so strangely? It's quite rude."

Because you remind me of my beloved wife, he thought.

The Reverend Cody Daniels had carpentered his house to resemble the forecastle of a ship, up on a bluff that overlooked a wide arid bowl flanked by hills that contained layers of both red and chalk-colored stone, giving them in the sunset the striped appearance of a freshly sliced strawberry cake. A sandstone bluff rose straight into the air behind the house, and on it he had painted a huge American flag, one that was of greater dimension than the roof itself. In the evening, Cody Daniels liked to walk back and forth on his front deck, surveying the valley below, sometimes gazing at the southern horizon through the telescope mounted on the deck rail, sometimes simply taking pleasure in the presence of his possessions — his canary-yellow pickup, his horse trailer, his cistern up on the hill, his silver propane tanks that ensured he would never be cold, the smell of the game he had shot or beef he had butchered dripping into the ash inside his smokehouse, the wood shell of a church that came with the property down on the hardpan, a building he had given a second life by putting pews inside it and a blue-white neon cross above the front door.

Some evenings, after the last wash of gold light on the eastern side of the valley had risen into the sky and disappeared like smoke breaking apart in the wind, he would focus his telescope on a gingerbread house far to the south and watch the events that seemed to unfold there two or three times a week.

When the evening star rose above the hills, Cody Daniels could see small groups of people moving out of the haze that constituted the Mexican border — like lice fleeing a flame, he thought, carrying their possessions in backpacks and knotted blankets, their children stringing behind them, not unlike nits.

He had heard about the woman who lived in the gingerbread house. The wets coming across the border knelt before her altar and believed the glow of votive candles burning at the base of a statue somehow signaled they had reached a safe harbor. Not true, Cody Daniels thought. Not as long as he had the power to send them back where they came from. Not as long as there were still patriots willing to act independently of a government that had been taken over by mud people who were giving away American jobs to the beaners.

Cody could have tapped just three digits into his phone console and brought the authorities down on the Asian woman's head. The fact that he didn't made him swell with a sense of power and control that was rare in his life. The Asian woman, without even knowing it, was in his debt. Sometimes she passed him on the sidewalk in town, or pushing a basket in the grocery store, her eyes aimed straight ahead, ignoring his tip of his hat. He wondered what she would say if she knew what he could do to her. He wondered how she would enjoy her first cavity search in a federal facility. He wondered if she would be so regal in a shower room full of bull dykes.

On the deck this evening, with the wind cool on his face, he should have felt at peace. But the memory of his treatment by the deputy sheriff, the one named Tibbs, was like a thumbtack pressed into his scalp. His eyes had the cupped look of an owl's from the Mace she had squirted into them. The baton stroke she had laid across the back of his calves flared to life each time he took a step. Then, for reasons he didn't understand, the thought of her slamming him against the truck, of forcing him on his face and kneeing him in the spine and hooking him up, brought about a weakening in his throat, a stiffening in his loins, and fantasies in which he and the woman were in a soundproof room that had no windows.

But Cody did not like to pursue fantasies of this kind, because they contained images and guilty sensations that made no sense to him. It was not unlike watching two or three frames of a film — an image of her hand flying out at his face, a fingernail cutting his cheek — and refusing to see what was on the rest of the spool.

Unconsciously, he rubbed the dime-sized pieces of scar tissue on the back of his fingers. Long ago, when he was hardly more than a boy riding freight trains across the American West, he had learned lessons he would take to the grave: You didn't sass a railroad bull; you didn't sass a hack on a county penal farm; and you didn't put tattoos on your body that told people you were nobody and deserving of whatever they did to you. You rinsed their abuse off your skin and out of your soul; you became somebody else, and once you did, you no longer had to feel shame about the person who somehow had brought degradation upon himself.

Then you did to others what had been done to you, freeing yourself forever of the role of victim. Or at least that was what some people did. But he hadn't done that, he told himself. He was a minister. He had an associate of arts degree. Truckers talked about him on their CBs. He handed out pocket Bibles to rodeo cowboys behind the bucking chutes. Attractive waitresses warmed up his coffee for free and called him Reverend. He wrote letters of recommendation for parolees. He had baptized drunkards and meth addicts by submersion in a sandy pool by the river that was as red as the blood of Christ. How many men with his background could say the same? And he had done it all without therapists or psychiatrists or titty-baby twelve-step groups.

But his self-manufactured accolades brought him no solace. He had been bested by Sheriff Holland's chief deputy and, in a perverse way, had enjoyed it. He had been threatened with bodily harm by the sheriff, as though he were white trash. And while all this was happening, an Oriental woman was openly aiding the wets and getting christened for her efforts as La Magdalena. Anything wrong with this picture?

Maybe it was time to let Miss Chop Suey 1969 know who her neighbors were.

In the fading twilight he drove in his pickup down the long, tire-worn dirt track that traversed the valley from his house to the county road that eventually led to the southern end of the Asian woman's property. He passed two abandoned oil storage tanks that had turned to rust, a burned-out shack where a deranged tramp sometimes stayed, and a private airstrip blown with tumbleweed, the air sock bleached of color. He turned onto the Asian woman's property and passed a paint-skinned gas-guzzler driven by two men who were sitting on a hillside, staring north at the Asian woman's compound. They were smoking hand-rolled cigarettes and wore new straw hats and boots that were curled up at the toes. One of them pulled on a bottle that had no label, and gargled with whatever was inside before he swallowed. The other man, the taller of the two, had a pair of binoculars hanging from his neck. His shirt was open on his chest, and his skin looked as brown and smooth as clay from a riverbank. Cody Daniels nodded at him but didn't know why. The man either ignored or took no notice of

Cody's gesture.

If you want to live in this country, why don't you show some manners? Cody thought.

He drove between the gateless walls of the Asian woman's compound and was surprised by what he saw. Mexicans were eating from paper plates on the gallery and the front steps and at a picnic table under a willow in the middle of the yard. Obviously, no effort was being made to conceal their presence. He got down from his truck and immediately saw the Asian woman staring at him from the gallery. She was the only person among all the people there who looked directly at him. She stepped into the yard and walked toward him, her eyes never losing contact with his. He felt himself clear his throat involuntarily.

"What are you doing here?" she asked.

"Introducing myself. I live up yonder, in the bluffs. I'm Reverend Cody Daniels, pastor of the Cowboy Chapel."

"I know who you are. You're a nativist and not here on a good errand."

"A what?"

"State your business."

"Who are all these people?"

"Friends of mine."

"Got their papers, do they?"

"Why don't you ask them?"

"I don't speak Spanish."

"You have a cell phone?"

"Yeah, I do, but the service isn't real good

here. Want to borrow it?" He felt the open door of his truck hit him in the back.

"Either call 911 or leave."

"I didn't come here to cause trouble."

"I think you did."

"I try to save souls, just like you. I saw y'all from my deck up there, that's all. I got a telescope. I'm an amateur astronomer."

She stepped closer to him. "Let me see your hands."

"Ma'am?"

"I won't hurt you."

"I know that," he said, half laughing.

"Then let me see your hands."

He held them out, palms up, in front of her. But then she turned them over and moved her thumbs across the scar tissue on the back of his fingers. "You were in prison, weren't you?" she said.

"I don't know if I'd call it prison." He paused. "I was on a county farm in New Mexico when I was a boy."

"You had your tattoos removed when you came out?"

"I did it myself. Burned them off with acid and took out the leftover flesh with nail clippers." He started to pull his hands away from her, but she held on to them. He grinned. "I know what you're gonna say. You're gonna tell me I had 'love' and 'hate' on my fingers, aren't you? Well, I didn't. I guess that shows how much you know."

"No, you had the letters B-O-R-N tattooed on your left hand, the letter T on your left thumb, the letter O on your right thumb, and L-O-S-E on your right hand. Who taught you such a terrible concept about yourself?"

"I had no such thing on there."

"Why do you feel guilty over things that weren't your fault? You were just a boy. People hurt you and tried to rob you of your innocence. You don't have to be ashamed of what happened to you. You don't have to be afraid of people who look different or speak a different language."

He felt himself swallowing. Through the wetness in his eyes, he saw the people in the yard and on the steps and gallery shimmer and go in and out of focus. "I'm not afraid of anything. If I ever catch up with the sonsof-bitches who did what they did, you'll see how afraid I am."

She squeezed both of his hands tightly in hers. "You have to forgive them."

He tried to pull away from her again, but she held on. He said, "I hope those men go to hell. I hope they burn from the top down and the bottom up. I hope Satan himself pours liquid fire down their throats."

"Would you drink poison in order to get even with others?"

"Sell that Dr. Phil douche rinse to some-body else. They draped me across a sawhorse. I was seventeen. You ever been raped? You wouldn't be so damn quick to advise if you had."

"Stay and eat with us."

"Are you out of your mind, woman? Let go of me."

But she didn't. She squeezed his hands tighter, her face staring intently up into his. He freed one of his hands and used it to pull her other hand off his and fling it from him. He got into his truck and started the engine and rammed the transmission into reverse. He steered by glancing over his shoulder, the pedal to the floor, scouring dirt out of the yard, so he would not have to look into the Asian woman's face again.

How had she gotten into his head? How did she know his history with such accuracy? He had always claimed he could read people's thoughts. But that wasn't true. He could read personalities, character traits, and especially secret designs that hid in the eyes of a manipulator. Every survivor could. That was how you became a survivor. But she was the real thing. She had seen into his past in a way no one ever had, and that thought made him grind his molars.

The purple haze he had seen earlier had spread across the valley floor, and he had to turn on his headlights to see his way down the dirt track to the county road. He had forgotten about the two Mexicans who had been smoking on the hillside earlier; he had even temporarily forgotten the rudeness one of them had shown Cody when he tried to say hello. The two men had gotten back into the gas-guzzler, and evidently had decided to stop and urinate at a spot where the dirt track was pinched on either side by big piles of rock.

He slowed his pickup and hit his high beams, drenching the two figures with an electric brilliance, carving their rounded spines, their splayed knees, the cupping of their phalluses, the amber arc of their urination out of the darkened landscape.

The license plate on the gas-guzzler was dented and filmed with a patina of dried mud and attached to the bumper with coat-hanger wire. Cody could see COAHUILA at the bottom of the plate. He mashed on his horn, holding the button down, clicking his high beams on and off, while the two men stuffed their phalluses back in their pants, their eyes glinting like glass.

The shorter of the two men walked toward Cody's truck, shielding his eyes from the glare with one hand. His jaw was as heavy-looking as a mule's shoe, his forehead ridged like a washboard, his hair and chin stubble the color of rust. "You got a problem, *chico?*" he said.

"*Chico?*" Cody said.

"That means 'boy,' " the man with orange hair said. "You got a problem, *chico* boy?"

"Yeah, how about getting your shitbox off the road? Also, find a public restroom and stop polluting the countryside. There's one at the truck stop up on the four-lane. It's got a dispenser of toilet-seat covers on the wall. The sign on the dispenser says MEXICAN PLACE MATS. That's how you'll know you're in the restroom."

"This is a funny guy here," the man called back to his friend. "Come up here and listen. He is very funny."

Cody looked in his rearview mirror and could see only a dim glow from the compound of the Asian woman. The stars seemed to arch overhead and stretch beyond the horizon and curve over the earth's rim. "I need to get about my business. How about it?" He lifted his finger to indicate their vehicle, but his hand felt disconnected from his wrist, lighter than it should.

"What is your business, *señor?*" said the man with a jaw like a mule's shoe, leaning in the window, his breath rife with onions and mescal, the whites of his eyes a watery red.

"I'm a preacher."

"Hey, *jefe,* the funny gringo is a preacher. That's why he called my car a shitbox and shone his headlights on us while we were relieving ourselves."

The second man approached Cody's window, touching his friend on the shoulder, indicating he should move aside. "That's right? You're a preacher?" he said.

"Reverend Cody Daniels. But I got to be getting on my way."

"You work with La Magdalena?"

"I'm just a neighbor making a neighborly visit. I live up yonder, in the bluffs. I got people waiting on me."

The tall man's shoulders seemed unnaturally wide for his thin waist. His profile made Cody think of an ax blade. "Why are you so nervous?" the man asked. "I do something to make you nervous? You have never seen somebody relieve himself on a road in the dark?"

"You got a pistol stuck down in your belt. That's what some might call carrying a concealed weapon. In this county I wouldn't mess with the law."

The tall man fingered his cheek, then pointed at Cody. "I think I know you."

"No, sir, I don't think that's the case."

The tall man jiggled his finger playfully. "You are like me, a hunter. I've seen you down on the border. You hunt coyotes. Except these are coyotes with two feet."

"Not me. No, sir."

"No? You're not the man who likes to look through a telescope?"

"I just want to be on my way."

"What did you see up there at the house of *la china?*"

"Of *la* what?"

"You seem like one stupid gringo, my friend. Do I have to say it again?"

"If you're talking about the Chinese woman, I saw the same thing you saw through your binoculars — a bunch of people stuffing food in their faces."

"You were watching us?"

"No, sir, I passed you on the road here, that's all. I wasn't paying y'all any mind."

"You're one big liar, gringo."

"That woman up yonder is your problem, not me."

"You're a *cobarde,* too."

"I don't know what that means."

"You're a coward. You stink of fear. I think maybe you're a *cobarde* that shot at me once. A man up in the rocks with a rifle. You were far away, safe from somebody shooting back at you."

"No, sir," Cody said, shaking his head.

"What we going to do with you, man?"

"I'm gonna turn out on the hardpan and drive around those rocks and let y'all be. You're right, sir, none of this is my business."

"That's not what's going to happen, man. You see Negrito over there? He drinks too much. He's a *marijuanista,* too. When he drinks and smokes all that dope, you know what he likes to do? It's because he was in jail too long in Jalisco, where he was provided young boys by his fellow criminals. Now when he drinks and smokes marijuana, Negrito thinks he's back in Jalisco. If you try to drive out of here before I tell you, you will learn a lot more about your feminine side than you want to know."

"Don't be talking to me like that. No, sir."

The shorter man, the one called Negrito, opened the passenger door and sat down heavily in the seat. He smiled and touched the side of Cody's head and ran one finger behind his ear. "You got gold hair," he said. He touched Cody's cheek and tried to insert the tip of his finger in his mouth. "Mexican place mats, huh? That's really funny, gringo."

"You get him out of here," Cody said to the tall man.

"*La china* is hiding a friend of ours, a man who has gone insane and is wandering in the desert and needs his family. You need to find out where *la china* is hiding our friend. Then you need to build a fire and pour motor oil on it so the smoke climbs straight up in the sky. If you call anybody, if you make trouble for us, we're going to get you, man."

"I won't do it," Cody said.

"Oh, you're going to do it. Show him, Negrito."

The man named Negrito fitted his hand over the top of Cody's head, his fingers splaying like the points of a starfish. When he tightened his fingers, the pressure was instantaneous, as though cracks were forming in Cody's skull.

84

"I crushed bricks with my hands in a carnival," Negrito said. "I ate lightbulbs, too. I could blow fire out of my mouth with kerosene. I snapped a bull's neck. I can punch my fingers through your stomach and take out your liver, man. Don't pull on my wrist. I'm just gonna squeeze tighter."

"Please stop," Cody said.

When Negrito released his grip, Cody's eyes were bulging from his head, tears running down his cheeks, his ears thundering.

"When I see the smoke climbing up from the bluffs, I'll know you'll have something good to report," the tall man said. "If I don't see any smoke, I will be disappointed in you. Negrito is going to stake you out on the ground in the hot sun. Your voice is going to speak to the birds high up in the sky. Maybe for two or three days. You will learn to yodel, man."

"I was just driving down the road. All I did was blow my horn," Cody said.

"Yes, I have to say you're a very unlucky gringo," the tall man said.

They were both laughing at him, their work done, Cody's self-respect in tatters, the person he used to think of as the Reverend Daniels gone from inside the truck.

"What you done to have this kind of luck, man?" Negrito asked, caressing Cody's cheek with the back of his wrist. "Maybe you just act like you're a funny man. Maybe you've

85

done some things you want to tell me and Krill about. Things that make you feel real bad. You're a nice boy. We're gonna be good friends." He leaned close to Cody's ear and whispered, his breath like a feather on Cody's skin. Then he withdrew his mouth and smiled. "You gringos call it pulling a train. But in your case, I'm gonna be the train, the big choo-choo in your life, man."

CHAPTER FOUR

Hackberry Holland had given the paper plate used by Krill to the FBI. That was on a Monday. The next day he heard nothing but marked it off to the workload that beset all law enforcement agencies. On Wednesday he began making calls, none of which were returned. Nor were they returned on Thursday. Late Friday afternoon Maydeen Stoltz came into his office. She had fat arms and wore too much lipstick and smelled of cigarettes and took a pagan joy in her own irreverence. Hackberry had been reading a book he had checked out of the public library. He closed it and let his arm rest on the cover. "That fed was on the phone," Maydeen said.

"Which fed?"

"The one who uses the department to wipe his ass on."

"Good heavens, Maydeen —"

"If it was me, I'd slap him upside the head, I don't care how old he is."

"Would you kindly tell me who we're talking about?"

"Ethan Riser, who'd you think?"

Hackberry rubbed his temples, his gaze fixed on neutral space. "What did Agent Riser have to say?"

"That's the point. He didn't say anything, except you should call him. I told him you were in your office. He said he didn't have time to talk with you right now. He said you can call him back later on his cell phone."

Hackberry tried to process what he had just heard, then gave up. "Thanks, Maydeen."

"Want me for anything else?"

"Nope, but I'll tell you when I do."

"I'm just passing on the conversation."

"Got it," he said.

A half hour later, Ethan Riser called again. "Why wouldn't you talk to me a while ago?" Hackberry asked.

"I had an incoming call from Washington. I thought I explained that to your dispatcher."

"Evidently not. Did your lab get some prints for us?"

"Come down to the saloon. I'll buy you a drink."

"You're in town?"

"Yeah, I have to be over in Brewster tonight. But I like the saloon and café you have here. It's quite a spot."

"I'm glad you were able to find time to visit.

You have a reason for not coming to my office?"

"Can't do it, partner. That's the way it is," Riser said.

"I see. My dispatcher is named Maydeen Stoltz. If you run into her, just keep going."

"Care to explain that?"

"You'll figure it out." Hackberry hung up the telephone without saying good-bye. He got up from his desk and went into Pam Tibbs's office. "Let's take a walk," he said.

When they entered the saloon, Riser was eating a hamburger and drinking beer from a frosted mug in a back booth. His gaze slipped from Hackberry's face to Pam's, then back to Hackberry's. "Order up. It's on the G," he said.

Pam Tibbs and Hackberry sat down across from him. The saloon was dark and cool and smelled of beer and pickled sausage and ground meat frying in the kitchen. The floor was built from railroad ties that had been treated with creosote and blackened by soot from prairie fires, the heads of the rusty steel spikes worn the color of old nickels. The mirror behind the bar had a long fissure across it, shaped like a lightning bolt, so that the person looking into it saw a severed image of himself, one that was normal, one that was distorted, like a face staring up from the bottom of a frozen lake. Riser drank from his beer, a shell of ice sliding down his fingers. "I like this place. I always stop here when I'm in the area," he said.

"Yeah, it's five stars, all right. How about losing the charade?" Hackberry said.

"I do what I have to do, Sheriff."

"I'm not sympathetic."

"Okay," Riser said, setting down his beer, pushing away his food. "The guy who ate off that paper plate doesn't have prints on file in the conventional system. But you knew that or you wouldn't have given it to us. You were trying to use us, Sheriff."

"I gave you the paper plate because I had a professional obligation to give it to you," Hackberry said.

"Deputy Tibbs, can you go up to the bar and get whatever you and Sheriff Holland are having and bring another beer for me?" Riser said.

"No, I can't," she replied.

Riser looked at her out of the corner of his eye. He finished his beer and wiped his mouth with a paper napkin. "This guy Krill is in the computer at Langley. Before 9/11 we didn't have access to certain kinds of information. Now we do. A couple of decades back, our administration had some nasty characters working for us in Central America. Krill was one of them. He was of low-level importance in the big scheme of things but quite valuable in the bush."

"What's his real name?" Pam asked.

"Sorry?" Riser said.

"Are you hard of hearing?" she asked.

"Sheriff, we have a problem here," Riser said.

"No, *we* don't have a problem," Pam said. "The problem is you treat us like we're welfare cases you keep at bay with table scraps. Sheriff Holland has treated you and the Bureau with respect. Why don't you and your colleagues pull your heads out of your asses?"

"I had hoped we might establish some goodwill here," Riser said.

"I think Pam has a point," Hackberry said.

"I don't make the rules. I don't make our foreign policy, either," Riser said. "Nobody likes to admit we've done business with crab lice. Our friend Krill's real name is Antonio Vargas. We don't know that much about him, except he was on the payroll for a while, and now he's off the leash and seems to have a special hatred toward the United States."

"Why?" Hackberry asked.

"Maybe the CIA paid him in Enron stock. How would I know?"

"You need to stop lying, Mr. Riser," Pam said.

"Ma'am, you're way out of line," Riser said.

"No, you are," she said. "We bagged up that guy's dirty work. You ever pick up human fingers with your hands? Anybody who could do what he did has a furnace inside him instead of a brain. For us, these guys are not an abstraction. We live on the border, in their midst, and you're denying us information we're entitled to have."

Riser picked up his hamburger and bit into it. He chewed a long time before he spoke, his face looking older, more fatigued, perhaps more resigned to serving masters and causes he didn't respect. "This saloon reminds me of a photograph or a place I saw on vacation once," he said.

"The Oriental in Tombstone," Hackberry said. "It was run by the Earp brothers. That was just before the Earps and Doc Holliday blew three of the Clanton gang out of their socks at the O.K. Corral, then hunted down the rest and killed them one by one all the way to Trinidad."

"You guys must have a different frame of reference, because I'm never quite sure what you're talking about," Riser said.

"The message is we don't like getting dumped on," Pam said.

"This has really been an interesting meeting," Riser said. He got up from the booth and studied the check. He wore a brown suit with a thin western belt and no tie and a cowboy shirt that shone like tin. He didn't raise his eyes from the check when he spoke. "I love this country. I've served it most of my life. I honor other people who have served it, particularly someone who was a recipient of

92

the Navy Cross. I also honor those who work with a man of that caliber. I'm sorry I don't convey that impression to others. I hope both of you have a fine weekend."

Pam and Hackberry said little on the way back to the department. Rain and dust were blowing out of the hills against the sunset, a green nimbus rising from the land as though the day were beginning rather than ending. Hackberry took down the flag and folded it in a military tuck and put it in his desk drawer. He started to pick up the book he had left on his desk blotter. He was not aware Pam was standing behind him. "Don't buy into it," she said.

"Into what?"

"Riser is putting the slide on us."

"He isn't a bad man. He just takes orders. Consider how things would be if the Risers of the world hung it up and let others take their place." There was silence in the room. "I say something wrong?" he asked.

"Your goodness is your weakness. Others know it, and they use it against you," she replied.

"You need to stop talking like that to me, Pam."

She glanced at the title of the book on his desk blotter. "You reading about Air America?" she said.

"I thought it wouldn't hurt."

"Is the Asian lady's name in there?"

"In fact, it is."

"You like her?"

"I don't think about her one way or the other."

Pam gazed out the window. Down the street, a neon beer sign had just lighted in a barroom window. The pink glow of the sunset shone on the old buildings and high sidewalks. Pickup trucks and cars were parked at an angle in front of a Mexican restaurant that had a neon-scrolled green cactus above its front entrance. It was Friday evening, and as always in the American Southwest, it came with a sense of both expectation and completion, perhaps with the smell of open-air meat fires or rain on warm concrete. "Hack?" she said.

Don't say it. Don't think about it, he heard a voice say inside him. But he didn't know if the voice was directed at Pam or him. "What?" he asked.

"It's pretty here in the evening, isn't it?"

"Sure."

"I didn't mean to embarrass you in front of Riser."

"You didn't."

She looked out the window again. "We're off the clock now. Can I ask you a question?"

No, that's not a good idea, he thought.

"Hack?" she said, waiting for his response.

"Go ahead." In his mind's eye, he saw the

motel room in the crossroads settlement north of the Big Bend; he even felt the primal need that had caused him to break all his resolutions about involvement with a woman who was far too young for him and perhaps interested only because he had become a paternal figure in her life.

"Do you think about it?" she asked. "At all?"

"Of course."

"With regret?"

He took his hat off the rack, glancing into the outer offices. "No, but I have to remind myself that an old man is an old man. A young woman deserves better, no matter how good her heart is."

"Why is it that I don't get to make the decision, that you have to make it for me?" she asked.

Because you're looking for your father, he thought.

"Answer me," she said.

"I'm still your administrative supervisor. You have to remember that. It's not up for debate. This conversation is over."

"I've seen your wife's picture."

He felt a tic close to his eye. "What are you trying to tell me?"

"The Asian woman. She looks like her, that's all."

"I think I'd better head for the house."

He started to put on his hat, although he

95

never did so unless he was going out a door. She stepped close to him, her thumbs hooked in the sides of her belt. He could smell her hair, a hint of her perfume, the heat in her skin. There was a glaze on her eyes. "What's wrong, Pam?" he asked.

"Nothing."

"Tell me."

"Nothing. Like you say, you'd better go to your house. It's the kind of evening when most people want to celebrate the sunset, have dinner, dance, hear music. But you'd better go to your house."

"That's just the way it is," he replied. Then he remembered those were the words Ethan Riser had used to defend behavior that Hackberry considered morally indefensible. As he walked away, he heard her draw in a deep breath. He kept his eyes straight ahead so he did not have to look at her face and feel the hole in his heart.

Hackberry seldom slept well and never liked the coming of darkness, although he spent many hours sitting alone inside of it. Sometimes he fell asleep in his den, his head on his chest, and awoke at two or three in the morning, feeling he had achieved a victory by getting half the night behind him. Sometimes he believed he saw the red digital face on his desk clock through his eyelids. But quickly, the haze inside his head became the dust on a road north of Pyongyang and a molten sun that hung above hills that resembled women's breasts.

Sometimes as he dozed in the black leather swivel chair at his desk, he heard an airplane or a helicopter fly low overhead, the reverberations of the motors shaking his roof. But he did not identify the sound of the aircraft with a law enforcement agency patrolling the border or a local rancher approaching a private airstrip. Instead, Hackberry saw a lone American F-80 chasing a MiG across the Yalu River, then turning in a wide arc just as the MiG streaked into the safety of Chinese airspace. The American pilot did an aileron roll over the POW camp, signaling the GIs inside the wire that they were not forgotten.

When Hackberry slept in his bed, he kept his holstered blue-black white-handled custom-made .45 revolver on his nightstand. When he dozed in his office, he kept the revolver on top of his desk, the handles sometimes glowing in the moonlight like white fire. It was a foolish way to be, he used to tell himself, the mark of either a paranoid or someone who had never addressed his fears. Then he read that Audie Murphy, for the last two decades of his life, had slept every night with a .45 auto under his pillow, in a bed he had to move into the garage because his wife could not sleep with him.

Sometimes Hackberry heard the wind in

the trees or the clattering of rocks when deer came down the arroyo on their way to his horse tanks. Sometimes he thought he heard a messianic homeless man by the name of Preacher Jack Collins knocking through the underbrush and the deadfalls, a mass killer who had eluded capture by both Hackberry and the FBI.

Hackberry tried to convince himself that Collins was dead, his body long ago eaten by coyotes or lost inside the bowels of the earth. Regardless, Hackberry told himself, Collins belonged in the past or the place in the collective unconscious where most demons had their origins. If evil was actually a separate and self-sustaining entity, he thought, its manifestation was in the nationalistic wars that not only produced the greatest suffering but always became lionized as patriotic events.

At 2:41 Saturday morning, his head jerked up from his chest. Outside, he heard a heavy rock bounce down the arroyo, the breaking of a branch, a whisper of voices, then the sound of feet moving along the base of the hill. He unsnapped the strap on his revolver and got up from his desk and went to the back door.

A dozen or more people were following his fence line toward his north pasture. One woman was carrying a suitcase and clutching an infant against her shoulder. The men were all short and wore baseball caps and multiple shirts and, in the moonlight, had the snubbed profiles of figures on Mayan sculptures. So these were the people who had been made into the new enemy, Hackberry thought. Campesinos who sometimes had to drink one another's urine to survive the desert. They were hungry, frightened, in total thrall to the coyotes who led them across, their only immediate goal a place where they could light a fire and cook their food without being seen. But as John Steinbeck had said long ago, we had come to fear a man with a hole in his shoe.

Hackberry stepped outside with his hat on his head and walked into the grass in his sock feet. In the quiet, he could hear the wind blowing through the trees on the hillside, scattering leaves that had been there since winter. *"No tengan miedo. Hay enlatados en la granja,"* he called out. *"Llenen sus cantimploras de la llave de agua. No dejen la reja abierta. No quiero que me dañen la cerca, por favor."*

There was no response. The people he had seen with enough clarity to count individually now seemed as transitory and without dimension as the shadows in which they hid. "My Spanish is not very good," he called. "Take the canned goods out of the barn and fill your containers with water from the faucet

99

by the horse tank. Just don't break my fences or leave the gates open."

There was still no response or movement at the base of the hill. But what did he expect? Gratitude, an expression of trust from people sometimes hunted like animals by nativist militia? He sat down on the steps and rested his back against a wood post and closed his eyes. Minutes later, he heard feet moving down the fence line, a squeak of wire against a fence clip, then a rush of water from the faucet by the horse tank. No one had opened a gate to access or exit the lot; otherwise, he would have heard a latch chain clank against the metal. He waited a few more minutes before he walked down to the barn. The boxed canned goods were still in the tack room. His two foxtrotters stood three feet from the tank, staring at him curiously. "How you doin', boys? Make any new friends tonight?" he asked.

No reply.

Hackberry went back inside the house. He dropped his hat on the bedpost and laid his pistol on the nightstand. Still wearing his clothes, he lay down on top of the covers, one arm across his eyes, and fell asleep, his thoughts about war and the irreparable loss of his wife temporarily sealed inside a cave at the bottom of a wine-dark sea.

Hackberry knew what he was going to do that

morning even before he got up. Saturday had always been the day he and his wife attended afternoon Mass at a church where the homily was in Spanish, then later, ate fish sandwiches at Burger King and went to see a movie, no matter what was playing. After her death, he had an excuse to drink, but he didn't. Instead, he lived inside his loneliness and his silent house from Friday night to Monday morning, his only companion a form of celibacy that he had come to think of as the iron maiden.

Today was going to be different, he told himself with a tug at his heart and perhaps a touch of self-deception. He fed his animals and drank one cup of coffee and shaved and showered and shined his boots and put on a new pair of western-cut gray trousers and a wide belt and a navy blue shirt. He strapped on his revolver and removed his dove-colored Stetson from the bedpost and went out to his pickup truck. The sun was below the hills, the north and south pastures damp and streaked with shadow, the stars and the moon just starting to fade back into the sky. *You're too old to act like this,* a voice told him.

"Who cares?" he said.

Don't use your legal office for your personal agenda or to make a fool of yourself.

"I'm not," he said.

If there was any reply in his debate with himself, he refused to acknowledge it.

When he cut his engine in front of the Asian woman's house, he could hear metallic scraping sounds in back. He walked around the side of the house and saw her scrubbing out the corrugated tank by the windmill with a long-handled brush. She wore oversize jeans that were rolled up in big cuffs, and a long-sleeve denim shirt spotted with water. She pushed a strand of hair out of her eye with the back of her wrist and looked at him.

"I need to ask you a question or two about the fellow who got loose from our man Krill," Hackberry said.

"I can't help you," she said.

"You gave assistance to this fellow when he was hurt. I saw the bloody bandages and the mattress in the bunkhouse. You didn't trust me enough to tell me that. Then you told Krill something to the effect that this fellow wouldn't be at your house again. Not at your *house,* right? But he might be somewhere in the vicinity. I think you don't want to tell a lie, Miss Anton, but for various reasons, you're not telling the truth, either."

She held his gaze for a moment and seemed about to speak, but instead, she bent to her work again. He took the brush from her hand. "You're doing it the hard way," he said. He lifted the tank on its rim and dumped out all the water lying below the level of the drain plug. Then he righted the tank, released the chain that locked the windmill blades, and began filling the tank again while scrubbing a viscous red layer of sediment from the sides and bottom. "This stuff forms from a mixture of water and leaves or dust or both, I've never figured it out. It's like most things around here. Little of what happens is reasonable. It's the kind of place people move to after they've been eighty-sixed from Needles, California."

"What do you expect me to tell you?" she asked.

"You don't need to, Miss Anton. I think I know the truth."

With a spot of dirt on one cheek and the wind dividing her hair on her scalp, she waited for him to go on. When he didn't speak, she placed her hands on her hips and stared at the horse tank. "Sheriff Holland, don't play games with me."

"The federal employee who was taken hostage by Krill is probably a single man with no family; otherwise, they would be down here looking for him or making lots of noise in the media. The fact that he sought sanctuary with you indicates he's either on his own or he thinks you can provide him with a network of pacifists like himself. It also means he's probably somewhere close by, up in those hills or in a cave. From what little you've said, and from what the FBI hasn't said, this fellow was probably working in a defense program of some kind, one that presented him with problems of conscience. Maybe I can sympathize with his beliefs and also with yours. But Krill tortured a man to death in my county. Your friend the federal employee probably has information that can help me find Krill. Also, I think your friend is in grave jeopardy. I need your cooperation, Miss Anton. You've seen war in the most personal way. Don't let your silence contribute to this man's death."

"You'll turn him over to the FBI," she said.

"What would be the harm in that?"

"He has information the government doesn't want people to hear."

"The government doesn't operate that way. Politicians might, but politicians and the government are separate entities," Hackberry said.

"I heard you were once an attorney for the American Civil Liberties Union. You hide your credentials well."

He didn't reply and used his palm to deflect the water jetting from the well pipe in order to clean the scrub brush. He could feel her eyes peeling the skin off his face.

"I make you smile? There's something amusing about my speech?" she said.

"Somebody else once told me the same thing. Sometimes she'd tell me that every day."

She looked at him for a long time. "Are you a widower?"

"Yes, ma'am."

"Very long?"

"Eleven years."

"I'm sorry."

"She was a great woman. She was never afraid, not of anything, not in her whole life. She never wanted people to feel sorry for her, either, no matter how much she suffered."

"I see," she said, obviously trying to conceal her awkwardness.

He flicked the drops off the end of the brush onto the ground. He glanced up at the salmon-colored tint in the sky and looked at the hills and could almost smell the greening of the countryside and the feral odor that hung in its pockets and cracked riverbeds. He wondered how a land so vast and stark and self-defining could be marked simultaneously by both dust storms and acreage that was probably as verdant as the fields in ancient Mesopotamia. He wondered if the writer in the Bible had been describing this very place when he said the sun was made to shine and the rain to fall upon both the wicked and the just. He wondered if the beginnings of creation lay just beyond the tips of his fingers. "Have breakfast with me," Hackberry said.

"Sir?"

"You heard me."

"I don't know if that would be appropriate."

"Who's to say it's not?"

"You think I'm hiding a fugitive from the FBI. You virtually accused me of it."

"No, you're not hiding him, but you're probably feeding him and treating his wounds."

"And you want to take me to breakfast?"

"Look at me, Miss Anton. You think I'd try to trick you in some way? Ferret out information from you under the guise of friendship? Look me in the eye and tell me that."

"No, you're not that kind of man."

He let the water tank fill to the halfway mark, then notched the windmill chain and shut off the inflow valve. "I know this spot on the four-lane that serves huevos rancheros and frijoles that can break your heart," he said.

Cody Daniels felt he was not only the captain of a ship but the captain of his soul as he peered through the telescope mounted on the deck rail of his house. The valley was spread before him, the American flag painted on the cliff wall behind him, the wind blowing inside his shirt. As he watched the arrival of the sheriff at the Oriental woman's compound, his loins tingled with a surge of power and a sense of control that was so intense it made him wet his bottom lip; it even made him forget, if only briefly, his humiliation at the hands of the Hispanics named Krill and Negrito. He was fascinated by the body language of the sheriff and the woman, she with her demure posturing, he pretending he was John Wayne, scrubbing red glop off the sides of the horse tank like nobody else knew how to do it. Maybe the sheriff was not only pumping his deputy, the woman who'd stuck a .357 in Cody's face, but also trying to scarf some egg roll on the side. *Yeah, look at her,* Cody told himself, she was eating it up. These were the people who'd treated him like butt crust, a guy who had founded the Cowboy Chapel? They were the elite, and he was a member of the herd? What a joke.

With one eye squinted and the other glued to the telescope, Cody was so enamored with his ability to dissect fraudulence and self-serving behavior in others that he didn't notice the two dark Town Cars coming up the dirt track on the hardpan. The cars rumbled across Cody's cattle guard and parked by his church house, their dust floating up in a cinnamon-colored cloud that broke apart on his deck. Seven men wearing either suits or expensive casual clothes and shades and jewelry and shined shoes or boots got out and walked up the wood stairs. Their faces had no expression. When they neared the top step, they looked at him with the nonchalance of people entering a public restroom.

One man in the middle of the group was

obviously not cut out of the same cloth as the others. He removed his shades and pinched the bridge of his nose. Then he extended his hand and smiled good-naturedly, with the authority of a man who was comfortable in any environment. "It's Temple Dowling, Reverend. I'm pleased we could meet," he said. "You have a fine place here. You're not afraid to display the flag, either."

The other men walked past Cody as though he were not there. "Where are they going?" he asked.

"Don't worry. They're professionals," Temple Dowling said.

"They're going into my house."

"Concentrate on me, Reverend. We're on the same side. This country is in danger. You agree with that, don't you?"

"What's that got to do with those guys creeping my house?"

" 'Creeping' your house?"

"Yeah, breaking into it. That's what it's called. Like burglary."

"I could tell you I'm CIA. I could tell you I'm NSA. I could tell you I'm with the FBI." Temple Dowling's hair was silver and black, thick and freshly clipped, the part as straight as a taut piece of twine. His face wore the fixed expression of a happy cartoon, the skin pink and creamy, his lips too large for his mouth. He reached out and took Cody's hand again, except this time he squeezed hard, his gaze locked on Cody's. Cody felt a ribbon of pain slide up his wrist to his armpit. "What are you doing?" he said.

"Congratulating you. I love to fly the flag. I love the people who fly it, too."

"But you're with the government, aren't —" Cody began, opening and closing his bruised hand, his words catching in his throat.

"No, I'm like you, a citizen soldier. We're looking for a man by the name of Noie Barnum. He's a misguided idealist who can do great harm to our country. A man such as yourself has many eyes and ears working for him. You can be of great assistance to us, Reverend."

"I don't have anybody working for me. What are you talking about?"

"You have a church house full of them."

"People in my congregation got their own mind and go their own way."

"We both know better than that. You put the right kind of fear in them, they'll do whatever you say."

"I don't want any part in this. You get those guys out of my house," Cody said.

"Reverend, let's be frank. You've stumbled into a world of hurt. Would you rather deal with people of your own race and background or Mr. Krill?"

"How do you know about him?"

"We watched you talk with him. Mr. Krill is the man who wants to sell Noie Barnum to Al Qaeda. Would you like that to happen?"

"You were spying on me?"

"What does it matter? You're working for us now."

"No, sir, I work for the Lord."

"You're saying I don't?"

The other men reemerged from Cody's house. "It's clean," one of them said.

"Answer my question," Temple Dowling said to Cody. "You're telling me to my face I'm not on the side of our Lord?"

"No, sir, I didn't say that. What's he mean, it's clean?"

"It means you're not hiding the man we're looking for. It means your computer doesn't indicate you're in touch with the wrong people. It means you just passed a big test. I'm going to give you a business card, Reverend, and I want you to call me when you find out where Mr. Barnum is. I also want you to keep me updated on what that Chinese woman is doing. That means I want to know about everything that happens down there on her property. You're going to be my pipeline into Mr. Krill's little group. Whatever he does, whatever he tells you, you'll report it directly to me."

"You're going too fast," Cody said.

"You're doing all this out of your own volition. That's because you're a patriot. I know

110

about that clinic bombing. You're a man willing to take risks. That's why I'm making you part of our team."

"I didn't have anything to do with that clinic business. No, sir."

Temple Dowling set his hand on Cody's shoulder. "We're going to take care of you. There'll be a chunk of cash in it for you, too. You've got my word. Give me a big hug."

"What?"

"Just kidding. I had you going, didn't I?"

Cody's head was swimming, a smell like soiled cat litter rising from his armpits. "No, sir," he said.

"No, sir, what?" Temple Dowling said.

"I'm not working for y'all. I'm not having any part of this."

"I have two affidavits that say you bought the oven timer that detonated the bomb at the clinic. It blinded and disfigured a nurse. I have pictures of her if you'd like to see them. I have a videotape of you in the crowd across the street. You couldn't stay away from your own handiwork, could you, sir? That's what I mean when I say you're a man who lives on the edge. You're not a suck-up, kick-down kind of guy. You know how to rip ass, Reverend. That woman won't be in the baby-killing business anymore, that's for sure." He glanced at his men and was no longer able to contain his laughter. All of the men had a merry expression in their eyes and were clearly enjoying themselves. "Reverend Daniels, you're a special kind of shepherd," Dowling said.

When his visitors had driven away, Cody could hear kettle drums pounding inside his head. He sat down on a wood bench, his spine bowed, his eyelids fluttering, his muscles as flaccid as if his bones had been surgically removed from his body. The only other time he had felt this level of despair was when two county-prison gunbulls had finished with him and lifted him off a sawhorse and dropped him on a workroom floor like a slab of sweaty beef. He wondered why people thought they had to die in order to go to hell.

CHAPTER FIVE

Late Sunday afternoon Pam Tibbs parked the department's Jeep Cherokee at Hackberry's front gate and walked up the flagstone steps to his gallery and knocked on the door. He answered in his sock feet, his reading glasses on his nose. "I called twice and you didn't answer, so I thought I'd drive out," she said.

"I was in the pasture," he said.

"Maydeen got a report on an illegal dumping and another one on a break-in at a hunting camp. Both instances involved two guys. The dumping turned out not to be a dumping."

"I'm not following you."

"Last night a motorist saw two guys prowling in a creek bed and thought they were dumping trash. It turned out they were rifling the back of a camper. They stole some clothes and shoes and sleeping bags and a propane stove and a first-aid kit. This morning a guy with a long, pointy beard, wearing a tattered suit coat, was seen busting the lock on the back door of a hunting camp. He sounds like the same homeless guy who's been getting into people's garbage by Chapala Crossing. Except this time he had someone with him. They cleaned about forty pounds of venison out of the game locker. The witness said the guy in the tattered coat looked like he belted his trousers with a piece of clothesline. Sound familiar?"

"Jack Collins is dead," Hackberry said.

"You're convinced of that?"

"He either died of his wounds underground or was eaten by coyotes or cougars. He wasn't a supernatural entity. He was a psychopath and misogynist who probably couldn't tie his shoes without a diagram."

"Then who's the guy who keeps showing up around here?"

"Another lunatic. We're not in short supply of them."

"The guy with the tramp was limping. Like maybe a guy who ran a long distance with no shoes on."

"The man who escaped from Krill?"

"You know that burned-out shack where the tramp with the beard was probably living?"

"What about it?"

"I checked it out. It was soaked with an accelerant. Who would go to that much trouble to burn a shack?"

"You really think Collins is alive?"

"I'm not sure. But I'm bothered that you won't accept the possibility. I think you want to believe that evil dies."

She couldn't tell if he was thinking about what she had said or if he had lost interest. The sun had gone behind a hill, darkening the inside of his house, and she couldn't see past him into the shadows. "Did I disturb you?" she said.

"Pardon?"

"You didn't invite me in. Are you with someone?"

"Do I look like it?"

"You tell me. Did you enjoy your Mexican dinner with China's answer to Mary Magdalene?" She didn't wait for him to reply. "It's a small town. Why don't you at least spend the gas money to go into another county?"

"You need to concentrate on other matters, Pam."

"You're eating out with a woman who's part of a homicide investigation. Maybe someone who's aiding and abetting."

"Come in."

"No."

"Don't be resentful toward her."

"I'm resentful toward you. You're letting her jerk you around. You're acting like a damn fool."

"You mean an old fool."

"Don't put words in my mouth. Don't you dare act like I've ever been disloyal to you."

He held his eyes on hers, refusing to concede an inch. She picked up his hand and pressed it against her left breast, clenching down on his wrist so he couldn't remove it. "Feel my heart."

"Don't do this, Pam."

"Don't you ever accuse me of disloyalty."

"I wouldn't do that, Pam. Never."

"Then why the hell do you hurt me?"

"I don't mean to."

"That's all you're going to say?"

"Yes, ma'am, that's about it."

"I want to hit you. With my fists. As hard as I can. I want to break the bones in your face."

"Go ahead."

Her eyes went in and out of focus, a nest of blue veins pulsing by her temple. "What do you want me to do now?" she said.

"About what?"

"About Preacher Jack Collins or whoever this tramp and his friend are. About doing my goddamn job."

"We start at the hunting camp. Later, I'd like to buy you dinner."

"In your dreams," she said. "I'll wait for you in the Jeep."

Inside a ravine snaking back through a collection of sandstone formations that resembled pillars in an ancient church, a man wearing a soiled panama hat tipped down over his brow and a pin-striped suit coat that was frayed white on the tips of the sleeves squatted at the opening to a cave. He stared into a cook fire that he had built inside a ring of stones, and he fed the fire incrementally, stick by stick, as though fascinated with either his power over the flames or an image he saw inside them. In the firelight, his face seemed dotted with lumps of proud flesh, his cheeks and throat streaked with the irregular stubble of a man who had shaved with a dry razor.

"Why are you grinning?" asked the man on the opposite side of the fire ring.

"No reason," the man in the suit coat replied.

But he was not telling the truth. Inside the flames, he saw a woman's hair and the paleness of her face and the redness of her mouth. He saw the wantonness of her smile, the lewdness in her eyes, the flash of an incisor tooth as she glanced at him from behind a blanket she had hung on the wash line dividing the boxcar where she and her son lived. He heard the heavy weight of a Mexican gandy dancer settling between her thighs.

"You're a mysterious fellow," said the man on the far side of the fire ring.

"How's that?"

"You have little to share, but you befriend a stranger who has nothing. You're willing to break the law to find food for a man you owe nothing."

"Maybe I stole it for myself."

"A man as poor as you is not a thief."

"Maybe I like your name."

"It's hardly original," said the man on the opposite side of the fire. His face was long and homely, his ears too large, his nose shaped like a big teardrop, his shoulders knobbed as though they had been turned on a lathe. His name was Noie Barnum.

"Noie restarted the human race," the man in the suit coat said. "Noie watched Yahweh hang the archer's bow in the sky. 'God gave Noie the rainbow sign / It's not by water, it's the fire next time.' You know that song?"

"I haven't heard it."

"Yahweh made a contract. He stopped the rain and stilled the water and brought Noie and the ark to land. Before the flood, man was not supposed to break the skin of an animal with a knife. After the flood, the lion was supposed to lie down with the lamb. But it didn't work out that way. That's why the land is cursed."

"You're either a closet college professor or you've spent a lot of time in the public library," Noie Barnum said.

"You wouldn't mock a fellow, would you?" the man in the suit coat replied. His teeth shone at the corner of his mouth when he spoke, but there was no rancor in his voice.

"No, sir, I think you're a good man. You and the Asian lady saved my life."

"Which Asian lady?"

"The one the Mexicans call La Magdalena."

"The papist?"

"I'm not sure what she is. I know she's
brave and she's kind. I think she's a lot like
you, Jack."

"I doubt that." Jack flipped a twig into the
fire, fascinated with its fate. He pried open
the blade from his pocketknife and stripped
the bark from a mesquite branch and sharpened the end into a point, then speared four
chunks of venison and watched them curl and
brown over the campfire. His fingernails were
rimmed with dirt, his shapeless trousers
stuffed inside the tops of his cowboy boots.
As he squatted on his heels, his buttocks
looked as thin as barrel slats. He opened a
can of beans and stuck them down in the
coals. He poured water from a canteen into
two aluminum cups and handed one of them
to Noie. "You hear that sound?" he asked.

"What sound?"

"Out yonder, to the southwest, just below
the evening star."

"I don't hear or see anything," Noie said.

"It's a helicopter. When it flies over, don't
look up. The light always reflects off your
face. Even starlight does. Ever see ducks or
geese change their flight pattern when you
glance up at them? They read the propensi-
ties down below a lot better than we do."

"Shouldn't we put out the fire?"

"These hills and canyons and dry washes are full of fires. The people in that helicopter are looking for white men. They're looking for us."

"Who are you, Jack?"

"You don't want to know."

From his belt loops, Jack pulled the piece of rope he had been using to hold up his trousers. He dropped it in the fire and watched it spark and then dissolve on the coals like a snake blackening and curling back on itself. He uncoiled a belt he had taken from the camper shell of the parked pickup and threaded it through the loops on his trousers, working the point around his skinny hips to the buckle, totally absorbed with the task.

"I didn't mean to offend you," Noie said.

"Why study on a wretch like me?" Jack said. The thropping sounds of a helicopter passed overhead, the airframe silhouetting briefly against the moon like a giant predator. Jack sat motionlessly on a rock, smiling crookedly from under the brim of his panama hat, until the helicopter and the downdraft of its blades had disappeared in the darkness. He tossed Noie a tin plate. "Eat up. White-tailed venison cooked on a mesquite fire with a little pepper and salt is about as good as it gets."

Pam and Hackberry's investigation into the theft at the hunting camp and from the camper shell of the pickup truck went nowhere. There were no recoverable prints and no witnesses who could provide any additional information or descriptive detail about the two men who had committed the break-ins. Early Monday morning Hackberry drove by himself to the burned shack where the tramp had occasionally been seen. But he was not the first to arrive there.

Ethan Riser was standing among several men holding a conversation between two parked SUVs. Even though the morning air was soft, the sun hardly above the hills, the ground moist with night damp, all of the men were in shirtsleeves and wore shades, as though the sun were blazing in the center of the sky. Only Riser bothered to look at Hackberry when he got out of the cruiser and approached the SUVs. "Be with you in a minute, Sheriff," Riser said.

"No, sir, I need to talk with you now," Hackberry said.

Riser separated himself from the group and walked beside Hackberry toward the pile of ash and charcoal that had once been a shack where a nameless tramp sometimes lived. "Are you here for the same reasons I am?" Hackberry said.

"What would that be?" Riser asked.

"Don't try to take me over the hurdles, Ethan."

"The federal employee we're looking for is

named Noie Barnum. If this guy falls into the wrong hands, he can do enormous injury to this country. Believe me, you cannot imagine the extent of the damage. I need your cooperation, and by 'cooperation' I mean you have to stop intervening in our affairs."

"Noie?"

"Yeah, like the spelling in the King James Bible," Riser said. "People in the southern mountains pronounce it 'No-ee.' "

"This is my county and my jurisdiction. You guys are our guests," Hackberry said.

"That's outrageous."

"So is federal arrogance."

"I have to get back to work."

"No, you don't," Hackberry said. "What's your interest in a burned-down shack?"

"That's not your concern."

"You think Jack Collins might have given refuge to Barnum?"

"If you've figured everything out, why bother asking the FBI?"

"I'm not asking the FBI. I'm asking you, man to man."

"We never found Collins's body. His case is still open."

"You think he burned his shack to get rid of his prints?"

"We haven't come to any conclusions about any of this, at least not that we can pass on."

"*We?* I asked you for an opinion about the

torching of the shack. It's not a difficult question."

"I think you should take your mind off world events. Do that for us, and we'll do our best to stay out of your hair."

Hackberry gazed at the gray and black humps of ash and charcoal and scorched boards and cans of food that had exploded in the heat and the strips of rusted corrugated tin protruding from the pile. A charred Bible had been raked out on the grass. The pages, all of them burned as black as carbon paper along the outer margins, were flipping in the wind. Hackberry turned his attention back to Riser.

"You didn't bag the Bible," Hackberry said.

"Why should I?"

"To see if Collins's prints are on it."

Riser removed a ballpoint from his shirt pocket. He seemed to study it a moment; then he started clicking it. "I can never get these things to work right."

"You already know whose Bible that is. It belongs to Collins, doesn't it?" Hackberry said.

Riser stuck the ballpoint back in his pocket and glanced at his watch and at his colleagues by the SUVs. "I hope all this works out for everybody. Be seeing you, Sheriff," he said.

"Something else happened here. Collins didn't burn the shack, did he?"

"How do you know that?"

"He's a religious fanatic. He wouldn't burn his Bible."

"You're too smart for your own good. I mean that in a kindly way."

"You guys did it."

"No, *we* did not do it."

"Or somebody from ICE or the Border Patrol or the DEA. But one of y'all did it. Tell me I'm wrong. I want you to."

"So maybe you're not wrong," Riser said. "Maybe a hothead got pissed off and wanted to send Collins a message. Maybe unlike you, not everybody is always in control of his emotions."

"You're telling me one of your people soaked private property with an accelerant and put a match to it, and you're telling me lawmen do this with regularity?"

"The U.S. Forest Service used to burn out squatters all the time."

"Nobody can be this dumb. Do you realize what y'all have done?"

"The Department of Justice isn't exactly Pee-wee Herman. We don't quake in our shoes because we have to hunt down a self-anointed messiah who probably hasn't changed his underwear since World War Two."

Hackberry walked over to the group of federal agents, still gathered between the two SUVs. "Which one of you guys torched the shack?" he asked.

They stared at him blankly from behind

their shades. "What shack?" one of them said.

"I dug up nine of Jack Collins's victims, all of them Asian, all female, some of them hardly more than children. He used a Thompson submachine gun, a full drum, fifty rounds, at almost point-blank range. Then they were bulldozed over behind the ruins of a church. One of them may have been still alive when she went into the ground. A Phoenix mobster sent three California bikers to pop him. Jack bribed their chippies to set them up and then turned the three of them into wallpaper."

"Sounds like the right guy might have got his house burned down," one of the agents said.

Hackberry walked back toward his cruiser, his face tight, his temples knotted with veins. Behind him, he heard one of the agents make a remark the others laughed at. But Hackberry didn't look back. Instead, he kept his eyes focused on Ethan Riser. "That bunch of Ivy League pissants back yonder?" he said.

"What about them?" Riser said.

Hackberry opened the door to his cruiser. "I thought you were different, that's all," he said.

"You should have stayed with the ACLU, Sheriff. At least they have an understanding of procedure and protocol," Riser said. "They try to think twice before they put their own agenda ahead of their country's security.

Where do you get off lecturing other people? Who died and made you God?"

"Nobody. And that's the problem every one of y'all has, Ethan. You wrap your lies in the flag and put the onus on others. Shame on every one of you," Hackberry said.

When he drove away, the back tires of his cruiser ripped two long lines out of the grass.

That evening Hackberry was about to relearn that the past wasn't necessarily a decaying memory and that its tentacles had the power to reach through the decades and fasten themselves onto whatever prey they could slither their suction cups around. When he returned home from work, he found an envelope stuck in his doorjamb. Inside was a silver-edged sheet of stationery folded crisply through the center. The note on it was written in bright blue ink, in a flowing calligraphy, the curlicues fading into wispy threads. It read:

Dear Sheriff Holland,

Congratulations on all your political success. My father always spoke fondly of you and I'm sure he would be very proud of you. Forgive me for dropping by without calling first, but your number was unlisted. Call my car phone if you can have drinks or dinner, or I'll try to drop by later or at your office.

With kindest regards,
Temple Dowling

Unconsciously, Hackberry glanced over his shoulder after reading the note, as though an old adversary lay just beyond the perimeter of his vision. Then he went into the house and tore the note and envelope into four pieces, then tore them again and dropped them in the kitchen waste can and washed his hands in the sink.

It was easier to cleanse his skin than rinse his memory of Temple's father, United States Senator Samuel Dowling. And Hackberry's thoughts about the senator were uncomfortable not because the senator had been mean-spirited and corrupt to the core, but because Hackberry, when he ran for Congress, had, of his own choosing, fallen under the senator's control.

The 1960s had been a transitional time in Texas's political history. Hispanic farmworkers were unionizing, and huge numbers of black people had been empowered by the Voting Rights Act of 1965. Hackberry had watched the changes take place from a distance, at least when he wasn't driving across the river to the brothels in Coahuila or Nuevo León, or staining the shaved ice in a tall glass one jigger at a time, with four inches of Jack Daniel's, adding a sprig of mint and a teaspoon of sugar, just before taking the first drink of the day, one that rushed through his body with the intensity of an orgasm. Both the Democratic ticket and Hackberry's first wife, Verisa, were delighted at the prospect of a handsome, towering war hero representing their district. Hackberry soon discovered that his addiction to whiskey and the embrace of a Mexican girl's thighs didn't hold a candle to the allure of celebrity and political power.

The attraction was not entirely meretricious in nature. Couched inside the vulgarity and the crassness of the new rich who surrounded him, and the attempts at manipulation of the sycophants, were moments that made him feel he was genuinely part of history. For good or bad, he had become a player in the Jeffersonian dream, a decorated former navy corpsman from a small Texas town about to take up residence at the center of the republic. Maybe Jefferson's dream had been tarnished, but that did not mean it was lost, he had told himself. Even George Orwell, describing a Spanish troop train leaving a station on its way to the front while brass bands were blaring and peasant girls were throwing flowers, had said that maybe there was something glorious about war after all.

Hackberry remembered one balmy summer night of the campaign in particular. He had been standing on a balcony at the Shamrock Hotel in Houston, wearing only a bathrobe, a tumbler of whiskey and ice in one hand. Far below, columns of electric light glowed beneath the surface of a swimming pool built in the shape of a four-leaf clover. Across the boulevard, in a strange blend of the rural South and the New American Empire, oil wells pumped up and down — *clink, clank, clink, clank* — like the steady and predictable rhythm of lovers copulating, while cattle grazed nearby in belly-deep grass and thunder leaked from banks of black- and plum-colored rain clouds overhead.

The hotel had been built by a notorious wildcatter who sometimes came into the Shamrock Room and got into brawls with his own patrons, wrecking the premises and adding to a mythos that told all of its adherents they, too, could become denizens of the magic kingdom, if only the dice toppled out of the cup in the right fashion. In forty-five minutes Hackberry was to address a banquet hall filled with campaign donors who could buy third-world countries with their credit cards. When he was in their midst, he sometimes had glimpses in his mind of a high school baseball pitcher who resembled him and who took a Mexican girl to a drive-in theater in 1947, knowing that as soon as he went into the restroom, he would be beaten senseless. But Hackberry did not like to remember the person he used to be. Instead, he had made a religion out of self-destruction and surrounded himself with people he secretly loathed.

On that balcony high above the pool, he had not heard the senator walk up behind him. The senator had cupped his palm around the back of Hackberry's neck, massaging the muscles as a father might do to his son. "Are you nervous?" the senator had said.

"Should I be?"

"Only if you plan to tell them the truth."

"What *is* the truth, Senator?"

"That the world we live in is a sweet, sweet sewer. That most of them would drink out of a spittoon rather than give up their access to the wealth and power you see across the boulevard. That they want to own you now so they don't have to rent you later."

Hackberry had drunk from the tumbler, the ice cubes clattering against the glass, the palm fronds moving in the breeze down below, the warmth of the whiskey slowing his heart like an old friend reassuring him that the race was not to the swift. "Telling the truth would be my greatest sin? That's an odd way of looking at public service, don't you think?"

"There's a far graver sin."

"What would that be?"

"You already know the answer to that one, Hack."

"A worse sin would be disloyalty to someone who has reached out and anointed me with a single touch of his finger on my brow?" Hackberry had said.

"That's beautifully put. Your wife said you bedded a Mexican whore in Uvalde last night."

"That's not true. It was in San Antonio."

"Oh, that's good. I have to remember that one. But no more local excursions. There will be time enough for that when you get to Washington. Believe it or not, it will be there in such abundance that you'll eventually grow bored with it, if you haven't already. Usually, when a man of your background screws down, he's not seriously committed to infidelity. It's usually an act of anger rather than lust. A bit of trouble at home, that sort of thing. It beats getting drunk. Is that the case with the girl in San Antonio?"

Hackberry had not answered.

"Fair enough. There's no shame in having a vice. It's what makes us human," the senator had said. Then he had patted Hackberry gingerly on the back of the head, after first leaning over the rail and spitting, even though people were eating at poolside tables directly below.

Those moments on the balcony and the touch of the senator's hand on his head had remained with Hackberry like a perverted form of stigmata for over four decades.

An hour after tearing up the message left by Temple Dowling, Hackberry glanced through the front window and saw a man park a BMW at the gate and walk up the flagstones to the gallery. The visitor had thick silver-and-black hair and lips that were too large for his mouth. He was carrying an ice bucket with a dark green bottle inserted in it. Hackberry opened the door before his uninvited guest could ring the bell.

"Hello, Sheriff. Did you find my note?"

"Yes, sir, you're Mr. Dowling. Leave the bucket and the bottle on the gallery and come in."

"Excuse me?"

"Guests in my home drink what I have or they don't drink at all."

"I was supposed to meet a lady friend, but she stood me up. I hate to see a good bottle of wine go to waste. My father said you used to have quite a taste for it."

"You want to come in, sir?"

"Thank you. And I'll leave my bucket behind." Dowling stepped inside and sat down in a deep maroon leather chair and gazed through the picture window, patting the tops of his thighs, a thick gold University of Texas class ring on his left hand. He wore a gray suit and a tie that was as bright as a halved pomegranate. But it was the composition of his face that caught the eye — the large lips, the pink cheeks and complexion that looked as though they had been dipped out of a cosmetics jar, the heavy eyelids that seemed translucent and were flecked with tiny vessels. "What a lovely view. The hills in front of your house remind me of —"

"Of what?"

"A Tahitian painting. What was his name? Gauguin? He was big on topless native women."

"I haven't studied on it."

Temple Dowling smiled, his fingers knitting together.

"Do I amuse you, sir?" Hackberry said.

"I was thinking of something my father said. He admired your élan. I told him I'd heard you'd had a lot of girlfriends. My father replied, 'Mr. Holland is a great lover of humanity, son. But let's remember that half the human race is female.' "

"I think maybe the senator misrepresented the nature of our relationship. We were not friends. We used each other. That's a reflection on me, not him."

"Call me Temple."

"I was a drunkard and a whoremonger, not a man who simply had girlfriends. I used the bodies of poor peasant girls across the river without thinking about the misery that constituted their lives. When I met Senator Dowling, I was arrogant and willful and thought I could play chess with the devil. Then the day came when I realized I had gravely underestimated Senator Dowling's potential. After I mentioned my father's political principles and his friendship with Franklin Roosevelt, the senator explained why my father had shot and killed himself. My father had taken a bribe. The people who bribed and later tried to blackmail him were friends of Senator Dowling. The senator took great pleasure in telling me that story."

"I'm not my father, Sheriff."

"No, sir, you're not. But you're not here out of goodwill, either."

"How much money do you think it would take to shut down the city of New York?"

"I wouldn't know, and I'm not interested."

"I don't mean to just disrupt it, like the 9/11 attacks. I mean to flood the tunnels and destroy the bridges and hospitals and poison the water supply and to spread fire and plague and anthrax and suffering all over the five boroughs. What if I told you that fifty thousand dollars spent in the right place by the wrong guys could turn New York into Dante's ninth circle?"

"What business are you in, sir?"

"The defense of our nation."

"Would you answer the question, please?"

"Unmanned aerial vehicles."

"Drones that fire missiles?"

"Sometimes. Other times they're observation vehicles. The cost to manufacture a Patriot missile is three million dollars. The cost of drones is nickels and dimes in comparison. A small drone can be powered with batteries and is invulnerable to heat-seeking missiles. They can fly so slowly that jet interceptors can't lock down on them. Hezbollah has used them inside Israeli airspace."

"What do you want from me?"

"Nothing. I'm here to offer my services."

"They're not needed, and they're not wanted."

"Somewhere out there in those hills is a man named Noie Barnum. He's an idealistic idiot who believes that sharing knowledge about our weapons will make for a safer world."

"My impression is that he was kidnapped and about to be sold to Al Qaeda when he escaped. He doesn't sound like a willing participant in any of this."

"So why doesn't he come in?" Dowling said.

"That's a good question."

"Barnum has told others he has 'problems of conscience.' His 'problem' is the fact that UAVs can cause collateral damage. I wonder what he thinks about the collateral influences of napalm and bombs dropped from B-52s. Or maybe he'd like more of our soldiers killed while digging ragheads out of their caves."

"Why are you here, sir?" Hackberry said.

"I want Noie Barnum in a cage. I don't want him in front of a microphone or a camera. I'd like to see him buried under concrete at Guantánamo, after his head was wrapped in a towel and half the Atlantic was poured into it."

"I'll pass on your remarks to the FBI the first opportunity I have."

"Sheriff, who do you think runs this country?"

"You tell me."

"Lyndon was put into office by Brown and Root. Lyndon is moldering in the grave, but Brown and Root merged with Halliburton and is still alive and well. You think our current president is going to rescind their contracts at almost every United States military base in the world?"

"I wouldn't know."

Temple Dowling stood up from his chair and removed a strand of cat hair from his sleeve. "My father said you were never a listener."

"You ever hear of Preacher Jack Collins?"

"No, who is he?"

"The most dangerous man I've ever met," Hackberry said.

"What does that have to do with Noie Barnum?"

"Jack may be feeding and protecting him. I'm not sure why. Maybe because the feds burned Jack's shack. Keep hanging around this area, and you might get a chance to meet him. If he chats you up, try to get it on tape."

"Why would I want to do that?"

"Because it's the only record people will have of your death. Thanks for coming by."

CHAPTER SIX

Using only starlight, Jack Collins and Noie Barnum made their way up a deer trail along the side of a bluff and into a narrow canyon that was threaded by a creek and strewn with chertlike yellow rock that had toppled from the ridges. Jack was in the lead, a nylon pack on his back, the straps pinching his suit coat tightly into his armpits, his body straining forward. Noie was limping badly, barely able to keep up, one arm tucked against his rib cage. There was a layer of fertile soil on the ground that sloped from the base of the cliffs down to the creek, and grass and wildflowers grew on it.

Jack paused and wiped his face and took his companion's measure. "You want to sit down, bud?" he asked.

"No, sir, I'm fine."

"You're a tough *hombre.*"

"I'm not in your class, Jack. You're a mountain goat."

Jack walked back down the trail to where

his companion was leaning on the twisted remains of a cedar tree, breathing through his nose. "It gets steep up yonder. Put your arm on my shoulder. If you hear a rattler, hold still and give him time to get out of your way."

"What if he doesn't?"

"Throw a rock at him."

"For real?"

"I have the feeling people didn't tell a lot of jokes where you're from."

A cabin stood at the head of the canyon. Next to it was a loading chute that had turned gray with dry rot. In back were a barn with a sliding door and, farther up the hillside, an aluminum cistern supported on steel stanchions. Jack helped Noie the rest of the way up the trail, then slung his pack on the cabin's porch and eased Noie down on the steps. "I'll open up and fire the stove and get some food started," he said.

"Who owns this?" Noie asked.

"Me."

"You own property?"

"A mess of it."

"You're quite a kidder, Jack."

"That's me."

Jack removed the door key from behind a wallboard, unlocked the cabin, and went inside. He stuffed newspaper and kindling and three chunks of firewood in the cook-stove and set them ablaze, then went outside and started the gasoline motor that powered the water pump and the electric lights. He slid open the barn door and gazed at an unpainted Trans Am that had lines of rust around the fenders, though it was mounted with four Michelin tires that looked fresh from the dealership. Then he returned to the cabin and opened two cabinets lined with canned goods and boxes of cereal and jars of preserves. He filled a skillet with corned beef and hash and dumped a can of spinach into a pan and set them on the stove. He went back on the porch and helped Noie to his feet. "I think your ribs are fractured," he said. "The pain will probably be with you six weeks at the inside. You take the bunk, and I'll make a pallet on the floor."

"Jack, I have no idea what's going on. Is this really your camp?"

"You haven't figured out who I am?"

"No, sir, I'm pretty confused."

"I was a longtime exterminator for Orkin. I still have my license. That's a fact."

"You're a pest exterminator?"

"That says it all," Jack replied.

"Why are you doing all this for me?"

"I like your accent. I never met a Quaker from Alabama."

In the early morning, Jack rose from his pallet and slipped on his boots and retrieved a flashlight and a shovel from the barn. The sky was bursting with stars as he labored up a path to a cave entrance that was not much wider than his hips. He squeezed through the opening, then stood up slowly, in a crouch, and flicked on the flashlight. The interior of the cave was as orange and pale as the inside of a pumpkin, the roof jagged and blackened by the cook fires of hunters and gatherers who may have been there before the Indians. On one wall, petroglyphs and images cut with stone tools depicted the slayings of both animals and people. Jack sometimes wondered if the battle in the stone mural had been fought over food or if the animals had been slain to ensure that the survivors would starve. There was another artifact in the cave that seemed to answer the question for him. A hole used to grind corn had been augered into a slab of table rock that ran the length of one wall. Jack believed the grinding hole proved the battle was not over game. In Jack's opinion, man killed because he had lost Eden. The bitterness was obviously so great that nothing short of mass fratricide could assuage it. Why else did people enjoy it so? Killing over food? Who was kidding whom? The throngs who attended blood sports weren't worried about the quality of the hot dogs.

The air inside the cave was cool and smelled of guano and damp clay and the field mice that nested on the ledges. Jack worked his way to the rear of the shaft, then set his light on the table rock and went to work, his dirty panama pulled down on his brow, his unshaved cheeks as lined as old parchment. The mixture of sand and clay and charcoal curdled up like old skin on the shovel's blade as he pushed the handle toward the rear wall, peeling the ground away in layers, tossing each shovel load to one side. When he was down less than a foot, he glimpsed a piece of black vinyl in the dirt. He got to his knees and began scraping the dirt out of the hole with his fingers, brushing off the vinyl, pushing his hands sideways into the dirt to find purchase on the outer edges of the bag, feeling the hard, familiar contours inside it. He dug faster, his heart beating, his throat tingling with anticipation, his breath loud inside the confines of the cave. He sculpted the bag free of dirt from head to foot, then fitted both hands under it and lifted it from the ground. A damp odor that was as cool and pungent as bruised nightshade rose into his face.

In his haste, he knocked the flashlight off the table rock, and the inside of the cave went black. He groped in the dirt until he felt the aluminum cylinder with his fingers, but when he pushed the switch on and off, nothing happened. The inside of the cave contained a level of darkness that only a blind man would understand. Jack felt as though his eyes had been scooped out of his head with a spoon.

He stared up the shaft, hoping to see a glimmer of starlight through the opening, but there was both a bend and a drop in the floor, and the darkness was so absolute that it seemed to flow like liquid through his eyes into his skull.

It was not unlike the inside of a cargo trunk his mother had kept in the boxcar where they had lived. "You cost me the trick, Jack. That's the only way Ma and you can get by," she would say. "It hurts me to do this. Why are you such a headstrong little boy? Why do you force Ma to do this to her only begotten?"

He dragged the bag behind him, feeling above with one hand to protect his head, the weight inside the bag slapping across the cave floor. Then he rounded the bend and saw the stars in the sky and felt a sense of release that was like an infusion of pure oxygen into his soul. He climbed through the cave opening into the breeze and the smell of creek water and wet grass and desert bloom, then pulled the bag through the hole after him. When he sat down on the incline, sweat was leaking out of his hat and drying on his face. He waited until he had caught his breath, then tore the garbage bag away from the hard outline. His hands were shaking when he unsnapped the series of latches on the top of the guitar case and pried the top up on its hinges. Set inside the velvet pink liner, just as he had left them one year ago, were his

Thompson .45 submachine gun, a box magazine, two fifty-round ammunition pans, and six boxes of cartridges. He touched the cold blue oiled smoothness of the frame and saw the vaporous whorls of his fingertips clouding on the steel and evaporating, like the melting of dry ice or hailstones. Did the ancient gods give power with the touch of a finger? he asked himself. Or did they absorb it from the beings they touched? Didn't Death depend on his victims in order to sustain his own existence? Jack wondered what Ma would think if she saw him now. He wondered if she would smile in awe when the electric arc leaped from the muzzle of his Thompson, when he cut down his enemies like a harvester ripping a scythe through wheat. Would she believe her son had become the left hand of God and be proud of him? Or would she run squeaking and skittering like a dormouse squeezing through its hidey-hole?

He entered the back of the cabin and removed fresh underwear and socks from a dresser, and a white dress shirt and an unpressed clean brown suit from the closet. He stripped off his soiled clothes and let them drop to the floor and wrapped his body in a quilt. Then he carried the guitar case and his razor and a bar of soap and the change of clothes down to the creek. He laid out his suit and underwear on a rock and sat down in the center of the creek, the current frothing around his chest, a cluster of deer watching him from an arroyo. He washed his hair and face and body and lathered his throat and cheeks and shaved by touch. Even though he climbed dripping wet onto the bank and dressed without drying off, his skin was as warm as a heated lampshade. The light had started to go out of the sky, but the evening star still hung low in the west, just above the hills, twinkling like a harbinger of a fine day.

He slipped on his boots and lay down on the quilt, the Thompson at his side, his head cushioned on his arm. The ground was patinaed with tiny wildflowers, and as he breathed their fragrance, he thought he could hear the wind whispering through the grass. The whispering grew in volume until it sounded like bees buzzing in a hive, or the whisperings of desperate girls and young women who had been trapped unfairly underground long before their time, all of them Asian girls whose sloe eyes pleaded for mercy and whose voices asked, *Why did you do this to us?*

I freed you from a life of degradation, he replied.

But his words were like the weighted tips of a flagrum whipped across his soul.

Early the next morning, Maydeen Stoltz

walked into Hackberry's office. She had a pink memo slip in her hand. "That was Bedford at the firehouse. He said he had a call maybe we should know about."

"Concerning what?"

Maydeen looked at the memo slip. "The caller gave his name as Garland Roark. He said he was an arson investigator with the Texas Department of Public Safety. He said he was compiling information about the incidence of arson along the border."

"Say that name again."

"Garland Roark."

Hackberry wrote it on a legal pad.

"So Bedford told him about the shack burning down, the one maybe Collins was living in," Maydeen said.

"Go on."

"The caller wanted to know how Bedford knew it was arson. Bedford told him the whole place stunk of kerosene. Then the caller asked if Bedford had any suspects in mind. Bedford goes, 'Not unless you count the FBI.' "

"Wait a minute," Hackberry said. "When did Bedford get this call?"

"A week ago, right after the fire."

"Bedford suspected the feds did it but didn't tell us?"

"Hold your water two seconds and I'll try to finish," Maydeen said.

"Excuse me."

146

"I asked Bedford the same question. He said a trucker saw a car with a government tag parked by the shack just before the flames went up. Bedford figured if the feds set fire to it, there was a reason. He thought maybe it was a stopover place for illegals."

"So why is Bedford calling us now?"

"He started wondering why this guy Roark didn't ask about the arson incidents involving wildfires. Like what was the big deal with a shack? This morning he called Austin and was told nobody by the name of Garland Roark worked at the Department of Public Safety."

"That's because he's dead," Hackberry said.

"You knew him?"

"Garland Roark was the author of *Wake of the Red Witch.* Jack Collins likes to appropriate the names of famous writers. He used the name of B. Traven, the author of *The Treasure of the Sierra Madre,* on several legal documents. Jack is quite the jokester when he's not murdering people."

"You want me to get Bedford on the phone?"

"Forget Bedford. Call Ethan Riser and fill him in. If he's not in, leave the information on his voice mail."

"Shouldn't you do that?"

"I'm done pulling Ethan's biscuits out of

the fire," Hackberry replied. "Ask Pam to come in here, please."

"Yes, sir."

A moment later, Pam Tibbs tapped on the doorjamb.

"Jack Collins knows the feds burned him out," Hackberry said.

"Is Riser aware of this?"

"He will be. You have any suggestions?"

She shrugged. "Not really. Collins is going to square it."

"You and I know that. But we're the only law enforcement personnel around here who have dealt with him head-on."

"So maybe Riser will learn a lesson and not be such a smart-ass."

"We're not going to let Collins make this county his personal killing ground."

She took a box of Altoids out of her shirt pocket and put one on her tongue. "Why did you want to talk to me, Hack?"

"You know how Collins thinks."

"You're asking me what his next move will be?" she said.

"I thought you might have an opinion, since he tried to machine-gun you."

"That's not a subject I'm flippant about."

"Neither am I," he said.

"Collins hunts like a cougar," she said. "He'll go to the water hole and wait for his prey."

"Where's the water hole?"

"Wherever he thinks the feds will show up," Pam replied.

"Where would that be?"

"You already know where."

"Tell me."

"The Asian woman gave refuge to Noie Barnum. The feds are probably watching her. One way or another, Collins will find that out."

"Want to take a ride?" Hackberry said.

She looked out the window at the flag popping on the silver pole in front of the building. In the north a line of rain mixed with dust was moving across the hills, but to the south the sky was blue, the early sun already hot and as yellow as egg yolk. "Why ask me? You're the boss man, aren't you?" she replied.

Two men driving a black SUV had parked their vehicle behind a knoll and set up a high-powered telescope with a camera attached to it on a flat spot that overlooked the valley where the Asian woman lived. They were both dressed in stonewashed jeans and alpine shoes with lug soles and short-sleeve shirts with many pockets. They were both tan and wore shades and had the body tone of men who swam or ran long distances or trained at martial arts or followed a military discipline in their personal lives. One of them opened a lunch box on a rock and removed a thermos of hot coffee and two ham sandwiches. Both men carried Glocks in black nylon holsters on their belts.

Ten minutes later, a rock bounced down from the knoll. The men turned around but saw nothing out of the ordinary. After they finished their sandwiches and poured themselves a second cup of coffee, they heard the pinging of a guitar string. They turned around and saw a solitary figure sitting on the bleached trunk of an uprooted tree, thirty yards up a wash, his face darkened by the brim of a panama hat stained with soot or grime, a guitar propped on one thigh. He picked at a treble string with his thumbnail while he twisted a tuning peg on the guitar's head. "Howdy," he said without looking up.

"Where the hell did you come from?" one of the men in shades said.

"Up yonder, past those boulders," the seated man replied.

"Mind telling us who you are?"

"Just another pilgrim."

"Where's your car, pilgrim?"

"Who says I have one?"

The men in shades looked at each other. "He teleported," one said.

"You cain't ever tell. I get around. You ever hear that song by the Beach Boys? It's called 'I Get Around,' " the seated man replied.

"I get it. You've been shooting the curl off Malibu."

"There aren't many places I haven't been."

"I dig your threads."

"This?" the seated man said, pinching his suit coat with two fingers.

"Yeah, I thought it might be an Armani."

"Could be. You fellows are FBI, aren't you? Or maybe DEA?"

The two men in shades and stonewashed jeans glanced at each other. "Looks like we've been made," one said.

"I can tell because you're wearing Glocks."

"What's your name, asshole?"

The seated man laid his guitar flatly across both thighs, his gaze focused on neutral space, the bumps and knots in his complexion like tan-colored papier-mâché. A closed tortoiseshell guitar case lay on the ground by his foot. It was of expensive manufacture, the kind of case that might contain a Martin or vintage Gibson. "I disturb y'all?" the seated man said.

"That guitar looks like a piece of junk."

"It is," the seated man replied. "It's got rust on the strings. They sound like baling wire."

"So how about playing it somewhere else?"

"Y'all think the government has the right of eminent domain?"

"Of *what?*"

"The right to burn down someone's house just because the government takes a mind to."

"I've got an extra sandwich here. You can have it. But you need to eat it downwind."

"You haven't answered my question. Somebody gave y'all the right to burn a man's house and his books and clothes and even his Bible?"

"What's it take, pal? You want me to bust your guitar over a rock? Do we have to walk you over the hill and put you in your car?"

The seated man set down his guitar, the bottom of the sound box grating in the sand. He rubbed his palms up and down on his thighs, the focus gone from his eyes, his lips compressed, downturned at the corners. The knees of his trousers were shiny from wear. "You boys aren't much of a challenge."

"Repeat that?"

The seated man lifted his face, the sunlight shining clearly on it. "You don't recognize me?"

"Why should we? Who are you supposed to be? Somebody from *America's Most Wanted?*"

"How'd you know?"

The two men stared silently at the seated man and the somber expression on his face and the uncut hair on the back of his neck lifting in the wind. Their irritability was obviously growing, but the seated man seemed to pay no attention to it. He grinned, his teeth as tiny as pearls. "Got you, didn't I? They say that Chinese woman down yonder works miracles. Y'all believe that?"

"Buddy, you just don't listen, do you?"

"You reckon she can mix her spit with dirt

and touch the eyelids of a blind man and give him back his sight? Because that's the kind of he'p both of y'all need. Like all benighted men, you're arrogant. You walk upon the precipice and never glance at your feet."

"In about ten seconds, I'll be forced to hurt you."

"You wouldn't be the first."

One of the men removed his shades and slipped them in a leather case, then began picking up rocks from the ground.

"If you'd read the Bible you burned, you would have learned how Joshua took Canaan for the Hebrews," the seated man said. "He always attacked at daybreak, with the sun rising on his back. His enemies had to look into the glare while he was killing them."

The man who had taken off his shades flung a rock at the seated man and struck the side of his face. The rock was sharp-edged and triangle-shaped and left a one-inch cut as thin as thread just below the seated man's eye, one that seeped blood like tears on ceramic.

"You get the message?" the rock thrower said. "Do I have to do it again?"

"Well, it's been nice talking to you," the seated man said. He stood up, silhouetted against the sun, the brim of his panama hat riffling in the wind. He lifted his guitar case from the ground and set it on the hard, barkless worm-scrolled apex of the tree trunk and began unsnapping the latches. When he turned around again, the two men he had mistakenly identified as federal agents stared at him openmouthed, their hands wooden at their sides, their expressions frozen like those of statues.

"It's a beaut, isn't it? I paid eighteen thousand for it. Same model you see John Dillinger carrying in that famous photograph."

"We can talk this out, pal," the rock thrower said.

"My biggest problem with you boys is your lack of respect. But maybe the devil can teach y'all manners."

Against the brilliance of the sun, the spray of rounds from the Thompson seemed like an eruption of lightning bolts from a black cutout. The few rounds that missed their target whanged off the rocks and ricocheted into the distance with a sound like the tremolo in a flopping saw blade. Then the man in the panama hat pulled the ammunition drum from the Thompson's frame and laid the Thompson and the fifty-round drum inside the guitar case and shut and latched the top. Before leaving, he took the remaining ham sandwich from the lunch box on the rock and unwrapped it from the wax paper and let the paper blow across the landscape. He ate the sandwich with one hand while he walked back to his vehicle, the guitar case knocking against his leg, the soles of his boots clopping on a series of flat stones like the feet of a hoofed animal.

When Hackberry and Pam arrived at the Asian woman's house, the air was dense and sparkling with humidity, coating every surface in sight, clinging to the skin like damp cotton, as though the sunrise were a source not of light but of ignition. The morning itself seemed divided between darkness and shadow, the clouds overhead roiling and black and crackling with electricity against an otherwise blue and tranquil sky. In the north Hackberry could see a great brown plume of dust lifting out of the hills, and he thought he could smell an odor like baitfish that had been trapped in seaweed and left stranded along the edge of a receding ocean, although he was hundreds of miles from salt water. His eyes burned with his own sweat as he watched the Asian woman approach from the backyard, wearing a white dress and a necklace of black stones.

"Here comes *Teahouse of the August Moon*," Pam said.

"Don't start," Hackberry said.

"I can't help it. This woman is a fraud."

"Time to be quiet, Pam," he said.

She turned and stared at the side of his face, her nostrils dilating. He stepped forward into the breeze, removing her from the periphery of his vision. He tipped the brim of his hat. "How you doin', Miss Anton?" he said. "Sorry to bother you, but we've got a problem with a guy by the name of Jack Collins."

"I don't recall the name," she replied.

"Collins is a mass killer. Some federal people burned a shack he was using. I think Jack aims to do some serious payback. Your place is probably under surveillance by the feds. I suspect Jack knows that. My bet is he'll be coming around."

"Why should this man know I'm under surveillance?"

"Krill knew to come here. Krill is a lame-brain compared to Collins. The Mexicans say he can walk through walls. Collins has killed people for years but has never been arrested or spent one day in jail. He murdered nine Thai girls down by Chapala Crossing. I dug them up."

"He's the one who did that?" Anton Ling said, her face frozen as though painted on the air, her eyes elongated and lidless.

"He tried to kill my chief deputy in her cruiser. He executed one of his own men in a cave we had cornered him in. He blew three outlaw bikers all over a motel room. He pushed a corrupt PI off a cliff up in the Glass Mountains. A little earlier in the day, he wiped out a whole collection of gangsters in a hunting lodge. He dressed as a cleaning woman in a San Antonio motel and murdered an ICE agent. Nobody knows his body count across the border."

Anton Ling seemed to listen less with shock or horror than with the fixed attention of someone revisiting a tape seen before. "You think he's a threat to the people who come to my house?"

"Probably not. They don't have anything he wants," Hackberry said.

"But he could be a threat to me?"

"Possibly."

"Well, I appreciate your telling me this. But I can't control what this man does or doesn't do."

"It's not all about you, Ms. Ling. Believe it or not, we'd like to get this guy in custody," Pam said. "Collins wears suits and fedoras he buys from the Goodwill. His face looks like it was stung by bumblebees. See anybody like that around?"

"No, I haven't. Otherwise I would have told you."

"Sure? So far you haven't been very forthcoming," Pam said.

"Madam, what did I just say?"

"You can call me Chief Deputy Tibbs, thank you."

"I'd like to invite you in," Anton Ling said to Hackberry. "But I have to go to San Antonio. Some of our people are in jail."

"Your people?" Pam said.

"Yes, that's what I call them. They're destitute, cheated out of their money by coyotes, hunted by nativist snipers, and generally treated as though they're subhuman. The particular woman I'm going to try to bail out watched her two-year-old daughter die of a rattlesnake bite in the desert."

"I think Pam was just asking a question, Miss Anton," Hackberry said.

"No, she was making a statement. She's done it several times now."

"Why is it we have to keep coming out here to protect you from yourself? To be honest, it's getting to be a drag," Pam said.

"Then your problem can be easily solved. Just leave and don't bother to come back."

"I think that's a good idea," Pam said.

Hackberry was not listening. The thunderheads had blotted out the sun, dropping the countryside into shadow. He had turned his head toward the southeast, where the wind was whipping dust off the hilltops and riffling the mesquite that grew down the slopes. His eyes fixed on a spot where rain had started to tumble out of the sky and a muted sound like crackling foil seemed to leak from the clouds. Hackberry opened and closed his mouth to clear his ears and listen to the sound that had started and now had stopped.

"What is it?" Pam said.

"Somebody was firing a machine gun," he replied.

"I didn't hear it," she said.

Because you were too busy talking, he thought. But he didn't say it. "You drive. Good-bye, Miss Anton. Thank you for your time."

"I'll follow you," she said.

"That's not a good idea," he said.

"My property line goes right through the hills. I have a right to know who's on my land."

"In this case, you don't. Stay here, please. Don't make me ask you again," he said.

He got in the passenger side of the cruiser and closed the door, not looking back, then glanced in the outside mirror. Anton Ling was already getting into a skinned-up pale blue truck seamed with rust, the front bumper secured by baling wire. "This stuff has to stop, Pam," he said.

"Tell *her*," Pam said.

"You two are more alike than you think."

"Which two?"

"You and Miss Anton. Who else?"

"Yeah?" she said, giving him a look. "We'll talk more about that later."

"No, we won't. You'll drive and not speak for me to others when we're conducting an investigation."

"Maybe I should turn in my badge, Hack. That's how you make me feel. No, I take that back. I can't even describe how you make me feel," she said. "You treated me like I was a fence post." She started the engine, then had to stop and concentrate on what she was doing.

"You're one of the best cops I've ever known," he said.

"Save it. You hide behind your years. It's a sorry excuse."

"My wife died on this date, Pam. I don't want to participate in this kind of conversation today. We're on the job. We need to give this nonsense a rest."

"I went out to the grave this morning. I thought you might be there."

He looked at her blankly. "Why did you go there?"

"I thought you might need somebody. I put flowers on her grave."

"You did that?"

She stared at the hills, her hands tight on the steering wheel, rain striking on the glass. Her expression was wan, her eyes dead. "I think you heard thunder," she said. "I don't believe anything is out there."

"You put flowers on Rie's grave?"

She would not speak the rest of the way to the place in the hills where Hackberry believed he had heard the staccato firing of a submachine gun. He took a bottle of aspirin from his shirt pocket and ate two of them and gazed out the window, his thoughts poor consolation for the spiritual fatigue that

160

seemed to eat through all his connective tissue.

Pam drove off the main road and up an incline dotted with cactus and small rocks and mesquite and yucca plants whose leaves were darkening in the rain. She squinted at a flat place between two knolls, the sky sealed with black clouds all the way to the southern horizon.

"There's a telescope on a tripod. It looks like it has a camera on it," she said.

"Stop here. You go to the left. I'll come around from the right," Hackberry said.

She braked the Jeep and turned off the ignition. "Hack?" she said.

"Yes?"

"Nothing," she said.

"Say it."

"I've got your back."

"You always do. That's why I wouldn't partner with anyone else," he said.

She looked directly into his face, her lips slightly parted, her teeth white. She made him think of a young girl outside a prom, her face tilted up, waiting to be kissed. Then she opened the door and stepped out into the rain, unsnapping the strap on her .357, her arms pumped and brown and glistening. She looked beyond him, down the incline, and lifted her chin as though pointing. He turned around and saw Anton Ling's pickup truck approaching from the dirt road, clattering across the rocks, the cactus raking under the bumper and oil pan. "Get down there and stop her," he said.

"Gladly," Pam said.

As soon as Pam began walking down the incline, Hackberry headed uphill between the two knolls toward the telescope and camera. He pulled his .45 revolver from its holster and let it hang loosely against his leg, his back straight so the pain that lived in his lower spine would not flare like an electric burn across his back and wrap around his thighs. He glanced once over his shoulder, then continued straight on toward the telescope, knowing already what he would find, knowing also that his nemesis, Jack Collins, had once again written his signature across the landscape with a dirty finger and had disappeared into the elements.

When Hackberry was little more than a teenage boy, in a battalion aid station at Inchon and later on the firing line at the Chosin Reservoir and even later in a giant POW enclosure the prisoners called the Bean Camp, he had acquired an enormous amount of unwanted knowledge about the moribund and the dead and the rites of passage from the world of the living into the land of the great shade. The opalescence in the skin, the wounds that had the glassy brightness of roses frozen inside ice, and the bodies stuffed in sleeping bags and stacked as hard as concrete in the backs of six-bys were the images a war poet might focus on. But the real story resided in the eyes. The marines and soldiers and navy corpsmen who were mortally wounded or dying of disease or starvation had stared up at him with a luminosity that was like ground diamonds, the pupils tiny dots, so small they could not have recorded an image on the brain. Then, in a blink, the light was gone, and the eyes became as opaque and devoid of meaning as fish scale. That was when he had come to believe that the dying indeed saw through the curtain but took their secrets with them.

The two men on the ground, dressed as casual hikers, must have thought they had walked into a Gatling gun. Their clothes were punched with holes from their shoes to their shirt collars. The spray of ejected shell casings showed no pattern, indicating the shooter had probably shifted his position and fired several bursts from different angles, as though enjoying his work. The fact that one man's hand was twitching at his side seemed almost miraculous, as though the hand were disembodied and the only part of the victim that was still alive.

"Pam! Call for the paramedics and the coroner and tell Felix and R.C. to get out here!" Hackberry shouted down the incline.

He holstered his revolver and walked past a downed tree, the root-ball impacted with dirt.

A worthless guitar, the strings coated with rust, lay on the ground. He gazed down a series of flat yellow rocks that descended like stair steps into a wide flume where an SUV was parked and a second vehicle had left a curlicue of tire tracks in the dirt. He strained his eyes against the distance and thought he saw a speck on the horizon that might have been a car, but he couldn't be sure. Then the speck was lost inside the bolts of lightning that leaped from the earth to the clouds like gold thread.

"Collins?" Pam said behind him.

"Who else kills like this?" he said.

"I think one of them is still alive."

"He's brain-dead. The twitching hand doesn't mean anything."

"Better tell her that," Pam replied.

He turned and saw Anton Ling on her knees next to the dying man, trying to resuscitate him, forcing her breath inside his mouth and down his windpipe, mashing on his chest with the heel of her hand. Her dress and hair and chin and cheeks were speckled with his blood. She turned his head to one side and drained his mouth, then bent over him and tried again.

"Miss Anton?" Hackberry said.

She didn't speak or even look up.

"This fellow is gone, Miss Anton," he said.

She stared up into Hackberry's face. Her mouth was smeared, her eyes slightly crossed.

"You gave it your best," he said, putting his hands under her elbows, lifting her up.

"Who did this?" she said.

"The man who calls himself the left hand of God."

"That's an insult to God," she said.

"Jack Collins is an insult to the planet," Hackberry said. "But Pam and I need to get to work."

"Are these federal agents?" Anton Ling asked.

"Maybe," he said. His knees popping, he squatted down, wincing at the pain in his lower back. He slipped the wallet from the back pocket of the man Anton Ling had tried to resuscitate. The leather was warm and sticky, and he had to wipe his fingers on a handkerchief before he opened it. Hackberry sorted through the credit cards, driver's license, and celluloid photo holders, then set the wallet down by the dead man's foot. He recovered the wallet from the second victim and did the same. He got to his feet, slightly off balance. "If Collins was trying to do payback on the feds, he screwed up."

"How?" Pam said.

"These guys worked for a security service out of Houston. My bet is they were doing scut work for Temple Dowling. He's a defense contractor and the son of a United States senator I was a hump for."

"I didn't catch that."

"I got politically ambitious back in the sixties."

"Everybody makes mistakes," Pam said.

"A mistake is something you do when you don't know better."

"What's the guitar doing here?" she said.

"Who knows? Collins is a harlequin. He has contempt for most of the people he kills."

Pam gazed down the incline. While Hackberry looked through the wallets of the two dead men, Anton Ling had gone back to her truck and was now walking back up the slope with a small silver bottle in her hand. She unscrewed the top and knelt by the man whose life she had tried to save. She put a drop of oil on her finger and drew the sign of the cross on his forehead.

"Miss Anton?" Pam said. "We shouldn't mess too much with the bodies until the coroner gets here."

"If you don't want me to, I won't," Anton Ling said.

Pam looked at Hackberry and waited.

"It won't hurt anything," he said.

Pam watched Anton Ling kneel by the second man and make the sign of the cross on his forehead with her thumb. Then Pam went back to the Jeep and returned with an oversize United States Forest Service canteen and a roll of paper towels. She poured water on a clutch of paper sections and squatted down by Anton Ling and began to wipe her hands and her face and then her hair.

"You don't need to do that," Anton Ling said.

"I know I don't," Pam said.

"I'm quite all right," Anton Ling said.

"Yeah, you are, ma'am. That's exactly what you are," Pam replied. "You're damn straight you're all right."

Anton Ling looked at her quizzically.

Hackberry walked down the slope to the Jeep. He scratched idly at his cheek with three fingers and wondered why men tried to puzzle through the mysteries of heaven when they couldn't even resolve the ones that lived in the human heart. He picked up the hand-held radio from the seat of the cruiser and called R.C. and Felix and asked for their ETA. When a tree of lightning burst on the horizon, he thought he saw a solitary figure standing as starkly as an exclamation point on the deck of a house high up on a plateau. But the raindrops were striking his hat as hard as marbles, and he had to concentrate on his call to Felix and R.C., and he paid no more attention to the solitary figure or the house that resembled the forecastle of a ship, a huge American flag painted on the sand-stone bluff behind it.

CHAPTER SEVEN

The Reverend Cody Daniels did not like sleep. During the waking day, he could deal with the past by constantly rebuilding his mental fortifications, alternately suppressing uncomfortable shards of memory or re-creating them so they didn't detract from his image of himself as the pastor of the Cowboy Chapel. Sleep was another matter. Sleep was a stone jail cell without windows or light, where any number of malformed creatures could reach out of the darkness and touch him at will, their fingers as gelatinous and clinging as giant worms. Sometimes the creatures in the dream pressed their faces to his and ran their tongues along his skin, their breathing labored in his ear, the invasion of his person so complete that he felt his entrails would burst, his pelvis would split apart.

When he woke, he would have tears in his eyes and would sit on the side of the bed in the dark and beat his fists on his thighs.

Almost twenty-four hours had passed since

he had looked through his telescope and had witnessed the machine-gunning of two men by a man wearing a rumpled suit and a panama hat. At first he had not believed what he was watching. The efficiency of the killer, the way he methodically hosed down his victims, blowing them all over the rocks and sand, had made Cody numb with fear and horror but at the same time had left him in awe of the shooter, a man with cheeks like emery paper and whose clothes and hat looked as though they had been stripped from a scarecrow.

Then Cody had watched the arrival of the sheriff, and the female deputy with the wide ass and big shoulders, and the Asian woman who had held his hands in hers and looked into his eyes and read his most private thoughts. But they were not witnesses. *He,* Cody Daniels, was. He had seen it all and could describe how the victims had raised their arms in front of their faces, their mouths pleading, their eyes squeezing shut, their coffee spilling to the ground. It was Cody Daniels who had experienced an almost omniscient oversight of events that others would have to guess at and reconstruct and debate and analyze in a laboratory. All he had to do was make one phone call, and the sheriff who had threatened to kick a nail-studded two-by-four up his hole would be treating him as a friend of the court, hanging on his words, the female deputy reduced to nothing but an insignificant functionary in the background.

Except Cody didn't make the call.

Why?

He knew all too well the answer. It was fear, the succubus that had fed at his heart all his life.

Temple Dowling had given him a business card and had told him to report whatever happened on the Asian woman's property. Krill and the degenerate named Negrito had weighted him with the same obligation, telling him to build a signal fire and pour motor oil on it, like he was an Indian in a loincloth in a John Wayne movie. Dowling claimed to have evidence that could send Cody to prison for the clinic bombing. Krill and Negrito's potential was even worse. No matter which course of action Cody chose, he had become a human piñata for people he despised, the rich and powerful on one side and a pair of pepper-belly sadists on the other.

Why had all this befallen him? He had bought the oven timer; he didn't set it. The others had said the bomb would go off in the middle of the night, that no one would be hurt, that the object was to scare the shit out of people who were killing the unborn. It was a noble cause, wasn't it?

But why had he gone to the scene immediately afterward, hiding in the crowd, fascinated, his head reeling with both exhilaration and guilt? Unfortunately, Cody got to see more than he had planned. He had watched dry-mouthed while the firemen and the paramedics pried the nurse from the rubble. Then he saw the glass and brick that had embedded in her face and eyes, and the blood that had fried in a black veil on one side of her head. He had tried to push his way back through the crowd, away from the paramedics loading the nurse into an ambulance only a few feet away. A fat white woman had blocked his way, virtually shoving him, her face blazing with anger. "Watch it, buster," she said. "I'll punch you in the mouth. I've seen you around here before."

She had terrified him. That night he had bought a bus ticket to San Antonio and since then had never picked up the phone when the caller ID indicated the call had originated in the East. But this particular dawn, Cody was strangely at peace. The air was cool, the sun still below the earth's rim, his bedroom filled with a softness that he associated with the promise of rain and the bloom of desert flowers. He had not done the bidding of either Temple Dowling or the blue-eyed half-breed Krill, and now almost twenty-four hours had passed without incident since he had witnessed the killings in the foothills below his house. Maybe these guys were all bluster, he told himself. Cody had dealt with meth-head bikers and gangbangers and perverts of every stripe on a county prison farm, including the two Hispanic hacks who had walked him out to the work shed where a solitary sawhorse waited for him under a naked lightbulb. What could Krill or Dowling do to him that hadn't been done to him before? Cody was a survivor. *Screw these guys,* he thought.

He rolled over in bed and let the soft blue coolness of the dawn seep inside his eyelids and lull him back to sleep. That was when he heard a sound that made no sense. Someone was brushing his teeth in Cody's bathroom. He sat up in bed and stared in disbelief at a man who was bent over the lavatory, jerking Cody's toothbrush like a ragged stick in his mouth, toothpaste and saliva running down his fingers and wrist.

The figure looked like a half-formed ape wearing a vest and striped trousers without a shirt or belt, his skin streaked with tufts of orange hair. A knife in a scabbard was tied flatly along his upper right arm with leather thongs. He stopped brushing and cupped water into his mouth and spat into the lavatory. "How you doin', man?" he asked.

"You're using my toothbrush."

"Yeah, it's a good one, man."

"How'd you get in?"

"You were supposed to make a signal fire.

172

How come you didn't do that? Krill is pissed at you."

"Signal fire for what?"

"About that crazy man who killed those two guys down below. He had a machine gun. You can hear it a long way, man. You didn't hear nothing?"

"I was gone. I didn't hear or see anything. All I know is what was on the news. Get out of here."

"A friend of ours says your truck was parked here all day yesterday. You calling our friend a liar?"

"Where's Krill?"

"Outside, looking through your telescope at *la china*. He's got a fascination with her. Know why that is?"

"No. I mean I don't care. I just want you guys out of my life."

"Krill's children were killed by a U.S. Army helicopter. They wasn't baptized. He thinks *la china* can do it for him. At least he's been thinking that up till now. Guess why Krill likes you?"

"Likes me?"

"Yeah, man, you're lucky. He likes you a lot, even when he's pissed at you. He needs you to do him a favor. You got a lot of luck."

"What kind of favor?"

"He wants you to baptize his kids."

"You said they're dead."

"Yeah, man, they're dead. They're gonna

be that way a long time."

"I cain't baptize dead people. Nobody can."

"Why not? They're the ones that need it most. I was baptized when I was born. It didn't do me no good. Maybe it's better to get baptized after you die. Then you can't fuck things up anymore."

"How long have his kids been dead?"

"A lot of years, man."

"Then they're buried, right? In Nicaragua or El Salvador or Guatemala or one of those other shitholes, right?"

"Not exactly."

Cody waited for Negrito to go on, his heart dilating with fear for reasons he didn't understand. Negrito was grinning at him, his eyes lit with a lunatic shine. "They're in a box," Negrito said. "He carried it around a long time, then buried it in the desert."

"They're what?"

"He's got them in a wood box. Their bones look like sticks inside skin that's all shriveled up. Like little mummies. When you shake the box, you can hear them rattle."

"That's sick."

"Say that to Krill and see what happens. He talks to them, man. Krill's brain is a couple of quarts down sometimes. That's why he's out here in a place that's like a big skillet. That's why all of you are here. It's a place for losers, man. You ain't figured that out?"

"Figured out what?"

174

"Why you live here. You, *la china,* the crazy man they call Preacher Jack. Krill understands. But you can't figure it out? You're saying you're not as smart as Krill?"

"Smart about what?"

"About who you are, man. About where you live. Krill says you're in the belly of God. That's what Krill thinks the desert is. You thought I was scary, huh? What you think now, man? Look at Krill. He takes scalps 'cause he's more Indian than white. You gonna tell him you ain't gonna baptize his kids 'cause they already turned into mummies? You got that kind of guts? I sure ain't."

"That's what it will take to get shut of y'all?"

"No, man. That's just a small part of it."

Negrito removed the knife from the scabbard tied down on his upper arm and began cleaning his nails as though he had forgotten the point of the conversation. His hand slipped, and the tip of the knife sliced open the ball of his index finger. He watched a thick drop of blood well from the proud tissue, then inserted his finger in his mouth and sucked the wound clean.

"Go on with what you were saying. What does Krill want?" Cody said.

"Your soul, man. What'd you think?" Negrito replied. "He collects souls that he wants to take with him into the next world. Why are you so stupid, my little gringo friend?"

■ ■ ■ ■

That same morning, Maydeen Stoltz walked
into Hackberry's office without knocking, her
mouth glossy with lipstick. She waited as
though gathering her thoughts, her love
handles protruding over her belt. "A guy who
refuses to give his name has called twice on
the business line and demands I put you on
the phone," she said.

"Demands?"

"I think he said, 'Get to it, woman.' "

"What's on his mind?"

"He wouldn't say. He claims you two go
back." She looked at him blankly.

"What are you not telling me?"

"His voice isn't one you forget. I think I
talked to him once last year."

"Collins?"

"How many sexist pricks call in on the business line?"

"If he calls again, put him through."

"I put him on hold. I also told him if I get
my hands on him, his brains are gonna be
running out his nose."

"You said that to Jack Collins?"

"If that's who he is."

"I'm going to pick up now. See if you can
get a trace."

"Watch yourself, Hack."

He winked at her and lifted the receiver to

his ear. Oddly, it gave off a sound like a high wind blowing through the holes in the earpiece. "This is Sheriff Holland. Can I help you?" he said.

"I thought I ought to check in. We haven't talked in a while."

The accent was what a linguist would call southern midlands, a dialect common on the plains west of Fort Worth and up through Oklahoma, the pronunciations attenuated, as though the speaker doesn't have enough oxygen in his blood. This speaker sounded like he had put a teaspoon of metal filings in his morning coffee.

"It's good to hear from you, Mr. Collins. I had you figured for dead," Hackberry said.

"In a way, I was."

"Can you clarify that? I'm not that fast."

"I did penance for one year. I ate from people's garbage and slept in caves and wore rags and washed myself with wet ash. I think you know why."

"I dug those girls up. I wish you could have shared the experience with me. I think you'd find your role as penitent a little absurd."

"Judge me as you will."

"Oh, I will."

"How about those two federal agents? Do you think they were innocent victims?"

"The two guys you capped? I've got news for you. They were PIs out of Houston, not feds. They didn't have squat to do with burning up your shack and your Bible."

"I'm sorry to hear that."

"Tell that to their families."

"No, I mean I'm sorry I wasted all that ammunition. There's been a right smart jump in the price of bullets since the election of our new president."

"You made a mistake coming back here, bub."

"I address you by your title, Sheriff Holland. I'd appreciate your showing me the same level of respect."

"In your way, you're an intelligent man. But you're also a narcissist. Like most narcissists, you're probably a self-loathing failure whose mother wished she had thrown her son away and raised the afterbirth. All of your power is dependent on the Thompson you use to overwhelm your victims, some of whom were Thai girls hardly older than children. How's that feel, Mr. Collins? You think authors such as Garland Roark or B. Traven would break bread with you?"

"I don't make claims for myself or impose myself on others."

"How about Noie Barnum? Does he know you're a mass killer?"

"Who says I know such a person?"

"You were seen with him while robbing food and camping gear from other people. I hate to disillusion you about your criminal abilities, but you have a tendency to leave fecal prints on whatever you touch."

"Noie is a decent man untainted by the enterprises you serve, Sheriff."

"That could be, but you're *not* a decent man, Mr. Collins. You bring misery and death into the lives of others and quote Scripture while you do it. I'm not a theologian, but if the Prince of Darkness has acolytes, I think you've made the cut."

"You're a damn liar."

"No, sir, you're the dissembler, but the only person you deceive is yourself. This time out, I'm going to burn your kite and expose you for the cheap titty-sucking fraud that you are."

"You won't talk to me that way."

"I just did. Don't call here again. You're an embarrassment to talk with." Hackberry eased the receiver back into the phone cradle. Maydeen appeared at the doorway and studied his face. "Get it?" he asked.

"Nope. He's using some kind of relay system."

"I was afraid of that. No matter. We'll see him directly, one way or another."

"I have a feeling you made sure of that," she said.

He leaned back in his swivel chair and put his boots on the cusp of the wastebasket and stretched his arms. "You got to do something for kicks," he said. "Can I buy you and Pam lunch?"

■ ■ ■ ■

Anton Ling had just pushed her grocery cart around a pyramid of pork and beans when another shopper wheeled his cart straight out of the aisle and crashed into her basket so hard that her hands flew in the air as though they had received an electric shock. A bag of tomatoes she had just sacked spilled over the top of the basket and rolled across the floor.

"Sorry, I didn't see you there," Cody Daniels said.

"You did that on purpose," she replied.

"No, ma'am, I certainly did not. I was looking for the Vi-ennas and soda crackers, and there you were."

"The what?"

"Vi-enna sausages. They don't have those in China?"

"Have you been drinking?"

"I have a diabetic condition. It causes my breath to smell like chemicals." He grinned at her stupidly, his face dilated and shiny. "It's colder than a well digger's ass in here."

"Why are you acting like this?"

"Here, I'll pick up your 'maters. Want to get a snack over at the Dog 'n' Shake? It's on me."

"Sir, you can hardly stand."

"Drunk on the love of the Lord, is what I call it."

"Don't touch my tomatoes. Don't touch anything in my basket. Just get away from me," she said.

She picked up her tomatoes from the floor and replaced them in her cart and got in line at the cash register. But when she went into the parking lot, Cody Daniels was waiting by her pickup truck. "We're both clergy, Miss Anton. We've got us a mutual problem, and we need to put our heads together and work out a solution."

"I'm not a cleric, Reverend Daniels. I think you're very confused and should go home."

"Easy for you to say 'should go home.' Krill was at my house. Krill wants me to baptize some dead children he's got buried out in the desert. He gave me the feeling you won't do it, and so it's getting put on me."

"Of course I won't do it."

"So why should it fall on me?"

"I don't know. Talk to Sheriff Holland."

Cody Daniels swayed slightly, obviously trying to concentrate. "Sheriff Holland threatened me. I'm not one of his big fans."

"Look at me."

"Ma'am?"

"I said look at me."

"What the hell you think I'm doing?"

"Why are you so angry at yourself and others?"

The sky was gray, and the wind was blowing in the parking lot, and pieces of newspaper were flapping and twisting through the air. Cody Daniels's eyes seemed to search the sky as though he saw meaning in the wind and the clouds and the flying scraps of paper imprinted with tracks of car tires. "I'm not angry at anybody. I just want to go about my ministry. I want to be let alone."

"No, you carry a terrible guilt with you, something you won't tell anybody about. It's what gives other people power over you, Reverend Daniels. It's why you're drunk. It's why you're blaming everybody else for your problems."

"I was saved a long time ago. I don't have to listen to anything you say."

She dropped the tailgate on the back of her truck and loaded her groceries in the bed, hoping he would be gone when she turned around again. She closed the tailgate and latched it with the chain, her gaze focused on a blue-collar family getting in their automobile, the children trying to pull inside the stringed balloons they had gotten at a street carnival. Cody Daniels had not budged. "Let me get by, please," she said.

"I could have dropped the dime on you any time I wanted and had you arrested," he said.

"For what?"

"Smuggling wets, aiding and abetting dope mules, maybe hiding out a fellow name of Noie Barnum, a guy who might end up in the hands of Al Qaeda."

182

She tried to walk around him, but he stepped in front of her. His breath made her wince. "I saw the man with the machine gun kill those two men down below your place," he said. "It was Preacher Jack Collins."

"So what?"

"If you ask me, not everything he's done is all bad."

"Say that again."

"Nits make lice."

"Excuse me, sir, but you're disgusting."

"Those Thai women didn't have any business in this country. Just like those Mexicans you're bringing in. Every one of them is a breeder, wanting to have their babies here so they can be U.S. citizens."

Anton Ling's eyes were burning, her jaw clenched. She held her gaze on him as though watching a zoo creature behind a pane of glass. He stepped back, a twitch in his face. "Why you staring at me like that?"

"It had to do with a woman, didn't it?" she said.

"What?"

"You hurt a woman very badly. Maybe even killed her. That's it, isn't it?"

"You spread lies about me, I'll come down there and —"

"You'll what?"

His face was contorted, his eyes hot and small and unfocused. "I just wanted to be your friend," he said. "You're putting Krill and that man Negrito on me while you're walking around with your nose in the air like you're some kind of female pope. La Magdalena, my cotton-picking ass."

She got in the cab of her pickup and started the engine. "Don't come around my home again. Don't presume about whom you're dealing with, either."

"*Presume?* What's that supposed to mean?" he asked. "You gonna call the Chinese army down on me?"

She drove away without replying, her truck rattling and leaking smoke at every rusted seam.

"*Presume* what?" he shouted after her.

Hackberry worked late that evening, and at dusk he removed his hat from the peg on his office wall and put it on and hung his gun belt and holstered white-handled revolver from his shoulder and drove out to the site where Jack Collins had machine-gunned the two PIs. The crime-scene tape that had been wrapped around the mesquite and yucca had been broken by wild animals, the brass cartridges from Collins's gun picked up from the ground, the blood splatter washed from the rocks by the previous night's rain, even the sandwich crumbs eaten by ants and the ants in all probability eaten by armadillos. Other than the broken yellow tape, impaled and fluttering among the creosote bush and agaves and prickly pear, there was little to indicate in the reddish-blue melt of the sunset that two men had pleaded for their lives on this spot less than thirty-six hours ago, their sphincters failing them, their courage draining through the soles of their feet, all their assumptions about their time on earth leached from their hearts, their last glimpse of the earth dissolving in a bloody mist.

What good purpose could lie in his visit to the site of an execution? he asked himself. Perhaps none. In reality, he knew why he was there, and the reason had little to do with the two gunshot victims. Hackberry had come to learn that wars did not end with a soldier's discharge. The ordeal, if that was not too strong a word, was open-ended, an alpha without an omega, a surreal landscape lit by trip flares that could burst unexpectedly to life in the time it took to shut one's eyes.

Hackberry had many memories left over from the war: the human-wave assaults; the .30-caliber machine-gun barrels that had to be changed out with bare hands; the Chinese dead frozen in the snow as far as the eye could see; the constant blowing of bugles in the hills and the wind furrowing across the ice fields under a sky in which the sun was never more than a gaseous smudge. But none of these memories compared to a strip of film that he could not rip from his unconscious, or kill with alcohol or drugs or sex or born-again religion or psychotherapy or good works or sackcloth and ashes. He did not see the filmstrip every night, but he knew it was always on the projector, waiting to play whenever it wished, and when that happened, he would be forced to watch every inch of it, as though his eyelids were stitched to his forehead.

In the filmstrip, Sergeant Kwong would finish urinating through a sewer grate on Hackberry's head, then extract him from the hole where, for six weeks, Hackberry had learned how to defecate in a GI helmet and survive on a diet of fish heads and weevil-infested rice. In the next few frames of the strip, Hackberry would stand woodenly in the cold, his body trembling, his eyelashes crusted with snow, while Kwong lifted his burp gun on its strap and fired point-blank into the faces of two prisoners from Hackberry's shack, their bodies jackknifing backward into an open latrine.

They died and Hackberry lived. The other prisoners in his shack were also spared. But all of them were made to believe their comrades' deaths were caused by them and their willingness to confess to imaginary conspiracies in order to free themselves from the holes in the ground where they shivered nightly.

If Hackberry had to face Sergeant Kwong's burp gun again, would he be less fearful than the morning he had watched his fellow POWs executed, their hands lifting helplessly in front of their faces? If he met Kwong on a street, would he let the past remain in the past? Or would he call him out, as would his grandfather Old Hack, pistol-whipping Kwong to his knees?

Hackberry would never know the answer to those questions. Kwong had probably gone back home after the war and repaired bicycles or worked on a communal rice farm. With regularity, he had probably battered and impregnated a peasant girl he bought from a neighbor. He had probably treated his children with both fondness and cruelty while he watched them grow into imitations of himself. If he ever thought at all about the crimes he had committed in the Bean Camp, it was probably only to ask himself if he had been too lenient on the foreigners who had caused him to leave his home and serve in the frozen wastes of North Korea. He would probably be amazed that a lawman on the South Texas border did not go through one day or night in his life without thinking of him.

Hackberry walked to the top of the incline where the two PIs had died, his binoculars hanging from his neck. He gazed through the lenses at Anton Ling's house and at the lightning rods on the peaked roof and at the gables and the wide gallery and the paintless weathered severity of the wood in the walls. The house reminded him of Old Hack's place, a displaced piece of Victorian design dropped by happenstance on the Texas Plains, as though its picket fence and latticework and baroque cornices could end tornadoes and prairie fires and ice storms that froze a man to the saddle, or stop rogue Indians from rope-dragging white families through cactus or hanging them upside down over a slow flame.

He moved the lenses across Anton Ling's gallery and the hanging baskets of impatiens and coffee cans planted with violets and petunias. Children were sitting on the wood steps, playing with a whirligig. A meat fire was smoking in the backyard, the windmill's blades ginning, and Mexican families were sitting at the plank tables under the fruit trees by the barn. Then he saw her emerge from the back door, a straw basket on her arm, and begin setting the table with plastic forks and knives and paper plates and jelly glasses. She wore cowboy boots and a navy blue dress with a long brocaded hem and silver trim at the neck, one like his dead wife, Rie, would wear, adding to the effect of her dark features and the highlights in her hair. Then he saw the Mexicans bringing colored glass vessels from the chapel to the tables, candles flickering. The Mexicans were singing songs, the words rising and falling in the wind, their work-seamed faces exactly like those of the people who had always surrounded Rie. He had to take the binoculars from his eyes and sit down on a rock, a pang not unlike a sharp stone piercing his heart.

Was he so foolish that he would try to re-create his wife inside the skin of the Asian woman? Would he never learn to accept the world for what it was, a place where the sunlight blinded us to the figures beckoning to us from the shade?

In that moment he wished Preacher Jack Collins would once again appear in the middle of his life, his cheeks unshaved, his fingernails half-mooned with dirt, his rumpled suit coat and sweat-stained dress shirt like those of a drunkard out to spoil a party, the Thompson pointed dead center at Hackberry's chest. You feared whiskey in your dreams or in a store window or behind a bar, not when you drank it, Hackberry thought. You feared death only as long as you held on to life. Mr. Death lost his dominion as soon as you faced and engaged him and dared him to do his worst.

None of these thoughts brought comfort to Hackberry Holland. The unalterable reality that governed every moment of his waking day was simple: The love of his life was dead, and he would never see her again.

CHAPTER EIGHT

Danny Boy Lorca's home was not so much a house as a collection of buildings and shacks and pole sheds in or under which he cooked his food or ate or slept or worked or got drunk. He smoked his own meat and grew his own vegetables, did his own repairs on his army-surplus flatbed truck, and washed his clothes in an outdoor bathtub and dried them on a smooth-wire fence. He seldom locked his doors, except on a shed whose walls were layered like armor plate from the roof to the ground with chrome hubcaps. The interior of the shed had nothing to do with mechanized vehicles. It was there that he kept the cases of Corona and the gallon bottles of Bacardi and Oso Negro he bought in Mexico and brought back into the States through a ravine where seventeenth-century Spaniards had carved Christian crosses on the rocks to commemorate a battle in which they had slain dozens of Indians.

When Danny Boy drank, he did it methodically and with dedication, his time frame open-ended, his progress from the first drink to the last as steady and unrelenting and disciplined as anyone's can be while he is systematically sawing himself apart. His benders lasted from a few days to a few weeks, and they always commenced when a clock inside him would go off without warning and a voice would whisper, *It's time.* Danny Boy never argued with the voice. He would fill a bucket with crushed ice he bought from a filling station down the road, unlock the shed where he kept his beer and liquor, and stuff a dozen bottles of Corona into the ice. Then he would sit down at a plank table that overlooked the miles of ancient topography to the south, pour three inches of Bacardi into a jelly glass, and snap the cap off a Corona, the foam sliding down the bottle neck and wrapping around his wrist like a white snake.

The first drink produced the second, then the third, and eventually he would lose count of his consumption and slip into a blackout in which his motor control still functioned but his soul went somewhere else. When his supply in the shed was gone, he would panhandle on the streets or swamp out bars in exchange for alcohol, sleeping in alleys or on the floor of a jail cell. The pattern never changed. The first two days of his bender were memorable. The rest of it was a void that he learned about later from police officers and bailiffs.

It was four A.M. when he began his current bender at the plank table behind his house. The sky was spangled with stars, the desert floor silvery and pale green and rustling with forms of life that no one saw in the daytime. The visions he had of the land and its great alluvial vastness were always a puzzle to him. Sometimes he thought he saw dinosaurs rearing their long necks out of a marshy bog, great tendrils of vegetation and root systems hanging from their mouths, while people wearing animal skins squatted by campfires up in the rocks. Someone had told him that his visions were nonsense, that dinosaurs were extinct long before man appeared on the planet. Danny Boy did not argue with his detractors. How could he? Even though he had once claimed the powers of a shaman, he had hidden, as a coward would, while a defenseless man was tortured to death. Any powers he had possessed had been taken from him and surely given to someone else. Danny Boy did not contend with his fate. He had failed. A shaman did not fear either this world or the next. But if his power was gone, why was he experiencing another vision, in this instance a figure walking up the long alluvial plain toward him, a man who seemed made of sticks? The figure was wearing a pale wide-brimmed hat and a shapeless business suit, the cuffs of his trousers stuffed inside the tops of his cowboy boots, an old-style holster slung at an angle on his hip, brass cartridges inserted in the leather ammunition loops.

Danny Boy watched the figure draw nearer, the toes of his boots cracking through the shell of baked clay along the streambed, the sky behind him a royal purple, the mesquite and piñon trees on the hillsides alive with birds that only minutes ago had been sleeping. Danny Boy drank the rum from his jelly glass and lifted the Corona bottle and swallowed until he could no longer taste the rum in his mouth, until his tongue was dead and his chest was warm and empty of fear. He rubbed at his eyes with the back of his wrist, hoping that when he stared back down the slope, the figure would be gone, just another gargoyle that took up temporary residence in Danny Boy's dreams and went away.

"Some people say insomnia is a disorder. I say it's not," the man said, the wind ruffling the brim of his hat and fanning open his coat over his flat stomach. "I say it's a mark of somebody who sees things as they are."

Danny Boy remained silent, his face as square and expressionless as a stone carving, his shoulders slumped, his hands resting palms down on the table, like animal paws.

"You know who I am?" the man asked.

Danny Boy seemed to think about the question. "Maybe," he replied. "But probably not. I get things mixed up in my head sometimes."

"It doesn't make any difference. I'm here. That's all that counts. It's a fine spot to stand on, too. What a vista."

"Where'd you come from?"

"Out yonder." The man looked over his shoulder and pointed at a distant spot on the horizon.

"Where you're pointing at is Mexico."

"I get around."

"Why you carrying a pistol?"

"For snakes and such. You getting a jump on the morning or tapering off from last night? You look like you got rode hard and put away wet."

Danny Boy thought about what the man had said. "I reckon some people's ways ain't the best," he replied. He looked without focus at the tops of his hands and at the grain in the table's planks. He kept waiting for the visitor to speak, but he didn't. "You want a drink?"

"I'm not keen on alcohol. Can I sit down?"

This time it was Danny who didn't speak. He felt the visitor's eyes roving over his face in the silence. "You spend some time in the prize ring?" the visitor asked.

"I was a club fighter."

"You took some hits."

"Not from fighting other pugs. We traveled from town to town, like wrestlers do. The owner wheeled the fights any way he wanted. We all knew each other and slept at the same motel."

"So what happened to your face?"

"For a hundred bucks, locals could go three rounds with me. I got half of the hundred to let them go the full three. I got sixty-five if I let them work me over." He tried to smile when he spoke, the scar tissue in his eyebrows stretching his eyes into the shape of a China-man's. "They'd knock my mouthpiece into the seats. All the time I was holding them up, and they'd be hitting me with everything they had. Their gloves would be shiny with my blood, and all the time they'd be thinking how they busted up a pro."

"What you did back then isn't important. You're not an ordinary guy." The visitor turned and looked behind him, down the slope, his gaze lifting into the stars. Then he looked at Danny Boy again. "What do you see out yonder?"

"Rocks and sand. A desert. Sometimes bad people bringing dope through the ravines."

"I'm not an ordinary fellow, either, so don't talk down to me. I came a long way to see you. I'm going to sit down now. But don't you disrespect me again."

"I don't know why you're talking to me like this," Danny Boy said.

"Because you just lied to me."

Danny Boy watched his visitor raise one

foot over the plank seat and sit down at the table, his body all angles, like coat hangers, his holstered pistol binding against his belt and thigh, the leather creaking. "I see an ocean sometimes," Danny Boy said. "I can hear the waves in the wind. Or maybe it's just the sound the wind makes in the trees. It sounds like water rushing through a canyon."

When the visitor made no reply, Danny Boy lifted his arm and pointed. "The turtle eggs used to hatch in the sand, right at the base of those cliffs. If they hatched in the sunlight, the baby turtles would try to run to the surf before the birds got them. Sometimes I hear the sounds the turtles make when the birds have got them in their beaks. Or maybe it's the birds squeaking."

"Is that what you see now?"

"Not no more. I see sand and cactus. I ain't got no power now. You're him, ain't you?"

"Depends on who you mean."

"Him."

"You lost me. Some folks get around, but I get around a lot. Is that what you mean, a guy who gets around?"

"There ain't anything here you want."

"I'll decide that."

Danny Boy watched his visitor's eyes and hands in the starlight. "I'm gonna put my jacket on. It's cold. At least for this time of year," he said.

"Why should I care what you do?"

"I just thought I'd say."

"Your name was in the newspaper. You saw a man tortured to death. He was a corrupt Mexican cop. The man who killed him was named Krill. I aim to find him."

Danny Boy lowered his eyes.

"Did you hear me?"

"I don't know where he's at."

"Are you afraid of him?"

Danny Boy felt his fingers curl up and touch the heels of his hands. His mouth and throat went dry, and he could feel a stone drop in his chest and settle in the bottom of his stomach.

"Cat got your tongue?" the visitor said.

"I hid in a ravine while he killed that fellow."

Danny Boy pulled the sleeve of his denim jacket up on one arm, then forgot what he was doing and stared emptily at his visitor. There were lumps on the visitor's face, as though insects had fed on it.

"Is that why you're a drunk, or were you a drunk before you hid in the ravine?"

"I don't make no claims about myself. I am what I am."

"So what are you?"

"What you're looking at, I reckon."

"A drunk Indian?"

Danny Boy felt a pain in one temple; it ran down through his eye like an electric current, obscuring his vision, as though a cataract had

197

suddenly formed on the lens. "This is my place. Everything you see here, it's mine. It's where I grew up."

"What's that mean?"

Danny Boy couldn't formulate an adequate answer to the question, but he tried. "My daddy drilled a deep-water well with an old Ford engine and grew corn and squash and melons. We sold them at the farmers' market every Saturday. We'd go to the picture show in the afternoon and sneak in our own popcorn and Kool-Aid in a quart jar. My mother was alive back then. We all went into town together in our truck, with us kids sitting on the flatbed."

"If there's some kind of allegorical meaning, it eludes me."

"You ain't welcome here."

"I want the man named Krill. Most of the illegals in this county come through your land or the Asian woman's. So get used to me being around. Krill hurt a friend of mine. His name is Noie Barnum."

"The guy named Krill ain't your problem."

"Explain that to me."

Danny Boy reached for his bottle of Corona, but the visitor pulled it from his hand. "You shouldn't drink any more," the visitor said.

"Look out yonder."

"At *what?*"

"Them."

The visitor turned and gazed down the slope at the scrub brush and yuccas and mesquite trees rustling in the breeze. Then he stared at the mauve tint in the darkness of the sky and at the silhouettes of the mesas and hills and at the stars disappearing into the false dawn. "You see turtles out there?" the visitor said.

"No, I see the women and girls who been following you."

"What'd you say?"

"All them Asian women and girls you killed. They're standing just yonder. The Ghost Trail runs right through here. My people keep them safe now. After I hid from the man named Krill, I couldn't see the Ghost Trail no more. But now I can."

"I'd think twice before I ran my mouth to the wrong fellow."

"They're pointing at you. There's nine of them. They want to know why you stole their lives. You didn't have nothing to gain. They were begging when you did it. They had their fingers knitted together like they were in church. They were crying."

The visitor reached out and tapped Danny Boy on the cheek with the flat of his hand. "I can hurt you, fellow."

"Put a bullet in me. I was on Sugar Land Farm. You cain't do no worse than has already been done to me."

"You know the line 'Don't tempt the Lord

thy God'?"

"But you ain't Him."

The visitor rose to his feet. The flap of his coat was hooked back on the butt of his revolver. He was breathing hard through his nose, his gaze wandering from one object to the next, as though his thoughts were of no avail to him. He stared at Danny Boy. "Sheriff Holland spat on me once. Did you know that?"

"No, sir."

"You know what it feels like when another man spits on you? I'm not talking about a woman, because they do that sort of thing when a man offends their vanity. I'm talking about a man doing it. You know what that feels like?"

"No, sir."

"Sheriff Holland did that to me. I could have shot him then, but I didn't. Know why?"

"No, sir."

"Because I'm a merciful man. Because when I deliver Sheriff Holland up to judgment, it won't be the result of an emotional reaction. It will be under circumstances of my choosing."

Danny Boy nodded, his gaze turned inward.

"Tell the sheriff I was here," the visitor said. "Tell him I keep my word. Tell him he'll know when it's my ring. Can you keep all that in your head?"

"Yes, sir, I can," Danny Boy said.

"That's good. You're a good listener." Then the visitor poured the jelly glass half full of rum and picked it up from the table and threw it into Danny Boy's face.

That same morning, Hackberry went to the office early, his mind clear after a good night's sleep, the wind cool out of the north, the broken sidewalks dark with night damp, the hills outside town a soft green against an ink-wash sky. He could smell food cooking at the Eat Café down the street. Pam Tibbs met him at the back entrance of the department. "Danny Boy Lorca just came in half drunk and asked me to lock him up," she said.

"You mean he wants to sleep it off?"

"No, he wants to be locked up. He says he had a visitor this morning."

Hackberry walked through the hallway and hung his hat on a wood peg in his office. "I hate to ask," he said.

"The guy didn't give his name. Danny Boy said he was carrying a pistol. He was wearing a suit and a hat and beat-up needle-nose boots. He said he'd be looking you up and you'd know when it was his ring."

"Why is Collins pestering Danny Boy?"

"That's not all that happened this morning. I was down at the café, and two SUVs loaded with some cowboy cutie-pies came in. Stonewashed jeans, mustaches, two or three days of beard, stylized haircuts. They looked like porn actors."

"Like the two guys Collins popped?"

"The guy in charge knew the waitress. He had on a blue suit and a silver western shirt without a tie, like he was one of the boys. After they left, I asked her who he was. She said that was Temple Dowling."

"Forget about Dowling."

She closed the office door and approached his desk. "It didn't quite end there. I heard him talking in the booth. I heard him use your name."

"We need to get to the point, Pam."

"He called you a drunk."

"That's what I used to be."

"That's not all of it. I heard him whispering, then all of them laughed."

"Blow it off. These guys aren't worth talking about."

"Then one guy said, 'He brought clap home to his wife?' Dowling said something I couldn't hear, and they all laughed again, loud enough that everybody in the café turned around and looked at them."

"What that man said isn't true. But I don't care whether he says it or not. If he does it in my presence, I'll do something about it. In the meantime, let's forget it and talk to Danny Boy." Hackberry took the ring of cell keys off a peg next to his hat.

"I followed them into the parking lot," Pam said.

"Did you hit somebody?"

"No."

"All right, then let it go."

"I took the motormouth aside, the one who said something about clap. He was the driver of one of the SUVs. I told him I wasn't going to cite him for his broken taillights, but if I ever heard him slander your name again, I was going to beat the living shit out of him."

"He had two broken taillights?"

"He did after I broke them."

"Pam?"

"What?"

"What can I say?"

"I don't know."

He stepped closer to her, towering over her, and cupped his hand around the back of her neck. Her skin felt hot against his palm. He could smell the shampoo in her hair and the heat in her body and feel the hardness of the muscles in her neck. "You have to stop protecting me," he said.

"You're my boss, and I won't allow white trash to tell lies about you."

"You really know how to jump-start a man's day," he said.

She lifted her eyes to his. Her mouth looked like a flower that had crumpled in on itself in the shade. "Think so?" she said.

He removed his hand from the back of her neck and tried not to swallow. There was a thickness in his throat, a tightness in his chest, and a weakness in his loins that he did not want to recognize. "Why would Collins bother Danny Boy?" he said hoarsely.

"He wants to hurt you."

"It's that simple?"

"You bet your ass," she replied.

They climbed up the spiral steel stairs in the back of the building and walked down the corridor to a cell whose outer wall was a checkerboard pattern of steel bands and cast-iron plates that had been painted white and were now crosshatched with scratch marks and stained by orange rust around the rivets. Danny Boy was looking out the window when they approached the cell. When he turned around, his head and neck were framed against the window, his body enveloped in shadow, so that his head seemed to rest, decapitated, upon a plate. "I don't want out," he said.

"Can't lock up a man who hasn't committed a crime," Hackberry said.

"I'll drink if I'm back on the street," Danny Boy said.

"Incarceration is not the best way to find sobriety," Hackberry said.

"I'm not like you. There's still liquor at my house. I'll drink it if I can get back to it. In a few days, I can go without it."

"Was Preacher Jack Collins at your house?"

"If that's his name."

"Who'd he say he was?"

"He didn't. I said 'You're him.' "

"What did he say to that?"

"Nothing. Like it wasn't important. Or it wasn't important that a guy like me knew. When I told him the girls he'd killed were out there in the desert pointing at him, he told me to watch my mouth."

"What else did he say?"

"He's after the guy named Krill. He thought I might know where he was at."

"What'd you tell him?"

"That I hid when that fellow was murdered."

"You listen to me," Hackberry said. "You think I should feel guilty because I hid from the Chinese soldiers who were trying to kill me? You remember the name of General Patton?"

"No, who is he?"

"He was a famous military leader. He said you don't win wars by giving your life for your country. You win them by making the other son of a bitch give *his* life." Hackberry tried to smile and lift Danny Boy's spirits, but it did no good. "What else did your visitor say?" he asked.

"He'd be looking you up."

"What else?"

"Nothing. He threw a glass of rum in my face."

Pam Tibbs tapped her ring on the steel door in order to direct Danny Boy's attention to her. "Jack Collins has a way of showing up in people's lives when they're unarmed and vulnerable," she said. "He wants to rob people of their self-respect because he has none for himself. Don't be his victim."

"Listen to her," Hackberry said. "You're a fine man. You have an illness in you that's not your fault. One day you'll wake up and decide you don't want any more of the old life. That's when you'll start getting rid of all the problems that kept you drunk. In the meantime, you're going to take a shower and put on some fresh jeans and a sport shirt I have in my closet, and then you and I are going to have a steak-and-egg breakfast down at the café."

"I saw the Oriental girls standing in the desert. There was nine of them. They're waiting for him," Danny Boy said.

"You saw them when you were drinking?"

"It don't matter what I was doing. They were there. Collins knew about my visions. He knew what was in them. No, that's not exactly right. He knows things don't happen in order, like past, present, and future. He knows things happen all at the same time, all around us, people we cain't see are still living out their lives right next to us. Not many people know that."

"Collins is a fraud. Don't pay attention to what he says," Hackberry said.

"If he's a fraud, who's he pretending to be?

You ever know anybody like him?"

Pam Tibbs looked at Hackberry and raised her eyebrows. She took the ring of keys from his hand, unlocked the cell, and swung the door back heavily on its hinges, the bottom scraping the concrete. "Time to hit the shower and get something to eat, Danny," she said.

By eleven A.M. the sun was bright and hot outside Hackberry's office window, the block-like sandstone courthouse on the square stark against a blue sky, the courthouse lawn green and cool-looking under the shade trees. A church group had opened a secondhand sale on the sidewalk in front of the Luna Theater, and people were going in and out of the courthouse and the old bank on the corner much as they had in an era when the town was supported by a viable agrarian economy. It was a good day, the kind when boys used to cut school to go bobber-fishing or tubing down a river. It was not a day when he wanted to deal with the unpleasant realities of his job or the vestiges of his past. But when a black SUV pulled to the curb in front of his office and Temple Dowling got out, followed by three of his men, Hackberry knew exactly how the rest of the morning would go.

There was a class of people who always supported law and order. They believed that police officers and sheriff's deputies and the law enforcement agencies of the United States government constituted a vast servile army with the same raison d'être as insurance carriers, tax accountants, medical providers, and gardeners — namely, to take care of problems that busy and productive people shouldn't be concerned with.

Hackberry watched Temple Dowling stride toward the front door of the building, coatless, his silver shirt crinkling like tin, a martial glint in his eyes, his creamy complexion moist in the heat. But it was the man's lips that Hackberry couldn't get out of his mind. They seemed to have the coloration and texture of the rubber in a pencil eraser. They belonged on the mouth of a man who was cruel, whose sentiments were manufactured, whose physical appetites were visceral and base and infantile all at the same time. Watching him stride up the walk, Hackberry decided he had been too kind in assigning Dowling and his peers to that innocent and insular group who treated police officers as they would loyal servants. Temple Dowling, like his father, the senator, was a man who knew the value of the whip and how to turn the screw in order to bend others to his will. The fates may have given Temple Dowling a face that would never allow him to ascend to the throne. But Hackberry guessed that in Dowling's view, the power behind the throne was gift enough.

Hackberry got up from his chair and met Dowling at the entrance to the building. "What's your problem?" he said.

"I have a grocery list of them," Dowling said.

The three men standing behind him had come to a stop. They wore western hats and sunglasses and had the physiques of men who worked out regularly in health clubs. They wore mustaches and a growth of beard that Hackberry guessed was deliberately maintained rather than shaved entirely off. Their hands were folded in front of them, their faces turned at a deferential angle so Hackberry would take note that they were not staring at him from behind their shades. One man had a puncture in his cheek that looked like a hole someone had made by inserting his thumb into putty. One man wore a tattoo inside the growth of beard on his throat. The third man had facial skin that was as dark as saddle leather and flecked with scars that resembled tiny pieces of brown string.

"Lose the entourage and come in," Hackberry said.

"These men go wherever I go."

"Not here they don't."

"Why do I continue to have trouble with you, Sheriff?"

"Because you asked for it."

"I had to replace both the brake lights on my vehicle this morning."

"Yeah, I heard about that. That's too bad."

"You're aware your deputy broke them?"

"Be advised I support my deputy in whatever she does. I'm pretty busy. You want to stand out here in the sun or come inside?"

"Here will be just fine," Dowling said. He wiped his forehead and upper lip with a handkerchief, then shook it out and wiped the back of his neck. He gazed down the street at the courthouse, a slick of sweat on one cheek, his eyes intense with the words he was preparing to speak. Hackberry realized Dowling's next remarks would be part of a performance that was not for him but for his employees. "I've lost two good men to a psychopath who should have been mulch the first time you saw him. This same man has murdered an untold number of people in this county, *your* county, but you don't seem to have a clue where he is, nor do you seem bothered by your ignorance. Instead of conducting an investigation, your personnel are vandalizing people's SUVs. I understand that mediocrity is a way of life in a place like this, but I won't abide incompetence when it comes to the welfare of my people or the security of my country. We'll do your work for you, but you need to stay out of our way."

"If you interfere in a homicide investigation, you're going to find yourself in handcuffs, Mr. Dowling."

"My father said something about you,

210

Sheriff, that maybe you should hear. He said you were one of those rare politicians to whom nobody had to pay money in order to corrupt. All they needed to do was appeal to your Don Quixote complex. He said the only payment you required was a chance to play the role of the knight-errant so you could self-destruct and absolve yourself of your petty sins. I think my father read you like a book."

"Tell you what, I changed my mind about something I told my chief deputy this morning. I said I couldn't care less if you tried to slander my name. But on second thought, some might think the elements in your lies refer to my dead wife, Rie, and the nature of my relationship with her. You did make those remarks, didn't you?"

"I didn't have to make them. Everyone who knew you already has."

"I don't like to humiliate a man in front of his employees, but for you, I'm going to make an exception. I'm probably in the top of the eighth inning or the bottom of the ninth, which means I don't have a lot to lose. You ever play much baseball, Mr. Dowling? If you crowd the plate with the wrong pitcher, you can bet the next pitch will be a forkball at the head, the kind that hits you like a dull-bladed guillotine." Hackberry smiled pleasantly and winked at him. "What do you think about that?"

"Considering the source? Not very damn much," Dowling said.

Hackberry went back inside his office, sat down at his desk, and did not look outside the window until he heard the SUV drive down the street. But the anger that had bloomed in his chest would not go away. A half hour later, the phone on his desk rang. He looked at the caller ID and answered. *"¿Qué tal?"*

"¿Qué tal?" Ethan Riser repeated.

"Yeah, what's up?"

"I know what it means."

"Say what's on your mind."

"This is a personal call and off the record."

"I'm the sheriff of this county. I'm sitting at my office desk, on the job, in my official capacity. Nothing that occurs here is off the record."

"You sound a little short."

"What do you want, Ethan?"

"I'm taking early retirement. I wanted to tell you that. Plus a couple of other things."

"Like what?"

"You're in the way."

"Say again?"

"This guy Noie Barnum is the Holy Grail. We want him, Krill and his people want him, Al Qaeda wants him, Temple Dowling wants him, and now Josef Sholokoff wants him."

"Why would a Russian porn dealer risk his immigration status by going into espionage?"

"Josef Sholokoff has been spreading drug and porn addiction around the country since he arrived in Brighton Beach. Why should doing business with third-world bedbugs bother him?"

"You said I was in the way."

"Guys like you are not team players. You're a hardhead, you don't chug pud, and you cause major amounts of trouble. Government agencies might say otherwise, but they don't care for guys like you."

"What difference should that make to me?"

"They won't have your back, bud."

"Have you been drinking?"

"I'm at a driving range. I wish I'd done more of this a long time ago."

"When do you retire?"

"Three months, more or less. Yeah, about three months."

"You're retiring but you're not sure when?"

"I'm terminal."

Hackberry leaned forward on his desk. Before he could speak, Riser cut him off. "I used to smoke three packs a day. Five years ago I quit and thought I'd gotten a free pass. I went in for a blister on my nose last week, and the doc said it was already in my liver and pancreas and had reached the brain."

"I'm sorry, Ethan."

"There's something I never told you about my history with the Bureau. You remember right after 9/11 when a planeload of bin

Laden's relatives was allowed to leave the country without being detained, except for the fifteen minutes we were allowed to interview them on the tarmac? I was one of the agents who went on board the plane. I should have resigned in protest then. But I didn't. I've always regretted that. Take this for a fact. When you get to the end of the track, you don't regret the things you did. You regret the things you didn't do. You're a good man, Hack. But good men are usually admired in retrospect, after they're safely dead."

After he had hung up, Hackberry sat for a long time in his chair, the right side of his face numb, a sound like an electrical short humming in his ear.

CHAPTER NINE

Anton Ling woke in the darkness to the
flicker of dry lightning and a rumble of
thunder that shook the walls of her house in
the same way that the reverberations of aerial
bombs could travel through the earth and
cause a house to rattle miles away. She went
to the kitchen and sat at the table in the dark
and drank a glass of warm milk and tried not
to think about the images reawakened in her
unconscious by the thunder and the yellow
ignition in the clouds.

The night was unseasonably cold, the sky
churning with clouds that looked filled with
soot. She thought she heard a coyote's wail
inside the wind, or perhaps the shriek of a
rusty hinge twisting violently back on itself.
An empty apple basket bounced crazily past
the water tank in the backyard. The tank was
overflowing, the blades of the windmill ginning, the stanchions vibrating with tension.
Had she been so absentminded that she had
forgotten to notch down the shutoff chain on

the crankshaft?

She put on a canvas coat and went outside and was immediately struck by the severity of the wind and a smell that was like creosote and wet sulfur and the stench off a smoke-stack in a rendering plant. She hooked the chain on the windmill and realized the doors were slamming on all her sheds, a loose section of the tin roof on the barn clanging against the joists, as though things were coming apart and indeed the center could not hold. Was the odor coming from across the border, where industry did as it wished? The clouds were black and billowing and lighted from the inside, like giant curds of smoke rising from wet straw set ablaze by a chemical starter.

When would she be freed of her dreams and the sensations and shards of memory that followed her into the day and fouled her blood and made her wonder if her entire mission wasn't that of a hypocrite? Why could she not accept the fact that amnesia did not necessarily accompany absolution?

Don't think about it, she told herself. *Pray for the maimed and the dead and ask nothing more from life than another sunrise, and maybe along the way do a good deed or two.* She couldn't change the past. Why did she have to revisit the same slide show over and over?

Gasoline and diesel, drums of it, with Tide detergent poured into the mix so that the liquid adhered to every surface it touched, a homemade form of napalm dropped end over end from a few hundred feet while tiny figures below raced from their huts into the trees or sometimes rolled burning in the rice paddies to smother the fire on their skin.

From a great distance, she had witnessed the B-52 raids in Cambodia and had heard the thump of the bombs and had felt the explosions through the soles of her shoes and had seen the surface of rice paddies wrinkle, but the tremolo that spread invisibly through the floor of a rain forest was little different from the vibration of a subway train passing under the streets of a metropolitan city. The fifty-gallon drums filled with diesel or gasoline or both were different; they were up close and personal, their effect unforgettable. She had helped slide them off the tailgate of a Chinook, had cupped her hands around their hard rims, had watched them suddenly detach themselves from the plane and drop as heavily as woodstoves through the air into a landscape of elephant grass and tropical trees and fields of poppies that bloomed pink and red against a backdrop of blue mountains. Then she had seen them explode in a village that was a resupply depot for the Pathet Lao, but also a home to people who ate monkeys and dogs and harvested rice with their hands, and who knew nothing of the global powers that had decided to use their country as a battlefield.

She went back inside the house and hung her canvas coat on a peg and checked the locks on the doors, then sat down on the side of her bed, her head bent forward, the images and sounds from her dream gradually disappearing. The wind gusted under the house, causing the floor and the walls to creak and a tin cup to topple into the kitchen sink. She got up from the bed to pull the curtain on the window just as a net of lightning bloomed in the clouds. By the corner of the old bunkhouse, she saw a shadow. No, it was more than a shadow. It not only moved; light reflected off it. She stared into the darkness, waiting for the electricity to jump in the clouds again. Instead, drops of rain began to patter on the roof and in the dust around the windmill and in the nubbed-down grass near the barn, and all she could see through her bedroom window was darkness and the sheen of rain on the bunkhouse and an empty dark space where she thought she had seen the outline of a man.

She opened the bottom drawer of her dresser and reached inside it and groped under a pile of folded clothes for an object she hadn't touched or even thought about in many months. She went into the kitchen and pulled open a drawer, and from a collection of screwdrivers and hammers and pliers and duct tape and wrenches and scattered nails, she removed a flashlight. Then she put on a baseball cap and unlocked the back door and went outside, this time without her coat.

She moved the beam of the flashlight along the side of the bunkhouse and the stucco cottage, then shone it on the railed horse lot and through the open door of the barn, the light sweeping against the stalls and wood posts inside. She crossed the yard and looked inside the bunkhouse, then inside the cottage. She searched behind the bunkhouse and worked her way back to the corner where she thought she had seen the figure.

The rain was ticking on her cap and her shoulders, spotting her clothes and running down the back of her neck. She walked toward the barn, the flashlight beam spearing the darkness and bouncing off the tools and dust-covered tack inside. She took a deep breath, oxygenating her blood, and stepped through the door into the heady odor of horse sweat and decayed manure and pounded-down clay that was green with mold.

"What are *you* doing here?" she said.

"Nothing," said the figure in the shadows, raising his arm against the glare of the flashlight.

"You were looking through my windows."

"I was not. I just wanted to talk. I didn't understand what you said there at the grocery store."

"About what?"

"You said I shouldn't presume. You said I didn't know who I was messing with. You thought I was threatening you? I wouldn't do that. You made me feel bad, like I was a bully or a freak or something. Ma'am, is that a pistol in your hand?"

"What does it look like?"

"We're kindred spirits."

"No, we're not. How long have you been out here?"

"Just a few minutes. Maybe I was gonna knock on your door. I know you stay up. I've seen those candles glowing in your chapel late at night."

"How did you see them?"

"I got a telescope on my deck. I do stargazing sometimes. It's a hobby I got."

"Where's your vehicle?"

"Down the road a mite."

"You're a voyeur, Reverend Cody. Get off my property. If you ever come on it again, I'll shoot you."

"Don't talk like that. You got me all wrong, ma'am."

"No, I don't. I think you're haunted by a terrible deed you did to a woman or a group of women. It's something so bad you can't talk about it to anyone. But that's your problem, not mine. Get out of here and never come back. You understand?"

"Yes, ma'am, if that's what you say."

She lowered the pistol and stepped aside.

When he ran past her, his face was disjointed with fear and humiliation, like that of a child caught in a shameful act. She went back inside the house and locked the door behind her and replaced the small-caliber pistol in the bottom drawer of her dresser. She took off her damp clothes and dried herself with a towel and put on a pair of pajamas and lay down on the bed, a pillow over her face. She was surprised at how quickly and easily she fell asleep. Outside, a bolt of lightning struck the top of a hill and turned a pine tree into a crisp red fingerprint against the unrelieved blackness of the sky.

Cody Daniels's waxed canary-yellow pickup was parked off the side of the dirt road, down by a creek bed whose banks were bordered by gravelly soil and cottonwood and willow trees. The rain had beaded on the wax, and when electricity leaped between the clouds, his truck looked like a bejeweled artwork, a thing of beauty and power and comfort that had always given him an enormous sense of pleasure and pride and control. But now Cody Daniels took no joy in anything — not his truck, nor his Cowboy Chapel, nor his title of Reverend, nor the house he had built up in the cliffs, where he had strode the deck like the captain of a sailing vessel.

He had not only been caught hiding in the Chinese woman's barn, he had been accused of voyeurism and driven from her property as a degenerate might. Worse, he could not explain to himself, much less to Anton Ling, why he had gone there. To tell her he was sorry for approaching her in the grocery store while he was drunk? Maybe. To tell her that no matter what he might have done in the past, he would not try to harm her? Maybe. To look through her windows?

He wanted to say no to his last question but found himself hesitating. Of course he wouldn't do something like that, he told himself. Never in his life had he ever entertained thoughts like that. Why would she think that of him? Why would he doubt himself now?

Because there was no question he had become obsessed with her. While he set out his prayer books in the Cowboy Chapel or tried to prepare a sermon, he wondered what kind of services she conducted inside that little room where racks of candles burned in rows of blue and red vessels. He wondered why none of the Hispanics, at least the legal ones, ever came to his church. What did he ever do to them? He wondered if Anton Ling possessed powers that would never be given to him. What was the line in Scripture? Many are called but few are chosen? That seemed like saying there was a collection of real losers out there and Cody Daniels was probably one of them.

Was that his lot? To have the calling but never feel the hot finger of destiny on his forehead? Was he cursed with the worst state of mind that could befall a man, envy of a woman, in this case an Oriental whose features and figure and grace turned his loins to water?

He turned his face toward the sky. *Why have you done this to me?* he asked.

If there was any reply, he didn't hear it. The only sound he heard was that of a heavy vehicle, one with a diesel-powered engine, grinding its way down a dirt track between two hills on the north side of the Chinese woman's property. He could see the headlights in the rain and the outline of the extended cab and the large bed in back. It was an expensive vehicle that could seat a driver and five passengers easily. What was it doing in these hills at this time of night? It was now dipping off the road, proceeding down a long incline that fed into flatland and a string of cedar fence posts with no wire.

Cody got into his pickup and rolled down the passenger window so he could watch the diesel-powered truck as it approached the back of Anton Ling's house, its headlights turned off.

Maybe they're part of her Underground Railroad or whatever the hell they call it, he told himself.

But he knew better. He opened his cell

phone and looked at the screen. No service. *Well, that's the breaks,* he thought. What had she told him? To get out, to never come back? Something like that. So, sayonara, see you tomorrow, or whatever they said over there. *Maybe next time you'll appreciate it when a good man comes around. Voyeur, my dad-burned foot,* he thought.

He clicked on his headlights, dropped his transmission into gear, and drove south into the rain, away from Anton Ling's property, the clouds crackling like cellophane behind him.

It was still dark when she woke and realized that the four men standing around her bed were not part of a dream. She could smell the mud on their boots and the rain and leaves on their hooded slickers. She could hear their weight shift on the boards in the floor. She could see their gloved hands and the heavy dimensions of their torsos and arms. The sense of physicality in the three men who stood closest to her was overwhelming, as palpable as a soiled hand violating one's person. The fourth man, who stood in the background, did not seem to belong there. He was much shorter, his physical proportions lost inside his raincoat. The only thing she couldn't see were their faces, which were covered with a camouflage-patterned fabric that had been drawn tight against the skin, the material creased with lines like a prune might have.

She sat up in bed, the sheet pulled to her waist, her heart beating high up in her chest. She waited for one of them to speak. But none of them did. The luminous clock on her dresser said 4:54 A.M. Another hour until sunrise. "The doors were dead-bolted," she said.

"Not anymore they're not," one man said. He was taller than the others, maybe wearing cowboy boots, a military-style wristwatch with no reflective surfaces strapped just above the glove on his left hand.

"I'm of no value to you," she said.

"What makes you think this is about you?" the man asked.

"The man you're looking for stayed here briefly. I gave him food and dressed his wounds. But he's not here anymore, and I don't know where he has gone. So I'm in possession of nothing you want."

"You never can tell," the man said.

She tried to look straight into his eyes and confront his sexual innuendo. But she could see nothing behind the holes in his mask. "How many of you are outside?" she asked.

"What makes you think anyone is outside?"

"There are at least two. One in front, one in back. Because you used four men to confront one woman inside the house, you have personnel to spare. So there are at least

225

two outside."

"You're a smart lady," the tall man said. "But we knew that when we came here."

"Then you know I'm not trying to deceive you. It wouldn't be in my interest or in the interest of the work I do. I have no personal agenda and nothing I need to hide from you."

"Maybe *I* know that. But others may not. You were in Laos and Cambodia. You were in Tibet, too. You did airdrops to the Tibetan resistance. Not many people have a history like that."

"More than you think."

"The Communists had their hands on you for a while. Where did that happen?"

"In Tibet."

"What was that like?"

"Not very pleasant."

"Your record indicates you gave them nothing and lived to tell about it. So others might take that to mean we shouldn't believe anything you say unless it withstands the test of ordeal. Don't make us go through that, ma'am."

"Do you think politeness in language excuses you from what you're doing? You break in to my home and wake me from my sleep and suggest you might torture or rape me, then address me as 'ma'am'? What kind of men are you? Does it bother you that you mask your faces in order to bully a woman?"

She realized she was saying too much, that

she was taking the exchange over the edge and ignoring the fact that her intruders wore masks because they did not plan to kill her. She tried to keep her face empty of expression, to not signal them in any way that she understood their thought processes or the methods they were considering using against her. It was time to distract them by giving them information they probably already had that would indicate she was telling the truth but be of no help to them. "The man you're searching for is probably with a homicidal lunatic by the name of Jack Collins."

"You have any idea where Collins might be?"

"Are you serious?" she replied.

In the silence, she could hear the tall man breathing and see the camouflaged fabric ruffling around his mouth. Why was he breathing through his mouth? In anticipation of what he was about to do? Was he about to make a decision that would take him and her across a personal Rubicon she did not want to think about?

"Collins is a religious head case. He seems to have obsessions with women in the Bible," the tall man said. "You might fit the bill. What's your opinion on that?"

Don't let him know you're afraid, a voice inside her said. "I think you're an idiot."

The short man standing behind the others peered through the corner of the window shade into the yard. He wore heavy boots that looked like they had elevated soles and heels. She saw his head tilt upward and guessed that he was checking for the first glow of dawn beyond the ridgeline. Then she realized that the tall man was watching the man at the window shade. The tall man was not in charge. He was waiting on the man at the window to tell him what to do.

The man at the window did not speak but made a rotating motion with his index finger, as though saying either "continue" or "wrap it up."

But which?

The tall man went to the closet and threw a robe on Anton Ling's bed. "Put it on," he said.

"What for?" she asked.

"Certain things have to be done. Don't make them harder than they already are."

"Who do you work for?"

"The country. The people who want it to remain free. You think protecting a traitor like Noie Barnum is a noble act?"

"I won't put a robe on. I won't move. I have no control over what you're about to do. But I won't cooperate with it."

The tall man leaned down and took her wrist in his hand. His fingers went easily all the way around it, as though he were compressing a stick in his palm. "Get up."

"No."

"You're making this personal, Ms. Ling. It's unwise."

"Don't use my name. I don't know you and have no intention of knowing you. Don't you dare address me as though you know me."

"I heard you were arrogant, a Mandarin princess or something." He jerked her up from the bed and knotted her hair in his fist, twisting it hard, pulling her head back until her mouth fell open. "We used to call this cooling out a gook. Is that what you want? Tell me. Tell me now." He twisted her hair tighter. "I don't like to do this. This is all on you. I can make it worse and worse and worse, to the point I start to enjoy it. Don't make me do that."

When he released her hair so she could speak, she gathered all the saliva in her mouth and spat it full in his face. Then he hit her so hard with his fist that two picture frames fell to the floor when she crashed against the wall. Two of the other men picked her up and shoved her toward the doorway. She thought she heard the sound of water running in the kitchen sink.

Cody Daniels kept his truck pointed south, slamming over the ruts, water splashing up on the hood and across the windshield. He had his radio tuned full-blast to an English-language station that broadcast from across the border to avoid FCC regulations, its signal reaching all the way to Canada. Twenty-four hours a day, it provided a steady stream of country music, evangelical harangues that left the preacher gasping into the microphone, and promotions for baby chicks, tulip bulbs, bat guano, aphrodisiacs, glow-in-the-dark tablecloths painted with the Last Supper, and miracle photographs of Jesus. Late at night it was the refuge for the insomniac and the ufologist and the sexually driven and those who loved the prospect of the Rapture. But right now, for Cody Daniels, it was a source of maximum electronic noise that he hoped would pound the name of Anton Ling out of his head.

He was pastor of the Cowboy Chapel, not the overseer for Asian females in Southwest Texas. Why didn't she go back where she came from? She had told him to get lost. All right, that's what he was doing. Live and let live. Besides, maybe the truck with the extended cab wasn't going to Anton Ling's. Maybe it was the Border Patrol rounding up stray wets. The wets traveled by night. Wasn't it reasonable for Cody to at least conclude the oversize pickup was on a government mission?

Except the Border Patrol usually operated by the numbers and didn't use pickup trucks to round up wets or drive down hillsides through private property in the dark.

Why did his mind always set traps for him?

His own thoughts were more intelligent and wily than he was. Again and again, his thoughts knew how to corner and bait him, as though a separate personality were constantly probing at him with a sharp stick.

Without thinking, without planning, as though his motor control had disconnected itself from his instincts, he removed his foot from the accelerator and depressed the brake pedal. He felt the truck slowing, the vibration in the frame diminishing as though of its own accord. Then the truck stopped as rigidly as a stone in the road. He switched off the radio and listened to the windshield wipers beating in the silence. He opened his cell phone, praying that this time the screen would show at least one bar.

No service.

Where was the sheriff? Where was the female deputy who had thrown him in the can? This was their job, not his. Who had dumped all this responsibility on Cody Daniels? He looked through the windshield at a long white streak of lightning that leaped from the hills into the clouds.

You? he asked.

No, God had more to do than concern Himself with the likes of Cody Daniels.

How do you know? a voice said, either inside or outside his head.

Cody put his truck into reverse and turned around in the middle of the road, wondering if the tattoo BORN TO LOSE that he had removed from his skin should have read BORN TO BE STUPID.

Two men held Anton Ling's arms while a third plunged her head into the water brimming over the sides of the sink. She clenched her mouth and held her breath and tried to twist away from the hand that pushed her head deeper into the water. She kicked sideways with her feet and pushed against the cabinets with her knees. All she accomplished was to drain herself of the energy and oxygen she needed to survive. After what was surely a minute, her lungs were bursting and air was bubbling out of her mouth and she knew she was only seconds away from both swallowing water and breathing it through her nostrils. Then the hand went away from the back of her neck and she reared her head above the level of the sink, gasping for air.

"Noie Barnum must know other people around here besides you. Who would he contact?" the tall man said. His gloved right hand and sleeve were dark with water. She realized it was he who had held her head down in the sink.

"He's a Quaker. Other Quakers."

"Where do they live?"

"There're none around here."

"Wrong answer."

"He's with Collins."

"Where's Collins?"

"I don't know anything about Collins."

"Hold her arms tighter," the tall man said.

"No, wait," she said.

"Your time is running out, Ms. Ling."

"Noie has no ties here. He is wherever Collins is. How could I know where Collins is when the FBI doesn't? You're making me do the impossible. I can't prove to you what I don't know."

"I got to admit I wouldn't want to be in your shoes. But you created this situation, not us. This is the way it stands: You went down the first time for exactly one minute and ten seconds. The second time you're going down for two minutes and twenty seconds. Think you can hold your breath for two minutes and twenty seconds?"

"I can't."

"Then you're going to die. Maybe you'll have a heart attack before you drown, so it won't be that bad. I'll let you fill up with air first. Nod when you're ready."

"My father flew with the original Flying Tigers. He was a friend of Claire Chennault."

"Who cares?"

"If he were here, you'd have to hide."

He plunged her face into the water and leaned his weight heavily on his hand, driving her forehead to the bottom of the sink, his gloved fingers spreading like banana peels on

233

the back of her head. Her skin broke against the porcelain, and blood curled around her face and rose in a smoky string to the surface. The more she struggled, the weaker she became. Her lungs burned as though someone had poured acid in them. She dug her knees into the cabinets and pushed herself backward with all her remaining strength. Then she realized that the incendiary raids she had lived through as a child, the pancake air crash she had survived on a Laotian airstrip, the ordeal she had endured at the hands of Chinese Communists, had been illusions, flirtations with a chimera who was a poseur. Death did not appear with a broad flapping of leathery wings; death came in the form of a stoppered silvery-green drain hole at the bottom of a flooded sink, while three men snapped her sinew and bones with their hands.

But something had just happened that neither she nor her adversaries could have anticipated. Her upper body was soaking wet, and the man on her left let his grip slip for just a second. When he tried to reposition his hands, she jerked free of him and fell backward to the floor, sucking air as raggedly into her windpipe as she would a razor blade.

The tall man reached down and grabbed the front of her shirt and pulled her to her feet. She could feel the sourness of his breath on her face. "Now, you listen," he said.

"You're making us waste time that we don't have. You're vain from your hairline to the bottoms of your feet, and you know it. You've turned your pride into a religion and convinced a bunch of ignorant peons you're a Catholic saint. Be assured, if you want to be a martyr, we'll arrange that. But in the meantime, you're going to tell us where Barnum is or prove to us you're as unknowledgeable as you claim. If you don't know where he is, give us the name of somebody who does. That will get you off the hook, *that* and nothing else.

"If you doubt me, tell me how you feel one hour from now, after I let my associates take you back in the hills. Maybe you saw ugly things in the Orient, the kinds of things my associates are capable of doing, but you *saw* them, they didn't happen to you. If they had happened to you, you wouldn't be here today. You would be either dead or in an asylum, unable to deal with your own memories of what was done to you. My associates have insatiable appetites. When they start in on you, you will renounce everything you ever believed in just to make them stop what they're doing for only one minute. You'll give up your lover, your family, your religion. I've seen them at work. I don't judge them for what they do. They are only satisfying the desires that to them are natural. But I never want to witness human behavior like that again. You don't know how kind I have been to you, Ms. Ling.

"There's another notion I want to dispel here. People in your situation convince themselves that a miracle is going to happen, that their pain will be taken away, that angels will protect them in their last agonizing moments. But it doesn't work that way. No God will help you, no plastic Madonna, no hallelujah choir will arrive singing the praises of Anton Ling. You'll die a miserable death, and no one will ever know where you're buried. Tell me what you want to do."

Her hair formed a tangled skein in front of her eyes and dripped water and blood on her face and shirtfront. Her eyes were crossed from shock and trauma, her bare feet slippery on the wet floor, her pajamas sticking like wet Kleenex to her skin. Her chest was still laboring with shortage of breath, her heart swollen as big and hard as a cantaloupe. "I know nothing," she said.

"Then enjoy your time in hell, bitch."

His hand reached out and settled almost lovingly on the nape of her neck. Then she twisted her body and back-kicked him with more strength and force than she thought she had.

He wasn't ready for it, and his upper body jacked forward with the blow, both of his hands grabbing his genitalia, a cry rising involuntarily from his throat. The man to her right tried to grab her, but she ripped her elbow into his rib cage, then kicked the tall man again, this time in the face. The third man grabbed her pajama top, tearing it down the back, but she pulled loose from him and got past the tall man and the man who had been holding her left arm. The inside of her head was roaring with noise, her hair matted with blood, her feet slipping on the floor. She felt a hand grab her neck, then fingers trying to find purchase inside the religious chain she wore.

The drawer holding the collection of tools and wire and duct tape was half open. She got her hand inside the drawer and picked up a screwdriver, a short one with a thick stub of a handle and a wide blade and perhaps a two-inch shank. She whirled and plunged it into the face of the man whose hand was tangled in her chain. The blade pierced the fabric of his mask right below his left eye, the shank sinking all the way to the handle, the wood and fabric pressing into the wound. The man screamed once, then touched the screwdriver's handle, his hand trembling, and began screaming again, this time without stop.

"You shut up! You eat your pain and shut your mouth!" the tall man said.

"I'm blind!"

"No, you're not. You're in shock. Shut your fucking mouth," the tall man said. Then he whirled around. "Get her!"

Anton Ling ran through the enclosed back porch and crashed through the screen into the yard, falling once, getting up, then plunging across the yard toward the barn, where her pickup was parked with the keys in the ashtray.

That was when another hooded man, even bigger than the others, a man whose breath smelled like snuff and spearmint, picked her up in the air, crushing her against his chest with his huge arms. "What do we got here?" he said, his lips brushing against her cheek through his mask. "A flopping goldfish, I'd say. We better slow you down a little bit. How about some hair of the dog that bit you?"

He carried her kicking to the horse tank by the windmill, his big hands and wrists notched into her rib cage.

Cody Daniels had turned the truck around in the middle of the road, his stomach churning with fear, his sweat as cold as ice water. He slowly depressed the accelerator, his right hand trembling on the gearshift, each jolt in a chuckhole like a piece of glass in his entrails. He wiped the sweat out of his eyes with his sleeve and swerved wildly around the pools of water in the road, wishing he would break an axle or tip off the shoulder's edge into a gulley. He prayed for the dawn to come, for lightning to strike Anton Ling's house and set it ablaze, for the FBI to descend from the sky in a helicopter. He had never been this afraid in his entire life. But why? Just because an oversize diesel-powered truck had come grinding down a hill? It was irrational.

No, it was not. Cody knew he had a talent, and it was not one to be proud of. He was con-wise. He knew how to read iniquity in others because it resided in him. He also had a tuning fork that vibrated when he was around dangerous people. And he understood that cruelty was not an occasional vice. If it existed in an individual, it was systemic and pervasive and always looking for a new prospect. Cody knew the oversize truck was coming for Anton Ling, and inside it were men in the employ of Temple Dowling, or maybe even Dowling himself.

The lessons he had learned in prison were simple. There were two kinds of people in the slams: screwups like himself and those who had not only gone over to the dark side but enjoyed being there and had no plans to return. The joke was the latter category was not confined to convicts. The worst people he had ever known had worn uniforms or used ballpoint pens to do damage that no burglar could ever equal. How did you recognize the Temple Dowlings of the world? That one was easy. They always mocked. It was in their voice, their use of difficult words, the way they twisted whatever came out of your mouth. They stole other people's dignity and made them resent themselves. He and his men had invaded Cody's home and treated him as though he were sewage, then had driven away as indifferently as if they had run over a bug.

Where did that leave him in the mix, a man who had helped blind and disfigure a nurse in an abortion clinic? He didn't like to think about that. His one serious fall was on a forgery charge. He had never deliberately hurt anyone. Why had he gotten mixed up with the people who had set off the bomb at the clinic? That one, too, was easy. They knew a useful loser when they saw one.

Maybe what was waiting for him under the thunderclouds up ahead wasn't a totally undesirable fate. Maybe this was as good a place as any to cash in. He had spent most of his life waking up with a headful of spiders, then spending the rest of the day pretending they weren't there. He had shot over the heads of Mexicans coming out of the desert, scaring the hell out of women with infants hanging in slings from their chests and backs. He had painted the American flag on the cliff above his house but had never been in the service. He was a religious hypocrite and a peckerwood bully. His mother took off with a trucker when he was three, and his father, whom he had loved, had placed him in an orphanage when he was nine, promising to return after working a pipeline job in Alaska. But he never saw his father again or heard what happened to him, if anything. Was everything a conspiracy against Cody Daniels? Or wasn't it more probable that he was simply unwanted and, worse, unwanted for a legitimate reason? Gravity sucked, and shit always slid down the pipe, not up.

He felt his foot pressing on the accelerator. He had never thought so clearly about his life. The thunder rolling through the hills, the smell of the ozone, the cold tannic odor of the rain and dust, the branches of the mesquite and scrub oak bending almost to the ground all seemed like the pages of a book flipping before his eyes, defining the world and his role in it in a way he had never thought possible. Let Temple Dowling and his men do their worst. What was so bad about ending here, inside an electric storm, inside a clap of thunder that was as loud as God slapping His palms together?

Cody had all of these thoughts and was almost free of his fear when he drove into Anton Ling's yard and his headlights lit up the scene taking place by the windmill. Then he remembered why he had been so afraid.

CHAPTER TEN

Two men were holding Anton Ling by her arms. Her bare feet were bloody, her wrists duct-taped behind her. They had just lifted her out of the tank. Four other men stood close by, watching. All of the men were masked and had shifted their attention from Anton Ling to Cody. The only person not staring at him was Anton Ling, whose head hung on her chest, her wet hair wrapped around her cheeks. Cody Daniels braked and stared back at the men staring at him. He felt he had walked into someone else's nightmare and would not be leaving it any time soon.

He opened the door and stepped out of his vehicle, the engine still running. The ground seemed to shake with thunder, pools of quicksilver rippling through the clouds. "Howdy, fellows," he said.

No one answered him. Why did they look so surprised? Hadn't they heard or seen his truck coming? Maybe the sound of the engine had gotten lost in the thunder. Or maybe

Temple Dowling's people had recognized his truck and had already dismissed his presence as insignificant. "It's me. Cody Daniels. What's going on?" he said.

"Turn off your engine and lights and get over here," a tall man said.

"I was just doing like y'all told me. Keeping an eye on the place and all. I don't think y'all should be doing this to Miss Anton."

"Did you hear me?"

"Yes, sir."

"Then cut your engine and your lights."

"Yes, sir, I'm on it," Cody said. He reached back in the cab and turned off the ignition and headlights. He looked at the sky in the east and the wind flattening the trees on the hillcrests and the darkness that seemed to extend to the edges of the earth. "Boy, this has been a frog-stringer, hasn't it? Where's Mr. Dowling at?"

"What are you doing here?"

"Motoring around and such."

"Motoring around?"

"Yes, sir."

"Take out your wallet and put it on the hood of your vehicle."

"You don't know me?"

The tall man approached him. "Don't make me repeat myself."

"See, I thought y'all might be the cops I called earlier. I saw the lights on down here, which didn't seem right, so I did a nine-one-

one and figured y'all were with Sheriff Holland. I expect he ought to be showing up any time now."

"You're a damn poor liar, boy."

"I'd appreciate it if you wouldn't call me that."

"Get on your knees and put your hands behind your head."

"That woman hasn't done anything to y'all. Why don't you leave her alone?"

The tall man drove his fist into Cody's stomach, burying it to his wrist. Cody doubled over, his breath exploding from his chest, his knees collapsing in the dirt. The tall man shoved him over with his boot, then stepped on the side of his face. "Who are you?"

"A guy who lives up in the cliffs."

"Who'd you call?"

"Nobody. I didn't call anybody. You cain't get service out here."

"You know a man name of Noie Barnum?" The tall man pushed his boot tighter into the side of Cody's face.

"I've heard of him. I don't know him."

"Where did you hear about Barnum?"

"From a man name of Dowling. I thought that's who y'all were."

"What did you see here this morning?"

"Nothing," Cody replied, his mouth mashed against his teeth.

"Sure about that?"

"I know better than to mess with the wrong folks."

The tall man did not release his foot from Cody's face. He seemed to be looking at a diminutive man in the background, perhaps waiting for instructions. Cody could feel the lugs and grit on the bottom of the tall man's boot biting into his cheek and jawbone. He could smell the soiled odor of the man's foot and sock and the oil that had been rubbed into the boot's leather. The pressure on Cody's skull and jaw was unrelenting, as though the tall man were on the edge of cracking Cody's facial bones apart.

Cody was not seeing the tall man now. He saw two prison-farm gunbulls walking him from the trusty dormitory to the shed with the sawhorse standing under a bare lightbulb. They were both drunk and laughing, as though the three of them were only having fun, not unlike kids putting a friend through a harmless initiation ritual. Maybe at first that was all they had intended to do — just scare him and knock him around for sassing one of them that afternoon, what did they call it, making a Christian out of a hardhead? He knew the reality was otherwise. These were men for whom cruelty was as natural a part of their lives as eating breakfast. Their only task had been to hide their intentions from themselves, to set up the situation, then to simply follow their instincts, not unlike flinging gasoline on a fire and stepping back to watch the results. Cody would never forget the lustful cry of release in the throat of the first gunbull who mounted him. He would also never forgive himself for being their victim, accepting what they did to him as though somehow he had deserved his fate.

"I didn't see anything here except six men tormenting a he'pless woman," he said.

There was a pause. "You saw what?" the tall man asked, twisting the sole of his boot on Cody's cheek.

"Saw a tall man that's got so much chewing tobacco in his mouth, he cain't swallow. Saw a li'l bitty fellow over yonder by the horse tank. Saw one man that's bleeding through a hole in his mask, like somebody seriously fucked up his face. Saw a big gray truck with a diesel engine and a stack on it. Saw a bunch of men that dress like they been in the military. Saw a bunch of men that wouldn't believe me when I said I called Sheriff Holland. I'm here to tell you the sheriff of this county is one mean motor scooter. He'll flat kick a two-by-four up your ass. I know. I've been in his jailhouse."

Cody thought the torque in his neck was going to snap his spinal cord. He could hear the windmill's blades spinning, a loose door banging in the barn, the thunder in the clouds retreating in the hills. Through the dirt and sweat and rain mist in his eyes, he could see a pale band of cold light appear beyond the hills in the east, as though the season were winter rather than spring. He heard someone snapping his fingers, as though trying to get the attention of the tall man. Then the boot went away from Cody's face.

"You're a lucky fellow," the tall man said, lifting Cody to his feet by his shirtfront. "But let me leave you this little reminder of what happens when you wise off to the wrong people." He drove Cody's head into the truck fender and dropped him to the ground.

Cody felt himself descending into a deep well, one that was cool and damp and colored by a sunrise that had the texture and pinkness of cotton candy. As though from a great distance, he could hear glass breaking, furniture being overturned, a telephone crashing through a window into the yard, a computer being smashed into junk. These things were not his business any longer. Somehow Cody Daniels had faced down and bested the men who had raped him when he was seventeen. That an event of that magnitude could take place in his life seemed impossible. All he knew was that after a few minutes at the bottom of the well, the truck with the diesel-powered engine drove away, and he found himself cutting the duct tape on Anton Ling's wrists and ankles, wondering if she was still alive.

■ ■ ■ ■

The 911 call came in to the department at 6:47 A.M. The caller said he was an emergency electrical worker who had been sent out to find a downed power line in the neighborhood and had been flagged down by a man claiming to be a minister. "Y'all better get out here. This guy isn't making much sense," the caller said.

"Neither are you. What's the nature of your emergency?" Maydeen said.

"The guy says there's a Chinese woman inside that almost drowned. The place looks torn to hell. There're two pickup trucks in the yard with the wiring ripped out of the dashboards. Maybe a bunch of those Mexicans went crazy."

"Which Mexicans?"

"The ones that come through here every night. Maybe now y'all can get off your asses and do something about it."

"What's your name?"

"Marvin."

"What's your last name, Marvin?"

"I didn't give it."

"Well, Marvin I-Didn't-Give-It, you keep yourself and your smart-aleck mouth there till a deputy sheriff arrives. You also keep this line open. You copy that, Marvin?"

"Yes, ma'am," he said. "Ma'am?"

"What?"

"I'm standing in the yard by the horse tank. There's blood in the water and on the side of the tank. There's something else, too. Hang on."

"Are you still there?"

"There's a car, maybe a Trans Am, driving up from the back of the property. It doesn't have any paint. A guy is getting out."

"What about him?"

"I don't know. A guy in a suit and a hat. A guy in a dress shirt. I don't know where he came from. There's no road back there."

"Have you seen him before?"

"I waved at him, but he's just standing there. His engine is running."

"Can you get the tag?"

"No, ma'am. He's got his door open and he's staring at me. He hasn't shaved in a while. His shirt is yellow-looking, like there's dried soap in it."

Then the caller went silent.

"Are you there? Stay with me, Marvin," Maydeen said.

"I don't know what he wants. He's just staring at me. His pants are stuck down inside the tops of his boots. Are y'all on your way yet?"

"Can you ask the driver who he is?"

"No, ma'am."

"Why not?"

"I'm not sure why not. This isn't a reg'lar

sort of guy."

"What do you mean by that?"

"The way he's staring at me. He's got a shoulder rig on."

"He's carrying a weapon?"

"Yes, ma'am, a big revolver in a shoulder rig. I can see it against his chest."

"Go to your vehicle, Marvin."

"I don't think he wants me to do that."

"Listen to me, Marvin. Take your cell phone from your ear and walk to your vehicle with it. But don't break the connection. Are you listening?"

"He's walking up to me, ma'am."

"Drive away, Marvin."

"No, ma'am. This is not the time to go anywhere. Jesus Christ, lady, get out here." There was a pause, then: "I'm from the power company. I'm not sure what's going on. The place is a wreck, isn't it? I think a lady in there might be hurt real bad. Sir, you cain't take the keys out of my truck. That's a company vehicle. They don't allow unauthorized personnel inside their vehicles. Sir, don't throw my keys up there. I'm gonna be in a heck of a lot of trouble."

The connection went dead.

Maydeen dispatched the paramedics and two deputies to the house, then called Hackberry at his home and told him of the 911 call. "The guy from the power company didn't

250

say who the minister was?" he asked.

"No clue."

"And nothing else about the guy in the Trans Am?"

"Just what I told you."

"Collins?"

"I've tried to call Marvin twice, but I go to voice mail."

"Call the power company and ask them to call the radio in his truck."

"Yes, sir."

"There was blood in the horse tank?"

"That's what the caller said."

"I'm on my way. Get Pam out there."

"She just walked in."

"Put her on, please."

"It's Collins, isn't it?" Maydeen said.

"That's my guess."

"You'll probably beat the ambulance there. Wait till I get R.C. and Felix out there for backup."

"Do what you're told, Maydeen."

"You're too goddamn old and stubborn for your own good, Hack. You're gonna get yourself killed."

Pam picked up the extension. "What's going on?" she said.

"We ROA at Anton Ling's place. Maydeen will fill you in. Get ahold of Ethan Riser and tell him Jack Collins is probably in the neighborhood. Put out an APB on a Trans Am with no paint on it. Include Collins's physical description."

"Copy that," she replied. "Hack?"

"What?"

"If you see Collins, forget the rules."

"We never forget the rules."

"Haven't you figured it out? That's exactly what Collins counts on."

Maydeen was right. Because Hackberry was driving from his ranch, he arrived at Anton Ling's property before the ambulance or the deputies from his department. The rain had stopped, and the great boundless baked emptiness of the land that was not unlike the floor of an ancient ocean seemed to have risen cool and green and washed from the storm, a blue and pink and turquoise rainbow arching over the hills, anchoring itself and its promise somewhere beyond the clouds.

Cody Daniels's truck was parked in front of the house, the ignition wires ripped out. The lineman's truck was parked close by, the driver's door open, the keys gone from the ignition. There was no movement either inside or outside the house. Hackberry walked to the barn and the bunkhouse and the stucco cottage and looked inside. There was no one there, and the Trans Am was nowhere to be seen. He pulled his revolver from its holster and entered the house through the kitchen door, the pistol hanging heavily from his hand. The contents of the cupboards and the pantry had been raked on the floor. Through a side door, he could see into the room that served as a chapel. The statue of the Virgin Mary had been broken in half, and the tiered rack of votive candles had been flipped over and the candles and glass holders smashed and ground into the floor. The small altar had been flung into the folding chairs, the white altar cloth grimed with footprints.

The only sound he heard was the wind flapping the curtains on the windows. Through a doorway, he could see the dining and living rooms. The pictures had been stripped from the walls and the dining table turned over, as though someone had been looking for something taped under it, the fabric on the stuffed chairs sliced open.

"This is Sheriff Holland! Who's in here?" he called.

"Sheriff?" a familiar voice said.

"That's what I said."

"It's Cody Daniels."

"Walk out here where I can see you, Reverend."

"Did you bring the ambulance?"

"Do what I say, please."

"Yes, sir, I'm coming," Daniels said, walking into the dining room. "They beat up Miss Anton and almost drowned her. We got to get her to the hospital. Sometimes people get pneumonia when they almost drown."

Hackberry still held his revolver, his eyes roving around the house's interior, searching over Cody Daniels's shoulder. "Where's Collins?"

"Is that his name?"

"Will you answer the question?"

"You're talking about the guy who killed all those Thai women, right? He didn't give us his name. He just asked who did this to Miss Anton. I told him I didn't have a clue."

Hackberry holstered his revolver and went into the bedroom. Anton Ling lay on a mattress that had been pulled off the bedsprings. Her dresser drawers had been dumped and her clothes pulled from the hangers in the closet. There was blood on her pillow, her clothes were drenched, and her eyes had the lack of focus that accompanies brain concussion. He knelt beside her. "Who did this to you, Miss Anton?"

"They all wore camouflage masks. Only one man spoke."

"What was Jack Collins doing here?"

"The man in the suit?"

"Yes, what did he say to you?"

"He wanted to know who the men were. He said he and I were on the same side. He touched my face with his hand. Cody told him not to do that, and for a minute I was afraid for Cody's life."

"Cody?"

"If it weren't for him, I'd be dead."

Hackberry looked over his shoulder at Cody Daniels and said, "Where's the guy from the power company, the one named Marvin?"

"The guy in the suit threw his keys on the roof and told him to hoof it. So that's what he did," Cody Daniels replied.

"The ambulance will be here in a few minutes, Miss Anton," Hackberry said. "I need to talk with the reverend, but I'll be right outside."

"I think I heard someone speak in Russian," she said. "But I can't be sure."

"You're pretty sure of that?" Hackberry said.

"Yes, I'd almost swear it was Russian, or at least East European."

As Hackberry got to his feet, tentacles of pain wrapped around his lower back and his buttocks, sinking into his viscera and then disappearing. He walked Cody Daniels toward the kitchen. "What were you doing out here?" he said.

"I wanted to see if she was all right. Then I left. That's when I saw this gray truck with an extended cab come down from the hills behind her fence line. It had a smokestack on it, one sticking up by the cab. The only guy I talked to had a mouth full of chewing tobacco and smelled like it, too."

"What time did you arrive on her property?"

"It was dark. I didn't note the time."

"You were looking in her windows?"

"I don't do things like that."

"You just drive out to other people's property in the middle of the night?"

"Yeah, in this case, that's what I did. I got a better question for you. When's that dadburn ambulance coming?"

"Why were you suspicious of the truck?" Hackberry said.

" 'Cause I thought they might be working for Temple Dowling."

"You know Dowling?"

"Dowling was at my house. He said he wanted me to spy on Miss Anton."

"Why would he select you for such a noble enterprise, Reverend?"

"Ask him."

"Don't worry, I will."

"You got the right to think anything you want of me, Sheriff. But I told you the truth. If you don't like it, that's —"

"Who were those guys?" Hackberry said.

"It wasn't Dowling or his people."

"If they wore masks, how can you be sure?"

"Dowling and his thugs invaded my house and threatened me on my deck. They would have recognized me. These guys didn't know who I was. What's so hard to understand about that?"

"Did Dowling offer you money?"

"He mentioned it."

256

"What else did he mention?"

"Sir?"

"I know the Dowling family. I know how they work. Is Temple Dowling blackmailing you?"

Cody Daniels's hand was resting on the kitchen drainboard. His fingers twitched slightly, then became motionless. "I guess you could call it that. No, it's not up for debate, that's exactly what he was doing." His gaze drifted from the side window to the yard. "There're your deputies and the ambulance coming. Can I talk to your chief deputy a minute?"

"No, you can't. Did you have a gun or a weapon of any kind when you came back to help Ms. Ling?"

"No, sir."

"You just did it?"

"Not exactly. My teeth were rattling like Chiclets."

"What does Dowling have on you, partner?"

"You've pulled my sheet. Take your choice."

"You went down for forgery, but that's not it, is it?"

"I got no more to say on the subject."

"It's the bombing at the abortion clinic, isn't it?"

"I need to talk to your deputy. It's important. At least it is to me."

"Go sit on the gallery and let your mind think cool thoughts. You know who said that?

Satchel Paige. He said the key to longevity was to have cool thoughts and not to eat fried food. Why don't you try that?"

"Why you got it in for me, Sheriff?"

"Because I think you helped blind and mutilate a defenseless woman. Because I think anyone who plants a bomb among unsuspecting people should be stuffed feet-first into a tree shredder."

The skin of Cody Daniels's throat prickled, as though it had just been windburned. "You really mean that?" he said quietly.

"Probably not," Hackberry said. "But I mean something right close to it."

"You're not one given to mercy, Sheriff. I don't think it's right to talk to people like that, even the likes of me," Cody Daniels said. He went outside and sat by himself on the front steps, his face wan, his gaze fixed on the apron of bare earth at his feet.

Hackberry helped the paramedics place Anton Ling on the gurney and take her out to the ambulance. Before they put her inside, she touched his wrist. "I could hear you in the kitchen," she said. "Don't be too hard on Reverend Daniels."

"He has no explanation for being at your house."

"It was his pride. I shamed and demeaned him in the parking lot at the grocery store. I treated him like human refuse."

"To my mind, that's not an unfair description of a clinic bomber."

"You're wrong about him," she said.

"We'll straighten up your house and lock the doors. I'll be up to see you at the hospital. In the meantime, I don't want you to worry about anything. We'll get the guys who did this."

"Maybe," she replied.

"What were they after, Miss Anton?"

"Noie Barnum."

"No, in the house. What were they looking for?"

"My guess is they're looking for technical material about the Predator drone."

"Is it there?"

She shook her head.

"Did Barnum have it on him?"

"To my knowledge, all he brought to this house were his wounds. He stayed in the cottage. I forgot to tell you something. I hurt one of the men who was holding me at the sink. I stabbed him just below the eye with a screwdriver. He'll have to go to a hospital or see a doctor."

"You're a tough lady, Miss Anton."

"You won't catch them."

"Pardon?"

"The men who did this to me have been with us a long time. They're in our midst every day. We just don't acknowledge their presence," she said.

A paramedic closed the back door of the

ambulance. Hackberry watched the ambulance drive away, then walked back to the windmill and watched Pam Tibbs and R.C. stringing crime-scene tape from the barn to the front of the house. R.C. was over six feet and had a skeletal frame that looked tacked together from the staves in an apple box, his stomach and buttocks flat, his waist twenty-eight inches, his face perpetually young, his mouth small like a girl's, his eyes always bright with surprise. He was chewing gum, snapping it in his jaw, his coned-up white straw deputy's hat slanted down over his brow. "Found a bloody screwdriver that somebody kicked under the counter in the kitchen, Sheriff," he said.

"Did you bag it?" Hackberry said.

"Yes, sir."

"Good. That must be the one Ms. Ling put in a guy's face."

"You want to make casts of those tire tracks?"

"That's a good idea."

"See the tracks on top of the truck tires? Those are Michelins."

"How do you know?"

"I can tell by the width and the tread. They're brand-new, too. Want to start checking the dealerships?"

"You can identify a Michelin tire just by looking at the tread marks?"

"I only mounted about five hunnerd of them."

Hackberry glanced at Pam. She brushed at her nose with her wrist, her eyes smiling.

"What are y'all laughing at?" R.C. asked.

"Nothing," Hackberry said.

"I say something wrong?" R.C. asked.

"No, not at all," Hackberry said.

"I was just making an observation," R.C. said, his cheeks reddening.

"We were laughing because you were two jumps ahead of us, R.C.," Hackberry said. "Don't tell the voters I said that, or they might take my star away."

"No, sir, they're not going to do that," R.C. said. "They think you're one of them bleeding-heart liberals, but they trust you to do the right thing more than they trust themselves. How's that for smarts?"

"On the subject of smarts, what's with shit-for-brains over there on the steps?" Pam asked, glancing in Cody Daniels's direction. The sun had broken through the clouds, and her bare arms looked brown and big in the sunlight as she unrolled and tightened the crime-scene tape, her dark mahogany hair that was either sunburned or white on the tips curled against her cheeks, her breasts as firm-looking as softballs against her khaki shirt.

"He says he wants to talk with you about something," Hackberry replied.

"I think I can forgo the pleasure," Pam replied.

"Anton Ling says he saved her life."

"If he did, it was by accident."

Pam went back to work, stringing the tape behind the barn and around the back of the stucco cottage and the bunkhouse. She secured it to a fence post on the far side of the main house and returned to the windmill, her hair moving in the wind, strands touching her mouth. In moments like these, when she was totally unguarded and unmindful of herself, Hackberry knew in a private place in the back of his mind that Pam Tibbs belonged in that category of exceptional women whose beauty radiated outward through their skin and had little to do with the physical attributes of their birth. In these moments he felt an undefined longing in his heart that he refused to recognize.

"Mind if I see what he wants?" Pam asked.

"Suit yourself," Hackberry replied.

"Come with me."

"What for?"

"This is the same guy who claimed I assaulted him. I don't want him telling lies about anything I say to him now."

"Then I'd leave him alone."

"Jesus Christ, Hack, first you tell me the guy wants to talk to me, then you tell me not to talk with him. In between, you tell me he saved someone's life."

"What are you laughing at, R.C.?" Hackberry said.

"Not a thing, Sheriff. I was just enjoying the breeze and the freshness of the morning. This cool wind is special. Lordy, what a fine day," R.C. said, folding his arms over his chest, gazing at the sunlit greenness and clarity of the hills, puffing out his cheeks, sucking his teeth.

"I'll talk to you later," Hackberry said.

"Yes, sir," R.C. said.

Hackberry walked with Pam to the gallery, where Cody Daniels was sitting on the steps in the shadow of the house, staring into space, a bandage taped to his forehead. "You wanted to say something to Chief Deputy Tibbs, Reverend?" Hackberry said.

"I'd like to do it in private, if you don't object," Cody Daniels replied.

"Say what's on your mind. We have work to do," Pam said.

Cody Daniels looked back and forth, his mouth a tight seam. He fiddled with his shirt buttons and made lines in the dirt with the heel of his shoe. Strands of his hair were stuck inside the tape on his bandage, which gave him the appearance of a disorganized and hapless child. "I apologize for the way I acted when you arrested me. I deliberately provoked you," he said to Pam.

She touched a nostril with one knuckle and huffed air out her nose. "Is that it?" she said.

"I also made some smart-ass remarks when I was in the holding cell. I'm sorry I did that."

"What smart-ass remarks?" Pam said.

"I said something to the sheriff. I don't remember it real clear. I should have kept my mouth shut, that's all."

"What remarks?" Pam said.

Cody Daniels wiped a piece of dirt off his face and looked at it. "Just idle, disrespectful stuff that doesn't mean anything. The kind of things an uneducated and angry man might say. No, 'angry man' doesn't cut it. The kind of thing a half-baked mean-spirited pissant might say. That's me I'm talking about."

"What did you say?"

"Sheriff?" Cody Daniels said, raising his eyes to Hackberry's.

"The man said he was sorry. Why not let it slide?" Hackberry said to Pam.

"Reverend, you've got about five seconds to get your head on right," Pam said.

"Cain't recall."

She pulled a braided slapjack from her side pocket and let it hang from her right hand.

"I said I'd rather belly up to a spool of barbed wire," Cody Daniels said. He knitted his fingers together and twisted them in and out of one another, his teeth clenched, breathing through the side of his mouth as though he had just eaten scalding food, patting the soles of his shoes up and down in the dirt. Hackberry could hear the blades of the windmill rattle to life as R.C. unchained the crankshaft and cupped a drink of water from the pipe.

"What did Sheriff Holland have to say about your remark?" Pam asked.

"He said something about kicking a two-by-four with nails in it up my ass till I'd be spitting splinters. Or something to that effect."

Pam brushed at her nose again, pushing the slapjack back into her pocket. "What do you think we ought to do with you?"

"You got me," he replied, shaking his head, his eyes lowered.

"Look at me and answer my question."

"Shoot me?"

"It's a possibility," she said.

"She's not serious, is she?" Cody Daniels said to Hackberry.

"You'd better believe it, bud," Hackberry said.

Pam and Hackberry went inside the house and, with two other deputies, began picking up the furniture and sweeping up the glass in the kitchen and the chapel. "Are we doing this because you're a Catholic?" Pam asked.

Hackberry reset the altar at the front of the chapel and picked up the broken pieces of the statue of the Virgin Mary and laid them on top of the altar. "We're doing this because it's the right thing to do," he said.

"Just thought I'd ask," she said.

"We protect and serve. We treat everybody the same. If others don't like the way we do things, they can run us off. End of discussion."

"Who spat in your Cheerios this morning?"

"Stop and consider the image that conjures up. Why don't you and Maydeen develop a small degree of sensitivity about the language you use? Just once, try a little professionalism." He propped his broom against the wall, knocking it into the wood.

"My uncle said I put him in mind of a cow with the red scours downloading into a window fan," she said.

Hackberry gave up. Through the window, he saw Cody Daniels rise from the steps and begin walking down the road toward the highway. Pam saw him, too, and seemed to lose her concentration. She stopped sweeping and blew out her breath. "Is there a shortcut to his place?" she asked.

"No, on foot it's four miles, most of it uphill," Hackberry replied.

"The sheriff in Jim Hogg told you Daniels was dirty on a clinic bombing back east?"

"He said Daniels was at least a cheerleader in the group. Maybe worse, who knows? He acts like he's dirty, though. If I had to bet, I'd say he was a player."

She propped her broom against the scrolled-iron candle rack and bit a piece of skin on her thumb. "Like you say, we treat

266

everyone the same, right?"

"That's the rule."

"The guy stood up. It's not right to pretend he didn't."

"I wouldn't say he stood up completely, but he made an effort."

"You mind? I'll make him sit behind the grille."

"No, I don't mind at all," Hackberry replied.

He watched Pam go out the front door and get in her cruiser and drive down the dirt road. She braked to a stop by Cody Daniels, rolling down her window and speaking to him over the sound of the engine. Daniels got in the backseat, ducking his head, like a man coming out of a storm into an unexpected safe harbor.

Go figure, Hackberry thought.

CHAPTER ELEVEN

Hackberry had never considered himself prescient, but he had little doubt about who would be calling him that evening. As the sun set behind his house, he sat down in a spacious cushioned swaybacked straw chair on his back porch, his Stetson tilted down over his brow, his cordless phone and a glass of iced tea and his holstered .45 on the table beside him. He propped his feet up on another chair and sipped from his tea and crunched ice and mint leaves between his teeth and then dozed while waiting for the call that he knew he would receive, in the same way you know that a dishonorable man to whom you were unwisely courteous will eventually appear uninvited at your front door.

He could hear animals walking through the thickness of the scrub brush on the hillside and, in his half-waking state, see a palm tree on the crest framed against a thin red wafer of sun imprinted on the blue sky. For just a moment he felt himself slip into a dream about his father, the University of Texas history professor who had been a congressman and a friend of Franklin Roosevelt. In the dream there was nothing about President Roosevelt or his father's political or teaching career or his father's death, only the time when Hackberry and his father rode horses into the badlands down by the border to hunt for Indian arrowheads. It was 1943, and they had tied their horses outside a beer joint and café built of gray fieldstones that resembled bread loaves. The land dipped away into the distance as though all the sedimentary rock under the earth's crust had collapsed and created a giant sandy bowl rimmed by mesas that were as red in the sunset as freshly excised molars.

The sun was finally subsumed by clouds that were low and thick and churning and the color of burnt pewter. In the cooling of the day and the pulsation of electricity in the clouds, dust devils began to swirl and wobble and break apart on top of the hardpan. For reasons he was too young to understand, Hackberry was frightened by the drop in barometric pressure and the great shadow that seemed to darken the land, as though a shade were being drawn across it by an invisible hand.

His father had gone inside the café to buy two bottles of cream soda. When he came back out and handed Hack one, the ice sliding down the neck, he saw the expression on his son's face and said, still hanging on to the bottle, "Something happen out here, son?"

"The land, it looks strange. It makes me feel strange," Hackberry said.

"In what way?"

"Like everything has died. Like the sun has gone away forever, like we're the only two people left on earth."

"Psychiatrists call that a world-destruction fantasy. But the earth will always be here. Hundreds of millions of years ago, out in that great vastness, there was an ocean where fish as big as boxcars swam. Now it's a desert, but maybe one day it will be an ocean again. Did you know there were probably whales that swam out there?"

"No, sir."

"It's true. Mythic creatures, too. See those pale horizontal lines in the mesas? That's where the edge of the sea was. You see those flat rocks up a little bit higher? That's where the mermaids used to sun themselves."

"Mermaids in Texas?"

"One hundred million years ago, you bet."

"How do you know that, Daddy?"

"I was there. Your dad is a pretty old fellow." Then he rubbed his hand on top of Hackberry's head. "Nothing is worth worrying about, Hack," he said. "Just remember how long this place has been here and all the people who've lived on it and maybe are still out there, in one form or another, maybe as spirits watching over us. That's what the Indians believe. Our job is to enjoy the earth and to take care of it. Worry robs us of our faith and our joy and gives us nothing in return. How about you and I go inside and play the pinball machine and order up a couple of those barbecue-chicken dinners? When we come back outside, one of those mermaids might be up there in the rocks winking at you."

That was the way Hackberry always wanted to remember his father — good-natured and protective and knowledgeable about every situation in the world that a man might face. And that was the way he had thought of him without exception every day of his young life, up until the morning his father had taken a revolver from his desk drawer and oiled and cleaned it and loaded each chamber with a copper-jacketed hollow-point round, then placed a pillow behind his head and cocked the hammer and fitted the barrel into his mouth, easing the sight behind his teeth, just before he blew the top of his skull onto the ceiling.

The sun had gone behind the hill when Hackberry's cordless phone rang and woke him from his dream. He checked the caller ID and saw the words "wireless" and "unknown." He clicked the "on" button and said,

"What's the haps, Mr. Collins?"

"I declare. You're on it from the gate, Sheriff."

"It's not much of a trick when you deal with certain kinds of people."

"Such as me?"

"Yeah, I think you definitely qualify as a man with his own zip code and time zone."

"Maybe I'll surprise you."

"Hardly."

"How's the Oriental woman doing?"

"Call the hospital and see."

"I would, but hospitals don't give out patient information over the telephone."

"Ms. Ling has had a bad time, but she's going to be all right. What were you doing at her place? Just happened to be in the neighborhood?"

"I have people watching it for me. Which is what you should have been doing."

"Thank you. I'll make a note of that. Are you done?"

"Pretty near but not quite."

"No, you're done, sir. And I'm done being your echo chamber. You're not Lucifer descending upon Eden in a Miltonic poem, Mr. Collins. You were a bug sprayer for Orkin. You probably skipped toilet training and have lived most of your life with skid marks in your underwear. I know of no instance when you've fought your fight on a level playing field. You consider yourself educated, but you understand nothing of the books you read. You're a grandiose idiot, sir. You'll end on the injection table at Huntsville or with a bullet in your head. I'm telling you these things for only one reason. Last year you invaded my home and tried to murder my chief deputy. I'm going to get you for that, partner, and for all the other things you've done to innocent people in the name of God."

"You need to be quiet and listen for a minute, Sheriff Holland. You probably have all kinds of theories about who hurt the Oriental woman and tore up her house. This defense contractor Temple Dowling has been looking for Noie Barnum all over the countryside, but I doubt it was him. There was a little man among that bunch in the truck. From what I could gather, he didn't have a lot to say, but he was the one giving orders. I suspect that's Josef Sholokoff. Do you call that name to mind?"

"Not offhand," Hackberry lied.

"I once worked for Josef Sholokoff. He tried to have me killed. He sent three degenerates on motorcycles to do the job. Some poor Hispanic maid had to scrub them off the wallpaper in a motel room. I always felt bad about that. I mean leaving her to clean up such a mess."

"Yes, you surely know how to write your name in big red letters, Mr. Collins. I don't think Ted Bundy or Dennis Rader or Gary

Ridgway or any of our other contemporary psychopaths quite meet your standards."

"There are different kinds of killers in the world, Sheriff Holland. Some do it out of meanness. Some do it for hire. Some do it because they're schizophrenic and attack imaginary enemies. Politicians have the military do it to increase the financial gain of corporations. Sholokoff takes it a step further. Ask yourself what kind of man would allow his people to vandalize a chapel and torture a female minister."

"Sholokoff has declared war on the Creator?"

"You could say that. He's a procurer. Is there anything lower than a man who lives off the earnings of a whore?"

"I don't think you have a lot of moral authority in that area, Mr. Collins. You're a murderer of innocent girls and women, which means you're a moral and physical coward."

"Could it be you who's wanting in courage, Sheriff, and not me? Did you sit with a weapon by your hand while you waited on my call? Were you that fearful of a homeless man?"

Hackberry's eyes swept the hillside, searching in the shadows that the trees and underbrush made on the slope. Then he examined the ridgeline and the trees growing up an arroyo and the outcroppings of sandstone and layers of table rock exposed by erosion, all

274

the places that a man with binoculars could hide in the setting sun.

"You used a generic term. You said 'weapon.' What kind of weapon would that be, Mr. Collins?" Hackberry said.

"Maybe I was just trying to give you a start."

"I always said you were quite a jokester."

"That's not what you just called me. You said I was a coward. I'm many things. But 'coward' isn't among them. A coward fears death. But Death is my friend, Sheriff Holland. You remember the poem by e. e. cummings? How does it go? 'How do you like your blue-eyed boy now, Mr. Death?' The poet was talking of Buffalo Bill. Will you be corrupted by the grave like Buffalo Bill? Or will you be freed by it? Can you say you have no fear of the black hole that awaits you?"

"Rhetoric is cheap stuff."

"Is it, now?"

"I'm going to sign off and ask that you not call again. I'll be seeing you down the pike. This time out, there won't be any warning."

"You're a judgmental man, Sheriff. As such, you may be the orchestrator of your own undoing."

"I don't think it's going to play out that way."

"Maybe you'll rethink your attitude."

The red dot of a laser sight appeared on the back of Hackberry's left wrist and traveled up his arm and across his chest. Hackberry sucked in his breath involuntarily, as though a black widow or tarantula had crawled across his body. He tried to get to his feet as the red dot paused on his heart, but he fell back in the chair, knocking over the iced tea, his back aflame. The red dot dropped to his loins and touched his scrotum and then was gone, all in under two seconds, so fast he wondered if he had imagined the event. He stared into the black-green shadows on the hillside while rocks clacked and spilled from somewhere near the ridgeline and the dial tone of his cordless phone buzzed like an electrified horsefly in his hand.

He lay sleepless in his bed most of the night, furious that he had let himself be bested by a messianic poseur and mass killer like Preacher Jack Collins, then doubly furious that, in his anger, he was giving away power to Collins and letting Collins rob him of sleep and peace of mind and, finally, self-respect. He had known reformers and Bible-thumpers all his life, and not one of them, in his opinion, ever proved the exception when it came to obsession about sexuality: To a man, they feared their own desires and knew after waking from certain kinds of dreams what they would be capable of doing if the right situation presented itself. Every one of them was filled not with longing but with rage, and their rage always expressed itself in the same fashion: They wanted control of other people, and if they could not have control over them, they wanted them destroyed.

The legacy of Salem did not go away easily. Vigilantism, the Klan, the acolytes of Senator McCarthy and others of his stripe formed a continuous thread from 1692 to the present, Hackberry thought. But that did not change the fact that Hackberry had failed miserably in dealing with Jack Collins, who killed people whenever and wherever he wished and seemed to walk through walls or leave no indicators of his presence except the funnel-shaped tracks of an animal.

The next morning did not go well, either. The previous day Ethan Riser had shown little interest in the events at Anton Ling's house, explaining that the break-in and the assault on her person did not constitute federal crimes and that Jack Collins's appearance and departure from Anton Ling's home provided no information or clue as to where he and Noie Barnum were hiding. "Let me call you back early tomorrow," Riser had said. "I'll try to find out where Josef Sholokoff is right now. If he's here, we can probably step into things and leave a lot heavier footprint."

"Why the sudden due diligence with Sholokoff and not our local residents?" Hackberry had said.

"Jack Collins is an aberration who will

probably self-destruct. Sholokoff is a contagious disease. If he can get his hands on a working model of a Predator drone or its design, Al Qaeda will have it in twenty-four hours."

"How would Sholokoff even know about Noie Barnum?"

"Temple Dowling used to be a silent business partner of his. We've had our eye on Dowling for a long time. He just doesn't know it. Or care. Weren't you associated politically with Dowling's father?"

"Yeah, I was, much to my regret. I'll expect your call early in the morning, Ethan," Hackberry had replied.

But Riser did not call back, and Hackberry's messages went unanswered. That afternoon another agent called Hackberry's office and told him that Ethan Riser had gone back to Washington.

"What for?" Hackberry asked.

"Ask him when he gets back," the agent said, and hung up.

Hackberry visited Anton Ling in the hospital but otherwise spent the rest of the day unproductively, still resenting himself for allowing Jack Collins to get inside his head. Or was something else bothering him as well?

That evening he drove to Pam Tibbs's house with a gallon of vanilla ice cream and a six-pack of A&W root beer packed in his cooler. He rang the doorbell, then sat on the front steps, staring into a street lined with bungalows and two-story frame houses that had been built during the 1920s, the porches hung with swings, the flower beds blooming, American flags hanging from staffs inserted into metal sockets on many of the wood pillars. It was a neighborhood that belonged to another era, one for which most Americans are nostalgic, but the people who lived in the neighborhood did not recognize it as such.

Hackberry heard the back screen slam, then a moment later, a man backed a waxed red convertible into the street and drove away, his attention concentrated on the traffic. Pam opened the front door. "Hi, Hack," she said.

He turned around and looked at her. She was wearing blue-jean shorts and a pink blouse and earrings and Roman sandals. "Hi," he replied.

"You want to come in?"

"Who was the guy in the convertible?"

"My cousin."

"I've never seen him. Does he live around here?"

"No."

"So where does he live?"

"He's a sales rep for a computer company. He travels a lot."

"People who travel a lot don't have addresses?"

"It's none of your business, Hack."

"You're right, it isn't."

She looked at the six-pack of root beer next to Hack's leg. The vapor on top of the cans was contracting, the beaded moisture on the sides running onto the porch. "What's in the sack?"

"Vanilla ice cream."

"You want to come in?"

"I should have called first."

"What's going on?"

"Nothing is going on. I thought you might like a root-beer float. It's that kind of evening."

"What kind?"

"When I was a kid, it was a treat to go to the A&W root-beer drive-in. We thought that was big stuff. Later-spring and summer evenings are the best moments in the year."

"Come inside."

"Another time."

"Come inside or I'm going to kick you in the small of the back as hard as I can."

He looked at the street in the gloaming of the day and at the darkness of the lawns in the shade, and he knew what had been bothering him since early that morning. A teenage boy on a bicycle was riding down the sidewalk, sailing a folded newspaper with the accuracy of a marksman onto each porch, whapping it solidly against the front door, the canvas bags slamming hard on his racks each time he banged over a peak in the sidewalk. The boy reminded Hackberry of himself, or maybe he reminded Hackberry of most boys of years ago, winsome in a way that was not calculated, full of expectation, full of innocent pride in their skill at lofting a tightly rolled, string-wrapped newspaper onto a front porch. But why was the boy throwing his route so late? Hackberry wondered. Why was the light so peculiar in tone — sepia-tinted, golden inside the branches of the trees, a smell like chrysanthemums pooling in the flower beds, more like autumn than spring?

"Hack?" Pam said.

"Yeah?"

"I'd really like some ice cream and root beer. It's very thoughtful of you to bring some by. Come in, won't you?"

Her mouth was red, her voice infused with a protective emotion that she rarely allowed anyone to see.

"Sure. That's what I was about to do," he replied.

She held the screen door open for him while he walked inside. He could feel her eyes slide across the side of his face when she latched the screen behind them. Then he heard her close the inside door and push the dead bolt into place.

"Why'd you do that?" he asked.

"Do what?"

"Lock the door."

"I didn't think about it."

"You think Collins will come around?"

"I hope he does. Except I don't think he's interested in me," she said.

"Then why did you lock the door?"

"Maybe I don't want to be disturbed by a couple of my busybody neighbors. You're acting a little strange, Hack."

"It goes with my persona. The VA gave me a D-minus on normalcy fifty years ago."

He went into the kitchen and set the root beer on the counter and put the ice cream in the freezer. His lower back felt like a junkyard that had fallen down a flight of stairs. He propped his hands on the edge of the sink and extended his legs behind him and leaned heavily on his arms, the pain slowly draining out of his spine and disappearing down the backs of his thighs into the floor. She placed her palm against the small of his back. "I hate to see you like this," she said. "I wish it was me instead of you."

"Like what?"

"In pain, depressed, unhappy. What did Collins say to you when he called your house?"

"It's not what he said. It's what he is. He loves death. That's his edge."

"So he'll have a smile on his face when we blow his head off."

"I met Jim Harrison once. He's a novelist. He made a remark in passing that I never forgot. He said, 'We love the earth but we don't get to stay.' On an evening like this, an irrefutable truth sometimes has a way of invading your soul. As a nihilist, Collins doesn't bear that burden. He seeks the dark hole in the ground that the rest of us fear. For that reason, we have no power over him. Even in killing him, we do his will. For that reason alone, I never believed in capital punishment. You said it when we first started dealing with Collins. He wants me to be his executioner."

She stretched her arm across his back and hooked her hand on his right shoulder and laid her face against his arm. "You were actually mad because my cousin was here?"

"No," he lied.

"He came to borrow money. His wife left him. He's a philanderer. No one else in the family will have anything to do with him." She exhaled and slipped her hand under his arm and squeezed it. "You and I were born by accident in different generations, Hack. But we're opposite sides of the same coin. Why do you keep thinking of yourself as old? You're handsome and youthful, and your principles have never changed. Why do you think people around here respect you? It's because from day to day you're always the same good man, one who never goes with fashion."

"There is no worse fate than for a young woman to marry a drunkard or an old man who is about to fall apart on the installment plan."

"Boy, do you know how to rain on a parade." She brushed her forehead back and forth on his shoulder. "What are we going to do, Hack?"

"About what?"

"Us."

"You want a root-beer float?" he asked.

"I feel like running off with my cousin. I probably would if he wasn't my cousin. I think right now I'd run off with Attila the Hun."

"You're the best, Pam."

"Best what?"

"The best of everything."

"I can't tell you how depressed that makes me feel."

The silence that followed seemed to envelop them, as though the inadequacy of the language they used in speaking to each other had come to define in an unalterable way the impossibility of their relationship. His cell phone vibrated in his pocket. It was R.C. "Maydeen told me to call you direct, Sheriff," he said. "I'm down in Coahuila in kind of a cantina."

"What are you doing in Coahuila?"

"I got a girlfriend in El Cibolo. On the way back, I blew out a tire and found out somebody had stolen my spare. I bummed a ride to this beer joint, except it's not exactly just a beer joint. There's some cribs in back, and up the street there's some reg'lar hot-pillow joints that need turnstiles on the doors. There was an *hombre malo* in here earlier, one I couldn't get a good look at, but he looked like he had a dent in his face. After these guys left, I asked this mulatto shooting pool who they were, and he said they were guys I shouldn't be asking about unless I was interested in guns that went south and cocaine that went north. He also said the guy they worked for was getting his ashes hauled up the street, a joint that specializes in girls in their early teens."

"Could the guy with the dent in his face be the one Anton Ling put a screwdriver in?"

"Maybe. He was back in the shadows, shooting pool on the edge of the light. All I could tell was that one side of his face looked caved in."

"Are there any Mexican cops around?"

"Not unless you count the two who're getting blow jobs out back."

Hackberry took a notepad and a ballpoint pen from his shirt pocket. "What's the name of this place?" he said.

R.C. was having a hard time focusing on the face of the mulatto drinking next to him at the bar, not only because of the mescal he'd knocked back a shot glass at a time and chased with Corona but because the light outside and inside the cantina was unnatural and seemed out of sync with the hour of the day and the geography of the countryside. The sun had gone down inside the clouds west of the mountains but had not died. Instead, a dull silver luminescence had pooled like smelted nickel in the clouds, accentuating the darkness of the valley and the poplar trees along the broken highway and the red-lit stucco houses along the street where the prostitutes sat in the windows, wearing flip-flops and loose dresses and no underwear because of the heat and the summerlike deadness in the air.

Though a big window fan sucked the cigarette smoke out of the cantina, the drain holes in the concrete floor smelled of stagnant water and spilled beer. R.C. could also smell the ammonia-like reek of the long stone trough in the *baño,* which had the words SOLO PARA URINAR painted over the open door. Most of the electrical lighting in the cantina came from the neon Dos Equis and Carta Blanca signs above the bar; but there was a purple stain to it, from either the gathering of the dusk in the streets or the tarnished glow inside the clouds west of the mountains, and the faces of the men drinking at the bar had the garish characteristics of cartoon figures. For R.C., the drinks the mulatto had bought him were coming at a high cost. His head was ringing, his heart was beating faster than it should, and the atmosphere around him had become as warm and damp and suffocating as a wool cloak.

Why was he having these thoughts and mental associations and seeing these images? he wondered.

The mulatto wore a smoke-stained, greasy wide-brimmed leather hat with a leather cord that flopped under his chin, and a leather vest without a shirt and striped suit pants without a belt and boots that had roweled spurs on the heels. Locks of his orange hair were flattened on his forehead; his eyebrows formed a solid line; his square teeth and the bones in his face and the thickness of his lips made R.C. think of a hard, compact gorilla. The mulatto filled his mouth with mescal and gargled with it before he swallowed, then pulled a bandanna from his back pocket and wiped his chin. "What'd you say you was doing here, man?"

"Trying to get my tire fixed," R.C. said.

"Yeah, me, too, man. That's how I ended up on a street full of *puta*. Getting my tire fixed. That's good, man. You ain't been in back yet?"

"I'm here 'cause a guy gave me a ride here."

"You want a ride, there's a *chica* out back will buck you to the ceiling." The bartender set a plate of sizzling onions and sliced green peppers and skillet grease and tortillas in front of the mulatto and went away. The mulatto rolled a tortilla full of onions and peppers and started eating. "Put something in your stomach, man. But don't drink no more mescal. You look like you been on board a ship in a bad storm. Hey, Bernicio, give my friend some coffee."

The bartender filled a cup from a tin pot that sat on a hot plate by the line of liquor bottles on the back counter. R.C. lifted the cup to his mouth, blowing on it, hardly able to swallow because it was so hot.

"What kind of work you do, man, besides drive around in Mexico and have flat tires?" the mulatto asked.

"I buy and sell livestock."

"Wild horses, huh?"

"Sometimes."

"For dog food?"

"I don't know what happens to them."

"You guys have shot most of them, *hombre.* There ain't many left. Where do you go to shoot them now? On the street of *puta?*"

"I'm just the middleman."

"You're wearing ironed blue jeans and a clean cowboy shirt with flowers printed on it. You got Tony Lamas on your feet. You got a shave and a new haircut, too. You're down here for *puta,* man. You ain't been buying no horses."

"I've got me a girlfriend here'bouts, but I don't call her what you just said."

"When you're in the sack with a woman,

288

hombre, it's for one reason, and the reason has got one name. Don't feel guilty about it. It ain't natural for a man to go against his desires."

R.C. drank again from the coffee cup, then set it down on the bar. His throat felt clotted, as though he had swallowed a handful of needles and could not blow them from his windpipe.

"Here, eat a tortilla," the mulatto said. "You ever have your throat blessed by the crossing of the candles on St. Blaise's Day? See, the priest puts the candles in an X on your throat, and for the next year you don't got to worry about choking on a bone or a piece of glass somebody put in your food. You okay, *rubio?*"

"Why you calling me that?"

" 'Cause you're *rubio* and macho, man. You're blond and strong and got cojones and can kick ass, I bet. Here, drink your coffee, then we'll go out back. It won't cost you nothing. I got a tab here. The best thing about my tab is I ain't got to pay it. You know why that is, man?"

R.C. could feel the skin on his face shrinking and growing hot, the beer signs and long bar and cuspidors streaked with tobacco juice slipping out of focus, the colors in the plastic casing on the jukebox dissolving and fusing together, the grin on the mulatto's face as red and wet as a split in a watermelon.

"I'll tell you why I ain't got to pay. I'm friends with La Familia Michoacána. You know who them guys are? They're religious crazies who cut off people's heads when they ain't transporting meth up to your country. We got your country by the balls, man. You need our dope, and you like to screw our women. But I'm gonna take care of you. Hang on to my arm. I'm gonna introduce you to a *chica* out back you gonna love. You can use my spurs on her, man."

R.C. felt himself falling to the floor, but the mulatto and a second man grabbed him and fitted each of his arms across their shoulders and carried him through the back of the bar, past a small dance floor and the stone urinal that was shielded only by a bead curtain, and into the alleyway between the cantina and the row of cribs that had canvas flaps on the doorways.

R.C. heard himself speaking as though his voice existed outside his body and he had no control over it.

"What's that you say?" the mulatto asked. "I couldn't hear. My ears are stopped up, and my mind is slow. It's 'cause of the way I grew up, working on a gringo ranch for a few pesos a day and eating beans that never had no meat in them. Getting slapped on the ear didn't help none, either. Okay, go ahead, I'm listening real good now."

R.C. heard himself speaking and then

laughing like he had never laughed in his life, his legs as weak as tendrils hanging from the bottom of his torso.

"Oh, that's good, *hombre*," the mulatto said, having listened carefully to R.C.'s words. " 'Mexico would make a great golf course if it was run by Texans.' But you're a narc, man, so guess who we gonna sell you to? You get to meet La Familia Michoacána. They don't mess around. When they catch informers or narcs pretending to be down here for *puta,* they put their heads out on the sidewalk with the blindfolds still on and sometimes a cigarette in their mouths. Believe me, man, when I tell you this. What's gonna happen to you ain't gonna be like life on no golf course."

Chapter Twelve

When Hackberry came through the front door of the cantina, he saw the bartender take note of him and Pam, then continue eating from a bowl of tripe, blowing gently on each spoonful before he placed it in his mouth. The bartender was seated on a stool, a napkin tucked inside the top of his shirt, his throat skin as coarse and wrinkled as a turkey's, his eyes like big brown buttons in a pie-plate face, his head shaved bald and a large black swastika, with red feathers for appendages, tattooed on the crown of his skull. He told Hackberry that he was sorry, but no, he had not seen anyone in the bar resembling Hackberry's young friend. His hands were big and square and looked like those of a bricklayer rather than those of a bartender. He continued eating, leaning forward over the bowl of tripe, careful not to spill any on top of his stomach.

"How long have you been on duty here?" Hackberry said.

"A few hours," the bartender replied. "But sometimes I got to serve food and drinks in the back. Maybe your friend was here but I didn't see him."

"In back?" Hackberry said.

"That's right, *señor*. We rent rooms to people who have traveled from far away. Sometimes they drink too much and want to rest before they drive home again."

"That's a very intelligent service you provide. How long does it take for you to carry a service tray to the back and return to the bar where your customers are waiting?"

"That depends, *señor*. Sometimes my customers take care of themselves. They are poor but honest, and they leave the money on the bar for whatever they drink."

"What's your name?" Hackberry asked.

"Bernicio."

"You have maybe a half-dozen customers in here. You can see everyone in the cantina from the front door to the back. My friend called me from here. He gave me the name of the cantina and directions to it. My friend is tall and looks very much like an Anglo. Don't offend me by pretending you were not aware of his presence."

"*Claro* that maybe he was here, but I didn't see him. I wish I had. Then I could be helpful. Then I could finish my supper."

Hackberry found himself trying to think through a peculiar manifestation of dishonesty that is considered normal in the third world and is totally antithetical to the average North American's point of view. The individual simply makes up his own reality and states that black is white and white is black and never flutters an eyelash. Appearance and denial always take precedence over substance and fact, and the application of logic or reason will never sway the individual from his self-manufactured convictions.

"Did you see a man with a wound in his face playing pool?" Hackberry asked.

"No, *señor.*"

"You were already shaking your head before I finished my question," Hackberry said.

"Because I have no information that can help you. The people who come here are not criminals. Look at those by the pool table. They're campesinos. Do they have the wary look of dishonest men?"

"I'm an officer of the law in the United States, Bernicio. I have friends who are officials here in Coahuila. If you have deceived us and put my friend in harm's way, you will have to answer both to them and to the United States government."

"Will you join me, you and the *señorita?* I can put onions and extra tortillas in the tripe, and we will have enough for three. I would like very much for you to be my guests and to accept my word about what I have said. I also hope you find your young friend. The

Americans who come here are not on a good errand, *señor*. I hope your friend is not one of these. I worked in Tijuana. Marines would be arrested by our police and moved from jail to jail in the interior and never seen again. Your government could do nothing for them. I served time in one of your prisons. It was a very nice place compared to the prisons here in Mexico. Fortunately, I am a Christian today, and I no longer think about these kinds of things."

Hackberry studied the swastika that was tattooed as large as a hand and clamped down on the bartender's shaved scalp. "Do you have to wear a hat when you attend church?" he asked.

Bernicio leaned forward, lifting the spoon to his mouth, his eyes focused close together, as though he were staring at a fly three inches from the bridge of his nose. *"Buena suerte, señor,"* he said.

Hackberry and Pam went back out onto the street. The dusk had settled on the countryside, and the sky was traced with shooting stars that fell and disappeared beyond the mountains in the south. Farther up the street, a band was playing in a cantina, and prostitutes were sitting on the steps of the brothels, some of them smoking cigarettes that glowed in the shadows and sparked brightly when the girls flipped them into the gutters. Across from where Hackberry and

Pam had parked their unmarked Cherokee was a squat one-story building constructed of rough stone with steel bars on the windows and a single tin-shaded yellow bulb over the entrance. Through the main window, Hackberry could see a beetle-browed man in a khaki uniform wearing a khaki cap with a lacquered black brim. The man was absorbed in the comic book he was reading, the pages folded back tightly in one hand.

"You want to check in with the locals?" Pam asked.

"Waste of time," Hackberry replied.

"It's like prayer. What's to lose?"

"It's not like prayer. The cops run the cathouses."

She was chewing gum, looking up and down the street, her hands propped on her hips. "This is what hell must look like."

"It is hell," he replied.

She glanced at him, then concentrated her attention on the police station across the street. He could hear her gum snapping in her jaw.

"I was a frequent visitor," he said. "Not to this place in particular but seven or eight like it. I was educated and had money and power and a Cadillac to drive. The prostitutes were hardly more than girls. Some of them were the sole support for their families."

"How many people were in a North Korean POW camp? How many of them spent months under a sewer grate in a dirt hole in winter?" When he didn't answer, she glanced at him again, still chewing her gum, shifting it from one side of her jaw to the other. "Let's stomp some ass, Hack. R.C. said the guy with the hole in his face worked for somebody who was visiting a cathouse?"

"Yeah, one that features teenage girls," Hackberry replied.

Krill was furious. He paced back and forth in the last silver glimmering of sunlight inside the clouds, staring at the open trunk of the gas-guzzler Negrito had parked behind the ruined adobe house where they were staying. In his right hand, he clenched a braided wallet, the shape as curved as his palm and pocket-worn the color of browned butter. "You smoked some bad weed?" he said to Negrito. "Something with angel dust or herbicide sprinkled on it? *¡Estúpido!* Ignorant man!"

"Why you say that, Krill? It hurts my feelings," Negrito said.

"You kidnapped a Texas deputy sheriff!"

"I thought he was valuable, *jefe.*"

"I'm not your *jefe.* Don't you call me that. I am not the *jefe* of *estúpidos.*"

"It's clear that he's a narc. Or maybe worse. Maybe he came down here because of us and the DEA informer we killed. We can sell the Tejano to La Familia Michoacána. They'll

297

cut his tongue out. He ain't gonna talk to nobody if he ain't got a tongue."

Krill ripped Negrito's leather hat off his head and slapped him with it, raking it down hard on his face. Negrito stared at Krill blankly, the orange bristles around his mouth and along his jaw and on his throat as stiff as wire, his lips parted, his emotions buried in a stonelike expression that seemed impervious to pain. Krill whipped the hat down on his head again and again, his teeth clenched. "Are you listening to me, *estúpido?*" he said. "Who gave you permission to act on your own? When did you become this brilliant man with a master plan for the rest of us?"

"You keep saying you're not my *jefe.* You keep saying we follow or we don't follow, that you don't care about these small matters. But when I use my perceptions to make a decision, you become enraged. I am a loyal soldier, Krill."

"You are a Judas waiting for your moment to act." Krill hit Negrito once more, and this time the leather chin cord with the tiny wooden acorn on it struck Negrito in the eye, causing it to tear.

"Why you treat me like this? You think I'm an animal and this is your barnyard and you can do whatever you want with me because I'm one of your animals?" Negrito said.

"No, an animal has brains. It has survival instincts. It doesn't always think with its penis. Who saw you leave the house of *puta* with the deputy sheriff?"

"It wasn't a house of *puta*. I don't got to go to houses of *puta*. It was a cantina. Bernicio the bartender drugged his coffee. We took the boy out the back. Bernicio is a member of La Familia and ain't gonna tell nobody about it. You worry about all the wrong things. Now you're taking out your anger on your only friend, someone who has been with you from the beginning."

The dirt yard where they stood was blown with tumbleweeds and chicken feathers and lint from a grove of cottonwood trees. A hatchet was embedded in a stump by an empty hog lot, and on the ground around the stump were at least two dozen heads of chickens, their beaks wide, their eyes filmed with dust. Someone had lit a kerosene lamp inside the ruined adobe house, and through the back window, Krill could see five of his men playing cards and drinking at a table, their silhouettes as black as carbon inside the window glass. He tried to clear his mind of anger and think about what he should do next. He gazed at the bound and gagged figure lying in an embryonic position inside the trunk of the gas-guzzler. *It is not smart to abuse Negrito anymore,* he told himself. *Negrito's stupidity is incurable and cannot be addressed effectively except by a bullet in the head. There will always be time for that, but not now. The others admire Negrito for his muscular strength and his ability to endure pain and the great reservoir of cruelty that he willingly expends on their behalf. Keep this Judas in full view and never let him get behind you,* Krill told himself, *but do not abuse or demean him anymore, particularly in front of the others.*

When Krill had finished this long thought process, he was about to speak in a less reproving way. But Negrito, being the man he was, began talking again. "See, everybody has been worried about you, man. Bringing that box out here with your children's bones in it, it's like you're putting a curse on us. The dead got to be covered up, Krill. You got to place heavy stones on their graves so their spirits don't fly around and mess up your head. The dead can do that, man. Even your kids. Baptism can't do them no good now. They're dead and they ain't coming back. That's why the earth is there, to hide the body's decay and to make clean the odors it creates. What you're doing goes against nature. It ain't just me that says it. You call me a Judas? I'm the only one who tells you the truth to your face. Those inside are not your friends. When you ain't around, they talk among themselves."

Krill squatted in the dirt and began pulling the photos and credit cards and the driver's license and Social Security card and the various forms of personal identification, includ-

300

ing a membership card in a state law enforcement fraternity, from the wallet of the Texan who lay bound in the trunk of the car, his mouth wrapped with duct tape, his forehead popping with sweat. Krill took a penlight from his shirt pocket and shone it on a photo of a girl standing in front of a church. The girl was wearing a sundress and a red hibiscus flower in her hair and was smiling at the camera. The church had three bell towers and a tile roof and looked like a church Krill had seen in Monterrey. Krill focused the penlight's beam on the driver's license and studied the photo and then shone the penlight on the Texan's face. Still squatting, he let the contents of the wallet spill to the ground and draped his hands on his thighs.

"What are you thinking, *jefe?*" Negrito asked.

Krill started to correct him for calling him *jefe* again, but what was the use? Negrito was unteachable. "Where is the Texan's money?" he asked.

"He must have spent it all."

Krill nodded and thought, *Yes, that's why it now resides in your pocket.* He stared at the Texan in the trunk and at the dust rising off the hills into the sky and at the chicken heads lying in the dirt. He could hear a sound inside his head like someone grinding a piece of iron unrelentingly against an emery wheel. He squeezed his temples and stared at Negrito.

"You know the dirt road that goes into the desert?"

"Of course."

"You have been there and can drive it in the dark, through the washouts and past the mountains where it becomes flat and no one lives?"

"I've done all these things many times, on horseback and in cars and trucks. But why are you talking about the desert? We don't need no desert. You know the place I use for certain activities. I'm telling you, this is a valuable man. Don't throw good fortune away. Make good things come out of bad."

"Do not speak for a while, Negrito. Practice discipline and be silent and listen to the wind blowing and the sounds the cottonwoods make when their limbs knock against each other. If you listen in a reverent and quiet fashion, dead people will speak to you, and you will not be so quick to dismiss them. But you must stop speaking. Do not speak unless you can improve the silence. *¿Entiendes?* Do not speak for a very long time."

"If you hear dead people talking to you, it's 'cause you're dead, too," Negrito said, his mouth gaping broadly at his own humor.

Krill gathered up the contents of the Texan's wallet and began sticking them back in the compartments and plastic windows. He closed the wallet in his palm and walked to the trunk of the car and tossed it inside.

While he did these things, he could feel the eyes of Negrito boring into his neck. He stared into the sweating face of the Texan. He could see the indentation in the tape where it covered the Texan's mouth. He thought he heard the Texan try to cry out when he slammed the trunk shut.

"This is what you need to do, Negrito," Krill said. "First, you —"

"You don't got to tell me. I'll get the shovel and take care of it. But it's a big waste of opportunity, man. And going out in the desert is a double waste of time and gas and effort. The others ain't gonna like this. We ain't been making no money, Krill. Everything we do is about your dead kids and getting even with the Americans 'cause their helicopter killed them. But how about us, man? We have needs and families, too."

Krill waited for Negrito to finish before he spoke, his face neutral, his white cotton shirt filling with air in the wind. "See, what you don't understand, my brother in arms, is that the Texan hasn't done anything to us. You fill the big wood canteen with water and put it in the car, and you put a sack of food with it. Then you drive the Tejano at least fifty kilometers into the desert and turn him loose. Later, you meet us in La Babia. With luck, all this will pass. If you hurt or sell the Texan, we will have no peace. Do you understand that now, my brother?"

303

"If that's what you say," Negrito replied.

"Good."

"And after La Babia?"

"Who knows? The Quaker belongs to us. We have to get him back. If you want to get paid, that's how we will all get paid. Then you can entertain all the *chicas* in Durango and Piedras Negras and Chihuahua. You will be famous among them for your generosity."

"You'll sell the Quaker to the Arabs but not the Texan to our own people?"

"The man Barnum has made machines that kill from the air, no matter what kind of conversion he claims to have gone through. All the gringos are makers of war and the killers of our people. Let them lie together in their own waste and eat it, too."

"I ain't never gonna understand you."

Krill watched Negrito enter the back of the farmhouse, the rowels on his spurs tinkling, the pad of orange hair on his arms and shoulders glowing against the light that fell from the kitchen. Unconsciously, Krill rested his palm against the car trunk and felt the exhaust heat in the metal soak into his skin and leave his hand feeling scorched and dirty.

The brothel where two SUVs with Texas plates were parked did not look like a brothel. Or at least it did not resemble the adobe houses or clusters of cribs on the far end of town where the street bled into the darkness of the desert and drunks sometimes wandered away from their copulations to bust beer bottles with their firearms out on the hardpan. The brothel frequented by the Texans was located at the end of a gravel lane and was actually an enclave of buildings that had once made up a ranch. The main house was built of stone quarried out of the mountains and had a wide terrazzo porch with large glazed ceramic urns that were planted with Spanish daggers and flowers that opened only at night. The colonnade over the porch was supported by cedar posts and covered with Spanish tile and tilted downward to direct rainwater during the monsoon season away from the house.

There was no lighting outside the building, which helped preserve the anonymity of the patrons. The night air smelled of flowers and warm sand and water that had pooled and gone stagnant and was auraed by clouds of gnats. Pam Tibbs pulled the Cherokee to a stop and cut the ignition. "How do you want to play it?" she said.

"We wear our badges and carry our weapons in full view," Hackberry replied.

"I've seen that purple SUV before."

"Where?"

"When I broke both of its taillights in front of the café."

"*That's* Temple Dowling's vehicle?" he said.

"It was when I broke his taillights. You're

surprised Dowling would be here?"

"Nothing about Dowling surprises me. But I thought the man with the hole in his face might have been working for the Russian, this guy Sholokoff."

"Let's find out."

"You feel comfortable going in there?" he asked.

She rested her hands on top of the steering wheel. Even in the starlight, he could see the shine on her upper arms and the sunburned tips of her hair. He could also see the pity in her eyes. "It's not me who's uncomfortable," she said. "When are you going to accept your own goodness and the fact that you've paid for what you might have done wrong when you were young?"

"When the mermaids come back to Texas," he said.

"Pardon?"

"It was a private joke between my father and me. Ready to make life interesting for the shitbags?"

"Always," she replied.

They got out on either side of the Cherokee and went inside the brothel. The living room was furnished with a red velvet settee and deep leather chairs and a cloth sofa and a coffee table set with wineglasses and dark bottles of burgundy and a bottle of Scotch and a bucket of ice. There was also a bowl of guacamole and a bowl of tortilla chips on the table. The only light came from two floor lamps with shades that were hung with pink tassels. Two mustached men Hackberry had seen before sat on the sofa, dipping chips into the guacamole and drinking Scotch on the rocks. A Mexican girl not over fifteen, in a spangled blue dress, was sitting on the settee. She wore white moccasins on her feet and purple glass beads around her neck. Her skin was dusky, her nose beaked, her Indian eyes as elongated as an Asian's. Her lipstick and rouge could not disguise the melancholy in her face.

"How are you gentlemen tonight?" Hackberry said.

"Pretty good, Sheriff. I didn't think you'd remember us," one of them said.

"You came to my office with Mr. Dowling," Hackberry said.

"Yes, sir, that's us. What might you be doing here?" the man said.

"Not a lot. Just driving around the countryside trying to find a deputy of mine who got himself kidnapped. Do you boys know anything about a kidnapped deputy sheriff by the name of R. C. Bevins?"

The two men looked at each other, then back at Hackberry. "No, sir," the first man said.

Hackberry could hear the clatter of pool balls in a side room. "Is that more of your crowd in there?"

"Yes, sir, they're with us. We'd help you if we could, Sheriff, but I think you've come to the wrong place."

"This is the wrong place, all right, but for reasons you evidently haven't thought about," Hackberry said.

"Sir?"

"How old do you reckon that girl is?"

"We don't make the rules down here. Nobody does," the second man said.

Both men were wearing skintight jeans and snap-button shirts and belts with big silver-and-gold-plated buckles, and they both had the styled haircuts and carefully maintained unshaved look of male models in a liquor ad or on a calendar aimed at homosexuals rather than at women. The second man had a deeper and more regional voice than the first, and a formless blue tattoo, like a smear, inside the whiskers that grew on his throat.

"Were any of y'all in a cantina earlier?" Hackberry said.

"Not us," the second man said.

"We're looking for a guy with a hole in his face. You know anybody like that?"

"No, sir," the first man said.

"I see," Hackberry said. "Is Mr. Dowling in back?"

Neither of the men spoke. The second man glanced at Pam Tibbs, then filled a taco chip with guacamole and stuck it in his mouth and chewed it while he took her inventory.

"What's in back?" Hackberry said.

"The whole menu," the first man said.

"You two guys go outside," Hackberry said.

"You've got no jurisdiction down here, Sheriff," the second man said.

"Who cares? I'm bigger than you are. You guys want trouble? I'll give it to you in spades."

The two men looked at each other again, then got up from the settee. "We'll honor your request, Sheriff Holland. We do that out of respect for you and our employer," the first man said.

"No, you'll do it because if I catch one of y'all putting your hands on this little girl, I'm going to kick your sorry asses all the way to Mexico City. And if I find out you're involved with the kidnapping of my deputy, I'm going to blow your fucking heads off."

Hackberry did not wait for their reaction. He walked into the side room, where two men were shooting pool inside a cone of light created by a tin-shaded bulb that hung from the ceiling. The pool table was covered with red velvet, the pockets hung with netted black leather, the mahogany trim polished to a soft glow. "You!" he said, pointing at the man about to break the rack. "Yeah, you! Put your cue down and look at me."

"*¿Hay algún problema?*"

"Yeah, you. Remember me?"

"Yes, sir, you're the sheriff."

"You were shooting pool at a cantina to-night."

"Maybe I was. Maybe not. So what?" There was a deep indentation below the pool shooter's left eye, as though a piece of the cheekbone had been removed and the skin under the eye had collapsed and formed a hole a person could insert his thumb in. But the injury was an old one. It was the same wound that Hackberry had seen in the face of one of Temple Dowling's employees when they came to his office.

"There's no maybe in this," Hackberry said. "You were in the Cantina del Cazador. You were shooting pool there. My deputy saw you in there and described you to me. In very few words, you need to tell me what happened to my deputy."

The pool shooter's shirt was open on his chest, exposing his chest hair and nipples and a gold chain he wore around his neck. "*¿Quién sabe, hombre?*"

"You *sabes,* bud. Or you'd better."

"I was in the cantina. I didn't see anybody who looked like a deputy sheriff. What else can I say?"

"Why'd your friends out front say you weren't there?"

"Maybe I didn't tell them."

"I can see you're a man who likes to keep it simple. So how about this?" Hackberry said. He pulled his white-handled blue-black .45

revolver from his holster and swung it back-handed across the pool shooter's mouth. The blow made a clacking sound when the heavy cylinder and frame and the barrel broke the man's lips against his teeth. The pool shooter dropped his cue and cupped both of his hands to his mouth, his face trembling with shock behind his fingers. He removed his hands and looked at the blood on them, then spat a tooth into his palm.

"*Chingado,* what the fuck, man!" he said.

"You *sabes* now?"

"What's going on here?" said a voice behind Hackberry.

Temple Dowling had come out of a bedroom down the hall. He wore slippers and a towel robe cinched around his waist. Lipstick was smeared on his robe, and his exposed chest looked pink and blubbery and his breasts effeminate. Two young girls were leaning out of the doorway behind him, trying to see what was happening at the front of the house. Hackberry could see a large man in a long-sleeve white cotton shirt and bradded jeans coming out of an office in back, a wood baton gripped in one hand.

Hackberry put his revolver in the holster and raised his left hand, palm out, at the man with the baton. "My business is with Mr. Dowling and his associates. Mix in it and you'll take their weight," he said.

"*¿Qué dice?*" the man with the baton asked

311

one of the girls who had stepped out of the bedroom.

"No sé," she replied.

"Está bien. It's all right, Hector," Dowling said to the Mexican with the baton.

"One of my deputies was kidnapped out of a cantina where your hired piece of shit with the bloody mouth was shooting pool," Hackberry said. "He denies seeing my deputy, even though my deputy described your man to me over his cell phone."

"Why would one of my employees have any interest in your deputy, Sheriff Holland?" Dowling said. "Are you down here about Jack Collins?"

"No."

"You're not?" Dowling said, looking confused.

"Why would I be looking for Collins on a street full of Mexican cathouses?"

"He's everywhere," Dowling replied.

"You've become a believer?"

"I haven't done anything to this man. I didn't say anything about him."

The register in Dowling's voice had changed, the vowels and consonants not quite holding together. The skin twitched under one eye as though a fly had settled on his skin. Hackberry wondered how many young girls had paid the price for the fear that Dowling had probably spent a lifetime trying to hide from others.

"Have you had an encounter with Collins?" Hackberry asked.

"I thought you knew."

"Knew what?"

"I put a reward on him. He killed two of my men. That's why I put the reward on him."

"You put a reward on Jack Collins?"

"For arrest and conviction. That's all the statement says. I didn't tell people to go out and kill him. It's what any employer or family member would do if their employees or family members were murdered."

"Have you seen him?"

"Last night there was a man outside my motel. My men tried to catch him, but he disappeared. He was wearing a dirty hat of some kind. He was in the shadows on the other side of the parking lot, under a sodium lamp. What do you call that kind of hat? A panama? It's made of straw and has a brim that dips down over the eyes."

Dowling seemed to wait, hoping that Hackberry would dispel his fears and tell him that the shadowy figure, for whatever reason, could not have been Collins.

"That sounds like Jack, all right," Hackberry said. "Congratulations, you've brought down perhaps the most dangerous man in America on your head. Jack's a real cutup. I've been trying to punch his ticket for over a year. Maybe you'll be more successful. You guys have any armored vests in your vehicles?"

"You're enjoying this."

"I guess it beats hanging in an upscale cathouse that provides services for pedophiles."

"Don't you dare talk to me like that."

"I was a whoremonger, Mr. Dowling. When I see a man like you, I want to shoot myself. I don't know if some of the girls I slept with were under the legal age or not. Most of the times I went across the river, I was too drunk to know what universe I was in."

Dowling was not listening. "Did you see anyone down here who looked like him?"

"Like Jack?"

"Who do you think I'm talking about, you idiot?" Dowling said.

"He paid a visit to my ranch just yesterday. He put a laser sight on me, but he didn't pull the trigger. That tells me he has something else planned for me. In your case, I doubt you'll see that red dot crawl across your skin. You'll see his Thompson for a few seconds, then you won't see anything at all."

A hulking Mexican woman appeared out of the back office and placed a highball in Temple Dowling's hand. Dowling looked at the drink as though he couldn't understand how it had gotten there. The two girls he had been in bed with were whispering under their breath, one translating to the other the conversation of the gringos, both of them trying not to giggle. *"Señor, este es muy malo para los negocios,"* the Mexican woman said.

Her words of concern about her business realities had no effect on Temple Dowling. Instead, his eyes remained fixed on Hackberry's, a lump of fear sliding down his throat so audibly that his lips parted and his mouth involuntarily made a clicking sound.

"I don't have any authority down here, Mr. Dowling," Hackberry said. "But when I get back to Texas, I'll make sure the appropriate agencies hear about your sexual inclinations."

"You're a bastard, Holland."

"You don't know the half of it," Hackberry replied.

CHAPTER THIRTEEN

Enclosure of any kind had always been R. C. Bevins's worst fear, the kind that is so great you never willingly confront it or discuss it with anyone else. Inside the darkness of the car trunk, while the gas-guzzler continued down a dirt or rock road of some kind, he tried to work his way forward and push his knees against the hatch and spring the lock. His wrists were taped together behind him, and the tape was wound around his ankles, forcing him to lie on his side, so he could not find purchase against a hard surface. There was a hole in the muffler, the engine's deep-throated sound rising into the trunk, the smell of the exhaust mixing with the dirty odor of the spare tire that R.C. could feel against the back of his head. He was finally able to touch the hatch with the points of his boots, but he was not able to exert any viable degree of pressure. The man named Negrito had done his job well. He had probably done it well many times before, R.C. thought.

He felt the car dip off the edge of the road and bounce heavily down an incline until it was on a flat surface again. Then he heard scrub brush raking thickly under the car frame, small rocks pinging under the fenders. R.C. strained against the duct tape, trying to stretch it to the point where he could slip one wrist free or work it over a boot heel so he could extend his legs and tear the tape off his wrists, even if he had to strip the skin from his thumbs.

Negrito was playing the radio, listening to a Mexican station that blared with horns and mariachi guitars. The car veered sharply, thudding off what was probably an embankment into a dry riverbed, jolting R.C. into the air, knocking his head against the spare tire. The gas-guzzler rumbled over rocks and tangles of brush while tree branches scraped against the fenders and doors and oil smoke from the broken muffler leaked through the trunk floor. The car swerved again, fishtailing this time, and came to a stop that caused the car body to rock on the springs.

Negrito waited until the song had ended, then turned off the radio and cut the engine. The night was completely silent except for the ticking of the heat in the car's metal. The driver's door opened with a screech like fingernails on a blackboard, and R.C. heard the tinkling of Negrito's roweled spurs approaching the trunk.

317

When Negrito popped the hatch, the sweet, cool, nocturnal smell of the desert flooded the inside of the trunk. But R.C.'s sense of relief was short-lived. Negrito's outline was silhouetted against the stars, a .45 auto strapped on his hip. "You okay, Tejano boy?" he asked. "I was worried about the way you was bouncing around in there. Here, I'm gonna get you out and explain our situation."

Negrito grabbed R.C. by one arm and the back of his belt and slid him over the bumper, letting him drop to the ground. "See, my friend Krill has got his head up his ass about a lot of things and don't know what's good for himself and others lots of the time. So I got to make decisions for him."

For no apparent reason, Negrito stopped talking and looked over his shoulder. From where he lay on the ground, R.C. could see that the car had ended up in a sandy wash, like a cul-de-sac, at the bottom of a giant hill that looked compacted of waste from a foundry. Negrito was staring into the darkness, turning his head from one side to the other. He picked up a rock and flung it up the incline and listened to it clatter back through the thinly spaced mesquite. "Maybe we got a cougar up there," he said to R.C. "But more likely a coyote. They come around, I'm gonna shoot them. They eat carrion and carry diseases. Like some of my girlfriends in Durango. What you think of that?"

Between Negrito's booted feet, R.C. saw an image that made his heart sink. On a level spot at the edge of the wash were at least five depressions, each of them roughly six feet long and three feet wide, the top of the depressions composed of a mixture of soil and dirt and sand and charcoal from old wildfires, all of it obviously spaded up and shaped and packed down by the blade of a shovel.

"See, I got to leave you here for a while and make some contacts," Negrito said. "You're gonna be safe till I get back. I like you, Tejano boy, but I got to make money and take care of my family. There's only one question I got to ask you. When I was a little boy working on this *turista* ranch in Jalisco, there was a gringo there who looked just like you. After he shot pigeons all day, he made me pick them up and clean them for his supper. While I did that, he screwed my sister. You think maybe that was your father?"

For a second, R.C. thought Negrito was going to pull the tape from his mouth so he could answer. Instead, Negrito's head jerked around and he stared again into the darkness, his nostrils flaring as though he had caught a scent on the wind, the thumb of his right hand hooking over the butt of his holstered .45. He walked up to the flat place and stood among the row of depressions, looking from one side of the hill to the other.

"*¿Quién está ahí?* Somebody out there want to talk to me?" he said to the wind.

He waited in the silence, then returned to the rear of the car, glancing once behind him. He squatted down and ripped the tape from R.C.'s mouth. "I'm gonna ask you this question once, no second chances," he said. "Be honest with me, I'm gonna be honest with you. You had somebody with you tonight? Or maybe you had somebody following you? 'Cause that's the feeling I been having all night."

R.C. tried to think. What was the right answer? "No," he said.

"That's the problem you gringos got. You're always trying to figure out what kind of lie is gonna work, like right now you're wondering how stupid is this Mexican man you got to deal with. I'm gonna be honest with you even if you ain't been honest with me. You're gonna have a bad night, man. You can cry, you can beg, you can pray, but only one thing is gonna happen to you, and there ain't no way to change that. Don't try to fight it. Tonight is gonna be a son of a bitch. Tomorrow, who knows? Maybe you're gonna catch a break."

"I'm not a narc," R.C. said.

"Maybe, maybe not. But the people I sell you to are gonna find out." Negrito stood up and opened one of the back doors of the car and returned with a shovel and a gas mask that had an extra-long breathing hose. "See this?" he said. "It's your chance to live. You just got to have a lot of self-control and not let your thoughts take over your body."

"Don't do this to me."

"It's out of my hands, Tejano boy. I was just having a drink in the cantina. You came into the wrong place and put your nose in the wrong people's business. Now you got to pay the price."

"The other guy said to turn me loose."

"You talking about Krill? He ain't never gonna know what happened to you. Krill thinks he's smart, but most of the time, his thoughts are in the next world, where he thinks his dead kids are." Negrito brushed a piece of dirt off R.C.'s cheek with his thumb and smiled. "You're a gringo cop who has a flat tire and ends up drinking in a whore-house that has a bartender who works for La Familia? I hope in the morning you get a chance to tell these other guys that story. It's a very good one, man. You got to tell them the joke about the golf course, too. They're gonna really laugh."

After Hackberry and Pam Tibbs left the bordello and got in the Cherokee, Pam remained silent for a long time. Then she started the engine and looked at him. "Where to?" she asked.

"Back to the cantina. That bartender was

lying," he said.

"I was a little worried in there."

"About what?"

"When you cracked that guy in the mouth."

"He'll get over it."

"I've never seen you like that."

"I don't like child molesters."

"You told those two guys in the living room you'd blow their heads off. I could hear you breathing when you said it."

"That's because I meant it."

"That's what bothers me."

"Let's get on it, Pam," he said.

On the way back to the cantina, Hackberry lowered the brim of his Stetson and shut his eyes, wanting to sleep for an eternity and forget the violence and cruelty and sordid behavior and human exploitation that seemed to become more and more visible in the world as he aged. According to the makers of myth and those who trafficked in cheap lies about human wisdom, the elderly saw goodness in the world that they had not been allowed to see in their youth. But Hackberry had found that the world was the world and it did not change because one happened to age. The same players were always there, regardless of the historical era, he thought, and the ones we heeded most were those who despoiled the earth and led us into wars and provided us with justification whenever we felt compelled to commit unconscionable acts against our fellow man. Maybe this wasn't a good way to think, he told himself, but when you heard the clock ticking in your life, there was no worse disservice you could do to yourself than to entertain a lie. Death was bad only when you had to face it knowing that you had failed to live during the time allotted you, or that you had lied to yourself about the realities of the world or willingly listened to the lies of others.

He felt his body rock forward when Pam touched the brake in front of the cantina.

"Take it easy in there, okay?" she said.

"I wonder what kind of night R.C. is having," Hackberry replied.

"You can really drive the nails."

"If we mess up here, R.C. dies. Inside that stone building on the corner are men in uniform who would gladly work in an Iranian torture chamber for minimum wage. The meth being funneled through this town probably originates with a bunch down in the state of Michoacán. These are guys who make the cops in the stone building look like the College of Cardinals."

She turned off the ignition and stared straight ahead, her hands resting on the wheel. "I wasn't criticizing you back there. I just worry about you sometimes. You don't handle regret very well."

"The person who does is dead from the neck up."

"One of these days I'll learn to keep my counsel."

"Watch my back. I don't want those *rurales* coming through the front door and planting one in my ear."

"R.C. is a tough kid. Give him some credit," she said.

"What's that mean?"

"Put it in neutral, Hack."

"Cover my back and lose the bromides."

"You got it."

Hackberry had already gotten out of the Jeep and crossed the sidewalk and entered the cantina before Pam had reached the curb. The bartender with the enormous swastika was stacking chairs on a table by the small dance floor in back. He grinned when he saw Hackberry. "Hey, amigo, you decided to come back and have dinner with me! Welcome once again. You brought the lady, too."

"Who wouldn't love a place like this? Excuse me just a second," Hackberry said.

"What are you doin', *señor?*"

"Not much. When I played baseball, I was a switch-hitter. I sometimes wonder if I still have it," Hackberry said. He pulled a pool cue off the wall rack and grasped the thinly tapered end with both hands and whipped the heavy end across the bartender's face. The cue splintered with the same hand-stinging *crack* as a baseball bat when it catches a ninety-mile-an-hour pitch at the wrong angle. The weighted end of the cue rocketed into the wall, and the bartender crashed over the table into the plastic-cased jukebox, blood pouring from his nose.

The bartender placed the flats of his hands on the floor and tried to straighten himself against the jukebox. Hackberry raised his right boot fifteen inches into the air and stomped it down into the bartender's face. The man's head pocked a hole the size of a grapefruit in the jukebox. "Where's my deputy?" Hackberry said.

"I don't know," the bartender said.

"You want another one?" Hackberry said.

Three men at a table by the dance floor got up quickly and went out the back door. A fourth man emerged from the bathroom and looked at the scene taking place by the jukebox and followed them outside. Hackberry could hear a whirring sound in his head and behind him the sound of Pam Tibbs chewing gum rapidly, snapping it, her mouth open. "Hack, dial it down," she said.

"No, Bernicio here wants to tell us where R.C. is. He just wants the appropriate motivation. Right, Bernicio? You have to explain to your friends why you cooperated with your gringo dinner guests." He brought his boot down again.

"Oh, shit," Pam said, her voice changing.

Hackberry turned and saw two Mexican policemen in unpressed green uniforms come through the front door and walk the length of the bar. Both of them wore lacquered-billed caps and were short and dark-skinned. Both wore brass badges and shiny black name tags on their shirt pockets and semiautomatic pistols on their hips. One of them wore thick-soled military boots that were spit-shined into mirrors, the laces starched white. He had tucked the cuffs of his trousers into the boots, as a paratrooper might.

"*¿Qué pasa,* gringo?" asked the policeman with the shined boots.

Hackberry opened his badge holder and held it up for both policemen to see. "My deputy was kidnapped from this cantina. We were having a discussion with Bernicio as to my friend's whereabouts. Thank you for your assistance."

"*Chinga tu madre. Tus credenciales valen mierda, hombre,*" the policeman in shined boots said.

"My badge is worth shit? I should fuck my mother?" Hackberry said. "I'm not sure how I should interpret that."

"*Venga,*" the policeman said, crooking two fingers.

"With respect, we're not going anywhere with y'all except maybe to find my friend," Hackberry said. He repeated himself in Spanish and then said in English and Spanish, "Right now we're wasting time that we don't have. My friend's life is in jeopardy. The man on the floor is a criminal. You know that and so do I. We are all officers of the law, separated only by a few miles of geography. I ask your cooperation, and I say all these things to you out of respect for your office and the importance of your legal position in the community."

"We are not interested in your evaluations of our community. You're coming with me, gringo," the policeman replied, this time in English, once again crooking two fingers. "You have no authority here, and you have assaulted an innocent man."

"How's this for authority, dickhead?" Pam Tibbs said, pulling her .357 Magnum from her holster and aiming it with both hands at the policeman's face.

"You are very unwise," the policeman said.

"That's right," Pam replied. She cocked the hammer on her revolver with her thumb. "I have little judgment. That's why I'm two seconds from flushing your grits."

"Flushing? What do you mean, 'flushing'?"

"Don't test her, partner," Hackberry said, surprised at the level of caution in his voice.

"No entiendo," the policeman said.

Hackberry could feel a band of tension spreading along one side of his head. It was of a kind that he had experienced only a few times in his life. It stretched the blood veins along the scalp into knotted twine. You felt it seconds after hearing the spatter of small-arms fire, a sound that was as thin and sporadic and innocuous as the popping of Chinese firecrackers. Or you felt it when someone shouted out the word "Incoming!" Or when it wrapped itself around your head like piano wire as a monstrosity of a human being in a quilted coat slathered with mud on the front and mucus on the sleeves pulled back the bolt on a Soviet-manufactured burp gun and lifted the muzzle into your face.

Hackberry could smell the stagnant water and expectorated tobacco juice under the drain covers in the concrete floor, and the stale cigarette smoke in the air and the residual odor of dried sweat that seemed layered on every surface of the cantina. From the cribs in back, he could smell a stench that was like fish roe in the sun and human waste leaching from an open ditch. He could hear a drunk singing in one of the cribs in the alleyway. He could hear his own heartbeat starting to crescendo in his ears.

"She'll kill you, buddy. Don't lose your life over a man who wears the tattoo of a self-important fool on top of his head," Hackberry said.

What followed was a phenomenon that Hackberry had seen perhaps no more than a dozen times in war and during his career as a lawman. Perhaps it could be called a vision of mortality. Or a moment when a person simply calculated his risk and evaluated what was to be lost or gained and then made his bet with full knowledge that his foot rested on the edge of the great precipice. Sometimes the heart-stopping pause that took place before the die was cast, when the filmstrip seemed to freeze inside the projector, dissolved into what Hackberry called "the blink." The blink was not in the eyes but deep down in the soul, and the effect was immediate and as real as the brief twitch, like a rubber band snapping, that shuddered through the person's face.

"I see nothing either exceptional or of value here," the policeman with shined boots said. "This is not worthy of official attention. Serious men do not waste their time on situations such as this. Good evening to you, *señor* and *señorita.*"

With that, he and his companion walked out of the cantina and into the street.

Hackberry heard Pam release her breath and ease down the hammer on her revolver and return it to its holster. "I don't want to ever relive that moment or even discuss it," she said.

"Neither does Bernicio," Hackberry said, looking down at the bartender. "Right?"

"Fuck you, man," the bartender said.

Hackberry knelt on one knee, the splintered felt-tipped end of the pool cue still in his hand. He glanced at the front door to ensure that the policemen had not returned. He knew at some point they would try to back-shoot him and Pam in the street or call their friends to devise a means to get even for having their faces put in it by a woman. You didn't shame a Mexican cop without running up a tab.

"You know where my deputy has been taken," Hackberry said. "Not approximately but *exactly*. If you claim to not have this information, I will not believe you. The continuation of your life depends entirely upon your ability to convince me that you know where my friend is. Do you understand the implications of what I have told you?"

"No, I do not understand these things. Your words are mysterious and confusing. Why are you doing this to me?" the bartender said, blood glistening on his upper lip.

"Because you're an evil man."

"No, *hombre,* I am not evil. I'm a worker. I am part of the revolution."

Hackberry placed his knee against the bartender's chest and leaned forward and forced the shattered end of the pool cue over his teeth and into his mouth. "In five seconds I'm going to push this down your windpipe and out the side of your neck. Look into my face and tell me I won't do it."

He could feel Pam Tibbs's hand clasp the top of his shoulder and squeeze. "Hack," she said softly.

He paid no attention.

■ ■ ■ ■

R.C. massaged his wrists, then picked up the
shovel by his foot, as the man named Negrito
had told him to do. The sky was black and
hazed with dust, and the shooting stars above
the hills looked like chips of dry ice that were
melting into nothingness. R.C thought he
heard a train whistle in the distance and the
sound of boxcars with their brakes on sliding
down an incline, the wheels shrieking against
the rails.

"What are you waiting for, Tejano boy?
Start digging," Negrito said.

R.C.'s hands were propped on the shaft of
the shovel, the worn, rounded, silvery tip an
inch into the dirt. Strips of severed duct tape
hung from his boots. He could feel his heart
beating against his ribs and a line of sweat
starting to run from each of his armpits. Negrito was squatted on a rise fifteen feet away,
his 1911-model United States Army .45
gripped casually on one knee, his fingers
loose around the trigger guard, completely
confident about the situation he had created.
His leather hat hung on the back of his neck,
the chin cord taut against his throat. He
picked up a dirt clod and threw it at R.C.'s
head.

"I've been kind to you," he said. "Don't
abuse my charity. I'm not a nice man when

331

I'm provoked."

"I cain't do it," R.C. said.

"Sí, puedes."

"I ain't. That's what I meant to say." Even to himself, R.C.'s voice seemed full of broken glass, his words thick, the worst fate he could imagine about to be realized only a few inches from where he stood.

"Meant to say what, Tejano boy?"

"I meant to say I ain't gonna dig my own grave," R.C. replied. "And I ain't no boy."

"It don't matter what I call you, man. You're gonna dig."

"No matter how it plays out, I ain't gonna he'p you. No, sir, I won't do it."

"That's what they all say. They buy a little time that way, and it makes them feel less bad about themselves. They want to believe their friends are gonna come over the rise and kill Negrito and take them home to their mothers and fathers and wives and husbands, but finally, they dig. You don't got to feel bad about it."

R.C. raised one foot and rested it on the top of the shovel blade, still gripping the shaft with both hands, his eyes stinging with sweat, a vinegary stench rising from his armpits. His heart felt as though it had been invaded by threadworms and was slowly being reduced to the point where it could no longer pump his blood.

"I make twenty-six thousand dollars a year.

I break up domestic fights and run in drunks and wets and nickel-and-dime meth mules."

"So?"

"Your friends won't pay money for me."

"You want me to shoot you, man?" Negrito raised the .45 and pointed it at R.C. and playfully sighted down the barrel. "Ever see one of these hit a kneecap? Or a guy's foot? I use hollow-points."

R.C. swallowed. Each time the gun's muzzle swung across his person, his colon constricted and his entrails turned to water.

"I'm gonna shoot you in a place that hurts like a son of a bitch, man," Negrito said. "Then you're going in the ground with all that pain while you try to breathe through the gas mask. Why you want to do that to yourself?"

R.C.'s head was spinning, bile rising from his stomach, his fear so great and his anger at himself and his despair so intense that he could feel himself walking through a door into a place where nothing mattered anymore. "I just remembered what you look like. I couldn't think of it. But it's real clear in my head now," he said, breathing hard through his mouth.

"Why you always got to talk, man? You are like a woman, always talking, filling the air with sounds that grate on the ear."

"I couldn't remember what you remind me of. At the cantina I was thinking about it, but

I couldn't get it straight in my head because I drank too much."

"What I remind you of?"

"An orange Brillo pad. Those steel-wool pads women use to clean grease and fish skins and fried crud out of skillets. After a while, the pads turn orange and blue with soap and rust and all the glop that's glommed up inside them."

"That's what I look like?"

"Yes, sir, I'd call it a match."

"Be quiet," Negrito said, rising to his feet.

"Like my mother says, looks is only skin deep."

"*Silencio,* foolish boy who does not hear or listen."

R.C. realized his tormentor was not interested in deflecting insults and that he had heard something out in the darkness. Negrito walked up the incline, away from the dry wash and the row of graves and the greasewood and the stunted willows along the bank and the tortoise-shaped sandstone boulders that were weathered through with holes the length of a man's arm. "Is that you out there, Mr. Crazy Man?" he said. "You want to fight Negrito? Come down and fight. I don't fear you."

R.C. watched, stupefied.

"The gringos fear you! But I don't! *¡Me cago en la puta de tu madre!* I take a shit in your mother's womb. How you like that?"

Negrito said.

"Who you talking to?"

Negrito said nothing in answer to R.C. He was standing on a slab of stone that was tilted upward on the slope, one pointy cowboy boot stationed in front of the other, his shoulders humped, his .45 hanging from his right hand. In profile, his right eye seemed to watch both the hillside and R.C. simultaneously, the way a shark's eye views everything in its ken, both enemy and prey, revealing no more emotionality than a flat coat button.

"Hey, *sacerdote* of the garbage dump and eater of your own feces! You think we treated your little Quaker friend bad?" he called out. "What if I bring you down here and make you suck my dick? I can do that to you, man, with great pleasure."

There was no reply from the hillside, and R.C. could see no movement among the shadows and mesquite and rocks and the dead juniper trees that looked like gnarled and polished bone. Negrito continued to stare into the darkness, his nostrils swelling, his profile as snubbed as a piranha's. He squeezed his scrotum with his left hand. "Come take it, *cabrón!*" he yelled.

The moon broke from behind a cloud and turned the hillside gray, the scrub brush pooling with shadows. "No? You prefer shooting women and people who ain't got no guns? You're a sorry Christian, Mr. Preacher. A

Christian without cojones."

"You know Preacher Collins?" R.C. said.

"The crazy man up there ain't gonna help you. So give that up," Negrito replied, backing down the slope, his gaze still concentrated on the hillside. "He's the hunter, the left hand of God. He don't have interest in a boy like you."

"But he's interested in you?" R.C. said.

"Of course. He knows we're brothers. Under our skin, we're no different."

"Brothers?"

"That's right, Tejano boy. Preacher and I are both dead. Our souls died many years ago. What do you see in my eyes?"

"Nothing."

"That's right. Nothing. And that's why you're gonna start to dig. Or maybe I'm gonna start shooting you in various places that will hurt more than you can believe."

"I done told you, I ain't gonna do it. So you'd better kill me, 'cause somewhere down the road, I'm gonna catch up with you. You damn betcha I will."

Negrito's eyes were rheumy, his face dull with fatigue, his mouth caked. He made a snuffing sound and rubbed his nose with the back of his wrist. "Release the shovel and get in the trunk of the car."

"What are you gonna do?"

"I got to dig your hole. That makes me very mad. You are lucky I am a merciful man."

R.C. let the shovel fall to the ground and started toward the gas-guzzler, glancing warily over his shoulder, then tripping and stumbling. He heard Negrito pick up the shovel.

"Look up there," Negrito said.

"At what?"

"The preacher up there in the rocks. See, against the moon. He wants to be your friend. The *sacerdote* who eats his own *mierda* has come to your rescue. Or maybe it's the sheriff you work for. Maybe this is your lucky day."

R.C. stared at the clumps of brush in the arroyos and at the layers of rock exposed by erosion in the hillside and at the tailings of a mine that spilled like rust down to the wash. He saw a shadow move across the moon. "That's a coyote," he said.

He turned around just as Negrito whipped the shovel with both hands through the air and almost flattened the concave steel blade on the back of R.C.'s head.

"I think you was right. It was just a coyote," Negrito said, staring up the hill.

Jack Collins lay below the crest of the hill, his belly and loins and legs stretched out on a flat rock that had ripples in it like water, his hat beside him, his eyes raised just above a pile of crumbling stone. Behind him, the two Mexican informers, cousins who did murders for hire, were talking quietly to each other, sometimes glancing up in his direction. They were restless men and did not like either indecision or complexity and often found themselves caught between their own self-protective instincts and their hesitancy to challenge the strange ways of the gringo *loco* whose lethality was a legend in Coahuila and Chihuahua. Finally, the one named Eladio approached the unshaved and unwashed American who dressed in rags and wore a heavy revolver on his hip, squatting down so as not to silhouette against the sky. "Señor Jack?" he said.

"Be patient," Jack said, peering down the opposite slope.

"Why don't we just go down there in the streambed and kill Negrito? I'll do it without no charge."

Jack looked back over his shoulder and grinned. "You boys were supposed to give me the man named Krill. We didn't come out here to hunt an orange ape."

"I thought Krill would be at the farmhouse. He's a very hard man to catch, boss. This is the place Negrito sometimes uses to bury his victims. It is fortunate that I knew that."

"So we're saved from your incompetence by the intervention of the fates, and that should make me feel good?"

"You talk too fast for me to understand sometimes, boss."

Jack worked his way backward on the rock

338

until he was well under the level of the hill-crest, then got to his feet. He dusted off his knees and the elbows of his suit coat and fitted on his hat, glancing at the strips of black cloud across the moon. He gestured for the other cousin to join him and Eladio. But minutes seemed to pass before he spoke. In the silence, he glanced at one man, then the other, and then into space, as though viewing two different screens in his head. "I pay you boys enough?" he asked.

"*Sí,*" both of them said, nodding.

"Krill has done great injury to a friend of mine. The one down the slope, the ape, isn't even a cipher."

"What is this 'cipher'? These kinds of words don't mean nozzing to us, boss," Eladio said.

"The fact you boys were raised up poor and ignorant isn't your fault. Most of y'all's mothers would have had you aborted if they'd had the money. But today there's no excuse for ignorance in an adult. People in mud huts watch CNN. The Internet is available in a street-corner café. You boys have access to the same knowledge a university professor does. I suggest y'all start showing a little more initiative regarding your self-improvement."

"We seek to please you, not to upset you, Señor Jack," Eladio said.

"You did very well following Temple Dowling for me. You did well learning of the machinations of Negrito with the young lawman. But you haven't given me Krill. Krill is the objective, not his monkey. Are y'all listening?"

"We ain't perfect, boss," the cousin said. His name was Jaime, and of the two Mexican killers, he was the less intelligent and the more recalcitrant.

Eladio looked angrily at his cousin, then turned his attention back to Jack, trying to undo any damage his cousin might have caused. "We can take Negrito alive and entertain him in ways he'll understand," Eladio said.

"Is he the kind of man who gives up reliable information when he's in pain?" Jack said. "Or does he lie and tell you what you want to hear?"

"You are very intelligent, Señor Jack," Eladio said. "Negrito has the strength of a mule and the brain of a snake. Pain means nothing to him. As a boy, he blew flaming kerosene from his mouth in a carnival. His *putas* say they can still smell it on him."

Jaime chewed on a weed and took a watch with a broken strap from his shirt pocket and looked at it. "Eladio is right. If Negrito ain't of no value, maybe it's time we took care of him and also the American you don't like at the whorehouse and get some sleep. What is of more importance? The cost of a bullet or the time we waste speaking of these men you say are worthless? Constantly talking of these men makes me resentful of myself."

Jack's face registered no emotion. It seemed as serene as a layer of plastic that had melted and cooled and dried in dirty lumps. He watched the lights in the sky and the dust that swirled off the desert floor and buttoned the top of his shirt with one hand as though expecting rain or cold. The Mexicans who worked for him were a mystery, an improbable genetic combination of Indian bloodlust and the cruelty of the Inquisition. The angular severity of their features, the way their skin stretched tautly on their bones, the greasy black shine in their uncut hair, the obsidian glint in their eyes at the mention of violence or pain made him wonder if they were remnants of a lost tribe from biblical times, perhaps an unredeemed race that had floated on the Flood far away from where Noah had landed on Mount Ararat. It would make sense. They were unteachable and killed one another with the dispassion and moral vacuity of someone who idly watches his children wander onto a freeway.

What was Jaime saying now? His lips were still moving, though no sound seemed to come from his mouth. Jack disengaged from his reverie and stared at him. "Repeat that?" he said.

"How come we ain't at least killed the *abusador de niños?* He was at the whorehouse. We could have done it easy. Not even

341

the *policía* would object to our killing such a man."

"I don't go in whorehouses," Jack said. "Also, don't speak to me of your policemen's virtue. They're jackals and will steal the coins off a dead man's eyes. What none of you seems to recognize is that your country is ungovernable. Your national heroes are peons who decorated trees with the bodies of their fellow peons. Do not tell me what I should do and not do."

"Señor Jack is very wise. We need to listen to him, Jaime," Eladio said.

"But we keep playing games with gringos who should be food for worms," Jaime said. "This man Holland is the enemy of Señor Jack, but we don't do nozzing about him. Why not kill Holland? It would give me great pleasure to do this for Señor Jack. What is so special about this man?"

Jack pulled the weed from Jaime's mouth and tossed it to one side. "Do not refer to Sheriff Holland by his last name only. His name is Mr. Holland or Sheriff Holland. Do you understand that?" he said.

Jaime started to speak, but Eladio squeezed his arm. "You are a man of honor. We will always follow you and do as you tell us," Eladio said.

"You wouldn't josh a fellow, would you?" Jack said.

"We are hurt deeply when you talk like that

342

to us, Señor Jack," Eladio said.

"Really?" Jack said. He gazed out at the desert and the nighttime glow of a distant town in the clouds. "That flatters and humbles me. I declare, you boys are full of surprises."

The two cousins waited for him to continue, neither of them meeting his eyes, Eladio's hand still locked on Jaime's forearm. "You didn't develop laryngitis on me, did you?" Jack asked.

"We are simple men, boss," Eladio said.

"That's why I like you. That's why I consider you not just friends but family. I wouldn't offend either of you for the world."

"Is true what you say?" Eladio asked.

"Cross my heart," Jack replied, his teeth showing in the moonlight. "But right now I want to see what this *hombre malo* Negrito is doing. He's a pistol, isn't he? A man that keeps his own private burying ground. Y'all surely grow some strange critters down here."

Jack walked back up the slope, then shook out a handkerchief and placed it on the ground and knelt on one knee so he could look down the far side of the hill without silhouetting. While he studied the scene down below, his right hand played with his revolver, lifting it partially out of the holster, reversing the butt, then reversing it again, dropping it back into the hardened leather with a dry *plop*.

"Come on up here and check this out," he said, motioning at the cousins.

The two Mexicans approached him, bent over, gravel rilling from under their cowboy boots, each of them attentive to the motion or lack of motion in Jack's right hand. Out on the hardpan, the gas-guzzler was driving away, its headlights lighting the scrub brush and cactus. "What is it?" Eladio said.

"I was just talking about strange critters," Jack said. He stood up and pointed down the slope. "Look yonder at that new grave. What's that sticking out of the dirt?"

Both cousins stared down into the moonlit wash, their foreheads knitted with thought. "An elephant's trunk?" Eladio said.

"It's the hose and filter on a World War Two gas mask. What do you boys think we ought to do about that?" Jack said.

R. C. Bevins had been raised in a fundamentalist church where the minister went to great lengths to instruct his congregation in the details of Jesus' crucifixion. His dedication to the macabre seemed equaled only by his dedication to busing as many congregants as possible to the local theater's showing of *The Passion of the Christ*. In his presentation, the minister included descriptions of long square-headed spikes that had pierced the victim's wrists — not his hands, the minister said, because the hands would have torn loose from the fastenings; not so the spikes through the wrists. The bones and tendons in the wrist were much sturdier and up to the task of supporting the victim's weight. Also, he pointed out, the spikes were not driven through the tops of the feet, as is often depicted. The knees were folded sideways on the perpendicular shaft, the ankles placed one on top of the other. A single long spike was adequate to pinion the two appendages together.

The minister also explained that death came by asphyxiation as a result of the tendons in the upper torso constricting the lungs and forcing the air back up the victim's windpipe. But for R.C., the worst detail was the minister's speculation that the trauma of being nailed to the cross and the cross being dropped heavily into a hole caused the victim to go into shock only to become conscious a few minutes later and discover that he was not waking from a nightmare but instead was anchored hand and foot to a cruciform of pain from which there was no escape.

That was how R.C. had woken under the ground, with the vague sense that something was wrong with his arms and legs, that he had heard a sifting sound of dirt and gravel sliding off a shovel blade, followed by a thump of stones being dropped heavily on top of him. His eyes were unable to see, his throat raw, as though he had not had water in days. When he tried to raise his head, he realized he was not only impaled by the earth but locked solidly inside it, the air that he breathed coming to him through a tube that smelled of rubber and canvas. The level of panic that occurred in him was like a violent electric surge throughout his body, except the electricity had no place to go.

The inside of the mask was soggy and foul with his sweat and his own breath, and no light at all came through the plastic eyepieces. He stretched out his fingers and for just a moment thought he might be able to work his hands through the dirt toward the surface an inch at a time. Then he discovered that by straightening his hands, he had allowed the overburden of the grave to press down on him more firmly, like an octopus tightening its tentacles on its prey.

Who were the fools who constantly taught about man's harmony with the earth? he asked himself. An uncle who had once worked in a Kentucky coal mine had told R.C. that the earth was not man's friend, that it was unnatural to enter the ground before one's time, and that if a man listened carefully, he would hear the earth creak in warning to those who thought they could tunnel through its substructure without consequence.

He could feel his fear going out of control and his breath beginning to rasp inside the mask, the weight of the earth and stones like knives around his heart. He tried to turn his thoughts into wings that could lift his soul above the ground and allow him to revisit scenes and moments he had associated with the best parts of his life: floating down the Comal River on a burning July afternoon, his wrists trailing in water that was ice-cold, the soap-rock bottom gray and smooth and pooled with shadows from the overhang of the cottonwood trees; dancing with a Mexican girl in a beer garden in Monterrey where Indians sold ears of corn they roasted on charcoal braziers, backdropped by mountains that were hazy and magenta-colored against the sunset; throwing a slider on the edge of the plate for the third strike and third out in the bottom of the ninth at a state championship game in San Marcos, the grass of the diamond iridescent under the electric lights, the evening breeze cool on his skin, a high school girl waiting for him by the bleacher seats, her hands balled into fists as she jumped up and down with love and pride at the perfect game he had just pitched.

His fondest memory was of his twelfth birthday, when his widowed mother took him on the Greyhound all the way from Del Rio to the state fair in Dallas. That evening he stared in awe at the strings of colored lights of the Ferris wheel and the Kamikaze printed against a blue sky puffed with pink clouds. High school kids screamed inside the grinding roar of the Tilt-A-Whirl and the Super Loops, and the air was filled with music from the carousel and the popping of balloons and target guns on the fairways. He could smell the aerial fireworks spidering in a purple and pink froth above the rodeo grounds, and the caramel corn and fry bread and candied apples and tater pigs in the food concessions. His mother bought cotton candy for him and watched him ride the mechanical bull, holding the cotton candy in her hand, smiling even though she was exhausted from the long day on the bus, her wash-faded dress hanging as limp as a flag on her thin body.

R.C. tried to fix the fairground in his mind so he could stay safe inside it, free of the grave and the weight on his heart, wrapped in the calliope's music and the shouts of children and teenage kids, his mother's smile on the edge of his vision, the electric glow of the amusement rides rising into an ethereal sky that was testimony to everything that was good and beautiful in the world.

If there was a way, Sheriff Holland would find him, he told himself. He had given the sheriff his location. It was only a matter of time before the sheriff found the bar and forced the bartender to tell him where R.C. had been taken. All R.C. had to do was hold on, to breathe in and out, to not let go of the fairgrounds and the best day of his life. The soul could go where it wanted, he told himself. It existed, didn't it? If it could fly from you at death, why couldn't it leave you while you were alive? He didn't have to abide the condition he had found himself in. Or at least he didn't have to cooperate with it.

When he swallowed, his saliva was bilious, and his eyes watered at the fate that had been imposed on him. In his impotence and rage and fear, he cursed himself for his self-pity.

He heard a shovel sink deep into the dirt and felt it graze his side, not unlike the tip of a Roman spear teasing the rib cage of an impaled man.

A moment later, the hands of two men began scraping the dirt away from his face and shoulders and arms and sides, lifting his head free, slipping the mask from his face, allowing him to breathe air that was as clean and pure as bottled oxygen. He could see the silhouette of a third man against the moon, a holstered thumb-buster revolver on his hip, his fingernails like the claws on an animal. He wore a sun-bleached panama hat that was grimed with finger smears on the front brim.

"Who are you?" R.C. said, unsure if he should have even asked the question, his face cold with sweat.

CHAPTER FOURTEEN

Hackberry looked through the front windshield at the long, flat, sunbaked rawness of the land and at the purple haze that seemed to rise from the creosote brush and the greasewood and the patches of alkali along streambeds that were hardly more than sand. In the distance, he could see hills in the moonlight and stovepipe cactus in the yard of an adobe house whose roof had collapsed. He looked through his binoculars at the hills and at the house and thought he could see a dirt road behind it that switchbacked up the side of the hill, but he couldn't be sure.

The bartender with the swastika tattooed on his scalp had given him and Pam Tibbs directions to the place where he believed Negrito was taking the young Texas lawman. When Hackberry had asked whether he was sure, the bartender had replied, staring at the broken pool cue Hackberry had almost stuffed down his throat, "It's where Negrito always disposes of people he has no more use for. It's the underground prison he likes to stand on top of. Maybe he comes back for them. Maybe that's where you will end up seriously *jodido,* that's what I hope."

Hackberry's cell phone vibrated on the Jeep's dashboard. He picked it up and put it to his ear. "Sheriff Holland," he said.

"It's Maydeen. Did you find R.C.?"

"Not yet."

"Let me try to get you some backup."

"There's nobody down here I trust."

"Hack, I called because I'm at the hospital. Anton Ling says she saw the guy she put a screwdriver in. He and another guy were in the hallway right outside her room."

"How did she know it was the guy she hurt? He was wearing a mask when she put the screwdriver in his face."

"She said she recognized the guy with him. She said she was mixed up in an intelligence operation of some kind years ago, and this guy was part of it. Felix and I are in her room now. She wants to talk with you."

"Put her on."

Hackberry heard Maydeen speaking to Anton Ling, then Maydeen got back on the cell. "She wants us to leave the room. When y'all get finished, I'll come back in. Felix will stay here the rest of the night."

"Tell Anton Ling that anything she wants to tell me, she can say in front of you."

"Don't worry about it, Hack. I need a cup

351

of coffee," Maydeen said.

A moment later, Anton Ling got on the cell. "I'm sorry to bother you with this, Sheriff Holland, but I needed to get something off my chest," she said.

"Miss Anton, in my department, we don't have private conversations, and we don't keep secrets from one another," Hackberry said. "I'm making an exception in this instance because your life may be in jeopardy."

"I didn't want your deputies to hear our conversation for the same reason. I have knowledge that can get people killed."

"Knowledge about what?"

"There was a political scandal years ago that flared and died. A reporter broke a story that the Contras were introducing cocaine into American cities to pay for the guns that were being shipped to Nicaragua. A couple of newspapers in the East debunked the story, and later, the reporter committed suicide. But the story was true. The guns were AK-47s and came from China. They were assembled in California and shipped south. The dope went to the West Coast first, then other places later. I was involved in it."

"Why didn't you tell someone about this?"

"No one cares. They didn't care then, they don't care now. It was *The Washington Post* and *The New York Times* that debunked the story."

"Do you know the names of the guys you

saw outside your room?"

"No, but I think they were here to wipe the slate clean. The man I recognized was a connection between the Contras and some dope mules in California."

"Do you know the name Josef Sholokoff?"

"I do. He was part of the drug deal with the Contras. There's no end to this," she said.

"To what?"

"To the grief I've caused others."

"People like us don't make the wars, Miss Anton. We just get to fight in them," he said. "I've lost a deputy sheriff down here in Mexico. For all I know, he's dead now. When I catch the guys who did this, I'm going to cool them out proper and not feel any qualms about it."

"I think you're not served well by your rhetoric."

"I've got a flash for you, Miss Anton. The only real pacifists are dead Quakers. Ambrose Bierce said that when reflecting on his experience at Shiloh."

"It's also cheap stuff. Good-bye." She broke the connection.

"Look up ahead," Pam said, steering down into the streambed. "There're tire tracks in the sand. They go through the backyard of that adobe house. This has to be the hill the bartender was talking about."

Hackberry turned on the spotlight mounted on the passenger side of the Jeep and shone it through the darkness. A yellow dog with mange on its face and neck, its sides skeletal, its dugs distended, emerged from the shell of the house and stared into the brilliance of the beam before loping away.

"You want to try the switchback up the hill or go around?" Pam asked.

"We take the high ground. Park behind the house. We'll walk over the hill and come down on top of them."

"Back there in the cantina, I saw a side of you that bothers me, Hack," she said.

"I don't have another side, Pam. You stand behind your people or you don't stand behind your people. It's that simple. We get R.C. back from this collection of cretins. When I was at Inchon, I was very frightened. But a line sergeant told me something I never forgot. 'Don't think about it before it happens, and don't think about it when it's over.' We bring R.C. home. You with me on that?"

"I'm with you in everything. But my words mean little to you," she replied. "And that bothers me more than you seem able to understand."

He didn't speak again until they had parked the Jeep behind the adobe house, and then it was only to tell her to walk behind him when they went over the crest of the hill.

The man wearing the hat and holstered thumb-buster squatted on his haunches, eye level with R.C. His breath was as dense and tannic as sewer gas. Two Mexicans wearing jeans that looked stitched to their skins stood stiffly on either side of him, like bookends fashioned from wire. "You have a bad moment or two down there?" the man asked.

R.C. nodded, meeting the strange man's eyes briefly.

"Enough to make you wet your britches?" the man asked.

"No, sir, I didn't do that."

The man lifted his chin and pinched the loose flesh under his throat. He was unshaved, and his whiskers looked as stiff as pig bristles. "What's it like under the ground, with a mask on your face and a lifeline anyone can pinch off with the sole of his boot?"

"Dark."

"Like the inside of a turnip sack, I bet."

"That comes right close to it."

"Your heart start twisting and your breath start coming out of your windpipe like you swallowed a piece of glass?"

"That pert' near says it," R.C. replied.

"I can sympathize."

"You been buried alive?"

"Not in the way you have."

"You either have or you haven't."

"When I was a little boy, my mother would stick me eight or nine hours inside a footlocker. I'd pretend I was on the spine of a boxcar, flying across the countryside under the stars. Did you have fanciful notions like that? Then you opened your eyes and thought somebody had poured an inkwell inside your head."

"Maybe your soul can go somewhere else. That's the way I figure it. That's how come people don't go crazy sometimes," R.C. said. Then he added, as though he were in the presence of a confidant, "I got wrapped up in a rubber sheet when I was a little baby and almost suffocated. My mother was in the yard and looked through the window and said I'd already turned blue. She ran inside and saved my life."

"You saying you had a real mother but mine was cut out of different cloth, maybe burlap?"

"No, sir, I didn't say that," R.C. replied, looking away.

"I wouldn't care if you did. Do you think I care about your opinion of my mother?"

"No, sir."

"What's the nature of your relationship with Sheriff Holland?"

"Sir?"

"You deaf?"

"I'm his deputy. My name is R. C. Bevins. I grew up in Ozona and Del Rio and Marathon. My daddy was a tool pusher in the oil field. My mother was a cashier at the IGA till the day she died. She went to work one day and never came home."

"Why should I care what your parents did or didn't do?"

" 'Cause I know who you are. 'Cause I know what happens to people when you get your hands on them. So if you do the same to me, I want you to know who I am, or who I was."

"Who do you think I am?"

"A stone killer who don't take prisoners."

"For somebody who was just dug up from a grave, maybe you should take your transmission out of overdrive."

"Maybe you should have practiced a little self-inventory before you murdered all them Asian girls."

"You're ahead of the game, boy. Best respect your elders."

"I ain't the one trying to get inside somebody else's thoughts, like some kind of pervert."

"You were in the whorehouse to play the piano?"

"If that's what it was, I was there because I blew out my tire. So don't go belittling me."

The man in the hat glanced up at the two Mexicans, his eyes amused, the soles of his boots grating on the gravel. "You thirsty?"

R.C. swallowed but didn't reply.

"You ever kill a man?"

"I never had to," R.C. said.

"Maybe that's waiting for you down the pike."

"If I got choices, it ain't gonna happen."

"You want a drink of water or not?"

R.C. sat erect and pulled his knees up before him, the dirt and pea gravel shaling off his clothes. "I wouldn't mind," he said.

The man with yellow fingernails that were as thick as horn signaled for one of the Mexicans to pass R.C. a canteen that was attached to a looped GI web belt.

"Does Sheriff Holland treat you all right?"

"We share commonalities. That's what he calls them, 'commonalities.'"

"In what way?"

"We both pitched baseball. I pitched all the way through high school. He pitched in high school and three years at Baylor. He got an invitation to the Cardinals' training camp. I wasn't as good as him, though."

"I declare."

"He has the Navy Cross and a Purple Heart. He treats everybody the same, black or Mexican or Indian or illegal, it don't matter. That's the kind of man he is."

"He sounds like a father figure."

"If he is, it's nobody else's business."

"The sheriff is a widower and doesn't have family close by. It must be a comfort for him to have a young fellow like you around. Someone he thinks of as a son."

"I got to use the restroom."

The man found a more comfortable position by easing his weight down on one knee.

"You might be hard put to find one out here," he said. He gazed into the distance, his eyes dulled over, seemingly devoid of thought. The collar of his white shirt was yellow with dried soap. "What if I gave you a choice, one that would he'p you define your loyalties in a way you wouldn't forget? That nobody would forget?"

R.C. had taken one sip from the canteen and had started to take another. But he stopped and set the canteen down on the edge of the grave and stared at it, his hand still cupped on the canvas snap-button pouch that held it. He waited, his eyes fixed in empty space, the wind flattening the mesquite along the banks of the streambed. He knew what was coming.

"Here's the situation as I see it," the strange man said. "The sheriff tried to kill me by firing a whole magazine down a mine shaft. He has also insulted me several times on a personal level without provocation, even though I have always treated him with respect. So principle requires that I do something in kind to him, otherwise I'll be guilty of what's called a sin of omission. Are you following me?"

"You're Preacher Jack Collins. Around here, that translates into 'crazy.' I don't have conversations with crazy people."

Collins shifted his weight and pulled his revolver from its holster and fitted his thumb over the hammer. "You'd better listen up, boy." He pulled back the hammer to full cock and touched the muzzle to R.C.'s temple. "With one soft squeeze, I can scatter your buckwheats all over that streambed. There will be a flash of light and a loud roar in your ears, then you'll be with your dead mother. I'll make sure the sheriff understands I did this as payback for what he's done to me. In that way, I'll rob him of any peace of mind for the rest of his life. But there's a problem with that choice. Other than not knowing how to stay out of a hot-pillow joint, you're an innocent boy and shouldn't have to pay the price for the sheriff's actions. So I'm going to create a choice for you that most people in your situation don't have."

Collins lowered the hammer and released the lock on the cylinder and tipped it sideways from the revolver's frame. He shucked the six brass cartridges into his palm. "Are you a gambling man?" he said.

"Whatever it is you're thinking about, I'm not interested."

"Believe me, you will be."

"Sheriff Holland is gonna hunt you down in every rat hole in Coahuila. Don't be talking down to me about no whorehouses, either. You got whores working for you as informants, and I suspect that ain't all they're doing for you, provided they're not choosy."

Collins stood up. "I'm going to put one in

the chamber and spin the cylinder. When I hand you the revolver, I'm going to cover the cylinder so you cain't see where the load is. If you'll hold the muzzle to your head and pull the trigger twice without coming down on the wrong chamber, I'll turn you loose. If you refuse, I'll pop you here and now."

"Why you doing this to me?"

"Boy, you just don't listen, do you?"

"Let me think it over. Okay, I have. Kiss my ass. And when you're done doing that, kiss my ass again."

"Why don't you have another sip of water and rethink that statement?"

"I don't need no more of y'all's mouth germs."

"Get up."

"What for?"

Jack Collins laughed to himself. "You're fixing to find out."

"I'm tired of all this."

"Tired?"

"Yeah, of being treated like a sack of shit. Just like I told that guy who took me out here, go on and do what you're gonna do. Fuck you, I couldn't care less. Hackberry Holland is gonna turn you into the deadest bucket of shit that was ever poured in the ground."

Jack Collins let the revolver hang loosely at his side, outside the holster. "Stand up and look me in the face."

R.C. got to his feet, his knees popping. He wiped the sweat and beaded rings of dirt from his neck and looked at his hand. His eyes drifted to the revolver in Preacher Jack's right hand. He closed his eyes and opened them again, forcing them wide, refusing to blink. On the edge of his vision, he thought he saw his mother watching him, a cone of cotton candy clutched in her hand.

"Just to set the record straight, the breed who buried you wasn't coming back. He's in Durango now, drunk out of his senses," Jack Collins said. "You would have died underground of thirst and starvation. If I had my druthers, I'd take a bullet anytime."

"I'll take a bullet just so I don't have to listen to you no more," R.C. said.

Jack Collins laughed again and picked up the canteen and looped the web belt over R.C.'s head, easing it down so as not to clip his ear. "Stay on the edge of the hillside and go due north for about three miles, and you'll hit a dirt road. Follow it eastward, and you'll intersect an asphalt two-lane that'll take you to the border."

R.C. stared at him dumbly, the backs of his legs shaking. He tried to think about what Collins had just said. The words made no sense. He felt as though the horizon were tilting sideways, the mountains going in and out of focus.

"You really thought I was going to cap

you?" Collins said.

R.C. didn't answer. He glanced sideways at the spot where his mother had been standing, but she had disappeared.

"I wouldn't do that to you, kid. You've got sand," Collins said.

With that, he and his friends walked away like Halloween trick-or-treaters who had lost interest in their own pranks.

A few minutes later, Hackberry Holland and Pam Tibbs came over the crest of the hill and looked down on the riparian landscape and the empty streambed that resembled a pale scar cutting across it, and the graves where the half-breed named Negrito had buried his victims, some of whom may have been alive when they went into the ground.

There was no one down below. Pam swept the area with her binoculars and then pointed at the north, handing the binoculars to Hackberry. In the moonlight, he saw a solitary figure walking alongside the streambed, a canteen slung from his shoulder, his shirttail hanging out, his shadow as sharp as a fence post on the ground. "R.C.," he said.

"How'd he get loose from the guy who kidnapped him?" Pam said.

"I don't know," Hackberry said. He focused the lenses on the southern horizon and thought he saw headlights dip over a rise and briefly reflect off a sandstone bluff and then disappear. "Let's find out."

They climbed back down the opposite side of the hill and drove north in the Jeep until they were out on the flats again and could drive past the hill and intersect the streambed R.C. was following. As they drove toward him, their high beams suddenly defining him among the pale greenery that grew out of the sand, burning the shadows away from the youthful angularity of his face, Hackberry experienced one of those moments doctors at the navy hospital in Houston defined as post-traumatic stress disorder but that Hackberry thought of as the natural entwining of events and people, past and present, that seemed to take place as one reached the end of his life.

The totality of a man's days eventually became a circle rather than a sum, and one way or another, he always ended up at the place where he had begun. Or at least that was what Hackberry believed.

As he looked through the windshield at R.C., he saw himself in the late summer of 1953, crossing the wooden pedestrian bridge at Panmunjom, the last man in a column of prisoners being returned from the camps south of the Manchurian border. He had been emaciated, barely able to walk and control his dysentery, his marine utilities stiff with salt and faded almost colorless. A photographer from *Stars and Stripes* took his picture with a big Speed Graphic camera, and later, the photo was picked up by the wire services and published all over the country above a cutline that began, "The last American soldier to cross Freedom Bridge . . ."

But he had not been the last man across Freedom Bridge. Others would follow and others would be left behind, perhaps four hundred of them who were moved by their captors across the Yalu River into Communist China and forgotten by the rest of the world.

Was it worth it? The great irony was that no one cared enough to even ask the question. The dates, the battles, the strafing of civilian refugees by American F-80s, the misery of the Chosin Reservoir, the red-hot thirty-caliber barrels they unscrewed with their bare hands, leaving their flesh on the steel, the systematic cruelty inside the gulag of prison camps in the north, Hackberry's time in a place called Pak's Palace, which had been housed in an abandoned brick factory where the North Koreans refined a method of torture known as Pak's Swing, all these things were smudged entries in a tragedy that had become little more than an inconvenient memory. But the participants never forgot the details of their experience, and like the Wandering Jew, they were condemned to remain their own history books, each containing a story they could not pass on to others and from which no one would learn anything of value.

Hackberry could see himself in R.C., walking down the flume of an ancient riverbed, staring back into the Jeep's headlights, his mouth cut with a grin, the soft white baked clay cracking under his weight. Youth was its own anodyne, Hackberry thought. For R.C., the world was still a fine place, his faith in his fellow man renewed by the arrival of his friends, his life unfolding before him as though it had been charted with the same divine hand that had placed our progenitors in an Edenic paradise. For just a second, Hackberry wanted to take all the experience out of his own life and give it to R.C. and pray that he would do better with it than Hackberry had.

He rolled down the passenger window. "Miss your turnoff to San Antone?" he said.

"I knew y'all would be along," R.C. said, grinning broadly, getting in the back. "What kept you? I was starting to get a little antsy."

"Bad traffic jam. What kept *us*? What the hell happened out here?" Hackberry said.

"This half-breed Negrito buried me after he almost took my head off with a shovel, that's what happened. Then Jack Collins and two Mexicans dug me up."

Pam put her foot on the brake. "Collins is down here?"

"He *was*."

"Where?" she asked.

"Him and the two Mexicans walked over a rise and just went *poof,* gone, just like that."

"Did they have a car?" Hackberry said.

"I didn't hear one. But the wind was blowing out of the north. Maybe I just didn't hear them start it up."

"What did Collins say to you?" Hackberry said.

"He said I had a choice. I could play Russian roulette or he'd pop me. When I told him I wouldn't do it, he gave me directions to the highway. I cain't figure it out. Maybe everything people say about him ain't altogether true."

"Don't fool yourself," Hackberry said.

"So why'd he cut me loose?"

"He told you to tell me something, didn't he?"

"He's got you on his mind, that's for sure, but he didn't send no message. No, sir."

Hackberry looked straight ahead at the countryside and at the stars that were going out of the sky.

"Did I miss something back there?" R.C. asked.

Collins wants me in his debt, Hackberry thought. But that was not what he said. "You did just fine, R.C. Who cares what goes on in the head of a madman?"

"I do. He's a scary guy."

"He is. He kills people."

"No, in a different way. His breath. It smells

like gas. His skin, too. It doesn't smell like sweat. He doesn't smell human."

The Mexicans say he walks through walls, Hackberry thought.

"Sir?"

"There's a town not far away. You hungry?"

"A twenty-ounce steak and five pounds of fries and a gallon of ice cream would probably get me through till breakfast," R.C. replied.

"You got it, bub," Hackberry said.

By dawn Hackberry was back home. He called Ethan Riser's cell phone and left a message, then slept four hours and showered and called Riser again. This time Riser answered. "I need you here, partner," Hackberry said.

"I got your message about Collins. We've contacted all the authorities in Coahuila."

"That's like telling me you just masturbated."

"Why do you go out of your way to be offensive?"

"Anton Ling told me she was involved in an arms-for-dope operation. The dope went into American ghettos, the guns went to Nicaragua. She says Josef Sholokoff was a player in the deal."

"I've heard all that stuff before."

"Is it true?"

"Maybe on some level it is. But it's yesterday's box score. Sholokoff is our worry, Sheriff. You worry about Collins and this guy Krill. It's clear they're both operating in your jurisdiction. Sholokoff is a separate issue."

Hackberry could feel his hand clenching and unclenching on the phone receiver. Through his window, he could see his horses running in the pasture and yellow dust rising off the hills, plum-colored rain clouds bunching across the sun. *He has cancer. He's at the end of his row. Don't insult him,* he heard a voice say.

"I'm against the wall," he said. "My deputy was drugged and buried alive. Federal agencies and their minions, people like Temple Dowling, are wiping their ass on my county, and I can't do anything about it. I'm throwing away the rule book on this one, Ethan."

"That's always the temptation. But when it's over, the result is always the same. You end up with shit on your nose."

"You coming down here or not?"

There was a long silence. "I'm tied up. I can't do it. Listen to me, Hack. Stay out of events that happened years ago. Stay away from this Anton Ling woman, too. She's an idealist who's full of guilt, and like all idealists, she'd incinerate one half of the earth to save the other half. She had a chance to return Noie Barnum to his own people — that's us, the good guys, we're not Al Qaeda. Instead, she chose to hide and feed him and dress his wounds and let him end up in the hands of Jack Collins. Are you going to put your bet on somebody like that? Use your head for a change."

That evening Danny Boy Lorca entered a saloon off a two-lane highway that wound through hills that resembled industrial waste more than compacted earth. The saloon was built of shaved and lacquered pine logs and had a peaked green roof that, along with the Christmas-tree lights stapled around the window frames, gave it a cheerful appearance in a landscape that seemed suitable only for lizards and scorpions and carrion birds. The saloon's name was spelled out in a big orange neon sign set on the roof's apex, the cursive words LA ROSA BLANCA glowing vaporously against the sky. The owner went by the name Joe Tex, although he had no relationship to the musician by the same name. When patrons asked Joe Tex where he had gotten the name for his saloon, he would tell them of his ex-wife, a big-breasted stripper from Dallas who had a heart of gold and a voice that could break windows and a thirst for chilled vodka that the Gulf of Mexico couldn't quench. The truth was, Joe Tex had never been married and had been a mercenary in Cambodia, operating out of Phnom Penh, where he had been close friends with the owners of a brothel that specialized in oral sex. The name of the brothel had been the White Rose.

Danny Boy had parked his deuce-and-a-half army-surplus flatbed and walked unsteadily across the gravel to the entrance, the drawstring of a duffel bag corded around his forearm, the weight in the bottom of the bag bumping against his hip as he scraped against the doorframe and headed for the bar.

Next door was a 1950s-style motel bordered with red and yellow neon tubing whose circular porte cochere and angular facade and signs gave it the appearance of a parked spaceship. The customers in the saloon were long-haul truckers staying in the motel; women who carried spangled purses and wore eyeliner and lip gloss and had mousse in their hair and whose voices seemed slightly deranged; locals who had been in Huntsville and were probably dangerous and not welcome at other clubs; and college boys looking to get laid or get in trouble, whichever came first.

Joe Tex dressed like a Latino, his cowboy boots plated on the toes and heels, his black cowboy shirt stitched with red roses. He smiled constantly, regardless of the situation, his teeth as solid as tombstones, the black hair on his forearms a signal to others of the power and virility wrapped inside his muscular body, one that pulsed with veins when he lifted weights in nothing but a jockstrap out back in 110-degree heat.

Danny Boy skirted the dance floor, walking as carefully as a man aboard a pitching ship. He set the duffel bag on the bar, the canvas collapsing on the hard objects inside.

"A beer and a shot?" Joe Tex said.

"I want to pay my tab," Danny Boy said.

Joe Tex took a frosted schooner out of the cooler and drew a beer from a spigot and set it in front of Danny Boy, then poured a shot glass up to the brim with Jim Beam and set it on a napkin next to the schooner. His expression made Danny Boy think of a profile carved on the handle of a Mexican walking cane — fixed, slightly worn, the paint chipping away. Joe Texas opened a drawer below the bar and looked in a metal box and removed a slip of paper columned with penciled sums. "Call it seventy-five even," he said.

"I got some dinosaur eggs. I want to sell them."

"If I was in the dinosaur business, wouldn't I have to be worried about something called the Antiquities Act?" Joe Tex's teeth were white against the deep leathery tan of his face when he smiled.

"These come from the back of my property. The government don't care what I dig up on my own land. I got two eggs, big ones." He raised the bag slightly by the drawstring, tightening the canvas against the shapes inside. "They're worth five thousand apiece. You can have them both for four thousand."

"That's how you're gonna pay your tab?"

"I saw a killing. It was done by a guy named Krill. I'm gonna put a bounty on this guy. I'm gonna put a reward on a guy named Noie Barnum, too, and maybe get him some he'p."

Joe Tex propped his hands on the bar. He seemed to gaze at the college boys and women and truck drivers sitting at the tables and the couples dancing by the jukebox without actually seeing any of them. He seemed to look at all the illusions that defined the lives of his clientele and maybe think about them briefly and then return to the realities and deceptions that made up his own life. "What are you doing this for, Danny Boy?"

" 'Cause I seen a murder and I didn't do nothing to stop it. 'Cause maybe I can make up for it by he'ping a guy name of Noie Barnum. He got away from this fellow Krill. He run right past me. Maybe he's hiding out with the one called the Preacher."

Joe Tex studied the tops of his fingers and the hair that grew from the backs of his hands along his wrists and under the metal band of his watch and the snap-button cuffs of his embroidered shirt. "This isn't the place to square a personal beef. The shot and the beer are on the house. Let's eighty-six the eggs. This isn't a souvenir shop."

Joe Tex walked away, his metal-plated boots making dull sounds on the duckboards. Danny Boy's eyes closed and opened as he tried to think his way through the haze and confusion that Joe Tex's words had caused in his head. He drank from the shot glass, a small sip at a time, chasing it with the beer, slumping forward for balance, one work-booted foot on the bar rail, his facial muscles oily and uncoordinated, the row of bottles on the back counter sparkling with light. The shot glass and the schooner seemed to go empty by themselves, his foot slipping off the rail as he stared wanly at them. "Hit me again," he said when Joe Tex walked past him to wait on a customer at the far end of the bar.

Danny Boy waited for his schooner and shot glass to be refilled, as though his level of desire were enough to make a reality out of a wish. But Joe Tex remained at the far end of the bar, talking to some college kids who were asking him about Big Bend National Park, and Danny Boy's shot glass and schooner did not get refilled. "Give me another one," he said to Joe Tex's back.

He rested his hand on top of the heavy, solid, thick shapes of the fossilized eggs and stared at the way Joe Tex's shirt stretched tightly across his shoulders, the tendon and sinew that tapered down to a thirty-two-inch waist, the wide belt he wore and the tight western-cut gray trousers and the polished Tony Lama boots. Couldn't Joe hear him? Danny Boy knocked on the bar with his knuckles. "Give me a beer and a sandwich," he said. "One of them ham and onion ones. Give me a shot, too."

But no one was listening to him. Not Joe Tex or the college kids or the dancers or the people drinking and eating at the tables. Didn't others understand the value of what he had found? The eggs proved a great antediluvian world was still out there, inhabited by stubby-legged creatures with reptilian necks. All you had to do was believe and you could see through time into the past and maybe even touch it with your hand. That's what happened when you went inside the desert and were absorbed by the rocks and the layers of warm air rising off the sand. You became part of a place where there was no past or future and where all things happened at the same time. "Hey, Joe, why you talking to them people?" he said. "I want a drink. Forget them kids. I want a fucking drink."

Did he just say that?

Joe Tex walked slowly toward him on the duckboards, a pocket of air forming in one cheek. He picked up the shot glass and schooner and set them in an aluminum sink filled with dirty water. The glass and the schooner sank down through the film of soap and grease and disappeared. "Time to go home, Danny," he said.

"I come here to pay my tab. I come here to drink like anybody else."

"Another time."

"I'll pay my tab tomorrow. I'll find somebody to buy the eggs."

Joe Tex lifted his hands and set them on the bar again. "I can get someone to drive you home, or you can sleep it off in back," he said. "That's it. We're done."

When Joe Tex walked away, Danny Boy felt like he was standing on a street corner by himself, watching a city bus lumber away from the curb, his reflection on the windows sliding past him, the passengers inside reading newspapers or talking to one another or listening to music through earphones as though he didn't exist. His lips were caked, his throat clotted, the veins tightening in his scalp, the bottles of rum and bourbon and tequila and vodka as mysterious and alluring as the radiance in a rainbow. "I been a good customer. I been your friend," he heard himself say.

Then he felt instantly ashamed at his plaintive tone, the pathetic role of victim once again his public mantle.

"Want a drink, chief?" a voice said.

When Danny Boy turned around, he saw a tall, clean-shaven man with wavy brown hair standing behind him. Three other men were sitting at a table behind the tall man, smoking cigarettes, drinking beer from the bottle. The tall man could have been a cowboy or a buyer of rough stock for a rodeo, but in reality, he probably did something else, Danny Boy thought, like manage a big-game ranch up in the Glass Mountains or cater to the needs of a rich man who hired others to do his work for him. He wore mirrored sunglasses and a sky-blue silk shirt and Wrangler jeans belted high up on his flat stomach. He had an easy smile and big hands with knuckles that looked like walnuts. Maybe he was a cowboy after all, Danny Boy thought, a regular guy who didn't mean anything by the word "chief."

"I'm tapped out," Danny Boy said.

"That's not just booze talking. You got some dino eggs in there?"

Danny Boy tried not to acknowledge the first part. "They come from the back of my place. I dug them up." He glanced at the bottles on the back counter and wiped his nose with a handkerchief. He watched the cowboy drink from the bottle of Mexican beer, his throat working smoothly, his cheeks glistening with aftershave, the label on the bottle gold and red and translucent and somehow beautiful. Danny Boy waited for the cowboy to offer him a drink.

"Maybe I could help you out," the cowboy said.

Danny waited, trying not to let his gaze

settle on the bottles of whiskey and rum and gin and vodka.

"Can I look at them?" the cowboy said, cupping his hand on the outline of the eggs.

"Maybe this ain't the place."

"I don't see any problem." The cowboy slipped a wallet from his back pocket and set it on the bar. The edges of a thick sheaf of crisp bills protruded from the braided edge of the wallet.

Danny Boy loosened the drawstring on the duffel bag and stuck his arm inside and slowly removed each dinosaur egg and placed it carefully on the bar. When he looked back into the cowboy's mirrored sunglasses, he saw the reflected image of a dark-skinned, truncated man in a dirty olive-colored T-shirt and canvas trousers he had probably pissed in without remembering.

"How much you want for them?" the cowboy asked.

"Two thousand for each."

"They look like a pair of petrified titties to me, and not very good ones, at that."

Danny Boy made a snuffing sound down in his nose and looked at the far wall and at the people on the dance floor and at the layers of smoke that flattened and sometimes swirled under the ceiling. "I could go eighteen hunnerd for each."

"And you're gonna use this money to round up a fellow name of Noie Barnum? You're kind of a specialist in solving big-picture problems? Tell you what, before you answer that question, how about one-fifty for both your busted titties here, and then you take yourself and your stink out of here? Have you noticed that your britches look like somebody shoved a wet towel in your crotch?"

Danny Boy stared at his reflection of the man trapped inside the cowboy's sunglasses. The trapped man's hair was cut in bangs, his skin so dark it looked as though it had been smoked on a fire; his emotionless expression was like that of a retarded man who absorbed insults without understanding the words; the scar tissue in his eyebrows and the gaps in his teeth and the rounded mass of his shoulders were those of a man who had been pounded into the ground for a lifetime, a hod carrier working under the scaffolding of a cathedral while stone dust filtered down on his head. He stared into the cowboy's sunglasses until the image of himself seemed to break into gold needles.

"I dug them up on my place," he said. "I'm gonna use the money to he'p this fellow Noie Barnum. I think you know who he is or you wouldn't be talking down to me."

The cowboy gripped Danny Boy's upper arm tightly with one hand, leaning over to whisper in his ear, his words wet with the smokeless tobacco tucked inside his lip. "I'm gonna walk you outside, boy, then we're gonna have a talk. In the meantime, you keep your mouth shut."

"I was a middleweight. I fought at the Olympia in L.A. I knew Tami Mauriello. He give me some pointers once. He sat in my corner and said I was as good as him. Tami almost nailed Joe Louis."

"You get your goddamn worthless stink-ass Indian carcass out front. You hear me, boy? You know what no God or law west of the Pecos means? It means this is still a white man's country."

The cowboy's teeth were clenched, his anger telegraphing through his grip, his breath wet against the side of Danny Boy's face.

Maybe it was the use of the word "boy" or the ferocity of his grip. Or maybe it was the years of contempt and ridicule and insult that Danny Boy had come to accept as a way of life, part of the tab that came with being a drunk and a swamper of saloons and bathrooms where people vomited in the lavatory and threw their paper towels on the floor and shit on the edge of the bowl. Or maybe it was none of these things. Maybe he just wanted to be seventeen again, fresh out of the Golden Gloves, lean and hard, his left as quick as a snake's head, his right hook under the heart enough to make a grown man's eyes beg.

This time Danny Boy's right didn't hook in to an opponent's rib cage; it went straight into the cowboy's mouth, breaking his lips against his teeth, knocking his mirrored shades off his face. The shock and pain in the cowboy's eyes could be compared to that of a man stepping out of a car and being hit by a bus. Before the man could raise his hands to protect himself, Danny Boy threw the whole factory at him: two left jabs, one in the eye, one high up on the cheekbone and the bridge of the nose, then a right delivered straight from the shoulder with his weight solidly behind it, his fist driving into the bloody hole he had already created in the bottom of the cowboy's face, breaking off his teeth at the gums, knocking a wad of blood and phlegm and smokeless tobacco down his throat.

All sound in the saloon stopped except for the voice of Willie Nelson on the jukebox. He was singing "Blue Eyes Crying in the Rain," his voice like a long strand of baling wire being pulled through a hole in a tin can. Danny Boy replaced the dinosaur eggs in the duffel bag and wrapped the drawstring around his forearm and started toward the door. The fight should have been over. The cowboy was sprawled backward on the floor, his nose and mouth dripping blood on his sky-blue shirt. Even Joe Tex, who usually broke up fights immediately, was observing silently from behind the bar, indicating that it was over, that all Danny Boy had to do now was walk out of the saloon.

That was how it should have gone. But it didn't. Danny Boy had taken only three steps when he heard the cowboy coming hard behind him. He turned, the duffel hanging from his left forearm, automatically setting himself, ready to unload with his right and this time click off the cowboy's switch.

Except the cowboy came in under the swing, gripping an antler-handled knife with a four-inch blade, the blade protruding from the heel of the hand and the fingers, his forearm and elbow raised in front of his face to absorb Danny Boy's next blow. Danny Boy tried to jump backward but tripped against a chair. He felt the knife go into his thigh like an icicle, all the way to the bone, thudding dully against it, a pocket of pain and nausea spreading out of the wound into his groin and stomach. He remembered hearing about an artery the heart depended on, and then he was outside himself, watching Danny Boy Lorca labor toward the door, his duffel bag swinging from his arm, his right leg as stiff as wood, the knife driven all the way to the hilt against his canvas trousers. Outside, bathed in the orange glow of a neon sign that advertised a Texas saloon and a Cambodian brothel, the entire world and the stars above it were draining down his leg into shale that creatures with long serpentine necks had probably once walked upon. It was a funny way to catch the elevator going south, he thought, just as the parking lot rose up and hit him between the eyes with the impact of a fist.

CHAPTER FIFTEEN

The attendant who stayed in the back of the ambulance with Danny Boy during the ride to the county hospital had acne on his forehead and on the bridge of his nose and on the point of his chin, so that his profile looked like it had been sawed out of a shingle with a dull knife. His skin and clothes were rife with the smell of nicotine, his hair flecked with dandruff, his arms as thin as sticks inside his shirtsleeves. The asphalt road was badly cracked, and Danny Boy's gurney and the equipment inside the ambulance were vibrating loudly, but the attendant seemed to take little notice.

"What do you call that artery in the thigh?" Danny Boy asked. "The one you don't want to get cut?"

"The femoral," the attendant said.

"Is that where he got me?"

"Guess."

"He didn't?"

The attendant untwisted the cellophane on

a piece of peppermint. "I got dry mouth," he said. "I'd offer you one, but you're not supposed to have anything right now."

"The artery is okay?"

"Jesus, buddy, what do you think?"

"I think I used to know you. Your nickname was Stoner or something like that."

"That doesn't sound familiar."

Danny Boy continued to stare at the attendant's profile. "I worked at a carnival in Marathon. I saw you at the free clinic. You were trying to get clean."

"Yeah, that could have been me. You were in a program there?"

"I went to the clinic 'cause of my headaches."

"The guy you decked, he's a private detective. He works for Temple Dowling." The attendant waited. Danny Boy stared at him without replying, the inside of the ambulance rattling each time the tires thudded across a tar-patched crack in the road. "You don't know who Temple Dowling is?"

"No."

"His father was a senator."

"Of what?"

The attendant shook his head. "The bartender told the cops you wanted to put a reward on a guy named Barnum. You know, same name as the circus?" He blew his nose on a tissue and stuck the tissue in his shirt pocket, sniffing, his gaze shifting sideways onto Danny Boy. "Maybe I know where he is. Or who he's with. You following me?"

"Tell the sheriff."

"Were you ever in N.A.?"

"What's that?"

The attendant sniffed again. "I sold some medical supplies to a guy. A guy I don't like to think about. He had me meet him at night out in the desert. You know who I'm talking about?"

"Maybe. What's his name?"

"If you meet this guy, you don't use his name."

"The one they call Preacher?"

"You said it, I didn't."

Through the back window, Danny Boy could see the reflection of the emergency lights racing along the sides of the highway. "That guy's a killer," he said. "You were selling him dope you stole?"

"Maybe I don't feel good about it."

"My leg hurts. I don't want to listen to this no more."

"I want to go to California and get clean and start over. Give me one of the eggs. I got the information you want."

Danny Boy looked at the attendant for a long time, his eyes going dull with fatigue. "My duffel bag is on the floor."

"You're doing the right thing, man. But I got to ask you something. Why you want to help this guy Barnum?"

" 'Cause I got to make up for something."

"Like what?"

"I was there when Barnum escaped from some killers. I saw the killers torture a man to death."

"For real?"

"Where's Noie Barnum?"

"I don't know the exact place, but when I gave the man in the desert the medical supplies, he looked at the north and said, 'It's fixing to rain snakes and frogs up yonder.' I go, 'Where up yonder?' He says, 'In the Glass Mountains. You ought to come up there and stand in front of a gully washer. It'd flat hydrate all that dope out of your system, make a man out of you.' " The attendant looked into space. "He's got a special way of making people feel small."

Danny Boy didn't reply.

"He made you feel the same way, didn't he?" the attendant said.

"Not no more he cain't," Danny Boy said.

It rained that night. To the south, a tropical storm had blown ashore on the Mexican coast, and the air smelled as dense and cool and laden with salt as seawater, almost as if a great displaced ocean lay just beyond the hills that ringed the town. Before Hackberry Holland and Pam Tibbs arrived at the hospital to interview Danny Boy, a bolt of lightning knocked out the power all over the county.

Flashes of white electricity flickered inside the clouds, and Hackberry thought he could smell tropical flowers and dried kelp in the wind and gas inside the trees on the hospital lawn. He was sure these were the musings of a self-absorbed old man, one who could not stop thinking about the past and the ephemerality of his life.

He and Pam Tibbs interviewed Danny Boy before he went into surgery, then tried unsuccessfully to find the ambulance attendant. Hackberry and Pam and their deputies and the surgeons and the other hospital personnel all did their jobs throughout the power outage, not thinking, just doing, never taking the time to wonder if any of it mattered or not. You did your job and you let the score take care of itself. How many times a day did Hackberry offer that same tired workhorse counsel to himself? Was that how one ended his days? Probably, he thought. No, there was no "probably" about it. If you thought about mortality in any other fashion, you'd go insane or put a gun in your mouth.

After the power came back on, he and Pam drove two blocks to a café on the courthouse square and had coffee and a piece of pie. Through the window, Hackberry could see the trees on the courthouse lawn and the mist blowing across the lawn and the streetlights shining on a bronze statue of a World War I doughboy, his '03 Springfield gripped in one hand, his other hand raised above his head as though he were rallying his comrades.

"You look tired," Pam said.

"You mean I look old."

"No, I don't mean that at all."

"I'm fine. I've never been better."

"Pray that liars aren't kept a long time in purgatory."

"Pam, you should have been a low-overhead dentist, someone who does fillings and extractions without the extra cost of Novocain."

She gazed out the window at the rain and at the drops of water beaded on the glass. Her eyelashes were reddish brown against the glow of the streetlamp; a wet strand of hair curved against her cheek. He couldn't tell if she was thinking about the two of them or all the events of the past few days. She seemed to read his thoughts. "Why does a mass killer make himself vulnerable to arrest by buying stolen medicine from a junkie in order to take care of a stranger?" she said.

"That's what every one of them does."

"Every one of who does what?" she said.

"All sociopaths. They do good deeds as a tribute to their own power and to convince others they're like the rest of us."

"You don't think Collins has any feelings about Noie Barnum?"

"I think the only genuine emotion he's capable of is self-pity."

"I don't like to see you bitter."

He placed his fork on the side of his plate and poured cream from a small pitcher on top of his half-eaten wedge of blueberry pie. He picked up his fork and then hesitated and set it down again. "By the seventh-inning stretch, this is what you learn. Evil people are different from the rest of us. Redneck cops, Klansmen, predators who rape and murder children, ChiCom prison guards, and messianic head cases like Jack Collins, all of them want us to think they're complex or they're patriots or they're ideologues. But the simple truth is, they do what they do because it makes them feel good."

"Would you have put that broken pool cue down that bartender's throat?"

"The bartender thought so. That's all that counts."

"Don't stop being who you are because of these guys. You've always said it yourself: Don't give them that kind of power."

Hackberry stared out the window at the electricity trembling on the tree above the bronze figure of the doughboy. The statue's head was turned slightly to one side, the mouth open, as though the doughboy were yelling an encouraging word over his shoulder to those following him across no-man's-land. Did they know what awaited them? Did they know the Maxim machine guns that would turn them into chaff were the creation of a British inventor?

Hackberry wondered who had erected the monument. He wanted to call them idiots or flag-wavers or members of the unteachable herd. But words such as those were as inaccurate as they were jaundiced and hateful, he thought. In our impotence to rescind all the decisions that led to war, we erected monuments to assuage the wandering spirits whose lives had been stolen, and to somehow compensate the family members whose loss they would carry to the grave. Who were the greater victims? Those who gave their lives or those who made the war?

He said none of these things and instead watched a man in a wilted hat park his car in front of the café and come inside.

"Ethan Riser is here," Hackberry said. "There's something I didn't tell you about him. He found out recently he has terminal cancer. No matter what he says tonight, he gets a free pass."

"Why didn't you tell me?"

"I don't think he wants other people to know. He's one of those guys who never shows his hole card, even when the game is over."

She pinched her eyes with her thumb and index finger, then widened them, the lines in her face flattening. "I'm not to be trusted?" she said.

"Don't do that."

"You treat me like I'm some kind of burden

you have to put up with, someone you have to instruct regarding decent behavior."

"Come on, Pam, stop it."

"You have no sense at all of the pain your words cause, particularly to someone who cares about you. Goddammit, Hack."

He let out his breath and tried to keep his face empty when he waved at Ethan Riser.

"Just go fuck yourself," she said.

"Did I walk in on anything?" Ethan said, not looking directly at either one of them, his smile awkward.

"How you doin'?" Hackberry said.

"Pretty good. Can I join you?"

"Yes, sir," Hackberry said.

"You sure?"

"Sit down, Ethan," Hackberry said, moving over, not looking at Pam.

"Lorca is out of surgery," Riser said. "It's nice to see you, Chief Deputy."

"You, too," Pam replied.

"Lorca told me about the ambulance attendant and the possibility of Jack Collins and Noie Barnum being in the Glass Mountains. I have the feeling you might be headed up there, Sheriff."

"I can't say I've given it any thought," Hackberry replied.

"I have trouble believing that," Riser said. "This time out, you and Chief Deputy Tibbs need to stay in your own bailiwick. I can't order you to do that, but I can ask you."

"Whatever we decide to do, we'll coordinate with the Bureau," Hackberry said.

"Ever hear how Pretty Boy Floyd died?"

"Shot down while running from some federal agents on a farm in Ohio?"

"Something like that. Except there's an unofficial account to the effect that he didn't die right away. He was wounded and lying on his back when the agents got to him. One agent asked him if he was Pretty Boy Floyd. Floyd answered, 'I'm Charles Arthur Floyd.' Then somebody gave the order to finish him off, and that's what they did."

"Why are you telling us this?" Hackberry said.

"It makes for a good story, that's all."

"It's not your style."

"Probably not," Riser said. "I'd sure like some of that pie."

"Ethan, did you hear me? That's not your style."

"I'm all talk. You know that. Miss, could I have a piece of that blueberry pie with some ice cream on it and a cup of coffee?"

"It's on us," Pam said.

"I appreciate it."

"Listen to Hack, Agent Riser."

"Of course."

The waitress brought the pie and ice cream and coffee, and Pam and Hackberry watched Ethan Riser eat. They also watched the way his eyes crinkled and the way his gaze seemed to probe the darkness outside the window, and each sensed in the other the embarrassment they felt while they watched a brave man try to mask the fact that he was under a death sentence.

"This area has never been quite real to me," Riser said. "It's a place where nothing is what it seems. A piece of moonscape where improbable people live and lunatics can hide in plain sight."

"All empires have their dustbins," Hackberry said. "It's the place we bury our sins."

"That's too deep for me."

"What do I know?" Hackberry said.

"A lot more than the Bureau wants to concede," Riser said. "They consider you a pain in the ass. Stay out of the Glass Mountains, my friend."

Pam drove Hackberry home in the rain. The fields were sodden on either side of the road, the sky black, the long lines of cedar fence posts and barbed wire glistening in the cruiser's headlights. "He's going to cool out Collins?" she said.

"I think that was all rhetoric. He's angry because he has to die. Ethan's a straight arrow. People like him make a pact with themselves and never violate it."

"I told you to go fuck yourself earlier."

"Forget it."

"No, I meant it. I just shouldn't have put it

that way."

"I see."

"Do you?"

"I'm old, Pam. You think it's honorable for an old man to take advantage of a young woman's affections? You want to become romantically involved with a man who would use a young and attractive woman, knowing eventually he would be a burden to her?"

"I think age doesn't have crap to do with any of it. With you, it's all about pride. You've never forgiven yourself for the mistakes of your youth, so you have to create a standard that's superior to everyone else's. It's not a lot different from the bad guys who are always trying to convince themselves of their own humanity."

"That's a rotten thing to say."

"Too bad."

He could feel his left temple throbbing again, and he knew that in the next few seconds, a sliver of pain as cold and hard as a stalactite would slide through his eye and the muscles of his left cheek. Up ahead, he saw his house suddenly illuminated by a bolt of lightning that struck in the trees behind his office, the same trees where Jack Collins had hidden and trained a laser sight on him. "You don't have to pull into the drive. Just drop me on the road," he said.

"You like walking in an electric storm?"

"In this case, I do."

"Too bad again," she said.

She drove across a wood bridge that spanned a creek running high with rainwater, the wild roses along the bank trailing in the current; then she turned in to his driveway and stopped at the picket fence that enclosed the front yard. "You think I'm unfair?" she said.

"I don't think anything," he said, getting out of the cruiser.

"There's an umbrella in the backseat."

"I've got my hat," he said, closing the passenger door.

She reached into the backseat and gathered up the umbrella and stepped out into the rain. She tried to pop it open, but the catch was jammed.

"Get back in the cruiser," he said.

But she didn't. She followed him up the flagstones to the gallery. She was wearing a department-issue campaign hat, and the rain was beating on the crown and the brim, rolling in rivulets down her shoulders and shirtfront. "I think I should resign, Hack. I think I should go back to Houston," she said.

"That's not going to happen."

"Who the hell are you to tell me anything?"

"I'm your boss, that's who."

"I can't tell you how bad you piss me off."

He walked back down the flagstones and took the umbrella from her hand and popped it open above both their heads. He could hear the rain thudding as hard as marbles on the nylon. "You're the most stubborn woman I have ever met. Why do you act like this?"

"Why do you think?"

"Come in."

"For what?"

"Just come in."

He put his arm over her shoulders and walked her up the steps and unlocked the door and held it open for her. The living room was unlit and smelled of the couch and the carpet and the drapes and the wallpaper and the polished hardwood floors; it smelled like a home; it smelled like a fine place to be while lightning flashed on the hillsides and the wind and rain blew against the window-panes and whipped an unfastened door on the barn and bent the trees and scattered the lawn with leaves and broken flowers. He dropped the umbrella on the rug and touched her face with his fingers, and in seconds felt her against him, her feet standing on top of his boots, her loins and breasts tight against his body, her hair wet against his cheek, her arms clenched around his back, all his personal resolve and his concerns about age and mortality and honor draining like water through the bottom of a paper bag.

"Oh, Hack," she said. "Oh, Hack, Hack, Hack."

From his deck Cody Daniels watched the

storm move out of the south and seal the sky, trapping the light between a blue-black layer of clouds and the desert floor and mesas that were pink and talc-colored and that made him think of pictures of ancient Phoenician ships he had seen. When the power outage spread across the county, he saw the reflected glow of the town flatten against the clouds and die, a surge of cool air rising from the valley floor into his face. Hailstones clattered on the hardpan and on the deck, dancing in a white haze, and in the smell of ozone and the drop of temperature, he felt as though the world were fresh and clean, as though every bad memory of his life were being washed away, every failure and personal affliction slipping over the edges of the earth.

If only things were that easy.

Cody started up his gas-powered generator and went back in the house to resume the most difficult task in his life — writing a letter to the FBI. He had attempted a half-dozen versions on his computer and had been unhappy with all of them. His language was either stilted and sounded self-serving, or it became so confused it was almost unintelligible. The last attempt was two double-spaced pages long and gave details about his recruitment into a small group of anti-abortion activists in northern Virginia. It wasn't a bad statement, except it indiscriminately included the names of his fellow travelers, some of whom may have been unaware of the group's ultimate goal.

He had gone out on the deck without saving the letter on his hard drive, and the power outage had wiped his screen clean. When he reentered the house, the lights burning dimly on the low wattage produced by his generator, he sat down at his desk and picked up a felt-tip pen and addressed an envelope to the Federal Bureau of Investigation in Washington, D.C., no zip code. He put his return address in the upper-left-hand corner of the envelope. Then he wrote the following letter on a yellow legal pad:

Dear Sirs,

I am the pitiful son of a bitch who bought the oven timer for the bomb that blew up the abortion clinic outside Baltimore three years back. I thought the bomb would go off in the middle of the night. But that doesn't help the woman who got her face blown off. I can't give you the names of any of the other people involved. This letter is about the evil deed done by one son of a bitch and one son of a bitch only, and as I have stated, that son of a bitch is yours truly,

Sincerely,
Rev. Cody Daniels

From outside, he heard the hiss of air

brakes and the sound of a tractor-trailer shifting down. He looked through the window and, in the rain-streaked fading of the twilight, saw an eighteen-wheeler parked by the Cowboy Chapel, its high beams on, the engine still hammering, and what appeared to be a lead car parked in front of it. Cody had seen the lead car before, without the clamped-on brace of yellow lights on the roof; it belonged to a musician, a man who stopped by on occasion at the Cowboy Chapel and drank coffee and ate doughnuts in the hospitality room Cody left open for truckers or travelers on their way to the Big Bend country.

Cody draped a slicker over his head and went down the wood steps to the coffee room in the back of the chapel. "Getting out of the storm?" he said to a small tight-bodied man sitting at the long table in the middle of the room, a chrome-plated guitar across his thighs.

"Hey, Reverend, I didn't see you, so I just come inside," the man said. "Hope you don't mind."

"That's what it's for. The name is Rector, isn't it?"

"Dennis Rector, that's me," the man replied. "I saw your nail gun there. You've been doing some carpentering."

"You play a Dobro?"

"You know your instruments. That's what it

is, resonator and all." The small man had the dark skin of a field hand and hair that looked like it had been cut with fingernail clippers. He wore lace-up boots and a tie-dyed T-shirt and denim work pants. His upper torso was bent like a question mark. "It's a Fender, built on the old National model. It feels like a Coca-Cola box packed with ice hanging from your neck."

Dennis Rector ran a steel bar up and down the neck of the Dobro and began playing a tune with the steel picks on the thumb and index and middle fingers of his right hand. "Recognize that piece? That's 'The Great Speckled Bird.' Same tune as 'The Wild Side of Life.' Same tune as 'It Wasn't God Who Made Honky-Tonk Angels.'"

Through the window, Cody could see two men sitting in the cab of the eighteen-wheeler. "What are y'all carrying?" he asked.

"Exotic animals. Want one?"

"You work for a zoo?"

"I guess you could call it that." Dennis Rector was smiling as though he possessed private knowledge that he might or might not share. "We supply a wild-game ranch up in Pecos County."

Cody nodded and didn't reply.

"You're not keen on them kind of places?"

"Live and let live."

"That's the way I figure it. Their misfortune and none of my own. You know you got some beaners parked down yonder on your road?"

"Pardon?"

"Some pepper-bellies in a beat-up old car with a busted headlight."

"Who are they?"

"Maybe a couple of people fucking. How should I know? I couldn't see them that good." The small man was still smiling.

"This is a church house, even if it's just the coffee room," Cody said.

"Sorry."

"Did you catch the tag?"

"I wasn't paying them much mind. They looked away from our lights when we passed. That's why I figure they were people making out. Mexicans tend to breed in the spring and domino in the winter."

Cody studied Dennis Rector from behind his eyelashes. "You from here'bouts?"

"Wherever I hang my hat. Jobs are kind of thin these days. Seems like there's less and less work for a white man. What's your feeling about that?"

"I never lost a job 'cause of my skin color."

"That sounds different from a couple of your sermons."

"Could I he'p y'all with something?"

"No, I just wanted to show my friends your church and get out of the storm."

Cody nodded again, looking out the door at the truck and the animals he could see behind the ventilation slots in the sides. "You mind locking up when you leave? I've got some work to do in the house."

The small man filled his mouth with a jelly doughnut, pushing the overflow back into his mouth with his wrist. His chrome-plated instrument swam with an oily blue light. "No problem, Reverend," he said.

Cody walked back up the stairs and across his deck into the house, forcing himself not to look back over his shoulder. He felt a sense of ill ease that he couldn't define. Was it the rawness of Dennis Rector's language? Or the fact that Cody had helped encourage the role of victim in many of his congregants? Or did he see a reflection of his former self in the lewdness of mind that characterized men like Rector? Why was a man like that playing "The Great Speckled Bird," a spiritual that was as deep-seated in southern religion as "The Old Rugged Cross"? Something wasn't a right fit.

There was also the business about the Hispanics parked on the road. He should have pumped Rector about them. Could the car have contained Krill and Negrito? It couldn't be them, could it? They were professional criminals, hunted by the local sheriff and the FBI and probably the Texas Rangers. Why would Krill and Negrito invest their lives in persecuting Cody Daniels, a mail-order minister who was awakened at two each morning by a blind woman with a disfigured face rattling his bedroom windows?

Just as the power went back on, Cody saw the eighteen-wheeler turn in a wide circle, led by Dennis Rector's car, and head south down the road, the edges of the trailer etched with chains of gold running lights. He folded the confessional letter he had written to the FBI and placed it in the envelope and licked the seal, his stomach churning, his head as light as a helium balloon. Then he sat at his desk, his head in his hands, and wondered how he had made such a catastrophe out of his life.

The wind was swirling out of the desert, the rain driving hard on the roof, dancing on the handrails of his deck, blowing in the blue-white radiance of the neon cross he had mounted above the entrance to the Cowboy Chapel. Maybe it was time to pile a few belongings into the cab of his truck, drop his letter to the FBI in a mailbox, and disappear inside the vast anonymity of the American West.

He could sell his truck in California and pick fruit in the San Joaquin, harvest beets up in Oregon and Washington, maybe lumberjack in Montana or get on a fishing boat in Alaska. If the law caught up with him, fine. If it didn't, that would be fine, too. Why not just roll the dice and stay out of the consequences? In the United States a person could get a new identity and start a new life as easily as acquiring a library card. He had to wonder at the irony of it all. In his fantasy, he was joining the ranks of the migrant workers he had railed against.

He went into his bedroom and began stuffing the clothes from his dresser and closet into a duffel bag. That was when he felt the air decompress around him and the cold smell of rain surge through the house, the joists and wood floors creaking as the temperature dropped inside. He turned around and stared into the faces of two men whose hats were wilted on their heads, their brown skin shiny with water, their clothes smelling like horses and wood smoke and sweat that had dried inside flannel.

"Why won't y'all leave me alone?" Cody said.

"You know," Krill said.

"I don't know anything."

"Yes, you know. Do not pretend you don't know. Do not make an insignificance of my children."

"I'm worthless as a minister. I'm no different from you. I he'ped put together a bomb that was used on an abortion clinic. I ruined a woman's life. I'm not worth shooting."

Krill was already shaking his head, indicating Cody's wishes had little to do with what was about to occur. Negrito was smiling broadly. "We told you we'd be back, man. But you don't listen," he said. "You got anything to eat? I'm really hungry. What was that about a bombing?"

"You got a hearing defect?" Cody said.

"End this silly talk and come with me," Krill said.

"Where?"

"Out into the rain, *hombre*."

"I'm no count as a pastor, no count as a man. That's not humility talking, either. It's the truth."

"*Venga conmigo.* Now. No more talking."

"You don't have to point a gun at me. I'm plumb worn out with people pointing guns at me."

"It's necessary, *hombre.* Your ears are wood, your thinking processes like cane syrup. It is clear you're of low intelligence."

"You want to hold a gun on me? Here, I'll he'p you."

"Let go of my wrist."

"Put one through my heart. I'm tired of y'all pestering me."

"Show him," Negrito said.

"Don't underestimate me," Krill said to Cody. "I have taken many lives. I have machine-gunned a priest."

"Then pull the trigger," Cody said.

Cody's hand remained clenched tightly on Krill's wrist. He could feel Krill's pulse beating against his palm. Krill's eyes were inches from his, the onions and wine and fried meat on Krill's breath as damp as a moist cloth on

Cody's face. "Are you going to help me?" Krill asked.

"Maybe, if you put the gun away," Cody said.

Krill's eyes were black and as flat as paint on a piece of cardboard. "It is as you request," he said, lowering his pistol. A curtain of rain slapped against the window and across the top of the church. "My car is parked behind your church."

"Let me put on my coat," Cody said.

"You will not try to deceive us?" Krill said.

"Why should I deceive you?"

"We know of your message to your flock. You have not been our friend. You make them feel comfortable with their hatred of us."

"I think maybe you aim to kill me when this is over."

"Would that be a great loss to the world?"

"Maybe not. But that doesn't mean I'd necessarily enjoy it."

"You are a very funny man," Krill said.

They went out the door and into the rain and down the stairs to the back of the Cowboy Chapel, where Krill's gas-guzzler was parked in the lee of the building. Krill opened the trunk and lifted out a large wood box tied with rope. Cody stared at the box and wiped his mouth. "They're in there?"

"Of course."

"I've always baptized by immersion," Cody said, the rain beating on his bare head.

"What does 'immersion' mean?"

"I take people down by the creek and put them under. If the water is low, I have to dam up the creek. If everything is completely dried out, we go to the river. The creek is probably running pretty good now."

"No, we aren't going to a creek."

"Then come inside," Cody said.

They walked through the lighted coffee room and into the chapel, both of Krill's hands cupped under the rope that bound the box, the weight hitting against his knees and sides. Cody removed his coat and wiped his face on his sleeve. He noticed that Negrito never touched the box, even though it was apparent that Krill was struggling with it. Krill set the box down heavily by the altar and untied the rope and let it snake to the floor.

The only light in the room came from a small stage hung with a blue velvet curtain. The interior of the chapel was immaculate, the pews gleaming, the floors polished. For some reason, as though for the first time, Cody realized what good care he had taken of the building. He had just installed new support beams under the peaked roof, heightening the effect of a cathedral ceiling, and had reframed the windows and painted birds and flowers on the panes. He had built a stage out of freshly planed pine in hopes that next year he could put on an Easter pageant and attract more children to his Bible-study classes. The air around the stage was as sweet-smelling as a green woods in spring, not unlike a deferred promise of better things to come.

"You have a very nice church here," Krill said.

"I'm going to get a pitcher of water out of the coffee room. I'm not gonna call anybody or give y'all any trouble. What I'm doing here might not be right, but I'm gonna do it just the same."

"What do you mean, 'not right'?"

"The papists anoint at death. We baptize at birth."

"These are considerations that are of no importance to me. Go get the water. Do not let me hear you talking on a telephone."

"Don't trust him, *jefe*. He's a capon, the friend of whoever he needs to please at the moment," Negrito said.

"No, our friend here has no fear. He has no reason to lie. Look at his eyes. I think he doesn't want to live. He's a sadder man than even you, Negrito."

"Don't talk of me that way, *jefe*."

"Then don't call others a capon, you who are afraid to touch the box in which my children sleep."

Cody went into the coffee room and filled a small pitcher with tap water. His head was pounding, his breath short, but he didn't know why. Was it just fear? Krill may have been a killer, but he was no threat to him. Krill was totally absorbed with the status of his children in the afterlife. What about Negrito? No, Negrito was not a threat, either, not as long as he was under Krill's control. So what was it that caused Cody's heart to race and the scalp to shrink on his head?

This was the first time he had ever done anything of a serious nature as a minister. And he was doing it at a time when he was about to flee his church and home and become a fugitive, just like the road kid who had forged checks and ended up on a county prison farm. He walked back into the chapel, knocking against a worktable he had fashioned from two planks and sawhorses, spilling a nail gun and a claw hammer to the floor.

Krill had opened the top of the wood box and was standing expectantly beside it, his gaze fixed on Cody. "How do you want to do it?" he asked.

Cody hadn't thought about it. The images that went through his mind were too bizarre to keep straight in his head. He looked into the box and swallowed. "Put them on the edge of the stage," he said.

"They're watching," Krill said.

"They're watching?"

"From limbo. They want to be turned loose. That's what you're going to do."

"Listen, I don't know about those kinds of

things," Cody said. "Don't make me out something I'm not."

"You have cojones, *hombre.* I misjudged you." Krill placed his children, one after another, on the apron of the stage. The oldest child could not have been over four when he died. The younger ones might have been three or two. All three were wrapped tightly in cloth and duct tape. Only their faces were exposed. Their eyes were little more than slits, their skin gray, their tiny cheekbones as pronounced as wire. There was no odor of decomposition. Instead, they smelled like freshly turned dirt in a garden, or like damp shade in woods carpeted with mushrooms.

"What are you waiting for?" Krill said.

"I feel like I'm doing something that's dishonest," Cody said.

"Your words make no sense. They are the words of a man with thorns in his head instead of thoughts."

"Your children are innocent. They never hurt anybody."

"Do not make me lose my patience, *hombre.* Do what you need to do."

Cody poured water from the pitcher on the thumb and the tips of his fingers and made the sign of the cross on each child's forehead. "I baptize these children in the name of the Father, the Son, and the Holy Spirit."

"That's good. I'm proud of you, man," Krill said.

411

"But it's me and these two men who need absolution, Lord. These children didn't commit any sin," Cody said. "I left a woman blinded and maimed for the rest of her life, and the two men standing beside me are covered with blood splatter. We're not worthy to touch the hem of Your garment. We're not worthy to baptize these children, either, particularly the likes of me. But You're probably used to hypocrites offering up their prayers, so I doubt if two or three more liars in Your midst is gonna make a lot of difference in the outcome of things."

"You better shut your mouth, gringo," Negrito said.

"I'm done. I'm sorry for what happened to your children, Krill. If y'all are fixing to kill me, I reckon now is the time."

He walked into the coffee room, his back twitching. Out the window, he could see the deck of his house glimmer in a bolt of lightning, like the bow of an ark sliding out of a black wave. He sat down in a folding chair, his back to the doorway that gave onto the chapel. A phone was on the counter by the sink, and for a moment he thought about picking it up and dialing 911. But what for? If Krill planned to kill him, he would do it before a sheriff's cruiser could arrive. Also, Cody would eventually have to tell the sheriff or one of his deputies about the clinic bombing, and Cody had no intention of going back to jail, or at least no intention to actively aid and abet his own imprisonment.

One minute clicked on the clock mounted on the wall, then two, then three. He heard Krill's and Negrito's boots walking across the chapel floor. He closed his eyes and clasped his hands between his thighs. He could hear his breath rasping in his throat. His fingers were trembling, his sphincter constricting. Then he heard the front door of the chapel swing open and felt a rush of air sweep through the pews. A moment later, he heard the gas-guzzler start up and drive away.

Cody opened his eyes and got up from the chair and began stacking dirty cups and saucers and plates in the sink and wiping down the long table in the center of the room. He had never thought the act of cleaning up a coffee room could be so pleasurable. Why had he spent so much of his life concentrating on every problem in the world rather than simply enjoying the small pleasures that an orderly life provided? Why did wisdom come only when it was too late to make use of it?

He poured a cup of coffee and put a small teaspoon of sugar in it and gazed out the window at the rain blowing off the hills and mesas in the west. Tumbleweed was bouncing as high as a barn, smacking his church, skipping through the yard, embedding under the stairs that led to his deck. A storm was a fine and cleansing thing, he thought, not to be feared or avoided but welcomed as one would a cool finger touching one's brow.

He heard the front door open a second time, and the wind cut through the chapel and blew a stack of hymnal sheets fluttering in the air. He set down his coffee cup but remained seated at the table. "I told y'all we were done," he called into the chapel.

A small, muscular man appeared in the doorway. "Brought some friends with me," Dennis Rector said. "You met them before, but they had masks on. Look, I'm just making a buck. Don't take this as personal."

CHAPTER SIXTEEN

Anton Ling opened the back door of her house to let in her cat and smelled the smoke inside the rain. She looked up into the bluffs and, in the blackness of the storm, saw a fire burning as bright and clean as the red point of flame on an acetylene torch. She dialed 911 and reported the fire, then got into her truck and headed down the dirt road for Cody Daniels's house, a fire extinguisher bouncing on the passenger seat.

Cody Daniels knew his fate was not up for discussion when he saw that the men who had followed Dennis Rector into the chapel had not bothered to mask their faces. What he had not anticipated was the severity of design they were about to impose on his person. They pulled back the velvet curtain on the stage in the chapel and lifted him above their heads, as college kids might at a fraternity celebration, trundling him on their extended arms and hands to the wood cross he had constructed for a passion play that had never become a reality. They were smiling as though Cody were in on the joke, as though it were a harmless affair after which they would all have a drink.

The man actually in charge was not Rector but a diminutive man who spoke in an accent that sounded like Russian. His chin was V-shaped, his teeth the color of fish scale, his nose beaked, his cheeks and neck unshaved, his maroon silk shirt unbuttoned on a chest that looked almost skeletal. He wore three gold chains on his neck and a felt hat cocked jauntily on his head. He had the face of either a goat or a pixie, although the purple feather in his hatband suggested a bit of the satyr as well.

"Have you seen my good friend the Preacher lately?" he asked.

The men had set down Cody on the stage so he could face the man in the cocked hat. "The killer? I saw him once at Miss Ling's house. But I don't know him," Cody said.

"I need to find my friend the Preacher and his companion Noie Barnum. I think Ms. Ling has probably told you where they are."

"No, sir, she didn't do that."

"Why should I believe you?"

"Why shouldn't you? I don't know anything about Barnum. I wish I had never heard of him."

"But you do know Temple Dowling."

416

"I wish I'd never heard of him, either."

"Did you know he was a pedophile?"

"No."

"When you went to work for him, he didn't ask you to find young girls for him?"

"I'm not gonna even talk about stuff like that."

"Before this is over, you'll talk about many things. We have all night."

Cody felt himself swallow. The man with the Russian accent sat down in the front pew and smiled and made a gesture to his men with his right hand. His men picked up the cross that had been propped against the back wall and laid it down on the stage, then spread Cody Daniels on top of it and removed his shoes. Cody had constructed the cross out of railroad ties, and he could smell the musky odor of the creosote and oil and cinders in the grain and feel the great hardness of the wood against his head and back and buttocks and thighs.

They're only going to scare me. They won't do this, a voice inside him said.

Then he heard the *pop* of the nail gun and felt a pain explode through the top and bottom of his foot. He tried to pull himself erect, but a man on either side of him held his arms fast against the cross's horizontal beam. He closed his eyes and then opened them and stared upward into the cathedral ceiling. For the first time in his life, Cody Daniels had a

417

sense of finality from which he knew there was no escape. "I shot over the heads of poor Mexicans coming into the country," he said. "When I was a boy, I made a fifteen-year-old colored girl go to bed with me. I wrote a bad check to some old people who let me charge groceries at their store. I stole a woman's purse in the bus depot in Denver. I took a watch off a drunk man in an alley behind the Midnight Mission in Los Angeles. I almost killed a woman outside Baltimore."

"What is he saying?" said the man with the Russian accent.

"He's sorry he's on the planet," said a man holding one of Cody's arms.

"See what else he has to say," said the man with the Russian accent.

Cody heard the nail gun again and felt his other foot flatten against the vertical shaft of the cross and try to constrict against the nail that had pinioned it to the wood. This time he thought he screamed, but he couldn't be sure, because the voice he heard did not seem like his own. The popping of the nail gun continued, the muzzle working its way along the tops of his feet and his palms and finally the small bones in his wrists. He felt himself being lifted up, the top of the cross thudding against the wall behind him, his weight coming down on the nails, the tendons in his chest crushing the air from his lungs. Through a red haze, he could see the faces of his executioners looking up at him, as though they had been frozen in time or lifted out of an ancient event whose significance had eluded them. He heard himself whispering, his words barely audible, his eyes rolling up into his head.

"What'd he say?" one man asked.

" 'I'm proud my name is on her book,' " another man said.

"What the fuck does that mean?" the first man asked.

"It's from the song 'The Great Speckled Bird,' " Dennis Rector said.

"What is this speckled bird?" asked the man with the Russian accent, standing at the foot of the stage.

"In the song, it's supposed to mean the Bible," Dennis Rector replied.

The man with the Russian accent gazed through the side window at the rain striking the glass.

"What do you want us to do, Mr. Sholokoff?" Rector asked.

"Is he alive?"

"I think he is."

"You think?" Sholokoff said.

"Just tell me what you'd like me to do, sir," Rector said.

"Do I have to write it down?"

"No, sir."

"Don't come into this county again."

"I come through here to deliver the animals

to your game ranches."

"You need to take a vacation, Dennis. Maybe go out into the desert for a while. Here, I have some money for you. I'll call you when it's time to come back to work."

Sholokoff began walking down the aisle toward the front of the church.

"I did what you wanted," Rector said. "You shouldn't treat me like this. I ain't somebody you can just use and throw away."

Sholokoff continued out the front of the church into the night without replying or looking back. Dennis Rector pinched his mouth with his hand and stared at Cody Daniels and the blood running from his feet and hands and wrists and down his forearms. He stuck Sholokoff's wad of bills into his jeans. "I'm gonna get the gas can out of my car," he said. "Did you guys hear me? Don't just stand there. Take care of business."

None of the other men spoke or would look directly at him.

A local rancher flying over the church saw the flames burst through the roof of the Cowboy Chapel and reported the fire before Anton Ling did. By the time she had headed up the road to the church, the volunteer fire department truck and Pam Tibbs and Hackberry Holland and another cruiser driven by R. C. Bevins were right behind her.

"Jesus Christ, look at it," Pam said.

The building was etched with flames that seemed to have gone up all four walls almost simultaneously and had been fed by cold air blowing through all the windows, which probably had been systematically smashed out. The fire had gathered under the ceiling and punched a hole through the roof that was now streaming sparks and curds of black smoke into the wind.

"Somebody used an accelerant," Hackberry said.

"You think it's the same guys who broke into Anton Ling's house?"

"Or Temple Dowling's people."

"You believe in karma? I mean for a guy like Cody Daniels."

"You mean is this happening to him because he was mixed up in the bombing of an abortion clinic? No, I don't believe in karma, at least not that kind."

"I thought maybe you did," Pam said.

"Who gets the rougher deal in life? Beggars on the streets of Calcutta or international-arms merchants?"

Pam's attention was no longer focused on their conversation. "Hack, Anton Ling is getting out of her truck with a fire extinguisher."

Hackberry saw Anton Ling run from her truck directly through the front door of the church, a ropy cloud of blue-black smoke funneling from under the top of the door-frame. Pam braked the cruiser behind the

421

pickup, and she and Hackberry and R. C. Bevins and two volunteer firemen ran up the steps behind Anton Ling.

When Hackberry went inside the church, the intensity of the heat was like someone kicking open the door on a blast furnace. The walls were blackening and starting to buckle where they were not already burning, the sap in the cathedral beams igniting and dripping in flaming beads onto the pews below. Hackberry could hardly breathe in the smoke. Anton Ling went down the main aisle toward the stage, the fire extinguisher raised in front of her. Through the smoke, Hackberry could see a man crucified on a large wooden cross at the rear of the stage, his face and skin and bloodied feet lit by stage curtains that had turned into candles.

Hackberry caught up with Anton Ling, his arm raised in front of his face to protect his eyes from the heat. "Give it to me," he said.

"Take your hand off me," she said.

"Your dress is on fire, for God's sake," he said.

He tore the fire extinguisher from her hands and pulled the pin from the release lever and sprayed foam on her clothing. Then he mounted the stairs at the foot of the stage, the heat blistering his skin and cooking his head even though he was wearing his Stetson. He sprayed the area around the man on the cross while the volunteer firemen, all of them wearing ventilators, sprayed the walls with their backpacks and other firemen pulling a hose came through the front door and horse-tailed the ceiling with a pressurized jet of water pumped from the truck.

"Let's get the cross down on the stage and carry it through the door," Hackberry said. "He's going to die in this smoke."

But when Hackberry grabbed the shaft of the cross, he recoiled from the heat in the wood.

"Sheriff?" R.C. said.

"What?"

"He's gone."

"No, the wounds aren't mortal."

"Look above his rib cage. Somebody wanted to make sure he was dead. Somebody shot nails into his heart," R.C. said.

The flashlights of the firemen jittered and cut angles through the darkness and smoke, the rain spinning down through the hole in the ceiling. "Nobody from around here could do something like this," one of the firemen said.

"Not a chance, huh?" Hackberry said.

"No, this kind of thing don't happen here," the fireman said. "It took somebody doped out of his mind to do this. Like some of those smugglers coming through Miss Ling's place every night."

"Shut up," Anton Ling said.

"If they didn't do it, who did? 'Cause it

wasn't nobody from around here," the fireman said.

"Give us a hand on this, bud. We need to get Reverend Daniels off these nails and onto a gurney. You with me on that?" Hackberry said to the fireman.

Outside, fifteen minutes later, Hackberry watched two paramedics zip a black body bag over Cody Daniels's face. The coroner, Darl Wingate, was standing two feet away. The rain had almost quit, and Darl was smoking a cigarette in a holder, his face thoughtful, his smoke mixing in the mist blowing up from the valley.

"How do you read it?" Hackberry said.

"If it's any consolation, the victim was probably dead when the nails were fired into his rib cage. Death probably occurred from cardiac arrest. The main reason crucifixion was practiced throughout the ancient world was that it was not only painful and humiliating but the tendons would tighten across the lungs and slowly asphyxiate the victim. The only way he could prolong his life was to lift himself on the nails that had been driven through his feet or ankles. Of course, this caused him to increase his own torment a hundredfold. It would be hard to invent a more agonizing death."

"I'd like to believe this poor devil didn't go through all that, that he died early," Hackberry said.

"Maybe that's the way it went down, Hack," Darl said, his eyes averted. "Did you know I got a degree in psychology before I went to med school?"

"No, I didn't."

"I wanted to be a forensic psychologist. Know why I went into medicine instead?"

"No, I don't," Hackberry said, his attention starting to wander.

"Because I don't like to put myself into the minds of people who do things like this. I don't believe this was done by a group. I think it was ordered by one guy and a bunch of other guys did what they were told," Darl said.

"Go on."

"The guy behind this feels compelled to smear his shit on a wall."

"Are you thinking about Krill?"

"No. The perp on this one has a hard-on about religion."

"How about Temple Dowling?"

"Stop it. You don't believe that yourself."

"Why not?"

"Dowling is inside the system. He's not a criminal."

"That's what you think."

"No, the problem is the way *you* think, Hack. You'd rather turn the key on a slumlord than a guy who boosts banks. You've also got a grudge against Dowling's father."

"Say that again about religion."

"I have to give you an audiovisual presentation? We're talking about a murder inside a church, on a cross. It was done by a believer."

"A believer?"

"Yeah, and he's really pissed."

"How about Jack Collins?"

"Collins is a messianic killer, not a sadist."

"You should have been a cop, Darl."

"That's what I did in the army. It sucked then and sucks now."

"Why?"

"Because arresting these bastards is a waste of time," Darl said.

Hackberry walked toward his cruiser, where Pam and R.C. were waiting. The hair was singed on the backs of his arms, and the side of his face was streaked with soot. The churchyard was filled with emergency vehicles, the red and blue and white flashers pulsing in the mist.

"Wrap it up here," he said to Pam.

"You tried to save him, Hack. When you went inside, you didn't know if the roof was coming down or not," she said.

"Call Ethan Riser."

"Riser is no help," she said.

"She's right, Sheriff. Them FBI people wouldn't take time to spit in our mouths if we were dying of thirst," R.C. said.

Hackberry opened his cell phone and found Riser's number and punched it in, then walked off into the darkness and waited for the call to go to voice mail. Surprisingly, the agent picked up.

"Ethan?" Hack said.

"Yeah, who'd you expect?"

Hackberry told him what had happened. "I need everything you can get me on Josef Sholokoff. I need it by noon tomorrow."

"Can't do it, partner."

"Cut this crap out, Ethan. I'm not going to put up with it."

"There're probably fifty agents in half a dozen agencies trying to shut down this guy. If you screw things up for the government, they're going to drop a brick shithouse on your head."

"Where are you?"

"In the Glass Mountains."

"Who's with you?"

"A friend or two."

"I think you're trying to take on Collins by yourself."

"Collins is long overdue for retirement."

"You don't know him. I do. Let me help you."

"I wish you'd been with me when we had bin Laden's family on the tarmac. But this one is all mine," Riser said.

"That's a dumb way to think."

"Did you ever hear of this black boxer who went up against an Australian who was called 'the thinking man's fighter'? The black guy scrambled his eggs. When a newsman asked how he did it, the black guy said, 'While he was thinking, I was hitting him.' "

"Don't hang up."

"See you around, Hack. I've been wrong about almost everything in my life. Don't make my mistakes."

Early the next morning, as Jack Collins listened to Noie Barnum talk at the breakfast table in the back of the cabin, he wondered if Noie suffered from a thinking disorder.

"So repeat that for me, will you? You met the hikers on the trail and you did what?" Jack said.

"I wanted to try out that walking cane you gave me, and I made it down the hill just fine and along the edge of the creek out to the cottonwoods on the flat. That's when my breath gave out and I had to sit down on a big rock and I saw the hikers. They were a very nice couple."

"I expect they were. But what was that about the Instamatic?"

"At least I think it was an Instamatic. It was one of those cheap cameras tourists buy. They said they belonged to a bird-watching club and were taking pictures of birds along the hiking trail. They asked me to take a snapshot of them in front of the cottonwoods. It was right at sunset, and the wind was blowing and the leaves were flying in the air, and the sky was red all the way across the horizon.

So I snapped a shot, and then they asked if they could take my picture, too."

"But you've left something out of the repeat, Noie."

"What's that?"

"The first time around, you mentioned this fellow's line of work."

"He said he was a Parks and Wildlife man. He didn't look to be over twenty-five, though. He said he and his wife were on their honeymoon. She had this warm glow in her face. They put me in mind of some folks I know back home."

"And where do they live?"

"He said Austin. I think. Yeah, that was it. Austin."

"Austin. That's interesting."

Jack got up from the table and lifted a coffeepot off the woodstove with a dishrag and poured into his cup. The coffee was scalding, but he drank it without noticing the heat, his eyes fastened on Noie. "You like those eggs and sausage?"

"You know how to cook them," Noie replied. "What my grandmother would call 'gooder than grits.' "

"You're a card, Noie. So this fellow was from a law enforcement agency?"

"I don't know if I'd call Parks and Wildlife that."

"And he lives in the state capital?"

"Yep, that's what he said."

"And you let him take your photograph? Does that come right close to it?"

Noie seemed to reflect upon Jack's question. "Yeah, I'd say that was pretty much it."

In the early-morning shadows, Noie's nose made Jack think of a banana lying in an empty gravy bowl. His long-sleeve plaid shirt was buttoned at the collar, even though it was too tight for him, and his suspenders were notched into the knobs of his shoulders like a farmer of years ago might have worn them. He was freshly shaved, his sideburns etched, his face happy, but his jug-shaped head and big ears would probably drive the bride of Frankenstein from his bed, Jack thought. Noie preoccupied himself with whittling checker pieces he kept in a shoe box, and he had the conversational talents of a tree stump. Plus, Noie had another problem, one for which there seemed to be no remedy. Even though he bathed every night in an iron tub by the barn, his body constantly gave off an odor similar to sour milk. Jack decided that Noie Barnum was probably the homeliest and most single man he had ever met.

"Did it strike you as unusual that this couple would want to photograph a man they'd known for only a few minutes?"

"My grandmother used to say people who are rank strangers one minute can turn out the next minute to be your best friends."

"Except we're not rank strangers to the law, Noie."

"That brings me to another topic," Noie said. "I know the government wants to get their hands on me, but for the life of me, I can't figure why you're running from them."

"You've got it turned around, pard. I stay to myself and go my own way. If people bear me malice, I let them find me. Then we straighten things out."

"I bet you give them a piece of your mind, too."

"You could call it that."

"You ever take your guitar out and play it?"

"My guitar?"

"You keep the case under your bed, but you never take your guitar out and play it."

"It sounds like it was tuned to a snare drum. That's because I tuned it."

Noie's expression had turned melancholy. He set down his fork and studied his plate. "That couple I met on the trail don't mean us any harm, Jack. Particularly toward a fellow like you. I don't know why you choose to be a hermit, but you're the kindest man I've ever known, and I've known some mighty good ones."

"I believe you have, Noie."

"I worry about you because I think you're bothered about something in your past, something you probably shouldn't be fretting yourself about."

Through the back window, Jack could see the rain from last night's storm still dripping off the barn roof and dew shining on the windmill and steam rising off the horse tank. The blueness of the morning was so perfect, he didn't want to see the sunlight break over the hill. "We've got us a fine spot here," he said. "Sometimes if you listen, you can hear the earth stop, like it's waiting for you to catch up with it. Like it's your friend and it wants you to be at peace with it. That's why I live alone and go my own way. If you don't have any truck with the rest of the world, it cain't mess you up."

Noie seemed to study the content of Jack's words, then he stared at his plate again and put his arms below the table. "I got blood on my hands," he said.

"From what?"

"Those Predator drones."

"It's not your doing."

"Those things have killed innocent people, Stone Age peasants who don't have any stake in our wars."

"That's just the way it is sometimes."

"My grandmother used to say there're two kinds of men never to associate with. One is the man who'll shed the blood of the innocent, and the other is a man who'll raise his hand to a woman. She always said they're cut out of the same cloth. They're of Cain's seed, not Abel's." Noie picked up his fork and waited for Jack to speak. Then he said, "Go ahead."

"Go ahead what?" Jack asked.

"You looked like you were fixing to say something."

"If you see that Parks and Wildlife guy again, don't be in a hurry to have your picture taken," Jack said.

"Where you headed?" Noie asked.

"I thought I might tune my guitar. I'll be up yonder in the rocks."

"Why are you taking your binoculars?"

"After a storm, there're all kinds of critters walking around, armadillos and lizards and such. They're a sight to watch."

That same morning Anton Ling received the most bizarre phone call of her life. "This is Special Agent Riser, Ms. Ling," the voice said. "You remember me?"

"I'm not sure," she replied. "You're with the FBI?"

"I was the supervising agent who talked to you after your home was invaded."

"I'd like to believe you're calling to tell me you have someone in custody."

"You don't think much of us, do you?"

"No, I don't."

"I don't blame you. I want to tell you a couple of things, Ms. Ling. We have a file on you that's three inches thick. I've tapped your phones and photographed you from a distance and looked with binoculars through your windows and invaded every other imaginable aspect of your privacy. Some of my colleagues have a genuine dislike of you and think you should have been deported years ago. The irony is you worked for the CIA before a lot of them were born. But my issue is not with them, it's with myself.

"I want to apologize for the way I and my colleagues have treated you. I think you're a patriot and a humanitarian, and I wish there were a million more like you in our midst. I think Josef Sholokoff was behind the invasion of your home. I also think we've failed miserably in putting his kind away. In the meantime, we've often concentrated our efforts on giving a bad time to people such as yourself."

"Maybe you're too hard on yourself, Mr. Riser."

"One other thing: Be a friend to Sheriff Holland. He's a lot like you, Ms. Ling. He doesn't watch out for himself."

"Sir, are you all right?"

"You might hear from me down the track. If you do, that'll mean I'm doing just fine," Riser said.

Ethan Riser closed his cell phone and continued up a deer trail that wound along the base of a butte with the soft pink contours of a decayed tooth. He passed the rusted shell of an automobile that was pocked with small-

434

caliber bullet holes and beside which turkey buzzards were feeding on the carcass of a calf. The calf's ribs were exposed and its eyes pecked out, its tongue extended like a strip of leather from the side of its mouth. The air was still cool from the storm, the scrub brush and mesquite a darker green in the shadow of the butte, the imprints of claw-footed animals fresh in the damp sand along the banks of a tiny stream. Ethan was sweating inside his clothes, his breath coming short in his chest, and he had to sit down on a rock and rest. Behind him was a young man dressed in pressed jeans and a white shirt with pockets all over it and canvas lug-soled shoes. He wore an unpretentious black-banded straw hat with the brim turned down and a western belt with a big, dull-colored metal buckle that fit flat against his stomach.

When the young man reached the rock where Ethan was sitting, he unslung a canteen from his shoulder and unscrewed the cap and offered Ethan a drink before drinking himself. "I got to be honest with you. I think this is a snipe hunt," he said.

"Hard to say," Ethan said, blotting his face with a handkerchief.

"That fellow was standing in the shade and wearing a hat when I took his picture. He could be anybody."

"That's why I want you to go back now. I've wasted enough of your time."

"You shouldn't be out here by yourself."

"It beats twiddling my thumbs in a motel."

"Let me treat you to lunch."

"What's farther up?"

"Jackrabbits and open space and some more hills. A game ranch or two, maybe one guy running cows. A gun club has a couple of leases where some oil-and-natural-gas guys bust skeet and drink whiskey. I think there might be a cabin that somebody uses during deer season."

"Who might that be?"

"Not somebody anyone ever paid much mind to. Ethan, you don't look well. Let's go back."

"I got no reason to. You're the one on his honeymoon."

"I shouldn't have ever told you about that fellow we ran into. On the homely scale, he was just this side of a mud fence. About as harmless-looking, too. If this guy is a threat to national security, we're all in deep doo-doo."

"You also said he talked like he had a mouthful of molasses. Noie Barnum is from northern Alabama."

"A Quaker from Alabama?"

"I grant you he's a strange duck. But compared to Jack Collins, he's as normal as it gets."

"My folks have always lived here'bouts, and they haven't heard any talk about hermits wandering around with Thompson machine guns."

A single-engine plane passed overhead, its shadow racing across the treetops and boulders on the sunny side of a hill.

"It's a fine day to be out and about, isn't it?" Ethan said.

"I cain't argue that."

"Help me up, will you?"

Ethan Riser's friend remained motionless.

"What are you looking at?" Ethan asked.

"I thought I saw a reflection of some kind up there on that hill." The young man removed a small pair of binoculars from a leather case on his belt and adjusted them to his eyes. "I declare, it's a book."

"A what?"

"Yeah, its pages are fluttering on top of a rock. Cain't anybody say people in Southwest Texas aren't literary. Stop looking at me like that, Ethan. There's nobody there. It's just a book somebody left on a rock."

Preacher Jack Collins was reading in the Book of Kings, the wind and sun on his face, when he glanced up long enough to see the single-engine plane coming out of the southeast, its wings tilting in the updrafts, its engine sputtering as though it were low on gas. He stepped backward into some piñon trees growing out of the rocks, his body motionless, his face pointed at the ground, his thumb inserted as a bookmark in the pages of his Bible. He heard the plane pass overhead, then the engine caught again, and when he climbed to the crest of the hill and looked between two boulders, he saw the plane disappearing over a long stretch of flatland, its wings level and parallel with the horizon.

Feds? Maybe. Probably a rancher who was burning the valves out of his engine with ethanol. Jack resumed reading in his comfortable spot among the rocks, the pages of the Bible as white as snow in the sunlight, the print on them as clear and sharp and defining as the lettering that Yahweh had seared with a burning finger in the Mosaic tablets. For Jack, there was no such thing as "interpretation" of the Scripture; there was also no such thing as "metaphor." These were devices that allowed the profligate and the libertine to consecrate behavior that made Jack's stomach curdle.

Homosexuality? Sodomy? Not exactly. It was a type of behavior that somehow remained nameless. It was more like a memory or the shadow of a person or an event that hid behind a corner on a long street he was forced to walk in his sleep. The street was uniformly gray, as though all the color had been leached out of the concrete and asphalt and stone. There were no people on the sidewalks or in the buildings, and when he crossed an intersection, he hoped to hear a roar of traffic or at least the footsteps of other pedestrians on a side street, but instead, he heard no sound except the pounding of blood in his ears.

In his dream, he would try to wake himself before he reached the last block on the street, but his willpower had no influence on his dream. At the corner of a building on the end of the street, a figure was moving into full view on the sidewalk. The figure wore a hooded workout jacket and a print dress and pink tennis shoes and a sequined belt, as though she had dressed randomly off the rack at a Goodwill store. Everything about her was in some fashion a frightening contradiction. She looked too young and pretty for the damage the world had probably done her. Her mouth was down-hooked at the corners, her brow dimpled with anger, her eyes lit with a quiet scorn that showed she was not only privy to Jack's most private thoughts but disgusted by them. Her meanness of spirit and the depth of her disdain for him did not seem to fit with the youthfulness of her face. How could he possibly understand the physiological riddle that she presented to him?

She beckoned to him, confident he would come to her, even as she removed her belt and wrapped one end around her palm.

When he would wake from the dream, he would sit on the side of his bed, his hands clenched between his knees, filled with self-loathing that seemed to have no cause.

The degradation that invaded his soul in his sleep never left him during his daylight hours, unless he could transfer its origins onto someone else. It might have seemed a twisted way to think, Jack told himself, but he did not invent the world, nor did he create the people who had bedeviled him without cause for a lifetime or gone out of their way to reject him.

It was the latter category that bothered him most. He did not subscribe to the belief that woman was man's downfall. Nor did he blame women for their vanity or the fact that guile was sometimes their only defense against man's exploitation of their bodies. No, it was the strange light in their eyes when they looked upon his person that caused a match to flare on the lining of his stomach. They not only feared him, they were viscerally repelled by him, a man who, in his entire life, had never referred to a woman in a profane or unseemly manner.

So he had found another kind of woman, one he could trust and who was worthy of a man people on both sides of the border referred to as the left hand of God. She lived inside the Scripture and was always waiting on the attention of his eyes when he turned to the thumb-creased pages where her story began but never ended. This woman did not have one name; she had many. She was Esther, who told Xerxes he would have to walk in her blood before she would allow him to harm her people; she was Rebecca, with the water jug on her shoulder, the strong-willed, intelligent wife of Abraham's son; she was the Samaritan woman with whom Jesus had the longest conversation in the New Testament; and ultimately, she was Mary of Magdala, who subsidized Jesus' ministry and stayed with him at the cross and became the first apostle of the new religion when she announced on Easter morning, "He is risen."

The figure who hid behind the wall at the end of the street could lay no claim upon Preacher Jack as long as he had his Testament.

He heard the plane again. This time it was coming out of the northwest, retracing its earlier flight path. He crouched inside the shade of the piñon trees and removed his panama hat and focused his binoculars on the side of the plane as it passed dangerously low over the crest with at least three men inside the cabin. Jack doubted they were feds. Feds didn't take unnecessary risks; self-important corporate douchebags who paid large sums of money to shoot captured animals on a game farm did. Just for fun, Jack picked up his submachine gun and aimed through the iron sights at the tail of the plane. "Pow," he whispered as softly as smoke.

Then he realized the distraction of the plane and his idle thoughts about game farms and douchebags had just cost him. Across the flatland to the southwest, two figures had emerged from a rocky basin and were headed in his direction. In fact, if they stayed on course, they would follow the creek up into the buttes to the natural fort where he had built his cabin.

He lay on his stomach, his elbows propped on grit, his binoculars aimed through the piñon branches. Both of the figures were men. One was young and athletic-looking, a canteen slung on his shoulder, wearing a hat that a tourist or rock collector would wear. The other man had meringue hair and a flushed face and was sweating and obviously slowing the younger man. The sun was white in the sky and had robbed the morning of all its redemptive qualities. These two men, particularly the older one, were not here to enjoy the Texas landscape.

What to do? Jack asked himself.

CHAPTER SEVENTEEN

Ethan Riser got up from the place where he had been resting and followed Caleb, his young friend from Austin, across the stretch of flatland that was streaked with alkali and dotted with green brush and that was now turning into a mirror under the hot sun. Ahead, he could see hills that gave shade and the promise of a cool alcove where the stone still smelled of predawn hours and flowers that opened only at night.

"What the hell?" Caleb said.

A group of at least five dirt-bike riders were headed across the hardpan, their engines whining like dentist drills, their deeply grooved tire treads scissoring the topsoil and weaving trails of dust and smoke in the air. Sometimes a biker roared over a knoll and became airborne, or gunned his engine and deliberately lifted his front wheel off the ground, scouring a long trench with his back tire. The collective cacophony the bikers created was like broken glass inside the eardrum.

Worse, at least to Ethan and his friend, the smells of exhaust and burnt rubber were the industrial footprint of modern Visigoths determined to prove that no pristine scrap of an earlier time was safe from their presence.

"This is one bunch that needs to get closed down in a hurry," Caleb said. He opened his badge holder and held it up in front of him so the sun would reflect off it. But the bikers either ignored his attempt to identify himself or were so committed to recontouring the area that they never saw him at all.

Just as Caleb took out his cell phone, the bikers were gone, as quickly as they had arrived, disappearing over a rise, their bandannas flapping, the roar of their exhausts echoing off a butte where piñon trees grew in the rocks.

"I'll make a deal with you," Caleb said.

"What might that be?" Ethan said. The armpits of his long-sleeve blue shirt were looped with sweat, his khaki pants hanging low on his stomach, his eyes squinting in the glare, even though he was wearing a bill cap. In spite of the semiautomatic on his hip, he looked like an old man who would not concede that disease had already taken him into a country from which no amount of pretense would ever allow him to return.

"We'll go one more mile, up into the shady spot," Caleb said. "We can sit by a little creek there. The Indians carved turkey tracks on some of the rocks thereabouts. They always point due north and south. That's how they marked their route, using the stars, never one degree off. You can set a compass on them. It's just a real fine place to cool our heels."

"Then what do we do?"

"We go back. It ain't up for grabs, either," Caleb said.

"I'll sit down with you a minute, but then I'm going on."

"Sometimes we have to accept realities, Ethan."

"That I'm worn out and can't make it?"

Caleb looked at the mottled discoloration in his friend's face. "I don't think Jack Collins is out here. If he is, we'll hear about it and come back and nail his hide to a cottonwood. In the meantime, it's not reasonable to wander around under a white sun."

"I spent seven months in a bamboo cage. The man next to me had a broken back and was in there longer than I was," Ethan said.

"In Vietnam?"

"Who cares where it was?" Ethan said.

In the distance, they heard the sound of a solitary dirt bike, the engine screaming as though the back tire had lost traction and the RPMs had revved off the scale. Then there was silence.

"Collins is here," Ethan said.

"How do you know?"

Ethan looked to the north, where turkey

buzzards were turning in a wide circle against a cloudless blue sky. "Know what death smells like?"

"Yeah, like some dead critter up there. Don't let your imagination start feeding on loco weed."

"Do you smell anything?"

"No, I don't."

"I can. It's Collins. It's Collins who smells like death. He's here. When you've got death in you, you can smell it on others."

Jack did not like what he was watching. Where did this bunch get off, invading a place that was *his,* one that could have been sawed loose from the edges of Canaan and glued onto the southwestern rim of the United States? Why was the government worried about working-class people crossing the border when a bunch like this were given licenses and machines to destroy public lands? Jack knelt on a sandstone ledge, the butt of his Thompson resting by his knee, the drum magazine packed with fifty .45 rounds, the clean steel surfaces of his weapon smelling slightly of the oilcloth he had used to wipe down and polish it last night. He longed to raise the stock to his shoulder and lead the bikers with iron sights and squeeze off three or four short bursts and blow them into a tangle of machines and spinning tires and disjointed faces, not unlike the images in the

Picasso painting depicting the fascist bombing of Guernica.

One of the bikers, as though he had read Jack's thoughts, veered away from his companions and roared up the hillside toward Jack's position, his goggles clamped like a tanker's on his face, one booted foot coming down hard on the dirt to keep his machine erect, his jeans stiff with body grease, his black leather vest faded brown and yellow under his naked armpits.

The biker throttled back his engine and swerved to a stop just twenty feet below Jack's position, smoke and dust rising behind him in a dirty halo. His teeth looked feral inside his beard, his chest hair glistening with sweat. Jack laid his Thompson on a clean, flat rock and stood up in full view. "How do, pilgrim?" he said.

"Were you flashing a mirror at me?" the biker asked.

"Not me."

"I think it *was* you. You got one of those steel signal mirrors? You being cute or something?"

"You probably saw the reflection off my field glasses."

"So you want to tell me what the hell you're doing?"

"Not much. Studying on the general state of mediocrity that seems to characterize the country these days. Did you know the United

States has the highest rate of functional il-
literacy in the Western world, even though we
have the most libraries? What's your thought
on that?"

"My thought is, I'm getting a crick in my
neck looking up at you. Who the fuck you
think you are?"

"The worst mistake you ever made."

The biker put a pinch of snuff under his
lip. "It's been good talking to you. Keep your
flopper oiled and cocked. The right girl is out
there waiting for you somewhere."

"Maybe you can he'p me with a theory I
have. It has to do with atavistic behavior. That
means a throwback to the way things were
when people hunted each other with rocks
and sharp sticks. Did you ever notice that
most of the fellows in biker gangs are strange-
looking? By that I mean way overweight, with
double hernias and beetle brows and pig
noses and bulging scrotums and hair growing
out of their ears. You'd think it would dawn
on them."

The biker pushed his goggles up on his
forehead with his thumb. There were white
circles around his eyes. "What would dawn
on them?"

"That ugly and stupid people find each
other."

The biker twisted the gas feed with his right
hand, revving his engine, making a decision.
"I hate to tell you this, pal, but I don't think

your opinion carries a lot of weight. If you haven't noticed, your suit looks like Sasquatch wiped his ass with it. You've got pecker tracks on your fly and enough dirt under your fingernails to grow tomatoes. If the wind turns around, I expect I'll have to put on a respirator."

Jack gazed across the flats into the distance. With his naked eye, he could not see the two hikers. The wind was up, out of the south, the piñon trees bending. The sound of a short burst might be mistaken for the backfire of a dirt bike or be lost altogether inside the wind. Yes, maybe this was an opportune moment. "You like tearing up the countryside, making lots of noise with your machines, smearing your scat on the morning? Look at me."

"What for?"

"The man who snuffs your wick is always the one you least suspect. You're tooling along, and you shoot off your mouth to the wrong fellow in the middle of a desert, and somebody stuffs a cactus plant up your ass. That's what the crossroads is all about."

"*You're* the wick snuffer?"

"Close your eyes and count to three and open them again. I have a surprise for you."

"Screw you," the biker said.

He turned his bike around and rode back down the slope, shooting Jack the finger just before heading across the flats, a fountain of gravel and silt flying from under his back wheel.

Jack let out his breath with a sigh. *Just two more seconds,* he thought. Oh well, maybe it was better that he kept his priorities straight. But before Jack could turn his attention to the hikers, the goggled, head-wrapped dirt biker had reconsidered and nullified his wise choice and spun his machine in a circle. He was headed back full-bore to the hillside, his thighs spread, his knees high, his shoulders humped, a simian throwback determined to teach a lesson to an unwashed, ignorant old man.

He veered north of Jack's position and bounced onto a narrow trail that would take him to where Jack was standing behind a boulder. Jack temporarily lost sight of him, then heard the biker gun his engine and mount a steep grade, gravel splintering off his back wheel.

Jack waited, his Thompson hanging from his right hand, his coat fluttering open in the wind, a half-smile on his face. The biker had reached the top of the grade and was bouncing up and down with the roughness of the trail as he approached Jack's position. Thirty feet below was a gully strewn with chunks of yellow chert and the dried and polished limbs of dead trees. Jack stepped out from behind the boulder and raised the muzzle of the Thompson at the biker's chest.

"I cain't blame you, pilgrim. Pride is my undoing, too," he said.

He never got a chance to squeeze the trigger. The biker saw the Thompson and threw his hands in front of his face, then plummeted off the trail straight into the gully, upside down, his machine crashing on top of him.

Jack walked to the edge of the trail and peered down at the biker and the wrecked bike, its front tire still spinning. "Ouch," he said.

The sun was blinding when Caleb approached the butte where he thought he had seen one of the bikers split off from the pack and power up the hillside. His eyes were stinging with salt, his mouth dry, and he wanted to stop and take a drink from his canteen, but he felt a cautionary sense he couldn't dispel. Why had the biker left his comrades? Who or what was up in the rocks where Caleb had seen book pages flipping in the wind? And why hadn't the biker come back down the hill? He cupped his hands around the sides of his mouth. "Hello up there!" he yelled. "I've got an injured man on the trail and need some help!"

He heard his voice echo in an arroyo that twisted toward the crest and opened into a saddle green with trees. "I don't have cellphone service," he called out. "I need somebody with a vehicle to go for help!"

Caleb began walking up the slope toward the boulder where he had seen the book. He heard slag sliding down the hill and clacking into a gully. A man appeared on a sandy patch of ground between a boulder and two piñon trees. He was wearing dark goggles and a bandanna on his head and a black leather vest that was discolored a sickly yellow under the armpits. The sun was shining in Caleb's eyes, but he could see that the man's face and arms and chest hair were streaked with blood.

"Did you spill your bike?" Caleb asked.

"I went off into the gully and busted my head. You say you got a hurt man with you?"

"He twisted his ankle."

"Let's take a look at him."

"Where's your dirt bike?"

"At the bottom of the gully."

"You cain't drive it?"

"No, it's finished."

"What's wrong with it?"

"It's broken."

"Maybe we can fix it. I'm a fair mechanic."

"I'm not?"

"We need your vehicle. I have to get my friend out of here. He's not well, and the heat has been pretty hard on him."

"That's what I said. Let's take a look at him."

"Maybe you should sit down. You've got

blood all over you."

"It's no problem. What's your friend doing out here?"

"He's an FBI agent."

"Is that a fact?"

"Where are the guys you were riding with?"

"Gone."

"They deserted you?"

"Are you a law dog, too, pilgrim?"

"Parks and Wildlife. I'm not sure I like the way you're talking to me."

"Don't Parks and Wildlife people carry weapons? I would. This area is full of rattlers."

"Where's the cut on your head? I don't see it."

"You're pretty damn inquisitive for a man asking other people's he'p. How far back is your FBI friend?"

"Not far. Are the other bikers coming back or not?"

"You cain't tell about a bunch like that. Y'all should know. They tear up the countryside wherever and whenever they want, and y'all don't do squat about it."

"They?"

The man in goggles pressed the back of his wrist to his mouth, as though his lip were split or his teeth had been broken or knocked out. Then Caleb realized there was nothing wrong with his mouth or teeth and that he was making a decision, one that would probably have irreversible implications for both of them.

"This is my neighborhood. You made your bed when you came into it," the man in goggles said.

"This is public land. It belongs to the people of Texas. We'll go wherever we please in it."

"Don't pretend you don't know who I am."

Caleb wet his lips and closed and opened his hands at his sides. "Give yourself up, Mr. Collins."

"You're honeymooning here?"

"What's it to you?"

"Answer me."

"I was recently married, if it's any of your business."

"Oh, it's my business, all right. You should have stayed with your woman. You've spat in the soup, fellow."

"I'm going to walk out of here now. When I come back, I hope you're gone. If you're not, you're going to be in custody."

Jack Collins thumbed the goggles off his face and threw them aside. He reached behind the boulder and lifted up the Thompson and pointed it at Caleb's midsection. "Why'd you wander in here, boy? Why'd you let the FBI use you?"

Caleb felt the muscles in his face flex, but no words came out of his mouth.

"You have cuffs or ligatures on you?" Jack

Collins said.

"No."

"Where's the agent?"

"In a cool place out of the sun. Let him be."

"What's his name?"

"Riser."

"Ethan Riser?"

"You know Ethan?" When Collins didn't answer, Caleb said, "You killed the biker?"

The bumps and knots and sallow skin and unshaved jowls that constituted the face of Jack Collins seemed to harden into a mask, as though his breathing and all the motors in his head had come to a stop. His eyes became lidded, without heat or anger or emotion of any kind. Then his chest began to rise and fall. "Sorry to do this to you, kid," he said.

"Buddy, before you —"

"Don't talk." Jack Collins's eyes closed, and his mouth formed into a cone, as though he were devolving into a blowfish at the bottom of a dark aquarium, a place where he was surrounded by water that was so cold he had no feeling at all.

Ethan was sitting on a flat rock inside an alcove that had a sandy floor and was protected on the north side by a big sandstone boulder. He heard an abrupt sound inside the wind, like a burst of dirty thunder, and for a moment thought the plane with the

455

sputtering engine had returned or the dirt biker had cranked up his machine and was gunning across the hardpan. Riser stood up and stepped from behind the boulder. Out of the white haze, he saw a figure walking toward him, a man wearing a leather vest with a panama hat slanted on his head, his face swollen with lumps that looked like infected insect bites, his trousers stuffed into the tops of his cowboy boots. The man was holding a Thompson submachine gun with his right hand. "Need to talk," he said.

Riser stepped back quickly behind the boulder and pulled his semiautomatic from the holster on his hip.

"You hear me? It doesn't have to end the way you think," the man called out.

Ethan inched forward and looked around the edge of the boulder. The man with the Thompson was gone, probably up in the rocks from which he could follow a deer trail over the top of the alcove or remain where he was and wait for Ethan to come out in the open.

"You sick down there?" the man said from somewhere up in the piñon trees.

"Come down here and find out," Ethan said.

"You're not calling the shots, Mr. Riser."

"Other people know where I am."

"No, I think you're out here on your own hook."

"Where's Caleb?" Ethan said.

"He's not here."

"Where is he?"

"He's somewhere else."

"You killed him?"

"I'm going to ask you a question. You need to think carefully before you answer. If you lie, I'll know it. Are you the agent who burned me out?"

"No. What did you do to Caleb?"

"Did you *order* my house burned?"

"That wasn't a house. It was a shack. You were squatting in it."

"Did you order it burned? Did you burn my Bible?"

"No, I had nothing to do with it. Where's Caleb?"

"Who told you where I was?"

"No one."

"It was your buddy Caleb, wasn't it? He and his wife took a picture of Noie Barnum and showed it to you."

"You've got your facts turned around, Collins. We received reports on you from the Border Patrol. They'd rounded up some illegals who'd seen you up here."

"Why would wetbacks take note of a fellow like me?"

"It's your BO. As soon as they mentioned it, we knew who they were talking about."

"Throw your piece out on the sand. Throw your cuffs out, too."

"You're a public fool, Collins. You're not a religious warrior or an existentialist hero. You're a basket case who probably killed his mother. You murder young girls and pose as a political assassin. Let me tell you a story. You know what the Feast Day of Fools was in medieval times? It was a day when all the lower-level dysfunctional people in the church were allowed to do whatever they wanted. They got sodden drunk, fist-fought in front of the altar, farted to hymnal music, buggered each other and each other's wives and sodomized animals or anything with a heartbeat, and had a glorious time. They got it out of their system, and the next day they all came to church hungover and were forgiven.

"Five hundred years ago there was a place for a pitiful fuck like you, but now there isn't. So you trail your BO around the desert and terrorize unarmed people and pretend you're the scourge of God. You need to sew bells on your suit, Collins. Maybe you can get a job as a jester in a medieval reenactment."

Ethan waited for Collins's response. The only sound he heard was the wind.

"I rumpled your feelings?" Ethan said. "Hypersensitivity usually goes back to a person's problems with his mother. Sexual abuse or constant criticism, that kind of thing. If so, we've got a special titty-baby unit we can get you into."

Ethan waited, his palm perspiring on the

458

grips of his semiauto. A gust of wind blew a cloud of alkali dust into his face. He wiped his eyes clear and tried to see above the top of the alcove without exposing himself to a burst of submachine-gun fire. He stepped back into the shade, letting his eyes readjust. Then he knew something was wrong. The alkali dust had not dissipated but had grown thicker. Above, he heard footsteps inside dry brush and the sound of tree branches being broken and dragged over a stone surface. He smelled an odor like greasewood burning and realized he had not been looking at alkali dust but at smoke from a fire, one that was being stoked into a blaze that was so hot, it immediately consumed whatever was dropped into it.

"You burn a man out of his house and excuse yourself by calling it a shack?" Collins said. "Now it's your turn, Agent Riser. See how you like it."

A rain of burning grass and tree limbs and trash scraped out of a deadfall showered down on the opening to the alcove, filling the air with smoke and soot and red-hot cinders. Then Collins pushed another load of dry fuel down on top of it.

"I can keep doing it all day, Mr. Riser," Collins said. "Or you can throw your weapon on the far side of the fire and walk out after it. I won't shoot."

"You were the right age for Vietnam. Where

were you when the rest of us went?" Ethan said.

"Those were your enemies, not mine. I never injured a man who didn't ask for it."

"How about Caleb?"

"Maybe he's still breathing. Come out of your hiding place and we'll go see."

Ethan charged through the flames, his clothes catching fire, his eyebrows and hair singeing. He whirled about, raising his semiauto, hoping for a clear shot at Preacher Jack. But the black silhouette he saw imprinted against the sky was armed with a magic wand that burst with light brighter than the sun, brighter than the fire eating Ethan's skin, even brighter than the untarnished shield to which he had dedicated most of his adult life. The Thompson seemed to make no sound, but its bullets struck his body with the impact of an entire hillside falling on top of him.

Jack Collins climbed down the slope, careful not to scrape the wood or the steel surfaces of his submachine gun on the rocks, and removed the semiautomatic from Ethan's hand and the cell phone from the pocket of his khakis. He flipped open the phone and idly reviewed the most recently dialed numbers. The first name to appear on the list was not one he was expecting to see.

Riser had been in touch with *her* only that morning. Why?

He tossed the cell phone into the fire, and for just a moment he thought he saw the face of the Chinese woman called La Magdalena rise from the flames.

Chapter Eighteen

Six hours later, Hackberry Holland sat numbly in his office chair, his forehead propped on his fingers, and listened to the sheriff of Brewster County read from the notes he had made at the crime scene. As in all crime-scene reports, the factual nature of the language served only to further depersonalize and degrade the humanity of the victims: The bodies had been discovered by the friends of the missing dirt biker; Ethan Riser was DOA; Riser's companion on the trail, Caleb Fry, was in a coma and barely alive; the dirt biker had died of either a broken neck or massive head trauma; the wounds to Ethan Riser indicated that he had been shot many times after mortality had occurred, to the degree that he had to be identified by his possessions.

"Are there any witnesses at all?" Hackberry asked. "Did anyone see Collins in the vicinity?"

"No, we've got no visuals on anything," the

sheriff in Brewster County said.

"Have you talked to the other bikers?"

"Yeah, they say their bud saw somebody flashing something at them from the rocks. Their bud was a lone wolf and liked to get into it with other people. By the way, we found his vest not far from where the agent died. Collins is here, isn't he? In my county?"

"That'd be my guess. Is the FBI there yet?"

"Like flies on shit. There's another detail I ought to pass on. There was a melted cell phone in the ashes of the fire. I suspect it was the FBI agent's. It was too deep inside the burn ring to have fallen there. Why would the shooter throw the guy's cell phone in the fire?"

"Fingerprints?"

"Maybe, but he didn't bother to pick up the brass."

"The day you understand Jack Collins is the day you check yourself in to rehab for the rest of your life," Hackberry said.

"Where do you think he's hid out?"

"The Unabomber lived in Lincoln, Montana, for ten years. He had no plumbing or electricity in his cabin. Forest Service personnel think he shot at their planes. The locals considered him a regular guy. Maybe Collins isn't hiding. Maybe he's out there in full view. It's a sign of the times. The standards for normalcy find a new low with each passing day."

"That's not funny."

"Who said it was?"

After Hackberry hung up, he called R. C. Bevins and Pam Tibbs into his office and told them of the conversation he'd just had.

"I'm sorry, Hack," Pam said.

"There is nothing for us to feel sorry about. We honor Ethan's memory by nailing the bastard who killed him," Hackberry said. "R.C., I want you to go up to Brewster and get a topography map and look up the land records of every piece of property within five miles of the crime scene."

"What am I looking for?" R.C. asked.

"Collins likes to take on the personae of obscure writers. Google the names on the land titles and see what pops up. Pam, you and I need to do something about Josef Sholokoff. For two years his name has been coming up in our investigation of Collins's background. Sholokoff used Collins as a hit man, and he was also the business partner of Temple Dowling. Plus, Anton Ling says Sholokoff was mixed up with shipping arms to the Contras in the 1980s. He's gotten a free pass for over twenty years, I think in part because he was a useful tool for some guys in the government."

"What do you want to do about him?" she asked.

"He's a Russian criminal. Maybe he needs a reminder of what life in Russia can be like,"

Hackberry said.

After Pam and R.C. had left his office, he felt no better for his rhetoric and could not rid himself of the words the sheriff in Brewster had used to describe the wounds to Ethan Riser's body. What had Ethan said to Collins that had filled him with such animus? Collins had always been cold-blooded and methodical when he killed, not driven by emotion or impetuosity. Before dying, Ethan had gotten to him. A remark about his mother? Maybe, but not likely. Collins had no illusions about the woman who had raised him. It was something else. Something that had to do with his image of himself. What greater bane was there for a narcissist than deflation of his ego? In his mind, Collins believed himself a Titan, a warrior-angel with a wingspan that could blot out the moon. Ethan had been well read, intelligent, and con-wise and had thought of Collins as a noisy, misogynistic nuisance who would eventually be greased off the planet. Somehow, before he died, he told Collins that in the great scheme of things, Collins had the wingspan of a moth and was hardly worth the effort of swatting with a rolled magazine. With luck, Hackberry might have a chance to deliver the same insult.

Something else was bothering him. Historians wrote of battles as epic events involving thousands of soldiers acting in concert, all of them directed by a brilliant strategist such as Alexander or Napoleon or Stonewall Jackson. But for the grunts on the line, the reality was otherwise. They took home a limited perspective, a few shards of memory, flashes of light, a name being called out, the whirring sound of a projectile flying past one's ear. In the larger context of the battle, the individual's perspective was little more than a sketch on the back of one's thumbnail. The invasion at Inchon saved United Nations troops from being pushed into the sea. But Hackberry remembered only one detail from it. A group of marines under the command of a young naval lieutenant had captured a lighthouse. They were aided by Korean civilians. Had they not held the lighthouse, the peninsula would have been lost. In retaliation, the North Koreans began executing civilians. Some of the civilians armed themselves with captured weapons and fought back at a railway station, where they filled suitcases from the baggage room with dirt and barricaded themselves inside. They should have survived, but they didn't. A shell from either a railroad gun or an offshore battery hit the depot and killed everyone inside. The shell must have contained phosphorus, because the bodies of the dead were burned uniformly black, as though they had been roasted on a slow fire, the skin swelling until it burst.

Hackberry had never forgotten the image of the dead Koreans and their frozen posture inside the ruins of the building. Nor would he ever forget the image of Ethan Riser dying in a spray of .45-caliber bullets fired into his face by Jack Collins. People said time healed. If it did, Hackberry thought, the pocket watch he had inherited from his father must have been defective.

"Pam?" he said through the open door without getting up.

"Yes, sir?" she answered.

"See if Anton Ling is home. If she is, tell her we're on our way out."

"What's up?" Pam said, standing in the doorway.

"It's time for Miss Anton to get honest about her past."

"You talking about that Air America bullshit?"

"No, arms to northern Nicaragua, courtesy of Josef Sholokoff. Would you stop using that language?"

Pam looked out the window at a woman coming up the sidewalk. "She must be psychic," Pam said.

Hackberry wasn't sure whether there was a thread of resentment or jealousy in Pam's voice. He had given up dealing with the mysteries of eros and was sure that at some linguistic juncture in ancient times, the words "error" and "erotic" had sprung from the same root. The truth was, he could not define his own feelings about either Anton Ling or Pam Tibbs. One reminded him of his dead wife, Rie, who would always remain the love of his life. The other woman, Pam Tibbs, was as brave as Rie had been and equally protective of him, even to the point of causing him public embarrassment, and the look in her eyes always told him that she saw the young man inside him and not the man who was almost eighty. Also, she gave no quarter in either love or war, and her level of loyalty was ferocious. No man could have a better companion as a lover or friend. He could have worse problems, he thought. But damn it to hell, an old fool was still an old fool.

Anton Ling walked past Maydeen and R.C. and Felix and a bail bondsman and Pam Tibbs and a drunk cuffed to a D-ring as though they were not there. "I just heard about Ethan Riser on the radio," she said.

"Chief Deputy Tibbs and I were just about to come out to your place," Hackberry said.

"Agent Riser called me this morning on his cell phone. I wish I'd gotten ahold of you."

"Called you about what?"

"He apologized for invading my privacy. He told me to be a friend to you. He sounded like a man making his peace. I asked him if he was all right. He said if I heard from him again, that would mean he was doing just fine. Why are all these people standing around here?"

"We work here," Pam said.

"Do you want to sit down, Miss Anton?" Hackberry said.

"No."

"How do you know Ethan was on a cell phone?" Hackberry asked.

"He was breaking up. Jack Collins just called me."

"Wait a minute. I don't understand. Collins called to tell you Ethan was dead?"

"No. He didn't mention anything about Mr. Riser. He asked me if I had given the FBI his location. I told him I didn't have any idea what he was talking about. He asked if I had learned of his whereabouts from the illegals who come to my house. When I told him I had no interest in either him or the FBI, he told me I was a Jezebel. On the way into town, I heard the news report about Agent Riser on the radio."

"Sit down," Hackberry said.

"No. I have to go."

"Where?"

"Home. Collins is insane. I have people coming tonight. He'll take his revenge on them."

"I doubt it. Come in and close the door, Deputy Tibbs."

"You're holding me?" Anton Ling said.

"The sheriff in Brewster County found

Ethan's cell phone inside the ashes of a bonfire that Collins set. Collins probably threw the phone there after he recovered the list of calls Ethan had made in the last few days. That's why Collins associated you with Ethan discovering his whereabouts. He also has a way of blaming women for most of his problems."

"Why were you coming out to my house?"

"We want Josef Sholokoff in a cage," he said.

"Then talk to the government agencies that have let him run loose all these years," Anton said.

"You recognized a man outside your hospital room. He was connected with smuggling guns into Nicaragua and introducing cocaine into the United States. He was with the guy whose face you put a screwdriver in. You've worked intimately with Sholokoff's people, and you have information about them that we don't. You have to give us some leads, Miss Anton."

"I don't have any."

"What you mean is you don't want to give us any," Pam said.

"Do I look like a professional informant?" Illogically, Anton said, "Most of the people I knew years ago are probably dead."

"This isn't Cambodia. We're sick of people working out their problems at our expense," Pam said. "It's time to get your head out of your ass, Ms. Ling."

"Why don't you get your head out of yours?" Anton said. "The electorate in this area puts people in office who belong on chain gangs."

"I guess that includes the sheriff," Pam said.

"You know what I mean," Anton said.

"No, I don't," Pam said. "We know you're sheltering illegals. We also know you were part of an Underground Railroad that hid them in Kansas back in the eighties. But we look the other way. Maybe you should decide who your real friends are."

Hackberry felt a pain spreading through his head as though someone were tightening a vise on his temples. "This isn't solving our problem," he said.

"The man I recognized outside my hospital room was a handler of animals," Anton said. "Exotic animals of some kind. I didn't like him. But I was part of the gun-smuggling operation, Sheriff Holland. I'm responsible for the deaths of innocent people."

"Did this guy supply exotic animals to game farms?" Hackberry asked.

"Maybe. He talked about it. I remember his complaining about driving a truckload of them into West Texas," Anton said.

"Where in West Texas?" Hackberry asked.

"This was twenty-five years ago."

"Where?" he said.

She shook her head. "I don't remember.

He probably didn't say. Wait a minute. He made a nasty joke once about a brothel in Phnom Penh. It specialized in . . . I don't care to talk about what it specialized in."

"Oral sex?" Hackberry said.

"Yes," she replied. "He said he had a friend in Texas who used to hang out in this particular brothel. The friend owned a nightclub in Texas."

"*La Rosa Blanca?* The White Rose?" Hackberry said.

"Pardon?" she said.

"Bingo," Pam said.

The orange neon sign on the roof of Joe Tex's saloon glowed against a turquoise sky that was bottom-rimmed in the west by strips of red and black clouds. The evening could not have been more beautiful. The wind was balmy and out of the south and smelled of distant rain. An obsolete windmill was clattering by an abandoned loading pen on the hardpan, like a beneficent reminder of a grand tradition as well as the potential the land held for all those who lived humbly upon it. Even the tractor-trailers wending their way down the two-lane through compacted hills that resembled ant mounds seemed like a testimony to the industrial success of a new nation rather than harbingers of pollution and the loss of Jefferson's agrarian vision.

There were few patrons in the saloon when Hackberry and Pam entered through the front door. Joe Tex was stocking his beer cooler behind the bar; Rosanne Cash was singing on the jukebox; the lacquered pine logs in the walls seemed to exude a golden light like warm honey. Joe Tex was smiling when he lifted his head from his work, his hair as shiny and black as a raven's feathers, his rolled shirtsleeves exposing his vascular arms. "My favorite sheriff and lady deputy," he said. "What are y'all having?" He propped his arms on the bar, waiting. The top of his white cowboy shirt was unsnapped, and his chest hair was fanned out on his skin like the points of a star. His eyes were so lidless in their intensity that he seemed incapable of blinking.

"Your name has come up in an investigation, Joe," Hackberry said, setting his hat crown-down on the bar. "Not that you did anything wrong. We just thought you could help us figure out a thing or two."

"Who was the shooter on the grassy knoll?" Joe Tex said.

"No, it has to do with the name of your saloon," Hackberry said.

"I remember now. Lime and soda and ice, right?" Joe Tex said. "How about you, Miss Pam?"

"Who was the White Rose?" she asked.

"My wife. She was a stripper in Big D. She

473

actually worked in Jack Ruby's old joint."

"We did some checking on that, Joe," Hackberry said. "Nobody can find any record of your being married."

"I guess that's their problem. My wife and I got hitched at a drive-by window in Matamoros."

"I heard you might have done some quasi-governmental work in Cambodia," Hackberry said.

"I'm not big on revisiting the past, Sheriff. I was a GI on the Mekong River. It took me to lots of places, most of them better forgotten."

"You fly in and out of the Golden Triangle at all?" Hackberry asked.

"I don't remember. I have a bunch of big blank holes in my memory when it comes to Indochina. I'll tell you one thing, though. I'm not ashamed of anything I did over there."

"I'm not questioning your service to your country," Hackberry said. "I'm interested in a man by the name of Josef Sholokoff. A man who works for him helped torture a local woman and maybe crucify Cody Daniels. That man was in the company of a guy who knows you, Joe. He used the name of your saloon. He used to deliver exotic animals to game farms. Does that ring any bells?"

"I guess I'm tone-deaf on that one."

"The White Rose was a whorehouse in Phnom Penh, right?" Hackberry said.

"Could be. Cherry Alley wasn't an open-air fruit market in Tokyo. But that doesn't mean I went there to find out. I got to get back to work."

"What you need to do is take the shit out of your mouth," Pam said. "I pulled Cody Daniels's feet and hands off the nails someone used to hang him on a cross inside a burning building. He was alive when his killers started the fire. With good luck, he died of smoke inhalation."

"I saw it on the news. You think something like that is lost on me? Years ago I knew some intelligence people. But I don't remember anything about some guy who hauled exotic animals around. Unless y'all got a warrant, get out of my establishment."

"You got a meth problem, Joe?" Hackberry said.

Joe Texas leaned across the bar. His skin was so dark that in the shadows, it looked like it had been removed from a tannery and kneaded and softened and fitted on his bones; his eyes stared out of the sockets like those of a man living inside a costume. "You don't have a clue about what you're dealing with," he said. "You want to end up a bump out there in the desert? Just keep fucking with the wrong people. You'll wish you were still drunk and humping underage Mexican whores, Sheriff. Y'all aren't the only people with access to security files. Get a warrant. In the meantime, I'm D-D-D. That stands for 'deaf, dumb, and don't know.' "

That night Hackberry went out to his barn and clicked on the interior lights. The row of bulbs on the ceiling glowed with a chemical-like iridescence inside the humidity. Bales of green hay bound with red twine were scattered on the concrete pad that extended between the stalls located on either side of the building, and a speed bag and an Everlast rebound board were mounted on the back wall of the rear stall. Hackberry's barn was not a bad refuge from the cares of the world. He began hitting the bag with a rotating motion, landing each blow on the heel of his fist, thudding the bag up into the circular rebound board before it could swing full-out on its cable, increasing his velocity until the bag became a blur, the rhythm as steady and loud as a drumroll.

But he could not clean Joe Tex's words out of his head. Hackberry had made no secret of his life as a drunk and an adulterer and a frequenter of brothels in northern Mexico. The age of the prostitutes had seemed insignificant at the time, as callous as that sounded. In daylight he would not have recognized most of them. Sometimes he went into a blackout, and when he woke sick and hungover in the morning, the only knowledge he had of the previous night came from his empty wallet and the mileage on his odometer. He suspected that the women or teenage girls who touched his body had done so with indifference if not with revulsion. The odium was his, not theirs. The man with a sprawling ranch and a Navy Cross and a Purple Heart hidden away in a seabag, the man who drove a Cadillac with fins and who had a law degree from Baylor, was the sybaritic visitor to a row of shanties built along an open sewage canal. Shame and dishonor were his flags, and self-loathing was his constant companion. His presence or his absence in the life of these girls or women was as significant as a hangnail they might clip off and drop outside into a waste bucket.

Even knowing these things, he had repeated the same behavior over and over and hadn't bothered to question himself about a form of immorality that went far beyond his unfaithfulness to Verisa, who'd had at least two affairs that he knew of, one with a banker in Victoria and one with an airline pilot who'd flown an F-86 in Korea. In Hackberry's mind, his greater sin was his sexual exploitation of girls and women who had no choice in the world. There was no way to excuse or rationalize his callousness toward the deprivation and sadness that constituted their lives. The fact that his behavior was documented in a security file was of no concern to him. The fact that a man like Joe Tex could have access to it and taunt him with it was.

He hit the bag one last time with the back of his fist and walked to the front of the barn and flicked on the outside flood lamp. His two foxtrotters were watching him from the far side of their water tank. "What are you guys up to?" he said.

Love That Santa Fe blew air through his lips, and Missy's Playboy whipped his tail back and forth across his hind legs.

Hackberry had nailed an apple basket against the side of the barn, roughly approximating the heart of the strike zone for a six-foot batter. He took a fielder's glove and a canvas bag of baseballs out of the tack room and carried them to the improvised mound he had constructed sixty feet from the apple basket. "Watch this," he said to the horses. "The batter is crowding the plate and staking out territory he hasn't earned. We're going to serve up a forkball to help him in his search for humility."

Hackberry spread two fingers on the ball, notching the stitches, hiding the pitch in his glove, then let fly at the basket, whipping the pitch overhand, throwing his shoulder and butt into it. The ball smacked into the wood, just wide of the apple basket, and the two horses whirled and plunged out of the light and into the darkness, making a wide circle and returning, their tails flagging.

"Okay, you got that out of your system?"

Hackberry said to the horses. "Now watch. This next one is a changeup, to be followed by a slider and then my favorite."

For the changeup, he held the ball in the back of his palm and floated it into the basket and then buzzed the slider wide and knocked a slat out of the basket.

"All right, forget the slider," he said. "The ball is getting thrown around the infield. The last guy to touch it before it comes back to me is the shortstop. This guy has no ethics at all. He's cut a hole in the pocket of his glove, and between his palm and the pocket is a wet sponge. When the ball comes back to me, it feels like it's been through a car wash."

Hackberry put two fingers in his mouth, then fired an in-shoot into the basket that sounded like silk ripping.

"What do you think of that, fellows?" he said.

He realized he had lost the attention of his foxtrotters and that they were looking at something out in the darkness, something just on the edge of the floodlight's glare.

"I didn't mean to give you a start," a voice said.

"Who are you?" Hackberry asked.

"Dennis Rector is my name. You're Sheriff Holland, right?"

"I was when I woke up this morning. What are you doing on my property?"

"I got a couple of hypotheticals to ask you."

"Where's your vehicle?"

"Out yonder, on the road, just about out of gas."

Dennis Rector walked farther into the floodlight. He was a small man whose head was shaved and whose skin was white and whose body looked molded from plastic. His jeans were too large for him and were rolled in big cuffs above his work boots. His shirt was torn and the side of his face scraped.

"You carrying a weapon, Mr. Rector?"

"No, sir. I'm not a violent man. But I know men who are. Men you're looking for."

"You're looking right into a flood lamp, Mr. Rector. But the pupils of your eyes are as big as inkwells. Can you tell me why that is?"

"I'm a truck driver, sir. I've pulled Monarch and Wolf Creek Pass when it was ten below, and I've gone sliding sideways on ice at forty miles an hour through Pagosa Springs. I've driven from Manhattan to Los Angeles in one haul, and I mean not ever shutting it down, either. I used to do whites on the half-shell, then I got into black beauties and have never quite got rid of their appeal. Those babies will flat cook your mush, I'm here to testify. Know a man name of Josef Sholokoff?"

"What about him?" Hackberry said.

"What about him, he asks," Dennis Rector said, as though a third party were there. "What this is about is I ain't no Judas Iscariot. I don't like getting treated as one, either. I don't like getting run through brambles and chased across the countryside like a fugitive from a chain gang is what I'm talking about. I shaved my head to disguise myself. I do not like this way of life."

"That's interesting. I think you might like our detox unit, Mr. Rector. You can get some medication and therapy and maybe enter a program. Let's take a walk up to the house, and I'll arrange some transportation, and in the meantime you can tell me about Josef Sholokoff."

"You can keep your detox and three hots and a cot, Sheriff, 'cause that ain't why we're having this meeting of the minds. I did what I was asked and got involved in something that just ain't my way. I know how things work. A bunch decides to do something really awful, and I mean awful, as bad as it gets, something that's worse than any nightmare, and one man gets blamed for it and becomes the stink on horse pucky."

"You have a point," Hackberry said. "There's a chair by the tack room. Take a load off, and I'll be right back with a couple of sodas. How's that sound?"

"I could use it, yes, sir."

Hackberry walked up to the house and called for a cruiser. Then he took two cans of ginger ale from the icebox and dropped two pieces of fried chicken in a paper bag and walked back down to the barn. He saw no sign of Dennis Rector. The moon was brilliant over the hills, the wind sweeping in the trees, his horses blowing in the pasture. The lights were still on inside the barn, and he heard a sound like the speed bag thumping irregularly against the rebound board in the rear stall, as though it were being struck by someone who did not know how to use it.

Then he noticed that the chair he kept on the concrete pad was gone and that the tack room door was ajar. He dropped the two cans of soda and the bag of fried chicken into the dirt and ran inside the barn and threw open the tack room door. The chair lay on its side. Above it, Dennis was still swinging from the impact of the drop, his throat wrapped tightly with horse reins, his arms twitching, his neck broken.

CHAPTER NINETEEN

Preacher Jack Collins was not in a good mood. Since the long drive from the cabin on the creek, he had said little to Noie Barnum. Also, he had offered no explanation for his and Noie's sudden departure, scowling whenever Noie asked a question, brooding and moving his lips without sound as though sorting out his thoughts with a hay fork. The decrepit stucco house they had moved into had been a home for bats and field mice and smelled of the damp earth under the floors. The toilet and sink and bathtub were streaked with orange rust and filled with the shells of dead roaches. In the back of the house was a butte that resembled a row of giant clay columns eroding side by side, creating an effect that was both phallic and effete. The front windows gave onto a long sloping plain and a junkyard that was surrounded by a twelve-foot fence with spools of razor wire on top. In the late-afternoon sun, the compacted and polished metal in the junkyard and the razor wire protecting it took on the sharpened brilliance of hundreds of heliographs.

Jack had flung his suitcase on a bunk bed, then brought his guitar case inside and set it on the kitchen table and unsnapped the top.

"What's that?" Noie asked.

"They were called trench sweepers in the Great War," Jack replied, setting the Thompson and two ammunition pans and box upon box of cartridges on an oily cloth. "They were manufactured too late to be used in the trenches, though. That's how guys like John Dillinger and Baby Face Nelson ended up with them."

"What are *you* doing with one, Jack?"

"Home protection."

"I don't get it."

"Get what?"

"Anything we're doing."

"There're people out there who want to hurt me. It's not a difficult concept."

"Hurt you why?"

"I'm hiding you, boy." Noie's adenoidal accent was starting to wear on him. Jack threaded a cleaning patch through the tip of a metal pod and dripped three drops of oil on the patch and pushed it down the muzzle of the Thompson. He worked the rod up and down, then inserted a piece of white paper in the chamber and looked down the inside of the barrel at the whorls of reflected light spinning through the rifling. "Did you ever take classes in speech or diction?"

"I was an engineering major."

"It shows."

"Pardon?"

Jack's eyes wrinkled at the corners. "Don't let my tone bother you. I got to stop fretting myself about our enemies. Some people aren't made for the world. That's the likes of us. That's why we're hunted."

"A man deals his own play. The world doesn't have much to do with it," Noie replied. "That's the way I look at it."

With his fingertips, Jack began loading one of the ammunition pans, lifting each .45 cartridge from its individual hole in a Styrofoam block and lowering it into a pod inside the circular magazine, as though he took more pleasure in the ritual than its purpose. "All I ever wanted from people was to be let alone. Learn it soon or learn it late, a man doesn't have peace unless he's willing to make war."

"Have you shot somebody with that thing?"

"They shot themselves."

"How so?" Noie asked, his throat clotting.

"They line up to do it. They cain't wait."

"That doesn't answer the question."

How was Jack to explain that he had two optical screens in his head? On one screen were people who caused him trouble or threatened his life. On the other screen was the backdrop against which they had originally appeared, but they were airbrushed from it. *Poof,* just like that. The alteration of the images had little to do with him. One side of his brain spoke to the other side. One side defined the problem; the other side took care of it. The people who disappeared from the screen designed their own fate and were responsible for their own diminution.

"Look out the front window," Jack said.

"At the two-lane?"

"I'm talking about the junkyard. You think anything inside it is of any real value?"

"Not unless you're keen on junk."

"But the man who owns the junkyard has razor wire on top of all his fences. That wire probably cost a lot more than anything anybody might steal off those rusted-out or compacted cars. The whole place is the automotive equivalent of a warthog. The wire deflates the value of the property around it and makes Nebraska look like the French Riviera. But nine out of ten people in this county would defend the guy's right to build a huge eyesore on the highway they paid to have poured."

"What's that have to do with your machine gun?"

"Not every asylum has walls."

"They're out to get us?"

"The government has been trying to put me out of business for twenty years. So has a guy by the name of Josef Sholokoff. His ex–

business partner, Temple Dowling, would like to see you dead, and Sholokoff would like to see you in a cage so he can sell you to Al Qaeda and screw Dowling. In the meantime, the likes of us are considered criminals. Am I getting through to you?"

"There's gunpowder residue on your cleaning patch."

"That's right."

"You fired your Thompson recently?"

Jack snapped the top back on the metal drum and began twisting the winding key. "The Oriental woman gave up our location to the FBI. At least that's my belief until I find out different."

"Miss Anton? She dressed my wounds. She wouldn't inform on me."

"How about on me?"

"You didn't harm her, did you?"

"No, I did not. But a couple of other guys paid her tab."

"What are you telling me?"

"You want to be back in Krill's custody? Time to take the scales from your eyes, son. Who do you think Krill used to work for? The United States government is who."

"What have you done, Jack?"

"Nothing. I told you that at the outset. Moses slew two hundred of his people for erecting the golden calf. He killed, but he didn't murder. His followers got what they deserved."

"Tell me if you killed somebody. Just say it."

Jack exhaled and stared into space, the lumps in his face spiked with unshaved whiskers. "Years ago I did something that still disturbs me, but you can make up your own mind about it. My mother was a prostitute. Most of her clients were gandy walkers or brakemen off a freight line that went past the boxcar we lived in. One guy in particular would come by every two weeks or so. He had a family in Oklahoma City, but that didn't stop him from topping my mother when he was on a bender. I'd have to wait outside, which I had more or less gotten used to, but on one occasion it was about fifteen above and snowing, and I spent an hour wrapped in a piece of canvas, crouched down out of the wind behind his car, which he kept locked because he didn't want a smelly little boy sitting on his leather seats.

"The next summer I was working as a dishwasher in town, and this same fellow came in and ordered the beef-stew special. He looked like he was just coming off a drunk and could have eaten a whole cow between two slices of white bread. That morning I'd swept up some broken glass off the back step and put it in the trash can. The glass was as fine as needles, but I mashed it up even finer and put it in his stew with a lot of potatoes. About thirty minutes later, he went down on

488

the sidewalk like he swallowed a handful of fishhooks. I heard he died, but I didn't go around asking questions about it."

Jack snapped the ammunition drum onto his submachine gun and laid the gun lopsidedly inside the guitar case. He wiped the oil off his fingers with a paper towel and gazed somberly into Noie's face, his eyes melancholy and shiny. Then as though he had been holding his breath underwater to the point where his lungs were bursting, his mouth fell open and his lips creased back in a broad smile. "Got you, boy! I had you convinced you were bunking with Jack the Ripper. My mother was an elementary teacher in Okemah, Oklahoma, and died of Huntington's chorea. My last job was at a Pee-wee Herman theme park. I couldn't hurt a fly."

"What about the submachine gun?"

"I've got a whole collection of rare firearms in Rio de Janeiro. One day I'll show them to you. You don't believe I'm a rich man, do you?"

"I don't know what to believe, Jack."

"That's because you're a good kid. Get out your checker set, and let's put on a pot of coffee and play a game or two."

The information that came in from the National Crime Information Center on Dennis Rector was of little value, other than to indicate that he had been arrested twice for DWI and once for domestic battery, and the United States Navy had given him a general discharge for the convenience of the service. His wallet contained an Arizona driver's license, a Social Security card, fourteen dollars, a condom, a GI can opener, a coupon for a box of cereal, a speeding citation that was four months old, a torn ticket to a concert in Branson, Missouri, and a photograph of the deceased in a navy uniform standing next to an Asian girl wearing a shift and flip-flops. Written in pencil on the back of the photograph were the words "With Luz, Mindanao, Aug. 6, 1982."

In his right-hand pocket Rector had been carrying seventy-three cents in change, three metal finger picks, and a half stick of gum wrapped in tinfoil.

Hackberry placed Rector's possessions in a manila envelope and gazed out the window at a pallid and sultry sky and hills that barely contained enough moisture to go with the greening of the season. What was the sum total of a man's life? Scraps of paper issued by the state? A photo taken with a peasant girl on the rim of the New American Empire on the anniversary of Hiroshima's bombing? A ticket to a country-music event at which the stage performers wore tasseled red, white, and blue costumes and offered up a meretricious tribute to a culture that celebrated its own vulgarity? A half stick of chewing gum?

Who was Dennis Rector, and what had he come to confess? How could a man who had acquired so little and left such a microscopic trace on the planet be so serious about himself that he would take his own life? What could he have done that was that bad? Hackberry picked up his desk phone. "Would you come in here, Maydeen?" he said.

Ten seconds later, she was standing in his doorway, pear-shaped, wearing a flowery western shirt with her department-issue trousers and a stitched belt and too much lipstick, her perfume flooding the room. "Are you gonna just stare at me or tell me what you want?" she said.

"If someone said to you 'I ain't no Judas Iscariot,' what would you say was on his mind?"

"Did you call him a Judas?"

"*I* didn't. To my knowledge, no one did."

"I'd say he sold out someone who trusted him, and his guilt was eating his lunch. Are we talking about the guy who hanged himself?"

"That's the guy."

"It seems like he had biblical stories on his mind. Like the crucifixion in particular."

"I believe you're right."

"You think he knew Cody Daniels?" she asked.

"He knew Josef Sholokoff, that's for sure."

"You think Sholokoff crucified Daniels?"

"I think it was either Sholokoff or Krill. Except a guy like Dennis Rector wouldn't have occasion to be mixed up with someone like Krill. So that leaves Sholokoff. Is Pam still at lunch?"

"She got a call from the Blue Bonnet Six. A guy skipped on his bill and stole the television set out of the room. Before he skipped, he tried to sell the owner something called a Dobro. What's a Dobro?"

"A guitar with a resonator in it. It's played with metal picks, like the ones I just put in this manila envelope."

"The guy who hanged himself played a musical instrument?"

"Evidently. Why?"

"Musicians make poor criminals. Outside of wrecking hotel rooms, they're amateurs when it comes to serious criminality," Maydeen said. When Hackberry didn't reply, she said, "Know why that is?"

"I think you're fixing to tell me."

"You'll figure it out," she said.

"Has R.C. called in yet?"

"No, sir."

"Let me know when he does. Tell me why musicians make poor criminals."

"They believe they have a gift, so they feel less inclined to steal. They also think they're special and they don't have to prove anything."

"I never thought of it that way," he said.

"My first husband was hung like a hamster. But after he recorded once with Stevie Ray Vaughan, you'd think he was driving a fire truck up my leg."

"I can't believe you just said that."

"Said what?"

"Out, Maydeen. And close the door behind you, please."

Hackberry walked to the saloon and ate lunch in the darkness of a back booth and tried to forget the image of Dennis Rector hanging from a barn rafter. But a larger issue than the suicide was bothering him. Hackberry believed that most crimes, particularly homicide, were committed for reasons of sex, money, power, or any combination of the three. Beginning with the murder of the DEA informant by Krill, the homicides Hackberry had investigated recently seemed to defy normal patterns. Supposedly, the central issue was national security and the sale of Noie Barnum to Al Qaeda and the compromise of the Predator drone. But that just didn't wash. The players were all people driven by ideology or religious obsession or personal rage that was rooted in the id. It was too easy to dismiss Preacher Jack Collins as a psychopath. It was also too easy to categorize Josef Sholokoff as a Russian criminal who slithered through a hole in the immigration process during the Cold War. Something much worse seemed to have come into the lives of this small-town society down here on the border, like a spiritual malignancy irradiating the land with its poisonous substance, remaking the people in its image.

Is that too dark and grandiose an extrapolation from the daily ebb and flow of a rural sheriff's department? Hackberry wondered. *Ask those medieval peasants who were visited in their villages by the representatives of the Inquisition,* he said to himself in reply.

He stared at the diamondback rattlesnake that the saloon owner kept in a gallon jar of yellow formaldehyde on the bar. The snake's body was coiled thickly upon itself, its mouth spread wide against the glass, its eyes like chips of stone, the venom holes visible in its fangs. The rattlesnake had been in the jar at least three years; its color had begun to fade, and pieces of its body were starting to dissolve in dirty strings inside the preservative. Why leave something that ugly if not perverse on top of a bar for that long?

Because the owner was making a statement, Hackberry thought. Evil was outside of us, not in the human breast, and could be contained and made harmless and placed on exhibit. Wasn't the serpent condemned to crawl on its belly in the dust and to strike at man's heel and be beaten to death with a stick? What more fitting testimony to that fact than a diamondback yawning open its mouth impotently six inches from the tattooed arm of a trucker knocking back shots of Jack and chasing them with a frosted mug of Lone Star?

Hackberry made a mental note to talk with the bartender. Then his cell phone vibrated on the tabletop. He opened it and placed it to his ear. "Sheriff Holland," he said.

"I called the office, Sheriff, but Maydeen said you were eating lunch," a voice said. "Hope I'm not bothering you."

Hackberry looked down at his plate of enchiladas and Spanish rice and frijoles that were growing cold. "Go ahead, R.C."

"I did what you said. I got a range-and-township map and looked up the title of every piece of land in a five-mile radius from the spot where that FBI man was killed. I Googled all their names and got a hit on one guy, but he's not a writer."

"What's the name?"

"W. W. Guthrie. Google took me to a folksinger by the name of Woodrow Wilson Guthrie."

"That's Woody Guthrie, R.C. He didn't just write folk songs. He published two books. One was *Bound for Glory*. It was made into a film. I think you just found the hideout of Preacher Jack."

"I'm on my way out there right now. I'll call you back as soon as I find out anything."

"What kind of help are you getting from the feds?"

"At the courthouse, one of them told me where the men's room was. Another one said he thought it might rain directly. That's the word he used — 'directly.' Like he was talking to somebody on *Hee Haw.* Are they as bright as they're supposed to be?"

"Probably."

"They sure know how to hide it," R.C. said.

Hackberry finished eating and left thirteen dollars on the table and used the restroom and dried his hands and picked up his hat from the booth and started toward the front door. Then he paused. "I almost forgot," he said to the bartender.

"Forgot what?" the bartender said. He was a big, dark-haired man with a deeply creased brow who wore a white dress shirt with the sleeves rolled up high on his arms.

"Can you put a bag over that snake jar the next time I come here?"

"Any reason?"

"Yeah, so I don't have to look at it while I'm eating."

"Who lit your fuse?"

"Did you read the paper this morning?"

"Something happen?"

"If I come in here again, refuse to serve me," Hackberry said. "I'd really appreciate that."

Halfway to the office, his cell phone vibrated again. "Sheriff Holland," he said.

"It's me, Sheriff."

"Yeah, I thought it might be you, R.C."

"How you doin'?"

"Fine."

"I'm parked at this cabin that's between a creek and a bluff. You cain't see it except from the air. Feds are all over the place, but I found something they missed. It's a checker. They didn't know what it was."

"I'm not quite tracking you."

"It's a homemade checker, one somebody carved out of wood. I'm not explaining myself real good. The property is in the name of W. W. Guthrie, but nobody around here seems to know what he looks like or where he's from. When the feds got here, the cabin and the house were clean. I went out to the barn and saw the same Michelin tire tracks we saw at Anton Ling's place. Then I went inside, and this fed was looking at a little round wood button that he found behind the kitchen door. You following me?"

"Not really."

"I'll try again. On the bottom of it were the initials N.B. For 'Noie Barnum.' On the top was a K. The fed didn't know what that meant. I told him it was K for 'king.' So he says, 'Yeah, it must have rolled behind the door.' So I went into the bedroom and found another one, except this one was wedged in the side of the dresser. That whole place was broom-sweep clean, Sheriff. The second checker, the one stuck in the dresser, wasn't left there by mistake. When I showed the fed what I'd found, he looked pretty confused."

"Noie Barnum isn't a willing companion of Jack Collins?" Hackberry said.

"Or he's covering his ass," R.C. replied.

Or he has his own agenda, Hackberry thought. "You did a fine job, bud. Come on in," he said.

Minutes later, he called both Maydeen and Pam into his office.

"Is this about my language?" Maydeen said. "If it is, I'm sor—"

"Forget your language. The feds have treated us like dipshits. Find out everything you can about Noie Barnum," he said.

Krill squatted down on a bare piece of ground a few feet from the common grave where he had buried his three children. The grave was marked by a Styrofoam cross wrapped with a string of multicolored plastic flowers. He upended an unlabeled bottle of mescal and drank from it against the sunset, the light turning to fire inside the glass. A copy of the *San Antonio Express-News* was weighted down on the ground with rocks he had placed on each corner of the front page, the paper riffling with wind. Krill drank again from the bottle, then pressed a cork into the neck with his thumb and gazed at the sun descending into a red blaze behind the hills.

Negrito squatted next to him, his greasy

leather hat flattening the hair on his forehead. "Don't pay no attention to what's in that newspaper," he said.

"They're gonna put it on us, *hombre.* It means trouble."

"*That* means trouble? What do you call killing a DEA agent?"

"He wasn't an agent. He was an informant and a corrupt Mexican cop. Nobody cares what we did to him. Reverend Cody was a minister."

"We didn't do it to him, man."

"But our prints are there, *estúpido.*"

"That ain't what's bothering you, Krill. It's something else, ain't it?"

"He baptized my children. Nobody else would do that. Not even La Magdalena. To treat him with disrespect now is to treat my children with disrespect."

"That don't make sense."

"Where's your brain? He had the power to set my children free from limbo. Should I tell them I care nothing for the man who did this for them? Can't you think? What is wrong with you?"

"You are making me confused. It makes my head hurt."

"Because you are stupid and self-centered. Go get the others and meet me at the car."

"Where are we going?"

"To get the men who did this to the minister."

"No, no, this is a bad idea. Listen to me, Krill. I'm your friend, the only one you got."

"Then follow me or go into the desert. Or to your whores in Durango."

"You're going after Noie Barnum. Some of the others might think you're gonna sell him and maybe forget to share the money."

Krill stood up to his full height and pulled Negrito's hat off his head. Then he slapped him with it, hard, the leather chin cord biting into the scalp. He waited a few seconds and hit him again. "We're going after the Russian. He should have been killed a long time ago. Don't ever accuse me of treachery again."

"How you know he did it?" Negrito asked, his eyes watering, his nostrils widening as he ate his pain and humiliation at being whipped by Krill.

"Because he hates God, stupid one."

"I hear this from the killer of a Jesuit priest?"

"They told us he and the others were Communists. There were five of them. I shot one, and the others shot the rest. It was in a garden outside the house where they lived. We killed the housekeeper, too. I dream of them often."

"Everybody dies. Why feel guilt over what has to happen to all of us?"

"You say these things because you are incapable of thought. So I don't hold your words or deeds against you."

"You hit me, *jefe.* You would not do that to an animal, but you would do it to me? You hurt me deep inside."

"I'm sorry. You are a handicapped man, and I must treat you as such."

"I do not like what is happening here. All this makes my head throb, like I have a great sickness inside it. Why do you make me feel like this, *jefe?*"

"It is not me. You are one of the benighted, Negrito. Your problems are in your confused blood and your tangled thoughts. For that reason I must be kind to you."

"I will forget you said that to me, 'cause you are a mestizo, just like me. I say we return to Durango. I say we get drunk and bathe in *puta* and be the friends we used to be."

"Then you must go and pursue your lower nature."

"No, I'll never leave you, man," Negrito said. "What does 'benighted' mean?"

Krill gestured toward the hills in the west, where the sun had become a red melt below the horizon and the darkness was spreading up into the sky. "It means the dying of the light," he said. "The benighted place is out there where the coyotes and carrion birds and Gila monsters live and the spirits wander without hope of ever seeing the light."

■ ■ ■ ■

At ten the next morning Pam Tibbs tapped on the doorjamb of Hackberry's office. She had a yellow legal pad in her hand. "This is what we've found out about Noie Barnum so far," she said. "There're a couple of holes in it. You want to hear it now or wait till Maydeen gets off the phone?"

"Who's she talking to?"

"The state attorney's office in Alabama."

"Sit down," Hackberry said.

"Barnum grew up in a small town on the Tennessee line and was an honor student in high school. His father died when he was three, and his mother worked at a hardware store and raised him and his half sister by herself. He was never an athlete or a class officer or a joiner of any kind. He won a scholarship to MIT and went to work for the government when he graduated. As far as anybody knew, he was always religious. When it came to girls and social activities, he was as plain as white bread and just about as forgettable. The exception came when he was seventeen. A three-year-old boy wandered away from the neighborhood, and the whole town organized search parties and went looking for him. Barnum found him in a well. He crawled in after him and got bitten in the face by a copperhead but carried the kid on his back four miles to a highway. By all odds, he should have died."

"What happened to the mother and the half sister?"

"The mother passed away while Barnum was at MIT. The half sister moved to New York and went to work for a catering service. Some stories came back about her, but no one is sure of the truth. She wasn't looked upon favorably in her hometown. She had been arrested in high school for possession of marijuana and was believed to sleep around. This is where it becomes cloudy."

"What does?"

"She used her father's last name when she moved to New York. Hang on," Pam said. She got up from the chair and went to the door. "Maydeen's off the phone."

When Maydeen walked into Hackberry's office, her expression was blank, as though she were looking at an image behind her eyes that she did not want to assimilate.

"What is it?" Hackberry said.

"The Alabama state attorney did some hands-on work for us," she replied. "He found a guy in a state rehab center who was the half sister's boyfriend. She died in the Twin Towers. She was called in to work on her day off because somebody else was sick. She was in the restaurant on the top floor. She was one of the people who held hands with a friend and jumped."

CHAPTER TWENTY

At the bottom of Danny Boy Lorca's land was a ravine that few people knew about or chose to travel. It led from Mexico into the United States, but the entrance was overgrown with thornbushes that could scrape the skin off a man or the paint from an automobile. The sides of the ravine went straight up into the sky and had been marked in four places by the lances of mounted Spaniards who littered the bottom of the ravine with the bones of Indians whose most sophisticated weapons had been the sharpened sticks they used to plant corn. The few illegals who used the ravine and even the coyotes who guided them swore they had seen Indians standing on ledges in the darkness, their faces as dry and bloodless and withered as deer hide stretched on lodge poles. The specters on the ledges did not speak or show any recognition of the nocturnal wayfarers passing between the walls. Their eyes were empty circles that contained only darkness, their clothes sewn from the burlap given them by their conquerors. No one who saw the specters ever wanted to return to the area, except Danny Boy Lorca.

He woke to the grinding noise of a car in low gear laboring up a grade and a brittle screeching that was like someone scratching a stylus slowly down a blackboard. When he went to his back door, he saw a gas-guzzler bounce loose from the ravine, its lights burning in the fog, strings of smoke rising from the rust in its hood. He saw the silhouettes of perhaps four men inside the vehicle.

He pulled on his boots and lifted his twenty-gauge from the antler rack on the wall and limped out onto the back porch. The fog smelled of dust and herbicide and a pond strung with green feces and someone burning raw garbage. The gas-guzzler was traversing his property, its engine rods knocking, its low beams swimming with dust particles and candle moths.

He walked toward it, a pain flaring in his thigh each time his foot came down on the ground, the shotgun cradled across the crook of his left arm. His twenty-gauge was called a dogleg, a one-barrel one-shot breechloader he had used to hunt quail and doves and rabbits when he was a boy. It was a fine gun that had served him well. There was a problem, though: He had not bought shells for it in years. He was carrying an unloaded weapon.

He limped through the chicken yard and past the three-sided shed where his firewood was stacked and through one end of his barn and out the other until he stood squarely in the headlights of the gas-guzzler. The driver touched his brakes and stuck his head out the window. "We got a little lost, amigo. Know where the highway is at?"

Danny Boy moved out of the headlights' glare so he could see the driver more clearly. "You got dope in that car?" he said.

"We're workers, *hombre*," the driver said. "We don't got no dope. We are lost. That canyon was a pile of shit. You got a cast on your leg."

"Yeah, and you got a bullet hole in your window," Danny Boy said.

"These are dangerous times," the driver said. "You have an accident?"

"No, a guy put a shank in me. Did you see the Indians in the ravine?"

"A shank? That ain't good. You said Indians? What is with you, man?" the driver said. He turned to the others. "The guy is talking about Indians. Anybody here see Indians?"

The other men shook their heads.

"See, ain't nobody seen no fucking Indians," the driver said. "We're going to Alpine. Come on, man, you need to stand aside with that gun and let us pass."

Danny Boy's gaze had been fixed on the driver's orange hair and whiskers and the gorilla-like bone structure of his face, so he had not paid attention to the man sitting in the passenger seat. At first the passenger's sharp profile and unnaturally wide shoulders and slit of a mouth were like parts of a bad dream returning in daylight. When Danny Boy realized who the passenger was, he felt his breath catch in his throat. He stepped back from the car window, gripping the shotgun tightly. "I seen you before," he said.

"You talking to me?" the passenger said.

It ain't too late. Don't say no more, a voice inside Danny Boy said. *They will disappear and it will be like they were never here.* "I remember your trousers."

"What about them?"

"Dark blue, with a red stripe down each leg. Like trousers a soldier might wear, or a marine."

"These are exercise pants. But why should you care about my clothes? Why are they of such consequence?"

Danny Boy had to wet his lips before he spoke. "I watched you from the arroyo. I heard that man screaming while you did those things to him."

"You're mixed up, man," the driver said. "We ain't from around here. You ain't never seen us."

"Let him talk," said the passenger.

"You tied the man's scalp on your belt," Danny Boy said. "You heard a sound up in

507

the rocks and looked up at where I was hiding. I acted like a coward and hid instead of he'ping that guy you killed."

"Many of our people use this place to enter Texas. We are workers trying to feed our families," the man said. "Why make an issue with us? It is not in your interest."

"Listen to him, *indio*," the driver said. "You can get that shotgun kicked up your ass."

"This is my land. That house is my home," Danny Boy said.

"So we're going off your land now," the driver said. "So get out of our way. So stop being a hardheaded dumb fuck who don't know not to mess with the wrong guys."

"You ain't gonna talk to me like that on my land," Danny Boy said.

"What I'm gonna do is spit on you, *indio*. I don't give a shit if you got a gun or not."

Danny Boy reversed the twenty-gauge in his hands and drove the stock into the driver's mouth, snapping back his head, whipping spittle and blood onto the dashboard and steering wheel.

"*¡Mátelo!*" a man in the backseat said. "Kill that motherfucker, Negrito."

"No!" the passenger in the front seat shouted, getting out of the car. "You!" he said, pointing across the top of the roof. "Put your gun away. We are no threat to you."

The driver was still holding his mouth, trying to talk. "Let me, Krill," he said. "This one deserves to die."

"No!" the passenger said. "*You,* Indian man, listen to me. You are right. This is your land, and we have violated it. But we mean you no harm. You must let us pass and forget we were here. I saw no Indians in the canyon, but I know they're there. I'm a believer, like you. We are brothers. Like you, I know our ancestors' spirits are everywhere. They don't want us to kill one another."

The passenger had walked through the headlights and was standing four feet from Danny Boy, his eyes roving over Danny Boy's face, waiting for him to speak.

"I was in Sugar Land with guys like you. You're a killer. You ain't like me, and we ain't brothers," Danny Boy said.

"Have it as you wish. But you're putting us in a bad position, my friend. Your fear is taking away all our alternatives."

"Fear? Not of you. Not no more." Danny Boy pushed the release lever on the top of the shotgun's stock and broke the breech and exposed the empty chamber. "See, I ain't got a shell in it. I ain't afraid of you. I ain't afraid of them guys in the car, either."

"*Está loco,* Krill," one of the men inside the car said.

The passenger folded his arms and stared into the darkness as though considering his options. "You got some real cojones, man," he said. "But I don't know what we're going to do with you. Are you going to turn us in?"

"When I can get to a phone."

"Where's your cell phone?"

"I ain't got one."

"You got a regular phone in your house?"

"No, I ain't got no phone."

"You don't have a telephone? Not of any kind?"

"You see a pole line going to my house?"

Krill stared at the house and at the barn and at the truck parked next to the barn. "The man you saw me kill out there in the desert? He was a corrupt Mexican cop who tortured my brother to death."

"Then you ain't no different from the Mexican cop."

"You are fortunate to have this fine place to live on. I had a farm once, and children and a wife. Now I have nothing. Don't judge me, *hombre*."

Krill pulled a long game-dressing knife from a scabbard on his side and walked to Danny Boy's truck and sliced the air stems off all four tires. *"Buenas noches,"* he said as he got back in the automobile. "Maybe one day you will understand men like us. Maybe one day the Indians who live in the canyon will tell you who your real brothers are."

"They ain't you!" Danny Boy shouted at the car's taillights.

In the gloaming of the day, Preacher Jack

Collins and Noie Barnum pulled into the drive-in restaurant on the state four-lane and parked under the shed and ordered hamburgers and fries and onion rings and frosted mugs of root beer. The evening was warm, the wind blowing steadily across the rolling countryside, the storm clouds in the south bursting with brilliant patterns of white electricity that made Jack think of barbed wire. He had not spoken since they had left the cottage on the hillside above the junkyard.

"You're not letting me in on where we're going?" Noie said.

Jack chewed on his food, his expression thoughtful. "You give much thought to the papists?"

"The Catholics?"

"That's what I just said."

"Not particularly."

"That Chinese woman, the one who dressed your wounds, is a puzzle to me."

"She's just a woman with a big heart."

"Maybe she's spread her big heart around a little more than she should have."

"If you read Saint Paul, there's no such thing as being too charitable."

"She may have been acting as a friend to the FBI. If that's true, she's no friend to us."

"You saying she's a turncoat?"

"I'd like to talk to her about it. Here's a question for you." From the side, Jack's eyes looked like glass marbles pushed into dough that had turned moldy and then hardened. The amber reflection in them was as sharp as broken beer glass but without complexity or meaning. In fact, the light in his eyes was neutral, if not benign. "You put a lot of work into whittling out that checker set. Each one of those little buttons was a hand-carved masterpiece. But two pieces were missing from your poke, and you didn't seem to give that fact any thought."

"I guess I dropped them somewhere."

"When you counted the checkers out, you didn't notice that two were gone?"

"Guess not."

"Too bad to lose your pieces. You're an artisan. For a fellow like you, your craft is an extension of your soul. That's what an artisan is. His thoughts travel through his arm and his hand into the object he creates."

"That's an interesting way to look at it."

"Think they might have fallen out in the trunk when we were moving?"

"I'll look first chance."

"You like your hamburger?"

"You'd better believe it."

"Does it bother you that an animal has to give up its life so we can eat types of food we probably could do without?"

"You know how to hang crepe, Jack."

"Think we'd be welcomed by the papist woman?"

"You know what I would really like, more than anything else in the world? I mean, if I could have one wish, a wish that would make my whole life complete? That would make me so happy I would never ask for anything else as long as I live?"

"I cain't figure what that might be, Noie."

"I'd like to make peace with the men who held me hostage and killed the Mexican man I was handcuffed to. I'd like to make peace with the Al Qaeda guys they were going to sell me to. I'd like to apologize to them for the innocent people I helped kill with the drones I helped develop. Most of all, Jack, I'd like to repay you for everything you've done. When they made you, they busted the mold."

Jack worked a piece of food out of his jaw with his tongue and swallowed, his gaze straight ahead. He sipped from his mug, grains of ice clinging to his bottom lip. An attractive waitress in a rayon uniform roller-skated past the front of the Trans Am on the walkway under the shed, but he didn't seem to notice. "Who's 'they'?" he asked.

"Pardon?"

"You said 'when they made you.' You didn't use God's name. Like it would be irreverent. Is that just a quirk, or are you saying I wasn't created by the hand of God?"

"I said it without thinking, that's all. It was just a joke."

"Not to me it isn't. Know why people use

passive voice?"

"I know that it has something to do with grammar, but I'm an engineer, Jack, not much on the literary arts."

"Passive voice involves sentence structure that hides the identity of the doer. It's a form of linguistic deception. Pronouns that have no referents are also used to confuse and conceal. A linguist can spot a lie faster than any polygraph can."

"You never went to college?"

"I never went to high school."

"You're amazing."

"That's a word used by members of the herd. Everything is either 'amazing' or 'awesome.' You're not a member of the herd. Don't act like you are."

"Jack, eating supper with you is like trying to digest carpet tacks. I've never seen the like of it. My food hasn't even hit my stomach, and I'm already constipated."

"Look at me and don't turn around."

"What is it?" Noie said.

"A highway patrol cruiser just pulled in five slots down. There're two cops in it."

The waitress came to the window and picked up the five-dollar tip and lifted the tray off the door and smiled. "Thank you, sir," she said.

"My pleasure," Jack said. He watched her walk away, his eyes slipping off her onto the side of the cruiser.

"We got to back out and drive right past them," Noie said. "Or wait for them to leave."

"I'd say that sums it up." Jack bit down on his lip, his face shadowed by the brim of his hat. He removed it and set it on the dashboard and combed his hair in the rearview mirror.

"What are you doing?" Noie said.

Jack got out of the car, yawning, rubbing his face, a weary traveler about to hit the road again. "Ask the cops for directions to the cutoff to I-10," he replied. He gazed up at the sky and at the network of lightning that was as spiked as barbed wire inside the clouds. "You can almost smell the salt and coconut palms on the wind. Mexico is waiting for us, son. Soon as we tidy up a few things. Yes, indeedy, a man's work is never done."

When Hackberry arrived at work early the next morning, Danny Boy Lorca was sleeping on a flattened cardboard carton in the alleyway behind the rear entrance, one arm over his eyes.

"Want to come in or sleep late and let the sun dry the dew on your clothes?" Hackberry said.

Danny Boy sat up, searching in the shadows as though unsure where he was. "I ain't drunk."

"Where's your truck?"

"At the house. Krill cut all my tires. I hitched a ride into town."

"Krill was at your house?"

"I busted his driver in the mouth. There was four of them together. They come up the ravine behind my property."

"You sure it was Krill, Danny? You haven't been knocking back a few shots, have you?"

"I'm going up to the café now and have breakfast. I told you what I seen and what I done."

"Come inside."

Danny Boy scratched at a place on his scalp and let out his breath and watched a shaft of sunlight shine on a dog at the end of the alley. The dog had open sores on its skin. "You ought to call the Humane Society and get some he'p for that critter. It ain't right to leave a sick animal on the street like that."

"You're a good man, Danny Boy. I meant you no offense," Hackberry said.

Danny Boy went inside and sat down by the small gas stove and waited, his work-seamed hands folded between his knees, his ruined face without expression, while Hackberry called Animal Control and fixed coffee and attached the flag to the chain on the metal pole out front and ran it up the pole, the flag suddenly filling with wind and popping against the sky.

"The guy named Krill said I don't know who my real brothers are," Danny Boy said.

"He did, huh?"

"His eyes are blue. But his hair and his skin are like mine."

"I see," Hackberry said, not understanding.

"He ain't got no family or home or country. Somebody took all that away from him. That's why he kills. It ain't for money. He thinks it is, but it ain't. He'd pay to do it."

"Why are you telling me this?"

"He believes the dead are more real than the living. That's the most dangerous kind of man there is," Danny Boy said.

An hour later, Hackberry called R.C. and Pam Tibbs into his office. "Here's the lay of the land," he said. "I've made six calls so far this morning and have been stonewalled by every fed I've talked to. My best guess is that Noie Barnum deliberately got himself kidnapped by Krill so he could infiltrate Al Qaeda's connections in Latin America. I'm not sure the FBI was in on it. Maybe Barnum is working for an intelligence group inside the NSA or the Pentagon or the CIA. Or maybe he's working on his own. Frankly, I don't care. We've been lied to over and over while serious crimes were being committed in our county. If any fed obstructs or jerks us around again, we throw his bureaucratic ass in jail."

"You sure you want to do that, Hack?" Pam said.

"Watch me."

"I don't get your reasoning, Sheriff. If Barnum wanted Krill to sell him to these Al Qaeda guys, how come he escaped?" R.C. said.

"Maybe Krill was going to piece off the action and sell him to a narco gang and wash his hands of the matter. So Barnum decided it was time to boogie."

"He wants to do all this to get even for what happened to his sister in the Towers?" R.C. said.

"Wouldn't you?" Hackberry asked.

"I'd do a whole sight more," R.C. replied.

"Right now we don't have eyes or ears out there. We need to find a weak link in the chain," Hackberry said.

"These guys are pros, Sheriff. They don't have weak links," R.C. said.

"We'll create one."

"Who?" R.C. asked.

"I saw Temple Dowling busting skeet by the Ninth Hole last night," Pam said.

It wasn't hard to find him. In the county there was only one country club and private golf course and gated community that offered rental cottages. All of it was located on a palm-dotted watered green stretch of rolling landscape that had all the attributes of an Arizona resort, the rentals constructed of adobe and cedar, the walks bordered with flower beds, the lawns flooded daily by soak hoses at sunset, the evening breeze tinged with smoke from meat fires and the astringent smell of charcoal lighter. The swimming pool glowed with a blue radiance under the stars, and sometimes on summer nights, a 1950s-type orchestra performed on the outdoor dance floor; the buffet-style fried-chicken-and-potato-salad dinners were legendary.

The club not only offered upscale insularity, it also allowed its members to feel comfortable with who they were and gave them sanction to say things they would not say anywhere else. Political correctness ended at the arched entranceway. On the links or in the lounge known as the Ninth Hole, no racial joke was too coarse, no humorous remark about liberals and environmentalists unappreciated. In the evening, against a backdrop of palm trees and golf balls flying under the lights on the driving range, in the dull popping of shotguns and clay pigeons bursting into puffs of colored smoke against a pastel sky, one had the sense that the club was a place where no one died, where all the rewards promised by a benevolent capitalistic deity were handed out in this world rather than the next.

The irony was that most of the members came from the Dallas–Fort Worth area or Houston. The other irony was the fact that the environs on which the club was built were part of the old Outlaw Trail, which had run from the Hole in the Wall Country in Wyoming all the way to the Mexican border. Butch Cassidy and the Sundance Kid and Kid Curry and Black Jack Ketchum and Sam Bass and the Dalton Gang had probably all ridden it. Thirty years before, wagon tracks that had been cut into the mire of clay and mud and livestock feces during the days of the Chisholm and Goodnight-Loving trails were still visible in the hardpan. When the topography was reconfigured by the builders of the club, the hardpan was ground up by earth-graders and layered with trucked-in sod and turned into fairways and putting greens and sand traps and ponds, for the pleasure of people who had never heard of Charles Goodnight or Oliver Loving or Jesse Chisholm and couldn't have cared less about who they were.

Deputy Sheriff Felix Chavez was twenty-seven years old and had four children and a wife he had married when she was sixteen and he was twenty. He was devoted to his family and loved playing golf and remodeling and improving his three-bedroom house. He was also a master car mechanic and a collector of historical artifacts and military ordnance. Because he often swung his cruiser off the main road and patrolled the country-club parking lot without being asked to do so, the management allowed him to use the driving range free whenever he wished, although the gesture did not extend to the links or access to the Ninth Hole. The consequence was that no one paid particular attention to him on the cloudy afternoon when he parked his cruiser by the clubhouse and got out and watched the golfers teeing off or practicing on the putting green. Nor did they think it unusual that Felix strolled through the lot, either checking on a security matter or enjoying a breezy, cool break in the weather. The drama at the club came later in the day, and Felix Chavez seemed to have no connection to it.

Temple Dowling was on the driving range with three friends, *whock*ing balls in a high arc, his form perfect, the power in his shoulders and thick arms and strong hands a surprise to those who noted only the creamy pinkness of his complexion and the baby fat under his chin and his lips that were too large for his mouth. The coordination of his swing and the whip of his wrists and the twist of his hips and buttocks seemed almost an erotic exercise, one that was not lost on others. "Temp, you're the only golf player I ever saw whose swing could make the right girl cream her jeans," one of his companions said.

They all roared, then sipped from their old-fashioneds and gin gimlets and turned their attention to the two-inch-thick bloodred steaks Temple had just forked onto the barbecue grill.

"What was that?" said one of the friends, a man with hair like an albino ape's on the backs of his wrists and arms.

"What was what?" Dowling said. He looked around, confused.

"I don't know," his friend said. "I thought I saw something. A red bug."

"Where?"

The friend rubbed at one eye with his wrist. "I probably looked into the sun. I think I need new contacts."

"It looked like it was fixing to crawl in your collar," another man said.

Temple Dowling pulled his shirt loose from his slacks and shook it. "Did I get it?"

"Nothing fell out."

"It wasn't a centipede, was it?"

"It was a little round bug," said the man with white hair on his arms.

Temple Dowling straightened his collar. "Screw it. If it bites me, I'll bite it back," he said. His friends grinned. He picked up a fork and turned the steaks, squinting in the smoke. "Right on this spot, before this was a country club, my father had a deer stand where he used to take his friends. I wasn't supposed to be there, but I snuck off to it and shot a nine-point buck with my twenty-two. Except I gut-shot him. He took off running, just about where that water trap is now. I had to hit him four more times before he went down. I was so excited I pissed my pants. I showed my father what I'd done, and he dipped his hand in the deer's blood and smeared it on my face and said, 'Damn if I don't think you've turned into a man. But we got to get you a thirty-thirty, son, before you shoot up half the county.' "

"Were you and your father pretty close, Temp?"

"Close as ice water can be to a drinking glass, I guess."

Dowling's companions nodded vaguely as though they understood when in fact they did not.

"My father had his own way of doing things," he said. "There was his way, and then there was his way. If that didn't work out, we did it his way over and over until his way worked. No man could ride a horse into the ground or a woman into an asylum like my old man."

The others let their eyes slip away to their drinks, the steaks browning and dripping on the fire, the golfers lifting their drives high into the sunset, a skeet shooter powdering a clay pigeon into a pink cloud against the sky. At the club, candor about one's life was not always considered a virtue.

"On your shirt, Temp," said the man with white hair on his wrists and arms. "There. *Jesus.*"

Dowling looked down at his clothes. "Where?"

One man dropped his gimlet glass and stepped away, his eyebrows raised, his hands lifted in front of him, as though disengaging from an invisible entanglement that should not have been part of his life. The two other men were not as subtle. They backed away hurriedly, then ran toward the Ninth Hole, coins and keys jingling in their pockets, their spiked shoes clicking on the walkway, their faces disjointed as they looked back fearfully over their shoulders.

Out on the county road, one hundred yards away, Felix Chavez walked from an abandoned mechanic's shed to an unmarked car, threw a rifle on the backseat, and drove home to eat dinner with his family.

Hackberry was dozing in his chair, his hat tilted down on his face, his feet on his desk, when the 911 call came in. Maydeen and Pam and R.C. had stayed late that afternoon. Maydeen tapped on Hackberry's doorjamb. "Temple Dowling says somebody put a laser sight on him at the country club," she said.

"No kidding," Hackberry said, opening his eyes. "What would Mr. Dowling like us to do about it?"

"Probably bring him some toilet paper. He sounds like he just downloaded in his britches," she replied.

"Maydeen —"

"Sorry," she said.

"Is Mr. Dowling still at the club?"

"He's in his cottage. He says you warned him about Jack Collins." She looked at a notepad in her hand. "He said, 'That crazy son of a bitch Collins is out there, and you all had better do something about it. I pay my goddamn taxes.' "

"Is there any coffee left?" Hackberry asked.

"I just made a fresh pot."

"Let's all have a cup and a doughnut or two, then R.C. and Pam and I can motor on out," Hackberry said. He stretched his arms, his feet still on his desk, and tossed his hat on the polished tip of one boot. "I'd better take down the flag before we go, too. It looks like rain."

"You want me to call Dowling back?"

"What for?"

"To tell him y'all are on your way."

"He knows our hearts are in the right place," Hackberry replied.

Forty minutes later, it was misting and the clouds were hanging like frozen steam on the hills when Hackberry and Pam arrived at the club in one cruiser and R.C. in another. Temple Dowling met them at the door of his cottage, a drink in his hand, his face splotched, his eyes looking past them at the fairways and trees and the shadows that the trees and buildings and electric lights made on the grass. The wind toppled a table on the flagstones by the swimming pool, and Temple

Dowling's face jumped. "What kept y'all?" he said. "Who's this woman Maydeen?"

"What about her?"

"She told me to fuck myself, is what's about her."

Hackberry stared at him without replying.

"Come inside. Don't just stand there," Dowling said.

"This is fine."

"It's raining. I don't want to get wet," Dowling said, his gaze focusing on a man stacking chairs behind the Ninth Hole.

"R.C., go up to the clubhouse and see what you can find out. We'll be here with Mr. Dowling. Let's wrap this up as soon as we can."

"Wrap this up?" Dowling said. "Somebody is trying to kill me, and you say 'wrap this up'?"

Pam and Hackberry stepped inside the cottage and closed the door behind them. "You say somebody locked down on you with a sniper's rifle?"

"Yeah. Why do you think I called?"

"And Maydeen told you to fuck yourself? That doesn't sound like her."

Dowling's eyes were jumping in their sockets. "Are you listening? I know a laser sight when I see one. Who cares about Maydeen?"

"Did your security guys see it?"

"If they had, Collins would be turning on a rotisserie."

"The last time a couple of your guys ran into Jack, they didn't do too well," Hackberry said. "The coroner had to blot them up with flypaper and a sponge. Did you call the feds?"

"You listen," Dowling said, his voice trembling with either anger or fear or both. He set down his drink on a bare mahogany table, trying to regain control of his emotions. The velvet drapes were pulled on the windows, the dark carpets and wood furniture and black leather chairs contributing somehow to the coldness pumping out of the air-conditioning ducts. "Collins has killed at least two federal agents. Nobody can do anything about him. Even Josef Sholokoff is afraid of him. But you have a personal relationship with him. If you didn't, you'd be dead. I think you're leaving him out there purposely."

"Jack Collins tried to kill Chief Deputy Tibbs. He knows what I'll do to him if I get the chance, Mr. Dowling. In the meantime, I'm not sure anything happened here. If Jack had wanted to pop you, your brains would be on your shirt."

Even in the air-conditioning, the armpits of Dowling's golf shirt were damp, his face lit with a greasy shine. He picked up his drink, then set it down again, clearing a clot out of his voice box. "I want to talk to you alone," he said.

"What for?"

"You'll see."

"Pam, would you wait up at the club?"

"I love your decor, Mr. Dowling," she said. "We busted some metalheads and satanists who were growing mushrooms inside a place that looked just like it."

Dowling went into the bedroom and returned with a cardboard file folder secured by a thin bungee cord. He removed the cord and laid the folder flat side down on a dining room table, his chest rising and falling, as though wondering if he were about to take a wrong turn into the bad side of town. "I was going to give you this anyway," he said. "So I'm not giving it to you as a bribe or a form of extortion or anything like that."

"I have no idea what you're talking about," Hackberry said.

Dowling lifted his glass and drank and set the glass down again, his words steadying in his throat. "Years ago, when you were going across the border, my father had you surveilled and photographed. And buddy, did he get you photographed. Through windows and doorways, in every position and compromising moment a man and woman can put themselves in. You used three cathouses and three cathouses only. Am I right?"

"I don't know. I had blackouts back then."

"Trust me, if my father said you did, you did. Nobody in the history of the planet was better at cooking up a witches' brew to destroy people than he was. He drove my mother mad and ruined his enemies financially and politically. In your case, he planned to blackmail you after you went to Congress. Except you married the union lady and got reborn with the proletariat and left the campaign."

"Why give me the photos?"

"I wanted to show you we're on the same side."

"We're not."

Dowling drank the rest of the whiskey in his glass, his cheeks blooming as though his soul had taken on new life. "Look, I don't have illusions about your feelings toward me. You think I'm a degenerate, and maybe I am. But I'm going to do something for you that nobody else can. You've made statements to people about your trips to Mexican whorehouses and the possibility that you screwed some underage girls. You were a whoremonger, all right, but not with young girls. If you had been, the photos would be in that file." Dowling pushed the folder toward Hackberry. "They're yours," he said.

"What about the negatives?"

"They're in there."

"And how about other prints?"

"There aren't any. I don't have any reason to lie. You may not like me, but I'm not my father."

"No, you're not," Hackberry said ambiguously.

"There's a barbecue grill on the patio out back. A little charcoal lighter and one match, and you can feed your mistakes to the flames."

"I tell you what," Hackberry said, sliding the folder back toward Dowling. "I'll provide you several phone numbers. You can give these photos to the San Antonio newspapers and my political opponents or ship them off to *Screw* magazine. Or you can thumbtack them to corkboards in Laundromats around town or glue them on the walls of washrooms and the sides of trucks. The Internet is another possibility."

"I thought I was doing the decent thing. I thought I'd put my own indiscretions in Mexico behind us. I thought you might hold me in a little higher regard."

"You profit off of war and people's misery, Mr. Dowling. My opinion about you has no weight in the matter. You're a maker of orphans and widows, just as your father was. You send others to fight wars that you yourselves will never serve in. Like a slug, your kind stays under a log, white and corpulent, and fears the sunlight and the cawing of jays. You have many peers, so don't take my comments on too personal a basis."

Dowling sat down in a straight-back chair, his hands cupped like dough balls. He was breathing through his mouth, looking upward, as though all the blood had drained out of his head. "You're a cruel, unforgiving man," he said.

"No, just a guy who has a long memory and doesn't allow himself to get bit by the same snake twice."

Pam Tibbs opened the front door without knocking and leaned inside. "Better come out here, Hack," she said. "R.C. talked to a caddie who saw a guy prowling around Mr. Dowling's SUV. R.C. is getting under it now."

The rain had stopped and the sky had started to clear and water was dripping off the fronds of the banana plants and palm trees and the roof of the shed on the driving range as they walked to the parking lot, Dowling's security men trailing behind them. In the waning of the sunset, they saw R.C. emerge from under the SUV, his uniform streaked with mud, one hand holding a serrated steel object. "It's either Chicom or Russian-made," he said. "The pin was wired to the wheel. One revolution would have pulled the pin and released the spoon."

"Where was it?" Dowling asked.

"This one was under the front seat," R.C. said.

"This one?" Dowling repeated.

"I thought I saw something back by the gas tank. I'll get a better light and check," R.C. said.

CHAPTER TWENTY-ONE

It took only two hours of worry and fear and the darker processes of the imagination to put Temple Dowling at Hackberry's front door.

"It's a little late," Hackberry said, a book in his hand.

"I'll tell you what I know, and you can do what you please with it. But you will not accuse me of being a murderer again."

"I didn't say that. I said you profited from it."

"Same thing."

"Do you want to come in or get off my property?"

Dowling sat in a chair by the front wall, away from the window, hands on the armrests like a man awaiting electrocution. He had showered and shaved and put on fresh clothes, but his face looked parboiled, his jaw disjointed, as though his mouth could not form the words he had to say. "I was a business partner with Josef Sholokoff," he said.

"In making and vending porn?"

"In entertainment. I didn't ask for details. It's a two-hundred-billion-dollar industry."

"What is?"

"Pornography. It's big business."

"You just said . . . Never mind. What about weapons?"

"I'm a defense contractor, but no, I don't work with Sholokoff. He does things off the computer with agencies that want anonymity. He's not the only one."

"Why does Sholokoff have it in for you?"

"He stiffed me on a deal, and I initiated an IRS investigation into his taxes. That's why he wants to get his hands on Noie Barnum. Josef will turn him over to Al Qaeda."

"What does he have to gain?"

"I hired Barnum. I thought he was a brilliant young engineer with a great future in weapons design. If Josef can compromise our drone program, I'll never get a defense contract again."

"You think Barnum would give military secrets to Islamic terrorists?"

"Of course. He's a pacifist and a flake or a bleeding heart, I don't know which. You don't think his kind want to flush this country down the drain? They want to feel good about themselves at somebody else's expense. What do you know about Barnum, anyway?"

Hackberry was sitting on the couch, half of his face lit by the reading lamp. He kept his expression blank, his eyes empty. "I don't know anything about him."

"No, you're hiding something," Dowling said.

"Like what?"

"I'm not sure." Dowling leaned forward. "You set me up."

"In what way?"

"At the country club. My father always said your best pitch was a slider. Son of a bitch. You took me good, didn't you?"

Hackberry shook his head. "You've lost me, Mr. Dowling."

"The grenade under my vehicle, the laser dot on my clothes. I must be the dumbest white person I ever met." Dowling waited. "You just gonna sit there and not say anything?"

Through the front window, Hackberry could see the hills and the stars and the arid coarseness of the land and the wispy intangibility of the trees in the arroyos and the glow of the town in the clouds. For what purpose had a divine hand or the long evolutionary patterns of ancient seas and volcanic eruption and the gradual wearing away of sedimentary rock created this strange and special place on the earth? Was it meant to be a magical playground for nomadic Indians who camped on its streams and viewed its buttes and mesas as altars on which they stood and stared at the western sun until they were almost blind? Or a blood-soaked expanse where colonials and their descendants had slain one another for four hundred years, where narco-armies waited on the other side of the Rio Grande, armed with weapons shipped from the United States, the same country that provided the market for the weed and coke and skag that went north on a daily basis? As Hackberry stared out the window, he thought he heard the rattle of distant machine-gun fire, a tank with a busted tread trying to dislodge itself from a ditch, the boiling sound napalm made when it danced across a snowfield. What did soldiers call it now? Snake and nape? What was the language of the killing fields today?

"You zoning out on me?" Dowling said.

"No, not at all. I was thinking about you and what you represent."

"Yes?" Dowling said, lifting his hands inquisitively.

"That's all, I was just having an idle thought or two. Good-bye, Mr. Dowling. There's no need for you to drop by again. I think your appointment in Samarra isn't far down the track. But maybe I'm wrong."

"My appointment *where?*"

Noie Barnum had experienced a recurrent dream for years that was more a memory than a dream. He would see himself as a boy again, hunting pheasants on his grandfather's farm in eastern Colorado. Noie had no memory of his father, who had died when he was three, but he would never forget his grandfather or the love he'd had for him. His grandfather had been a giant of a man, and a jolly one at that, who dressed every day in pressed bib overalls and, even though he was a Quaker, wore a big square beard like many of his Mennonite neighbors. When Noie was eleven, his grandfather had taken him pheasant hunting in a field of wild oats. The plains rolled away as far as Noie could see, golden and gray and white in the sunshine, back-dropped by an indigo sky and the misty blue snowcapped outline of the Rocky Mountains. He remembered telling his grandfather he never wanted to leave the farm and never wanted to go back to the little town where his half sister was not allowed to bring her female date to the high school prom.

His grandfather had replied, "It doesn't matter where we live or go, Noie. The likes of us will always be sojourners."

"What are sojourners?"

"Folks like me and you and your mother and sister. We're the descendants of John Brown. We have no home in this world except the one we create inside us."

Just then two pheasants had burst from the stubble, rising fat and magnificent and thickly feathered and multicolored into the air, their wings whirring, their strength and aerial agility like a denial of their size and the laws of gravity.

"Shoot, little fellow! They're yours!" his grandfather had said.

When Noie let off the twelve-gauge, the recoil almost knocked him down. Unbelievably, the pattern hit both birds; they seemed to become broken in midair, dysfunctional, their wings crumpling, their necks flopping, their feet trying to hook the air as they tumbled into the stubble.

That night Noie had cried, then the sun rose in the morning as though he had wakened from a bad dream, and for years he did not think about the birds he had killed.

But after 9/11, the dream came back in a mutated form, one in which he no longer saw himself or his grandfather. Instead, he saw curds of yellow smoke angling at forty degrees across an autumnal blue sky and two giant birds on a window ledge entwining their broken wings and then plunging into a concrete canyon where fire trucks swarmed far below.

Noie woke from the dream, raising his head off his chest, unsure where he was, staring down the long dirt road that led to an unpainted gingerbread house.

"Who's Amelia?" Jack asked.

"My half sister. I must have dozed off. Where are we?" Noie said.

"Right up from the Chinese woman's place.

Does your sister live in Alabama?"

"No, she died nine years ago."

"Sorry to hear that. I was an only child. It must warp something inside you to see your sibling taken in an untimely way."

"I don't like to talk about it."

"That's the way I figure it. We all get to the same barn. Why study on it?" When Noie didn't reply, Jack said, "You scared of it?"

"Of what?"

"Dying."

"There are worse things."

"Cite one."

"Letting evil men harm the innocent. Not doing the right thing when honor is at stake. Why are we parked here?"

"Since we're wanted all over the state of Texas, I thought it might be a good idea to wait until it was dark before we drove into the yard of somebody who knows us."

"I don't think this is smart, Jack."

"Many a man has tried to put me in jail, but I've yet to spend my first day there."

Jack got out of the car and unlocked the trunk and came back with a suitcase that he set on the hood.

"What are you doing?" Noie asked.

"Changing clothes."

"On a dirt road in the dark?"

Jack began stripping off his soiled white shirt and unbuckling his trousers and slipping his feet from his battered cowboy boots, not replying, intent upon the project at hand, whatever it was. His chest and shoulders and arms and legs were white in the moonlight, and scars were crosshatched on his back from his ribs to his shoulder blades. He buttoned on a soft white shirt and pulled on a pair of tan slacks and slipped a pair of two-tone shoes on his feet, then unfolded a western-cut sport coat from the suitcase and pushed his arms into the sleeves. He sailed his wilted panama hat up an arroyo and knotted on a tie with a rearing horse painted on it and fitted a blocked short-brim Stetson on his head. He turned toward Noie for approval. "You know the mark of a man? It's his hat and his shoes," he said.

"You look like the best-dressed man of 1945," Noie said. "But what in God's name is on your mind, Jack?"

"Options."

"Can you translate that?"

"An intelligent man creates choices. A stupid man lets others deal the hand for him."

"You're not going to hurt that woman, are you?"

"You must think pretty low of me."

"Not true. But I got to have your word."

"That's what my mother used to say, right before she made me cut my own switch and skinned me into next week," Jack said.

The front porch light was on when they parked in the yard of the gingerbread house and knocked on the screen door. "Just an advanced warning, Noie," Jack said. "I think some lies are being told about me. So don't necessarily believe everything this lady says."

"What lies?"

"If people faced the truth about how governments work, there would be revolutions all over the earth. So they blame the misdeeds of the government on individuals. I happen to be one of those individuals. You never read Machiavelli up there at MIT?"

"*¡Venga!*" someone called from the kitchen.

"You heard her," Jack said.

They went inside and sat on the couch. A heavyset Mexican woman with a wooden spoon in her hand and her hair tressed up in braids came into the living room. Jack's Stetson was propped on his knee. He rose from the couch, his hat hooked on one finger. "Where's Ms. Ling?" he said.

"She went to the store. She'll be right back. I'm Isabel," the woman said.

"Mind if we wait?" Jack asked.

"The people are coming. If you don't mind them, they won't mind you," Isabel said.

"What people?"

"*La gente.* The people."

"Yeah, I got that. But what people?"

"The people who always come. You can sit at the tables in back if you want. I already put Kool-Aid out there. You can help me carry out the food," Isabel said.

"We don't mind in the least," Noie said. "Do we, Jack?"

Jack's expression made Noie think of a large yellow squash someone had just twisted out of shape.

They carried out lidded pots of beans and fried hamburger meat and plates of hot tortillas smeared with margarine. They set them on the plank tables under the trees and helped light the candles affixed to the bottoms of jelly jars. In the distance, they could see the headlights of several vehicles headed up the dirt road toward them.

"You have a bunch of wets coming through here?" Jack said.

"No, no wets," Isabel said, wagging a finger. "These are not wets, and 'wets' is not a term we use. You understand that, *hombre?*"

"When is the lady of the house due back?" he asked.

"Any time now. Sit down. We have plenty of food for everyone."

"We're not here to eat," Jack said.

"You should. You look like a scarecrow," Isabel said.

Jack stared at her back as she walked away.

"What are you thinking?" Noie asked.

"That woman has a figure like a garbage can with a pair of bowling pins under it."

"What lies would Miss Anton be telling about you, Jack?"

"Eat up and don't worry about it."

A caravan of cars and pickup trucks pulled into the yard, and Mexican working people filed around the sides of the house and through the front door without knocking and out the back door and sat at the tables and began filling their plates, talking incessantly, paying no attention to either Jack or Noie. Through the window of the chapel, Noie could see several of them placing their hands on the base of a wooden statue. "Why do they do that?" he asked.

"They're ignorant pagans is why. Didn't you ever read Ernest Hemingway?"

"I don't think so."

"You don't *think* so? What do you people read in college? Hemingway said Spain was a Catholic country but not a Christian one. Same with this bunch."

Noie hoped the people sitting near them did not know too much English.

Several children began battering a piñata with a broom handle, tearing apart the papier-mâché and colored crepe paper and stringing pieces of wrapped candy over the dirt apron under the tree. Several girls and young women sat down across from Noie and Jack, their backs turned, watching the children, sometimes reaching behind them to pick up a jar of Kool-Aid or a rolled tortilla. Jack was eating frijoles with a spoon, watching the women and girls, a smear of tomato sauce on his chin, the lumps in his face as swollen and hard-looking as cysts. The hair of the women and girls was so black it had a purple tint in it, like satin under a black light. Their skin was sun-browned, their teeth tiny, their eyes elongated, more Indian than Mexican. Their faces and throats were fine-boned, their features free of cosmetics; they looked like girls and young women from the Asian rim who might have just arrived in a new land where they would bear children and be cared for and loved by husbands who considered them a treasure and not simply a helpmate or a commodity.

Jack tore a section of paper towel off a roll on the table and wiped his mouth with it and balled it up in his hand. His eyes seemed to go in and out of focus; he pressed a thumb into his temple as though someone had shot an iron bolt into it.

"You have a migraine?" Noie said.

Jack didn't answer. He seemed to be counting the number of girls and women sitting on the other side of the plank table. There were nine of them. The wind had come up, fluttering the candles inside the jelly jars, blowing the hair of the women and girls into strands, like brushstrokes in an Oriental painting. The piñata finally exploded from the blows of the broom handle, showering candy on the ground, filling the air with the excited screams of the children. Jack's eyes were hollow, his mouth gray, his hands like talons on the tabletop.

"You don't look too good," Noie said.

"Are you saying something is wrong with me?" Jack said, glaring into Noie's face. "You saying I got a problem?"

"No, I was wondering if you were sick. Your eyes are shiny, like you've got a fever, like you're coming down with something." Noie tried to touch Jack's forehead.

"Mind your damn business, boy."

"That's what I'm doing. If you live with someone who's sick, you ask about him."

"It's the dust and the insect repellent and the stink coming out of that pot of tripe. I told you to eat up."

Jack kept huffing air out his nose, then leaned over and spat into the dust. But he didn't raise his eyes again and kept his gaze focused on his plate. "Where's that Amerasian or Chinese woman or whatever she is?"

"Don't speak rudely of Miss Anton. She's a fine woman. What's gotten into you?" Noie said.

"We have to go."

"It was your idea to come here. It's a grand night. Look at the stars. Look at the children playing. You should have a family, Jack. You'd see things different."

"Best shut your mouth, son."

"Sticks and stones."

"I cain't believe I've become a warder for a moron."

Jack stared at the women and girls again and pressed his fist under his chin to keep his hand from shaking. Now Noie had no doubt about the origins of Jack's discomfort. He lowered his voice when he spoke. "These are poor and desperate people, Jack. Why are you upset by them? Their kind are the salt of the earth. Come on, you're a better man than the one you're acting like."

Jack rose from the bench and picked up Noie's paper plate and their uneaten food and threw it in the garbage can. "You can get in the car or walk, I don't care which," he said.

"There's Miss Anton now," Noie said. "Why don't you talk with her? I'm like these others, I think she's a holy woman. We're already here. What's to lose? It's just like giving witness at a prayer meeting."

"You like to quote Saint Paul, do you? 'I put no woman in authority over a man.' Did he say that or not? He understood the treachery that's inherent in their nature. Tell me he didn't say that?"

"Paul was talking about cultists in Corinth who belonged to a temple dedicated to the worship of Diana. They were courtesans and were behaving as such in the church. Stop acting like you're unlettered."

"A pox on you," Jack replied.

Noie stood up and smiled as Anton Ling headed for their table, but she didn't acknowledge him. She had parked her truck by the barn and was coming hard across the horse lot, past the windmill and the water tank, amid the tables and the seated diners and the children who were still hunting for the pieces of candy they had scattered on the ground. She paused only long enough to pick up the broom handle the children had used to burst the piñata.

"What are you doing here?" she said to Jack.

The women and the girls at the table scattered.

"To determine if you betrayed me to an FBI agent by the name of Ethan Riser," Jack said.

"Betrayed *you?* Are you insane?"

"Agent Riser tried to kill me. With no provocation."

"You murdered him. You also shot a man from Parks and Wildlife."

"I defended myself against them."

"Listen to me, Mr. Barnum," Anton said. "I don't know why you're with this man, but he's a mass murderer. He killed nine Thai girls with a submachine gun. He's a coward and a bully and mean to the bone. Stand up, Mr. Collins."

"I tried to be your friend, woman. I came to your house when Josef Sholokoff's men attacked you."

"Don't you ever address me as 'woman.' "

"How dare you sass me?"

"How dare you be on the planet?" she said,

and swung the broom handle down on the crown of his head just as he was rising from the bench. Then she attacked in serious mode, gripping the bottom of the handle to get maximum torque in her swings, slashing the blows on his ears and shoulders and forearms and forehead, any place that was exposed, cracking him once so hard on the temple that Noie thought the blow might be fatal.

"Miss Anton!" he said. "Miss Anton! Ease up! Please! You're fixing to kill him!"

Jack stumbled away from the table, blood leaking out of his hair, one arm crooked to protect his face. She followed after him, hitting him in the spine and ribs, finally breaking the broom handle with a murderous swing across the back of his neck. "Go into the darkness that spawned you, you vile man," she said. "Find the poor woman who bore you and apologize for the fact of your birth."

Jack fell to one knee. He had left his hat behind him, on the table, crown down. He seemed to look at it with longing, as though he had left behind the better part of him. Noie picked him up and helped him to the Trans Am, staring back over his shoulder at Miss Anton and the Mexicans standing in the backyard, their faces lit by the porch light and the candles flickering on the tables. Noie pushed Jack into the passenger seat. "I'll drive," he said.

"You're going with me?"

"What's it look like?"

Jack was smiling, his face threaded with blood running from his forehead. "You're a good kid."

"The hell I am." Noie started the engine and headed south down the dirt road, the headlights bouncing off mesquite that grew on the hillsides.

"I know a stand-up young guy when I see one," Jack said.

Noie accelerated, aiming over his knuckles at the road in front of him.

"Did you hear me?" Jack asked.

"Yeah, I heard you. Everything you've said. Night and day. I hear you. Boy, do I hear you. You killed an FBI agent and shot somebody from Parks and Wildlife?"

"They dealt the play. I didn't go looking for them."

Noie's jawbone tensed against his cheek in the dash light, but he said nothing in reply.

"You picked me up out of the dirt back there even though your ribs haven't mended. I know how much broken ribs hurt. There're not many kinds of pain I haven't experienced. But pain can be a blessing. It gives you fire in the belly you can draw on when need be, and it allows you to understand others, for good or bad. You hearing me on this, son?"

"I'm not your damn son."

"Have it your way."

"You have to help me find Krill."

"Why rent space in your head to a half-breed rodent?"

"I want Krill in leg irons," Noie said, looking away from the road into Jack's face. "That's the only reason I'm on board. You got that?"

"You believe I killed those Thai women?"

Noie's hands tightened on the wheel, and he looked at the road again. "Did you?"

"What's the deal with Krill?"

"He can take me to Al Qaeda. He was going to sell me to them. Then he decided to sell me to some narco-gangsters because it was easier."

"I think I'm seeing the landscape a little more clearly. Your sister died on 9/11?"

"In the Towers."

"If I he'p you find Krill and maybe even these asswipes from Al Qaeda?"

"I'll stay with you. I'll be your friend. I won't let you down."

"Turn east at the highway. We're not going back to our place. I'll show you a road through a ranch into Coahuila. Only a few wets know about it."

"But we leave everybody else here alone? Right? We find Krill but that's it?"

"You're preaching to the choir," Jack said. "All I've ever wanted was to be left alone. I never stole, and I never went looking for trouble. How many people can say that?"

Noie looked back at him. "I know you've done some dark deeds, but I can't believe you mowed down a bunch of innocent women. I just can't believe that."

"Believe whomever you want. I'm tired of talking. I've tired of everything out there."

"Out where?"

"There, in the dark, the voices in the wind, the people hunting and killing each other while they scowl at the likes of me. If I study on it, I have moments when I want to write my name on the sky in ways nobody will ever forget. That's the burden you carry when you're born different. You told me once your sister grew up bisexual or whatever in that small southern town y'all come from. Did she have a good time of it there? I think you've got more of me inside you than you're willing to admit, Noie."

"You're wrong."

Jack gazed silently through the front window, his forehead crosshatched with lesions, his thoughts, if any, known only to himself.

CHAPTER TWENTY-TWO

Anton Ling called in the report on Noie Barnum and Jack Collins's visit to her property five minutes after the two men had left. Maydeen Stoltz immediately called Hackberry at his home.

"Which way did they head?" he said.

"South, toward the four-lane."

"Get out traffic stops ten miles on either side of where they would enter the four-lane. Then call the FBI and the Border Patrol. Did Noie Barnum seem coerced?"

"Not according to Ms. Ling. She says Barnum heard her accuse Collins of murdering Ethan Riser and the Thai women, and Barnum left with him voluntarily. You think this is Stockholm syndrome or whatever they call it?"

"I doubt it."

"No matter how you cut it, Barnum isn't a victim?" Maydeen said.

"Not to us, he isn't," Hackberry replied.

"Ms. Ling says she beat the shit out of

Collins with a broom handle. You want me to check the hospitals?"

"Waste of time," Hackberry said. "I'll see you tomorrow."

"What do you think his next move is, Hack?"

"He's going to call either the department or my house."

"What for?"

"He made a public fool of himself at Anton Ling's," Hackberry replied.

"I don't get it."

"We're the only family he has."

"Yuck," she said.

The next morning Hackberry went to his office early and dug out the three-inch-thick file on Jack Collins and began thumbing through only a small indicator of the paperwork that one man had been able to string across an entire continent. The paperwork on Collins, who had never spent one day in jail, included faxes from Interpol and Mexico City, NCIC printouts, FBI transmissions, analytical speculations made by a forensic psychologist at Quantico, crime-scene photos that no competent defense attorney would allow a jury to see, autopsy summations written by coroners who were barely able to deal with the magnitude of the job Collins had dropped on them, witness interviews, crime-lab ballistic matches from Matamoros to San Antonio, and the most fitting inclusion in the file, a handwritten memo by a retired Texas Ranger in Presidio County who wrote, "This man seems about as complex as a derelict begging food at your back door and I suspect he smells about the same. I think the trick is to make him hold still long enough to put a bullet in him. But we've yet to figure out a way to do it."

What did it all mean? For Hackberry, the answer was simple. The system couldn't handle Jack Collins because he didn't follow the rules or conform to patterns that are associated with criminal behavior. He wasn't addicted to drugs or alcohol, didn't frequent prostitutes, and showed little or no interest in money. There was no way to estimate the number of people he had murdered, since many of his homicides were committed across the border, but he was not a serial killer. Nor could he be shoved easily into that great catchall category known as psychopaths, since he obviously had attachments, even though the figures to whom he was attached lived in his imagination.

Preacher Jack was every psychiatrist's nightmare. His level of intelligence and his wide reading experience allowed him to create a construct in which he shared dominion with the Olympians. His narcissism was so deeply rooted in his soul that he did not fear death because he thought the universe could not continue without his presence. He was messianic and believed he could see through a hole in the dimension and watch events play out in the lives of people who were not yet born.

With gifts like these, why should Preacher Jack fear a law enforcement agency? Like the cockroach and the common cold, he was in the fight for the long haul.

The irony was that in spite of his success in eluding the law for almost two decades, Collins shared a common denominator with his fellow miscreants: He needed law enforcement to validate who he was. Intuitively, he knew his own kind were by and large worthless and would sell him out for a pack of cigarettes if they thought they could get away with it. All career criminals wanted the respect of the cops, jailers, social workers, correctional officers, and prison psychologists whose attention gave them the dimensions they possessed in no other environment.

There was another consideration in regard to what went on in the mind of a man like Preacher Jack. His visit last night at Anton Ling's home reminded Hackberry of a similar event that had taken place in Jack's life the previous year, in San Antonio. Jack had become obsessed with a Jewish woman by the name of Esther Dolan and had invaded her home and indicated to her that he had chosen her as his queen. When she had recovered from the shock of his presumption, she called him a dog turd off the sidewalk and picked up a stainless-steel oatmeal pot and almost beat him to death with it.

Pam Tibbs leaned inside his door. "Guess who's on the phone," she said.

"Texas's answer to B.O. Plenty."

"Who?" she said.

"Collins?"

"I've already started the trace," she said.

"Have the feds called back this morning?"

"Nope."

Hackberry gazed at the blinking light on his telephone, then picked up the receiver. "What's the haps, Jack?" he said.

"I thought I'd check in."

"We figured we'd be hearing from you."

"You omniscient, Mr. Holland?"

"It's Sheriff Holland to you."

"I like to keep abreast of your activities, since you seem intent on doing me harm and forgetting I saved the life of your young deputy, what's-his-name, Bevins."

"No, I think you're calling because you became a human piñata out at Anton Ling's place, in front of dozens of poor Mexicans who are now convinced there's a serious problem in the Anglo gene pool. Just before you called, I was thinking about a pattern that seems to follow you around, Jack. Remember Esther Dolan in San Antone? She's the lady who drove you from her house with knots all over your head. Then there was that good-looking gal, the country singer, Vikki Gaddis. She sprayed wasp killer in your eyes and took your pistol away from you and shot you through the foot. Why is it you keep getting into it with women who kick your ass? Do they remind you of your mother?"

"Good try, Sheriff. But I'm afraid you don't know much about my upbringing."

"You like to read novels. I've got a story for you, better than any fiction. Did you know that when Ma Barker and her son Fred were surrounded by the FBI, they executed each other with submachine guns? They sat across from each other in straight-back chairs down by the Everglades and blew each other all over the walls. How about that for a tight mother-son relationship? They were even buried in the same casket."

"You fear a woman's wrath, Sheriff Holland? The man who does will surround himself with manipulators and prostitutes and will never have a real woman in his life. The level of his anger hides the degree of his need. I thought you were wise in the ways of the world, but I'm starting to have my doubts."

"Ethan Riser was my friend, you arrogant son of a bitch."

"Ah, now we get down to the real issue."

"You emptied your magazine into him after he was dead. His face was unidentifiable. He said something to you before he died, something you couldn't abide, didn't he? What was it, Collins? That you were despised inside the womb?"

"To be honest, I couldn't quite make out Agent Riser's words in all that shooting. The Thompson makes a heck of a racket."

Hackberry could feel his hand gripping the phone receiver tighter and tighter, a bilious taste welling up in his throat. "No, it wasn't about your mother. It wasn't about your pathetic sex life, either. It had something to do with your vision of yourself, the Orkin man posing as Jesus. Ethan was a student of both history and Shakespeare. He reached back into his own reference and used it on you, didn't he? What made it doubly injurious was the fact that you acquired your literary background the hard way, and he used it to make you look like a fool. He called you a clown, didn't he? A collection of tattered rags flapping in the wind, a stick figure with a carved pumpkin for a head. That's you, Collins. Everyone knows it except you, you moron. Even the dead people who follow you around know it. You're an object of pity. You think women like Gaddis and Dolan and Ling would be in a room with you unless you were holding a gun on them? Don't call here again, even to surrender yourself. A phone conversation with you is like someone putting spittle in my ear. I don't know how else to describe it. You have that effect on people."

Hackberry replaced the receiver in the phone cradle and stared at it, his hand shaking on the desk blotter.

"That was a beaut," Pam said from the doorway. "Think you got to him?"

Hackberry shook his head. "There're no handles on Collins. I had no design in mind."

"You could have fooled me."

He looked at her for a long time. "Be careful," he said.

"Of Collins?"

"Of everything. We can't lose our good people."

"Nothing is going to happen to me," she said.

"Don't say that. It's bad luck."

She came into his office and closed the door behind her. "The minister from my church dropped by. He said he wanted to warn me about a rumor he'd heard."

"What did you tell him?"

"That whatever it was, it was probably true, and I wasn't interested in hearing it."

He folded his hands behind his head and put one boot on the corner of the desk. "You're heck on wheels, kiddo."

"Call me that after quitting time and I'll hit you."

"I believe it," he replied.

In the darkness the game ranch was a surreal place that seemed more like African dry land drenched in moonlight and shadowed by an enormous mountain that was over six thousand feet in elevation. The sand in the streambeds was white, the rocky sides of the declivities as sharp as knives, the land rustling with desert greenery and tabled with slabs of sedimentary rock that looked like the marbled backs of albino whales. The steel fence that enclosed the ranch seemed to roll for miles across the countryside, and the mesh was so thick that it took Krill's men twenty minutes to scissor an opening in it with the bolt cutters. Out in the darkness, they could hear large animals banging around in the brush, hooves clattering on rocks, and they wondered if the noise would give warning to Josef Sholokoff and his entourage at the big stone house in the valley.

Krill led his men single-file through the slit in the fence, his M16 now equipped with a bipod and slung on his right shoulder, his eyes locked on the lighted compound down below. The wind was up, bending the trees and the tall grasses, which was not good for men threading their way through trees and foliage. When the wind blew, everything in the environment moved, even the shadows, everything except Krill and his men. But bad luck was an element to which a man adjusted and did not allow himself to be overcome by. Negrito was another matter. Suddenly, he had become an expert on all matters of importance and would not shut up: "This place has got rattlesnakes and Gila monsters in it . . . Those big animals you hear snuffing, that's rhinos. One wrong step and *squish* . . . A *puta* for one of the Russian's men told you where he was at? How dependable is that? What if he ain't there? What if we kill a bunch of guys and don't get the Russian? We got to wipe the slate clean, Krill. We turn the house down there into a cemetery."

"Once again you have shown your great wisdom," Krill said. "But now you must be quiet."

"I am operating as your loyal lieutenant and adviser, my *jefe*."

"Yes, yes, I know. But you talk like a bat flapping its wings in a cave, filling the air with sound that means nothing. You must cease this constant talking. It's like glass in my ears."

Negrito's BB eyes seemed to grow closer to the bridge of his nose. "I'm here to serve you, nothing more. I worry about this mission. We are killing the Russian because he killed the minister who baptized your children. But this all has it origins with La Magdalena. If she had baptized them as you asked, we would not be having these problems. The Russians are dangerous. If you kill one of them, you kill them all. They come out of prisons worse than Mexico's. They fuck their mothers and kill their children. Many of them were in insane asylums."

"Where do you get these ideas, *hombre?*"

"You don't listen to the new music, the *narcocorridas.* The *narcocorridas* tell us all about these guys. That's why our people have to be vicious and show no mercy."

"Look up there on the hillsides, above the stone house. Those two men are Sholokoff's guards. Let your actions replace your words, Negrito. Take Lupa and Mimo with you and do your job."

"Stay here and I'll bring you back their ears. I don't need Mimo and Lupa to do it, either."

Krill waved a finger back and forth. "No, you don't bring back ears."

"You took the scalp of the DEA agent."

"Because he killed my brother. Because I had to bring an offering to my brother's grave so he could rest. You do not bring back trophies from these men. They are only doing what they are told."

"Wait and see," Negrito said.

"Everything with you is an argument." Krill pulled Negrito's leather hat off his head and started to hit him with it but instead simply shook his head and handed the hat back. He waited several seconds before he spoke, the heat dying in his chest. "The moon is going behind the mountain. As soon as the shadow falls on the house, kill Sholokoff's guards and come back to me. You are very good at what you do, Negrito. Do not fail me."

"I will never fail you. When the rooster crows and the sun rises, you will see me at your side and know I have been your loyal servant and follower."

The moon slipped behind the crest of the mountain, dropping the valley into black shadow. Negrito and the two other men filed down a game trail and climbed silently over a table rock and disappeared into a thicket that was rife with thorns, never hanging their clothes on one of them, never rustling a branch. Krill unslung his assault rifle and knelt in the grass and waited, his gaze roaming over the lighted stone house and the swimming pool steaming behind it and a children's swing set whose chains made a tinkling sound in the wind.

His M16 had been stolen from an armory in Mexico, along with crates of ammunition and United States Army .45 automatics and bayonets and grenades and flak vests and other forms of military ordnance that Krill considered of no value. But the M16 was indeed a wondrous product of American manufacturing genius. It was lightweight, simple in design, easy to disassemble, rapid-firing, and soft on the shoulder. In semiauto mode, it could snap off shots individually with lethal accuracy or, on auto mode, hose down an entire room in seconds. The newer ones seldom jammed, and in the dark, the shooter could easily drop an empty magazine and replace it with a fresh one. Krill had jungle-clipped a twenty-round and thirty-round magazine together, so when his bolt locked open on an empty chamber, he could invert the two magazines and jam the full one into the loading slot without ever missing a beat.

Argentinean and American advisers had taught him how to shoot and care for the M16 and how to aim in the dark and not silhouette on a hill and how to crawl through wire on his stomach and sink mines in the trails used by the Sandinistas. They had also taught him the use of the M60 machine gun, a weapon whose murderous effectiveness had never ceased to amaze him. What his advisers had not taught him was how to live with the virus the guns had given him, because that was what it was, he told himself, a virus, one that produced an insatiable bloodlust that was like walking around in a warm pink mist and always wanting more of it.

He looked at the luminescent numbers on his wristwatch. Seventeen minutes had passed. He wondered what was keeping Negrito and the others. Lupa and Mimo were not killers by nature, but they would do as they were told and would not question the morality of the orders, as was almost always the case with poor men who became soldiers. Lupa had earned his nickname, "the magnifying glass," because of the cheap spectacles he wore in order to read and his attention to details that were of no importance. Like Lupa, Mimo had been a farmer in Oaxaca before the prices for corn had gone to virtually nothing, but he was also a drunkard who drank huge amounts of liquor, made from sugarcane, that could be bought for a few cents a bottle. Neither man was dangerous or violent in himself, and both men together did not form another personality that was necessarily dangerous. But under the direction of Negrito, they would commit any number of heinous acts as long as they believed they were committing them in the interest of their families. Mexico was not a country, Krill thought. It was a revolution that had never stopped. The only things in it that stayed the same were the killings and the river of narcotics flowing to the north. The poor suffered and worked in sweatshops and lived in hovels and abandoned their children to live on the streets of Mexico City. Why did they not all rise up and kill their masters? Krill had no answer. Could it be that they were holy in their passivity? As with Negrito, these were ideas he could not fathom, at least not adequately. Maybe that was why Negrito had become his companion and lieutenant. This last conclusion was a disturbing one, and he did not want to dwell further on it.

He saw Mimo and Lupa coming through

the trees and tall grass, bent down, their un-shaved faces as severe as those of men staring into an ice storm.

"*¿Qué pasa?*" Krill asked.

Their eyes avoided his. Lupa looked over his shoulder.

"*¡Dígame!*" Krill said.

"*Muerto,*" Lupa said.

"*¿Quiene?*" Krill asked.

"*Ellos,*" Mimo replied.

"Do you think I am stupid? What did you do out there?" Krill said in English.

Neither man replied. They squatted and kneaded their thighs as though they had run a long distance. They wiped their noses on their hands and felt in their pockets for tobacco or chewing gum, then looked with relief over their shoulders when they heard Negrito coming through the brush, bent low, a button-down shirt wadded in his hand.

"What happened out there?" Krill said.

"We took care of them guys. Like you told me. The second guy fought," Negrito replied.

"What is in your hand?"

"Nothing anybody's gonna miss. At least them guys ain't."

"Do not play games with me, Negrito."

"Krill, we are doing these things out of loyalty to you. We ain't getting paid. Why are you on my case, man?"

"Put the shirt on the ground and open it."

"I am at your orders. But you make a big

thing out of nothing. You didn't want no ears. So I took their noses. They were dead. What does a dead man care about a nose? What's he gonna smell? There ain't no flowers in a grave, at least the graves these guys are gonna have."

"The second man? You said he fought. He alerted others?"

"He couldn't talk, know what I mean?" Negrito drew a finger across his throat. "But he fought hard just the same. I think he was Russian. The Russians got cojones like base-balls. You got to kill them guys really dead. Krill?"

"*¿Qué pasa?*" Krill answered, overwhelmed by the processes of Negrito's mind.

Negrito seemed to stare at the stone house and the light falling out of the windows on the patio and the windmill palms and um-brella trees and the dark surface of the swim-ming pool. The wind gusted, wrinkling the water, rustling the limp chains on the swing set. His brow furrowed. "Me and Lupa and Mimo was talking," he said. "The inside of that house is like a bank. There's got to be cash all over it. Maybe cocaine, too. We do everybody in there, man, then take what we want."

"No."

"What do you mean 'no'? Come on, *cabrón.* We suppose to work for nothing? It ain't fair. We're amigos. We have always shared. But you can't share nothing."

"Go back on your own if you don't like our mission."

"I will never leave you."

"Then do as I say."

"And what is that? To let the Russian's friends hunt us down? We're gonna kill them all, right? If we kill them all, why not take what should be ours? All of this land belonged to our ancestors. Now it is owned by everybody except us."

"You are a logical man. But we do not have an issue with anyone but Josef Sholokoff. I do not want his possessions. We avenge Minister Cody. We made fun of his manhood, but it was he who set the souls of my children free. For that I honor his memory. Do not intrude upon my purpose here."

Negrito raised his big hands and turned in a circle like a baboon attempting a pirouette. "Then let's kill the Russian and be gone. I am tired of this place. Do you want me to do it? I would do it with great pleasure. I am tired of talking about baptism and souls while we don't get paid for the work we do. I am not a mystic. I believe in the knife and gun and dealing seriously with my enemies."

"You also believe in the shovel."

"You speak of my cemetery? I signal our adversaries of our potential."

"You keep a museum under the ground for your pleasure. As a ghoul would. *Vámonos*,"

Krill said. He slung his rifle over his shoulder and walked off through the brush and started down the incline, Negrito's close-set pig eyes slipping off the side of his face.

As Krill approached the stone house, he forgot about Negrito and began to think about the challenge at hand. When the two guards Negrito had killed did not report in, others would be sent outside to find them. In the meantime, Krill had to find a spot that would allow him a clean shot through the front window. He thought he could hear the sound of a television coming from the front of the house, but in the wind he couldn't be sure. His informant had told him that Sholokoff was staying at the house with no more than four men. Two of those were already taken care of. If Krill could get a clear shot at Sholokoff and kill him instantly, he might not have to kill his men, too. Few hired killers were willing to risk their lives for a dead employer. But if they chose to avenge their employer's death, they would share the fate of their comrades on the hillside, Krill thought, and the choice would be theirs, not his.

He stayed in the shadow of the mountain and found a flat place up on a bench behind a rock, perhaps thirty yards from the front of the house, with an unobstructed view through the picture-glass living room window. He removed a small pair of binoculars from a pouch on his web belt and focused them through the glass. A diminutive, gray-headed, wizen-faced man in a belted scarlet robe was watching television from a reclining chair. His wiry beard and angular features made Krill think of a ferret or a toy constructed of Popsicle sticks and glue. How could one so small possess so much wealth and exert so much power over others? Krill wondered. Why did the gringos allow this tiny man to do so much damage in their country? The narcotics he sold were the poor man's hydrogen bomb. But that was their business and not his. Krill wrapped his left forearm in the rifle sling, fitted his right hand in the pistol grip, and looked through the iron sights. Behind him, he could hear Negrito breathing in the darkness, an aura of dried sweat and tobacco and wood smoke emanating from his body.

"*¡Qué bueno, hombre!*" Negrito said.

"Do not talk," Krill said, shifting the bipod on the rock, depressing the barrel slightly so the hood on the front sight formed a perfect circle around Sholokoff's tiny head. He tightened his finger on the trigger, letting out his breath, his cheek flush against the dull black finish of the rifle stock.

"*Chingado,* go ahead!" Negrito said. "Burn the whole magazine. It's time we got out of here. I want to fuck my woman tonight."

Krill had released his finger from the trigger and was staring numbly down the incline at the window. Two little girls and a little boy had just run from a side room and climbed into Sholokoff's lap. Negrito leaned over Krill's shoulder to see better, his loins brushing against Krill's buttocks, his body odor and the smell of onions and garlic and fried meat on his breath enveloping Krill in a toxic cloud.

"Fuck, man, do it," Negrito said. "I hear a plane. Them hunters come in and out of here all the time. They got a landing strip on the other side of the house."

"Shut your mouth," Krill said.

"You ain't thinking straight. We already killed two guys. You got to finish the job, man. Sholokoff has many friends. We cannot have this man hunting us. Do it now, *jefe.*"

"Take your hand off my shoulder."

"Then shoot."

"You will not give me orders."

"Then give me the rifle."

"Remove your hand and take your odor out of my face."

"Look at the plane. It's dipping out of the sky. You have to choose between our families and these worthless people. You worry about my odor? What is wrong with you, man?"

"You are like an empty wagon rattling across a bridge," Krill said. "You speak craziness and nonsense. You are like the demoniac babbling among the swine. We do not kill children. Have you learned nothing? Do you understand nothing except killing?"

"We did not put the children here. This is not our fault. Lupa and Mimo and me will do everything that is necessary inside the house. You will not have to see or hear anything that happens down there. One day you will be right in the head, but now you are not. So we will do these things for you and forget the bad words that you have spoken."

"You will do nothing without my permission."

"Take the shot, Krill. Please. You can do it. I've seen you shoot the head off a dove at a hundred meters. Concentrate on the Russian and don't worry about the children. They will be all right. But we cannot leave this man alive."

Krill's head was pounding, his ears filled with whirring sounds that were louder than either the wind or Negrito's incessant talking. Had it been like this for the soldiers in the helicopter who had machine-gunned the clinic built by the East Germans? Had they seen Krill's children playing in the yard and wondered if they should not abort their mission? Had they fired on the building in hopes that they would not hit the children? Or had they given no thought at all to what they were doing? Did they simply murder his children and fly back to their base and eat lunch and drink warm beer under a palm-shaded table, staring idly at a smokeless blue volcano in the distance? Was that what happened when they slew the innocent children he had loved from the first breath they had drawn?

He bent over the rifle again, feeling the sling tighten on his left arm, his mouth filled with a taste like pennies, a brass band thundering in his head. The little boy was seated firmly in Sholokoff's lap, watching the television. Krill raised the rifle barrel until the hood on the front sight circled Sholokoff's head like the frame on a miniature photograph. He took a breath and waited a split second and then exhaled slowly, slowly, slowly, his left eye squinted shut, his right eye bulging like a child's marble, his index finger tightening as though it had a life of its own.

Suddenly, he stood erect, pulling his hand from the trigger guard as though it had been shocked with a cattle prod. His teeth were chattering, his breath catching in his throat. *Murderer,* he thought he heard a voice say. *Assassin! Man who brought death to his own children.* He stared wide-eyed at Negrito.

"You look sick, *cabrón.* You look like your mind has flown into the darkness," Negrito said.

"We go back through the grass and out the fence," Krill said. "We are through with this. We will deal with Sholokoff at another time."

"I cannot believe what you are doing," Negrito said. "You're letting us down, man. You are making a great mistake that each of us will pay for. It ain't fair. You are betraying us, Krill."

Krill was already walking deep into the mountain's shadow, his M16 reslung on his shoulder, his eyes empty, like those of a man who has looked into a mirror and is unable to recognize the image staring back at him.

CHAPTER TWENTY-THREE

Hackberry Holland did not learn of the killings near the Santiago Mountains from another law enforcement agency, because they were not reported the night they occurred or the following morning, either. He learned of them from a questionable source, one in whom he had already induced a sizable dose of paranoia. In fact, he had a hard time concentrating on the telephone conversation. It was raining, and he had forgotten to take down the flag outside his office window. The flag, soggy as a towel, hung twisted and forlorn against a gray sky, its chain vibrating against the pole like a damaged nerve. "Mr. Dowling, I've heard nothing about a shooting in this county or anywhere around here," he said. "It's been surprisingly quiet."

"Of course you didn't. Josef doesn't want cops crawling all over his property," Temple Dowling replied.

"You say two men were killed?"

"Right. Two security guys. Somebody cut their noses out of their faces."

"Sounds a bit strange, doesn't it? I mean, why is it you know about this but nobody else does?"

"Because maybe I got one or two people inside Josef's organization."

"What do you want me to do about this unreported homicide that only you seem to know about?"

"Go out to the game ranch. Investigate the crime. Stuff a hand grenade up his ass. What do I care? Why not just do your fucking job?"

"Because somehow you're at risk?"

"Josef believes I put a hit on him."

"Listen to what you're saying, Mr. Dowling. Two guys got killed outside Sholokoff's house, but no attempt was made to harm anybody inside the house. Does that seem like a rational scenario to you?"

"That's because a bunch of hunters had just flown in. Look, my source says Josef went apeshit. He had his grandchildren in the house." There was a pause. "His guys are coming after me."

Hackberry could hear the tremor in Dowling's voice, the frightened boy no longer able to hide behind arrogance and cruelty. "First, you have your own security service, Mr. Dowling. Why not make use of it? If a crime occurred in the place you describe, it's out of my jurisdiction. Second, maybe it's time for you to grow up."

"Time for me to —"

"Everybody dies. Why not go down with the decks awash and the guns blazing? You've probably made millions profiteering off of war. Get a taste of the real deal and scorch your name on the wall before you check out. It's not a bad way to go."

"You're a son of a bitch."

Hackberry rubbed his forehead and started to hang up, then placed the receiver against his ear again. "If you think you're in danger, get out of town."

"I'm already out of town. It doesn't matter. Sholokoff has a network all over the country."

"I think you're imagining things."

"You don't understand Josef. He doesn't just do evil. He loves it. That's the difference between him and the rest of us. Jack Collins is probably a lunatic. Josef isn't. He creates object lessons nobody ever forgets. He has people taken apart."

"He does what?"

Perhaps due to his fundamentalist upbringing, R. C. Bevins was not a believer in either luck or coincidence but saw every event in his life as one that required attention. The consequence was that he never dismissed any form of human behavior as implausible and never thought of bizarre events in terms of their improbability. The sheriff had once told

R.C. that if a UFO landed on the prairie, two things were guaranteed to happen: Everyone who witnessed the landing would grab his cell phone to dial 911, and R.C. would knock on the spaceship door and introduce himself.

R.C. had pulled into a convenience store and gas station on a county road just south of the east-west four-lane that paralleled the Mexican border, and had gone inside and bought a chili dog and a load of nachos and jalapeño peppers and a Dr Pepper and had just started eating lunch at a table by the front window when he saw a pickup stop and let out a passenger. The passenger limped slightly, as though he had a stitch in his side. He wore shades and an unlacquered wide-brim straw hat, like one a gardener might wear. His nose was a giant teardrop, his jeans hiked up too high on his hips, his suspenders notched into his shoulders, the way a much older man might wear them. The man went into the back of the store and took a bottle of orange juice and a ham-and-cheese sandwich from the cooler and a package of Ding Dongs from the counter. He paid, sat down, and began eating at a table not far from R.C.'s, never removing his shades. R.C. nodded at him, but the man did not look up from his food.

"Bet you could fry an egg out there," R.C. said.

"That about says it," the man replied, chewing slowly, his mouth closed, his gaze seemingly fixed on nothing.

"My uncle says that during the drought of 1953, it got so dry here he saw a catfish walking down a dirt road carrying its own canteen."

"That's dry."

"You looking for a ride? 'Cause the bread-delivery man is fixing to head back to town."

"No, I'm visiting down the road there. South a piece." The man drank from his orange juice and wiped his mouth with a paper napkin and began eating his sandwich again.

"Did you see any salt and pepper up there at the counter?" R.C. asked.

"I think I did. Where the ketchup and such are. In that little tray."

"You want some?"

"No, sir, I'm fine."

R.C. went to the counter by the coffee and cold-drink dispensers and began sorting through the condiments. "Do y'all have any hot sauce?" he said to the cashier.

"It's there somewhere," the cashier replied.

"I sure cain't find it."

The cashier walked over and picked up the hot sauce and handed it to R.C. He was a short man with a sloping girth who always showed up at work in a dress shirt and an outrageous tie and with polished shoes. He had a tiny black mustache that expanded like

578

grease pencil when he grinned. "Glad it wasn't a snake."

"Keep looking straight at me," R.C. said.

The cashier's face clouded, but he kept his eyes locked on R.C.'s.

"You know that old boy over yonder?" R.C. said.

"I think he was in yesterday. He bought some Ding Dongs and a newspaper."

"He was by himself?"

"He came here with another man. The other fellow stayed in the car."

"What'd the other guy look like?"

"I didn't pay him much mind."

"What kind of car?"

The cashier looked into space and shook his head. "It was skinned up. It didn't have much paint on it. I don't know what kind it was."

"You ever see it before?"

The cashier rubbed his eye. "No, sir," he said. "Are we fixing to have some trouble here? 'Cause that's something I really don't need."

"No. Did the guy in the car buy gas with a credit card?"

"If he did, I didn't see it. He got air."

"What?"

"He went to the air pump. I remember that 'cause he was the last to use it. Somebody ran over the hose, and I had to put an out-of-order sign on it. Ain't nobody used it since."

R.C. went back to his table and set the bottle of hot sauce down, then snapped his fingers as though he had forgotten something. He went outside to his cruiser and picked up a clipboard off the seat, then walked past the air pump. The concrete slab around it was covered with a film of mud and dust that had dried into a delicate crust. A set of familiar tire tracks was stenciled across it. "Michelins," R.C. said under his breath.

R.C. went back to his table with the clipboard. "I got to do these dadburn time logs," he said to the man at the next table.

"I bet that's what we'll all be doing when somebody drops a nuclear missile on us," the man said.

"I never thought of it like that. I think you got your hand on it."

"Hope we get some rain. This is about the hottest place I've ever been," the man said.

"You know what General Sherman said when he was stationed here? He said if he owned both Texas and hell, he'd rent out Texas and live in hell," R.C. said.

The man tilted up his orange juice and drank it empty, swallowing smoothly, never letting a drop run off the side of his mouth. R.C. went back to eating, his long legs barely fitting under the table, his jaw filled with food, one eye on his clipboard. "This stuff is a royal pain in the ass," he said. "I'm going back on patrol. If they want my time logs filled out, they can fill them out their own self."

"If I were you, I'd put the times in there somebody wants and not worry about it. That's how organizations are run. You just got to make things look right. Why beat yourself up over it?"

"You sound like a guy who's been around."

"Not really."

"Where you staying at, exactly?"

"A little vacation spot a buddy of mine has got rented. It's just a place to go hunting for rocks and arrowheads and such."

"Look, is somebody coming to pick you up? You looked like you were limping."

"I'll hitch a ride. People here'bouts are pretty nice."

"I don't mind driving you home. That's part of the job sometimes."

"No, I was in an accident a while back. I don't like to start depending on other people. It gets to be a habit too easy."

R.C. picked up the remnants of his nachos and chili dog and threw them in the trash, then sat down at the table with the man, who was now feeding a Ding Dong into his mouth. "You seem like a right good fellow," he said. "The kind of guy who don't want to hurt nobody but who might get into something that's way to shit and gone over his head."

"I wouldn't say that."

"I always figured if a guy makes a mistake,

he ought to get shut of it as quick as he can and keep on being the fellow he always was."

"That could be true, but I think you've got somebody else in mind."

"You're not from Texas, but you're from down South somewhere, right?"

"Me and a few million others."

"But you weren't raised up to keep company with criminals. It's got to grate on you. I reckon that's why you hitched a ride here today."

"You want a Ding Dong?"

"Not right now," R.C. said, and fitted one end of his handcuffs onto the man's left wrist and snicked the ratchet into the locking mechanism. "Mind if I call you Noie?"

"I've answered to worse."

"You have a friend who drives a Trans Am that has Michelin tires on it?"

"Can't say as I do."

"Where's Preacher Collins at, Noie?"

The man squinted thoughtfully and scratched at an insect bite on the back of his neck with his free hand. "Who?" he said.

"You're not going to believe this," Maydeen said, standing in Hackberry's doorway.

He looked up from his desk and waited.

"R.C. says he's got Noie Barnum hooked up in the back of his cruiser," she said.

Hackberry stared at her blankly.

"He says Barnum walked into a conve-

582

nience store down by the four-lane," she said. "He'd hitched a ride to have lunch there."

"How does R.C. know it's Barnum?"

"He says the guy looks just like his photo, except he's a little leaner. He's got a limp and maybe has some broken ribs."

"The guy admits he's Noie Barnum?"

"R.C. didn't say. He just says it's him."

"What about Jack Collins?"

"R.C. said there were Michelin tire tracks where Collins's car was parked yesterday. I didn't get it all, Hack. Want me to notify the FBI?"

"No."

"You don't?"

"Did you hear me?"

"Yeah, I did. How about losing the tone?"

He stood up from his desk, staring out the window into the brilliance of the day, at the wind whipping the flag on the pole, at the hard blueness of the sky above the hills. His right hand opened and closed at his side. "Tell R.C. to bring him through the back."

"Hack?"

"What is it?"

"You always say we do it by the numbers."

"What about it?"

"Pam told me about you almost shoving a broken pool cue down a bartender's throat in that Mexican cantina."

"R.C.'s life was hanging in the balance. Why are you bringing this up?"

"I could have done the same thing to the bartender, maybe worse, and so could Pam or Felix and a few others in the department. We wouldn't be bothered about it later, either. But we're not you. All of us know that, even though you don't. You go against your own nature."

"Where's Pam?"

"In the restroom, the last time I saw her."

"Believe it or not, Maydeen, sometimes I have my reasons for doing the things I do. We're not the only people who want to get their hands on Noie Barnum. The less anyone knows about his whereabouts, the safer he is. You got me?"

"Yes, sir, I expect so."

Hackberry looked down the street to see if R.C.'s cruiser had turned into the intersection yet. He tried to clear his head, to think straight, to keep the lines simple before he gave up his one certifiable chance to nail Jack Collins. "Fill in Pam and get the trusties out of the downstairs area. I want the prisoners in the cells at the end of the upstairs corridor moved to the tank. Barnum goes into total isolation. No contact with anyone. His food is brought to him by a deputy. No trusty gets near him. We're in total blackout mode regarding his presence. Simply said, he doesn't exist. You copy that?"

"I guess that means no phone call."

He gave her a look.

"Got it, got it, got it," she said.

Hackberry went out the back door and waited for R.C. The alleyway was empty in both directions. *Think,* he told himself. *Don't blow this one.* Why would Barnum be in a convenience store by himself? Collins wouldn't allow him to go wandering about on his own. They either had a fight or Barnum got sick of Collins's egomaniacal rhetoric and decided to take a stroll down the road and find some other company. But why had he stayed with Collins in the first place? To find Krill? To find some Al Qaeda operatives in Latin America and even the score for the death of his half sister? That made more sense than anything else.

R.C.'s cruiser turned in to the alleyway, the flasher off. Hackberry looked at all the rear windows of the building. He saw a face at one of the windows in the upstairs corridor. A deputy or a trusty? R.C. helped his prisoner out of the backseat of the cruiser, and the face went away. The prisoner's wrists were cuffed behind him, the tendons in his neck corded with either embarrassment or anger. In the sunlight, there were pinpoints of sweat on his forehead.

"I'm Sheriff Holland, Mr. Barnum," Hackberry said. "You *are* Noie Barnum?"

"Your deputy called me Noie. But I didn't tell him that was my name."

"Have it any way you like, sir. You're in

protective custody, but you're not under arrest. Do you understand the difference?"

"Yes, you're saying I don't have the constitutional right to a phone call or a lawyer."

"No, I'm saying this is a safe place for you."

"I think I'd just rather hike down to that café we passed and have a piece of pie and a cup of coffee and be on my way, if you don't mind."

"That's not an option, Mr. Barnum. I also need to advise you that you're starting to piss me off."

"I don't see why."

"I'll explain. You're one skip and a jump from being charged as an accessory in several homicides, all of them involving your companion Jack Collins. I dug up nine of his female victims. When we get time, I'll show you their postmortem photographs. The photos don't do justice to the realities of an exhumation — the stench of decomposition and the eight-ball stare and that sort of thing — but you'll have some sense of what a spray of forty-five-caliber bullets can do to human tissue."

"It's true?" the prisoner asked.

"What?"

"What you just said. Jack did that?"

Pam Tibbs had just come out the back door. "Who the hell you think did it, son?" she asked.

The prisoner tried to hold his eyes on hers,

but his stare broke, and he sucked the moisture out of his cheeks and swallowed.

Pam and Hackberry took the handcuffed man up the steel spiral stairs to the second floor and walked him down the row of cells to the end of the corridor. Pam whanged her baton against a cell door when two men came to the bars. Hackberry unhooked the prisoner, and he and Pam Tibbs stepped inside the room with him.

"You have a lavatory and a toilet and a bed and a chair and a window that lets you see the street," Hackberry said. "I apologize for all the graffiti and drawings of genitalia on the walls. We repaint every six months, but our clientele are a determined bunch."

"The other cells have bars. Why am I in this one?"

"The only people you're going to talk to are us, Mr. Barnum," Hackberry said. "I have a feeling you and Preacher were holed up down by the border or just on the other side of it. But chances are he's taken off. Is that right? He's way down in Coahuila by now?"

"You call him Preacher?"

"I don't call him anything. Others do," Hackberry said. "You're a Quaker, right?"

"A man's religion is a private matter."

"You deny your faith?" Hackberry said.

"No, sir, I don't. As you say, I'm a Quaker."

"And your namesake sailed out on the Flood?"

"Yes, sir, my christened name is Noie. Same spelling as in the King James."

"Can you tell me, with your background, why in the name of suffering God you hooked up with a man like Jack Collins?"

"Because he befriended me when nobody else did. Because he bound up my wounds and fed and protected me when others passed me by."

"Do you know how many innocent people have been hurt or killed because they think you have the design for the Predator drone?" Hackberry said.

"I escaped from a bunch of Mexican killers. They'd held me prisoner for weeks. How could I be carrying the design to a Predator drone? How could anyone have ideas that are that stupid?"

"An FBI agent by the name of Ethan Riser called you the modern equivalent of the Holy Grail," Hackberry said. "The design is in your head. You're a very valuable man, Mr. Barnum. Ethan Riser could probably explain that to you better than I, except he's dead. He's dead because Jack Collins blew his face and skull apart with a Thompson submachine gun. Ethan Riser was a good man and a friend of mine. Have you ever seen anybody machine-gunned, Mr. Barnum?"

"I found out about your friend when it was too late to do anything about it."

"Are you a deep-plant, sir?" Hackberry said.

"A what?"

"You know what I mean."

"No, I was about to go public with some information about the numbers of innocent people we've killed in the drone program, but I went into the desert first to think about it. That's when I got kidnapped by Krill and his friends. They found my government ID and a letter from a minister about my concerns over the Predator program, and they thought they'd sell me to Al Qaeda. Then they decided that was too much trouble and they'd sell me to some Mexican gangsters. That was when another fellow and I broke loose."

"You thought you were going to bring down Al Qaeda by yourself?"

"I was aiming to get some of them, that's for sure. But I was done helping kill third-world people. I got to say something here. I don't know everything that goes on in Jack's head, but somewhere inside him, there's a better man than the one you see."

"Keep telling yourself that crap," Pam said.

"Chief Deputy Tibbs isn't very objective about Jack, Noie. That's because he tried to machine-gun her," Hackberry said.

Noie Barnum looked at her blankly.

"What do you know about Josef Sholokoff?" Hackberry asked.

"I don't recall anybody by that name."

"He's a Russian criminal who wants to sell

you to the highest bidder," Hackberry said. "We think he may have crucified a minister by the name of Cody Daniels. You ever hear of him?"

"No, I haven't," Noie said. "A fellow was crucified?"

"You seem blissfully ignorant of all the wreckage swirling around you. Does that bother you at all?" Hackberry said.

"You're damn right it does. You stop talking to me like that."

"There's a ranch about six miles below the four-lane. The south end of the property bleeds into Mexico. I think that's where y'all were hiding out. Jack is probably long gone, and he's not driving that Trans Am anymore, either. But I need to know. Is that where y'all were holed up?"

"Ask Jack when you catch him."

"We don't abuse prisoners here," Pam said, stepping closer to Barnum, one finger barely touching his sternum.

"Ma'am?" he said.

"I just wanted you to take note of that fact," she said. "It's why I'm not pounding you into marmalade. But you open your mouth like that one more time, and I promise you, all bets are off."

Downstairs, five minutes later, Pam came into Hackberry's office and closed the door behind her. "I'm backing your play, Hack, whatever it is. But I think you're taking an awful risk here," she said.

"We don't owe the feds diddly-squat," he replied. "We apprehended Barnum. They didn't. As far as I'm concerned, they're on a need-to-know basis. Right now I don't figure they need to know anything."

"This is a national security issue. They're going to eat you alive. If they don't, your enemies around here will."

"That's the breaks."

"God, you're stubborn."

"I got a call from Temple Dowling. He says Josef Sholokoff believes Dowling put a hit on him."

"Why's he think that?"

"Because somebody killed a couple of Sholokoff's men at his game farm."

"Why didn't we hear anything about it?"

"Sholokoff didn't report it."

"What did you tell Dowling?"

"To get out of town. That he was on his own," Hackberry said.

"What's the problem?"

"I was pretty hard-nosed with him. Maybe I took satisfaction in his discomfort."

"Dowling is a pedophile and deserves anything that happens to him."

"He said Sholokoff takes people apart."

"In what way?"

"Physically, piece by piece," Hackberry said. He realized her attention was focused outside the window. A man in rumpled slacks, wearing canvas boat shoes without socks and his shirttail hanging out, was crossing the street hurriedly, a brown paper bag folded under his arm. "What's wrong?" Hackberry asked.

"That guy out there. He was just released."

"What about him?"

"He's a check writer. Loving and Jeff Davis counties have bench warrants on him, but they didn't want to pay the costs for getting him back."

"I'm still not following you."

"He was waiting to be taken downstairs when R.C. brought Barnum in. I remember he was watching us move everybody down to the tank. He was at the window, too, looking down in the alley."

"He probably wouldn't know who Barnum is."

"No, I saw his jacket. He was in Huntsville. He got clemency on a five-bit for sending his cell partner to the injection table. He's a professional snitch."

Hackberry thought about it. "Leave him alone. If he has any suspicions, we don't want to confirm them."

"Sorry, I had my hands full up there."

"Forget it," he said.

She looked at him for a long time before she spoke. "You want them to come after Barnum, don't you?"

"I haven't thought about it. I'm not that smart," he said. "You think I made a target out of Temple Dowling?"

"You're in the wrong business, *kemo sabe,* but I love you just the same," she replied.

What a difference a day and a change of topography could make, Temple Dowling told himself as he gazed through the lounge window of the Santa Fe hotel he and three of his men had checked in to. The evening sky was turquoise and ribbed with pink clouds, a rainbow arching across a canyon in the west, the sun an orange ball behind the mountains. The bartender brought him another vodka Collins packed with shaved ice and cherries and lemon and lime slices, and when Temple lifted it to his lips, the coldness slid down his throat like balm to his soul. Somehow his feelings of failure and humiliation at the hands of that clown Holland had evaporated during the flight to New Mexico. In fact, Temple was confident enough to smile at his foibles, as though someone else had temporarily occupied his skin and admitted his fear of Josef Sholokoff. It was nothing more than a silly lapse, Temple told himself. He had been tired, worn out by worry, beset on all sides by an army of incompetent employees and government bureaucrats and hayseed cops, Holland in particular. Why had Temple's father ever thought that idiot could be a congressman, a man who probably couldn't find his dork unless he tied a string on it? Temple sipped from his Collins and dipped a taco chip in a bowl of guacamole and chewed on it. Then an image he didn't want to remember floated before his eyes — being discovered by Holland and his chief deputy in the Mexican brothel with two underage girls.

He quickly transformed his emotion into one of righteous outrage. Temple Dowling didn't turn them into prostitutes. Poverty and hunger did. Was that his fault? Should they starve? Would that make the world a better place? What gave Holland the right to look down on him? Wasn't he intelligent enough to understand that most men who are attracted to children seek innocence in their lives?

He stopped, his mind seizing up as though he had experienced a brain freeze. He shouldn't have used the word "children." He was never attracted to children. He was not a pedophile. He just wanted to be with teenage girls while they were blooming into women. What finer creation was there than a young girl? What greater tragedy was there than seeing them left to the mercies of America's street culture? Or seeing them turned over to degenerates like Sholokoff, who made addicts of them and used them in porn films? Why was Temple Dowling the scapegoat? He had never treated a woman or girl badly in his life.

He drank his glass empty. The sky had darkened over the mountains, as though a lavender rain were starting to fall where the sun had just set. Where were his men?

"Would you like another, sir?" the bartender asked. He wore a white jacket and a red bow tie and black pants. His face had no color, not even the shadow of a beard, but his hair was as black and liquid in appearance as melted plastic.

"Yeah, hit me again," Temple replied. "What's all that noise next door?"

"It's a young people's organization of some kind." The bartender's cheeks were sunken, his mouth like a button.

"Listen to it. That's a lot of kids."

"Can I order you something from the grill?"

"They seem to be having fun," Temple said, still distracted by the celebratory mood next door.

"The hotel gives them the space for their meetings one night a week."

"That's pretty nice." Temple gazed out the door at the teenagers going in and out of the lobby, the shadows of the potted palms sliding off their skin and hair and the flowers some of the girls were wearing.

"It's called Alla-something," the bartender said.

"Can you order me a steak?"

"Yes, sir. Right away."

"I like it pink in the middle," Temple said.

He worked on his vodka and waited for his food and listened to the pianist play "Claire de Lune." The pianist was dressed in a summer tux with a red boutonniere, his long fingers floating above the keys in a cone of blue light. Santa Fe was a grand place to be. The Spanish ambience, the wooden colonnades and earthen jars on the terrazzo entrances to the shops along the street, the stars twinkling above the vastness of the mountains — why should a man be afraid in a country as wonderful as this? Or why should a man be ashamed of what he was? He agreed with the liberals and libertines on this one. A man didn't choose his sexual inclinations. They chose him. Didn't Jesus say there are those who are made different in the womb?

The girl who came into the lounge from the lobby and sat down next to him at the bar had the face of a pixie, with a pug nose and an uplifted chin and thick dark red hair that was tied in back. She wore a sequined cowboy shirt and tight stonewashed jeans tucked into boots that came almost to her knee. "Hi," she said.

"Hi," Temple said.

"Can you help me out?"

"You kill anybody?"

"I'd like to. At least if I have to go back in there."

"Where?" he asked.

"To the Alateen meeting."

"What's Alateen?"

"A meeting that's a guaranteed cure for insomnia. I got sentenced to it by the court."

"Why'd the judge send you there?"

"My boyfriend totaled his car and left me unconscious inside it. My boyfriend is not only a needle-dick but a lying shit. I told the judge if he believed my boyfriend, he was a shitbird, too, but I wasn't sure whether he qualified as a needle-dick. What's that music?"

"Debussy, I think. You know, Claude Debussy?"

"Who's that?"

"He was a great composer."

She was chewing gum, her eyes rolling, her mouth indolent and somehow vulnerable. The sound of her gum wet and smacking in her cheek made him swallow. She smiled lazily, one eye crinkling at the corner. "Will you buy me a drink?"

"Are you legal age?"

"Why do you think I asked you to buy me one?"

"What are you having?"

"I don't care. Something with candied cherries in it. Something that's cold and warm at the same time."

When the bartender served the steak, Temple ordered another Collins for himself and an old-fashioned for the girl. The bartender lowered his eyes with his hands folded, not unlike an undertaker who doesn't want to broach a difficult subject.

"She's my niece," Temple said. "Nobody would believe she's twenty-two."

"Very well, sir," the bartender said, and went to the end of the bar and took a tumbler from a rack on the back counter.

"That was impressive," the girl said. "I had an uncle like that. He could get people to do things for him and make them feel like they were doing themselves a favor. You know how he'd do that?"

"Tell me."

"He already knew what they wanted to do. They only needed permission from someone. It was usually about money. Or maybe sex. But one way or another, they were coming across for him. He used to say, 'Put a smile on their faces, and they'll follow you over a cliff.' "

"What happened to him?"

"Nothing. He owns a bunch of massage parlors in Los Angeles. Is that a Rolex?"

Temple looked at his watch, then realized how long he had been in the lounge. Where were his men? They had been acting strangely ever since two of them had been dumb enough to get themselves popped by Preacher Jack. "I never noticed. I have about a dozen watches I wear. Do you ride horses?"

"Sometimes. I barrel-raced when I was in Four-H. I was a hot-walker at Ruidoso Downs. Talk about a horny bunch. You ought to be in the bar after the seventh race."

"Yeah, but that's not your crowd. I bet you go to college."

"If that's what you call working at the McDonald's inside Wal-mart. How about that for being a two-time loser? Your steak is getting cold."

"You want one?"

"I'm a vegan. My whole life changed after I gave up meat and milk products. I thought my needle-dick boyfriend was the problem, but I think it was my diet."

"What problem?"

"My organisms were messed up."

"Beg your pardon?"

"Meat and cheese and barnyard shit like that are toxic to your erogenous development." The waiter placed a coaster in front of her and set down her old-fashioned. She wrapped her gum in her napkin. "Anyway, thanks for the drink. I can't take that group next door. You know their problem?"

"No," he replied.

She took a drink from her glass and her eyes brightened and her cheeks filled with color, in the same way a thirsty plant might respond immediately to water. He could feel the coldness of her breath when she exhaled. "They feel unloved," she said.

"You have a lot of insight for such a young woman."

"Yeah, that's why I'm in charge of the french-fry basket."

"You smell like orange blossoms."

"Maybe that's because I'm chewing an orange rind." She turned on the stool toward him, her knee hitting his. She let her eyes hold on his. "I bummed a ride here with a friend, but he's gonna stay at the meeting for another hour. I live six miles away, and I don't have money for a cab. I'd like a ride, but when I get home, I go in by myself."

"You're the captain of your soul?"

"No, I'm just not somebody's backseat fuck."

He picked up a small cooked tomato on the tines of his fork and placed it in his mouth and chewed slowly. "I wouldn't ever say or even think something like that about you," he said.

"So you're gonna give me a ride?"

"If you'll do one thing for me."

Her eyes shifted sideways with a level of dependence that made his heart drop. "What's that?" she said.

"Walk through the open-air jewelry market with me. I'm a sucker for Indian junk. I need an expert hand to guide me."

"You have a daughter?"

"No."

"I thought that's what you were gonna tell me."

"Why?"

"Most of the time they say I remind them of their daughter. They can't do enough for you."

"Who?"

"The kind of guys who like to grope young girls in the back of the church bus," she replied, picking up her purse. "Think I'm kidding? Ask yourself why any middle-aged man wants to make a career out of being a youth minister or a park director or a guy who teaches leather craft to rug rats. Because he likes the way the restroom smells after little kids have pissed all over the bowl? Give me a break."

"How *old* are you?"

"Buy me a veggie burger and I'll tell you. Let's go, I won't bite," she said, squeezing his arm.

CHAPTER TWENTY-FOUR

Krill had parked the car in a grove of dead fruit trees no more than fifty yards behind the house of the woman Negrito kept referring to as *la china.* After the setting of the sun, the wind had dropped, and the sky had turned as stark as an ink wash. The gingerbread house and trees and windmill and barn and horse tank, even the hills, seemed drained of color and movement of any kind. The horses and chickens were gone from the yard, and there was no birdsong in the trees. The only sound Krill could hear as he and Negrito approached the house was water ticking from a rusted pipe that extended over the surface of the horse tank. A nimbus of dust hung above the house like a great cloud of gnats.

Krill stopped and knelt on one knee behind a car that had no wheels or glass in the windows and whose metal was still hot from baking in the sun all day. He stared at the house and the absence of electric lights or movement inside. Negrito knelt beside him, the leather cord of his hat swinging under his chin, the heavy gray fog of his odor puffing out of his clothes. "Krill, you got to tell me," he said.

"Tell you what?"

"Why we are here. I don't see no percentage, man."

"There isn't one. Not for you, anyway, my old friend."

"The others have deserted you, but still you talk down to me like I'm the enemy and not the *maricones* who ran away."

Krill placed his hand on Negrito's shoulder, which felt like a flannel sack filled with rocks. "Like me, you are a killer. But killing is not a problem for you. You sleep without dreaming and rise each morning into a new day. But I relive all the times I watched the light go out of my victims' eyes. My thoughts have become my enemies."

"That's why there are whores and tequila in Durango. A trip there will ease your problems, *jefe.*"

"I have to talk to La Magdalena."

"You want to sleep with her? That's what's going on? You think there's something special about a Chinese woman in bed? They ain't no different from our women. You love them at night, and in the morning they make your life awful."

"Poor Negrito. Why do you always think

with the head of your penis?"

" 'Cause it ain't never let me down, man," said Negrito, and cupped his hand on Krill's shoulder. "Come on, tell me the truth. Why you got to talk to this woman if you ain't looking to poke her?"

"To confess my sins, *hombre.* To rid myself of the faces I see in my sleep."

"It ain't a sin to kill people in a war. We were farmers and cattle workers until the war came. The people we killed had it coming. What is the big loss when a Communist is killed?"

"My children died because of me."

"That don't make no sense, Krill."

"I used to blame the army and the Americans and those from Argentina who first gave us our guns. But I took the pay of corrupt political men and did what they told me. I killed the Jesuit and the leftists. You know these things are true, Negrito, because you were there. The helicopter machine-gunned the clinic, but I was their brother in arms. I helped bring a curse on our land."

"No, your head is screwed up, Krill. That woman ain't no priest. Whatever you confess to her, she's gonna tell the cops. Then they're gonna hunt us down. They don't want nobody to know what we done down there."

"There's something strange going on in that house," Krill said.

"What's strange is your head. It glows in

the dark. I think you got too many chemicals in it. Remember those nights in Juárez?"

"The woman's truck is by the barn, but there is no one moving in the house, and no electric light is turned on. But look through the window of the chapel. The candles are burning in front of the Virgin's statue."

"Of course. She burns candles all the time. That's what people like her do. They burn candles. The rest of us work and sweat and sometimes take bullets, but *they* burn candles."

"No, this one has been to war, Negrito. She is not one to go off somewhere or take a nap while an open flame burns in her house."

"You make a complexity of everything," Negrito said. "You are a man who cannot bear to have a quiet and simple thought. You constantly construct spiderwebs so you can walk through them."

"Look on the far side of the fence, beyond the barn, where the grass is tall."

"It's grass. So what is the great mystery about grass?"

"There is a channel through it. The wind is not making the channel. Somebody walked through there."

"Animals did. Deer or horses. They cross the field by walking on it. It took you a long time to figure that out?"

"No horses are in that field. And deer do not make paths on flat land, only on hillsides, where their feet have to find the same spot every day."

"See what I mean? A simple visit to the home of this pretender *sacerdote* becomes a torture of the brain."

"The back door is ajar, Negrito. There is something wrong in that house. You stay here and guard my back. You keep the rifle, but do not use it unless absolutely necessary. If everything is normal, I will come to the door and wave to you with my right hand, not my left."

"*Claro,* man. My head is starting to hurt again with all your cautions. I cannot stand this. We were never afraid before. I told you from the beginning, this woman who wears men's trousers was bad luck. But your obsession has no bounds."

"Then leave. Go to Durango. Bathe in the diseased fluids of your whores," Krill said.

Negrito was breathing heavily, the whiskers around his mouth as thick as a badger's. His pupils were no bigger than pinheads, the skin around his eyes wrinkled and flecked with scales. "You make me want to do something that's very bad."

"You want to be me, Negrito, to leave your own body and live inside mine. And because you are a killer by nature, you believe a bullet can give you my heart and brain."

"I am a loyal servant and follower and brother, not an assassin. I want you to be you

606

and the leader you used to be, Krill, not a self-hating fool ruminating on his sins."

"If I wave with my left hand from the door, rather than my right, what message will I be sending you?"

"I see only one message in any of this: that of a man being led with a ring through his nose by the Chinese *puta*."

"You are brave in ways that few men are, Negrito. But do not try to think anymore. For some men, thinking is a dangerous vanity. You must accept that about yourself."

Krill stood and walked toward the back entrance of the house, a holstered .357 Magnum hanging from the right side of his web belt, his skinning knife in a scabbard on his left. He stepped up on the back porch and listened, then felt a breeze on the back of his neck and heard the windmill come to life and water running into the horse tank. But where were the horses? Or the illegals who came almost every evening for food or benediction at the house of La Magdalena?

He paused at the back door and listened again. The windmill was stenciled against the black and gray patterns in the sky, and tumbleweed was bouncing through the yard, hanging in the fences, skipping by the junked car where Negrito was crouched with the M16. Krill pushed open the door and stepped inside.

Through the hallway, he could see her sitting very still in a straight-back chair, her hands resting on her knees, her hair tied in a bun. In the gloom, he could hardly make out her features. Her face was so still that in profile, it looked like it had been painted on the air. He eased his .357 from its holster and waited, his left foot in front of his right, breathing slowly through his mouth, the checkered grips of his revolver hard inside his palm.

He stepped backward, never taking his eyes off the Chinese woman, his left arm extended out the door. He opened and closed his hand so the fading light would reflect off it, then moved his arm up and down so Negrito could plainly see that he was signaling with his left hand and not his right. *Please remember what I told you,* he thought. *This is the moment I have to count on you, Negrito. This is when your skills will be of the greatest necessity.*

Krill went down the hallway and could see the woman watching him from the corner of her eye.

"Magdalena?" he said, his voice hardly audible.

She continued to stare straight ahead, her hands absolutely still.

"*¿Qué pasa?*" he said. He glanced over his shoulder. Where was Negrito? "*Señora,* look at me," he said. "It's Krill. I want to make

608

confession. I murdered a Jesuit priest. I must have absolution. You can give it to me."

He stepped into the room and felt the barrel of a gun touch the back of his head. "Bad timing, greaseball," a voice said.

There were four men inside the room, all of them wearing beige-colored gauzy masks with slits for the nose and mouth and eyes. One man stood against the far wall, his left hand on the shoulder of a girl not over ten years old. With the other hand, he held the stainless-steel four-inch blade of a clasp knife under the girl's throat. The girl's eyes were wide with terror and confusion, and her bottom lip was trembling.

The man holding the gun to the back of Krill's head removed the .357 from his grip. "Who's with you?" he said.

"A shit pile of people. They're going to cook you in a pot, too," Krill said.

"That's why you came in by yourself?"

"Who are you guys?" Krill said.

"Your worst nightmare, fuckhead."

"In my nightmares there are no guys like you. I don't have space in my head for guys in Halloween masks or guys who frighten little girls with knives. These are not the guys of nightmares. These are clowns and eunuchs who were born with penises but no cojones. Why would guys like these be in anybody's nightmares? That would be a great mystery to me."

"Antonio, don't speak to these men," the woman said.

"I was just clarifying my thoughts to myself, Magdalena. These men and their cleverness are a great mystery to me," he said. The yard was empty, the light dying in the trees, the windmill spinning against a horizon that looked as though the clouds were dissolving and running down the sides of the sky. Then he saw Negrito moving from behind the barn and around the front of the house, bent low, his greasy leather hat pulled down tight on his head, the M16 gripped with both hands, his heavy, truncated body moving with the fluidity of an animal's. In the distance, he thought he heard the thropping sound of a helicopter's blades.

"Take me but leave the child," the woman said to the man holding the gun to Krill's head.

"That's not a problem," the man replied. "But this guy is. Who is he?"

"A man seeking forgiveness. He's no threat to you," she said.

"You a coyote, buddy?" the man with the gun asked.

"No, *hombre.* I'm a Texas Ranger. I've been shooting the shit out of guys like you for many years."

"You're a real wit, all right. So smart you came in here and stuck your head in a mousetrap."

Then Krill heard banging and shuffling noises at the front of the house, booted feet coming down hard on the gallery, and a door flying back against a wall. Krill felt his heart drop. Two more men, each wearing the same masks worn by the men inside the house, were pulling and shoving Negrito into the living room. Blood leaked in a broken line from under the brim of Negrito's leather hat, running through one eyebrow, streaking the stubble on his cheek. His face was lit with a grin as wide as a jack-o'-lantern's. "*¡Qué bueno!* Everybody is here!" he said. Then Negrito saw the expression on Krill's face, and his grin faded. "These *cobardes* come up behind me. I'm sorry, Krill," he said.

"So you're the one they call Krill. We've heard about you," the man behind Krill said.

The helicopter passed overhead and circled over a field and began to descend on the rear of the property, the downdraft flattening the grass, blowing dust and desiccated cow manure in the air.

"Hey, Krill, I know who these guys are. They're Sholokoff's people," Negrito said.

"No, we have no interest in these people or the business they conduct," Krill said.

"Ain't that right?" Negrito said to his captors. "You work for that Russian prick. We know all about you. I hear a couple of your guys are missing their noses. Be nice to me, and maybe I'll tell you where their noses are

611

and you can glue them back on."

Negrito, Negrito, Negrito, Krill thought.

The man behind Krill stepped back and looked at both Krill and Negrito like a photographer arranging a studio portrait. "This is quite a pair," he said.

"What do you want to do?" said the man holding the knife to the little girl's throat.

"Take the girl in the kitchen."

"And?"

"What do you think?"

"I don't know, man. I don't know if this gig has parameters or not."

"There's a key sticking out of the lock in the pantry door. What does that tell you?"

"Lock her inside?"

"Brilliant," the man with the gun said. "Then take the woman to the chopper."

"What about these two?"

"That's a good question," the man with the gun said.

"I've got a question for you," Negrito said.

"*You've* got a question? Wonderful. What is it, greaseball?" the man with the gun said.

"If you're born without cojones, does that mean you're automatically a queer, or is it something you learn? 'Cause I believe every guy who ever called me a greaseball was probably a *maricón.* Know why I think that? 'Cause when I was in jail in Arizona and Texas, it was always the Aryan Brotherhood guys who were trying to get me in the sack.

That's right, man. Macho gringos like you was the main yard bitches in every joint I was in. I tell you what, man. 'Cause you look like a nice guy, I'm gonna do something for you. You surrender to me and Krill, I'll fix you up with some punks that ain't got a feather on them. You gonna dig it, man."

"We're wasting time here, Frank. What's it gonna be?" one of the other men said to the man with the gun.

"We split the difference," Frank replied. "Krill is the guy who kidnapped the Quaker. Josef will want to talk to him. The ape seems to have a death wish."

"Listen to me, *hombre,*" Krill said. "Negrito is a good soldier. He can be of value to you. He will never give up information to the FBI. Pain means nothing to him. His only defect is he runs his mouth when he shouldn't. But he can be a valuable man to your employer."

"I see your point," the man with the gun said. "We're all just making a buck. We shouldn't let it get personal. I totally understand where you're coming from."

No one in the room moved. In the silence, Krill could hear the little girl whimpering. The man who had been holding a semi-automatic on Negrito put it away and looked at the .357 he had taken from Krill. It was nickel-plated and had black checkered grips, and each chamber in the cylinder was loaded with a hollow-point round. "Your name is Negrito?" he said.

"That's my nickname. It's 'cause I'm mestizo."

"Do you mind riding in a helicopter?" the man asked.

Negrito shrugged and gazed out the window, his eyes dulling over, his mouth downturned at the corners.

"Because we don't want you to be uncomfortable. Can you handle heights? You don't get airsick or anything like that?"

Negrito looked at Krill. "We had some fun, didn't we, amigo? They're gonna remember us for a long time. Don't let this guy get to you. We're better than any of them. We're stronger and smarter and tougher. Guys like us come back from the dead and piss in their mouths and shit in their mothers' wombs."

Krill stood frozen, the sound of the helicopter blades growing louder and louder in his head, the dust swirling in the downdraft, the rain clouds forming into blue horsetails, the windmill shuddering against the sky, all of these things happening simultaneously as the man with the .357 lifted the barrel and fired a solitary round through one side of Negrito's head and out the other.

Hackberry Holland was reading a biography of T. E. Lawrence under a lamp by his front window when he heard thunder rolling in the clouds far to the south, reverberating in the hills, where occasionally a flash of dry lightning would flicker and then die like a wet match. The book was written by Michael Korda and dealt with the dissolution of empires and a new type of warfare, what came to be known as "wars of insurgency," all of which had their model among the sand dunes and date palms of Arabia. As Hackberry read the lines describing the white glare of the Arabian desert, he thought of the snow that had blanketed the hills south of the Yalu the first morning he had seen Chinese troops in their quilted uniforms, tens of thousands of them, many of them wearing tennis shoes, marching out of the white brilliance of the snowfield, heedless of the automatic-weapons fire that danced across the fields and the artillery rounds that blew geysers of snow and ice and dirt and rock in their midst.

He closed the book and placed it on his knee and stared out the window. Not far down the road, he could see a tree limb that had fallen across the telephone line that led to his house. Just as he got up to check the phone, he saw a cruiser turn off the road into his drive, its emergency bar rippling, its siren off. Hackberry stepped out on the front porch and watched R. C. Bevins get out of the cruiser and walk toward him on the flagstones, his face somber. "You tried to call?" Hackberry said.

"Yes, sir, your phone's out. Your cell must be off, too."

"It's in my truck. What is it, R.C.?"

"We've got a homicide at the Ling place. The victim appears to be Hispanic. From the exit wound in his head, I'd say somebody used a hollow-point. A ten-year-old girl had been left in Ms. Ling's care and saw it all. When her mother came for her, she found the girl locked in a pantry. Ms. Ling is gone."

"What do you mean, gone?"

"From what the little girl said, there were six guys in masks. They took Ms. Ling and a friend of the dead man on a helicopter."

"How long ago?"

"A couple of hours."

"Did you print the victim?"

"Yes, sir."

"Get a priority with AFIS."

"Pam is already on it. Who do you reckon are the guys with the chopper?"

"Josef Sholokoff's people."

"The little girl said the dead man and his friend spoke Spanish. She also said the friend had a pistol on one hip and a long knife on the other."

"What else did she say about him?"

"She said he was tall and that he had funny shoulders. She said they were too wide, like he had a stick pushed sideways inside his shirt."

"That's Krill."

"What would he be doing at Ms. Ling's place?"

"I don't have any idea, none at all."

"You okay, Sheriff?"

"How long have you been trying to get me?"

"About fifteen minutes. There wasn't no way you could know the line was down."

"Was Ms. Ling hurt?"

"The little girl said a guy shoved her down. The same guy held a knife at the little girl's throat. She said they all had gloves on, and the shooter called the dead man a greaseball. You think these are the same guys who crucified Cody Daniels?"

"What's your opinion?"

R.C. scratched at his eyebrow. "I think we got a special breed on our hands," he said. "I think all this is related to that Barnum boy we got locked in our jail. I'm not sure if we done the right thing on that."

Pam Tibbs was waiting for Hackberry when he arrived at the jail. She was not wearing makeup, and there were circles under her eyes. "What do you want to do?" she asked.

"About what?" he said.

"Everything."

"Did you talk to the FBI yet?"

"I reported the homicide and the kidnapping. I didn't mention our boy in isolation," she said.

"You're uncomfortable with that?"

"I don't know what you're doing, Hack. I don't know what the plan is."

"They're going to call."

"The abductors are?"

"You bet."

"Then what?"

"We've got what they want. As long as Barnum stays in our hands, Anton Ling will be kept alive."

"Hack, they wouldn't have grabbed her if we hadn't locked up Barnum."

"You don't have to tell me."

"Where are you going?"

"To take a nap," he said.

He went up the spiral stairs and pulled a mattress from a supply locker into an alcove off the corridor and lay down on his side with his head cushioned on his arm and fell asleep with far more ease than he would have guessed, knowing that his dreams would take him to a place that was as much a part of his future as it was his past. He remembered the words of the writer Paul Fussell, who had said he joined the army to fight the war for its duration and had discovered that he would have to fight it every day and every night for the rest of his life. In his dream, Hackberry returned once again to Camp Five in No Name Valley and the brick factory called Pak's Palace outside Pyongyang. The dream was not about deprivation or the harshness of the weather or the mistreatment visited upon him by his captors. It was about isolation and abandonment and the belief that one was totally alone and lost and without hope. It was the worst feeling that anyone could ever experience.

In the dream, the landscape changed, and he saw himself standing on a precipice in Southwest Texas, staring out at a valley that looked like an enormous seabed gone dry. The valley floor was covered with great round white rocks that resembled the serrated, coral-encrusted backs of sea tortoises, stranded and alone, dying under an unmerciful sun. In the dream, he was not a navy corpsman but a little boy whose father had said that one day the mermaids would return to Texas and wink at him from somewhere up in the rocks. All he saw in the dream was his own silent witness to the suffering of the sea creatures.

"Jesus Christ, wake up, Hack," he heard Pam Tibbs say, shaking his arm.

"*What?* What is it?" he said, his eyes filmed with sleep.

"You must have been having a terrible dream."

"What'd I say?"

"Just the stuff people yell out in dreams. Forget it."

"Pam, tell me what I said."

" 'He takes people apart.' That's what you said."

The telephone call came in one hour later.

CHAPTER TWENTY-FIVE

From his office window, he could see flecks of rain blowing in the glow of the streetlights, the traffic signal at the intersection bouncing on its support cables, the electrical flashes in the clouds that ringed the town. "Don't try tracing this," the voice said.

"You're too slick for us?" Hackberry replied.

"You know what we want. Deliver him up and there won't be any problem."

"By now you've probably figured out I'm a bit slow on the uptake. What is it you think I have?"

" 'It' is a Quaker with a hush-puppy accent who by all rights is our property."

"Somebody snitched us off, huh?"

"Spying on you hasn't been a big challenge, Sheriff. You seem to leave your shit prints everywhere you go."

"Should we decide to deliver up our Quaker friend, what are y'all going to do for us?"

"Give you your Chinese girlfriend back, for

one. For two, you'll get her back looking just the way she did the last time you saw her. Are you getting the picture?"

"I don't know if it's the electrical storm or that peckerwood speech defect, but you're a little hard to understand."

"We have another guest here, a guy whose father you did scut work for. We're gonna let him be a kind of audiovisual aid for you. Hang on just a second. You're gonna like this."

The caller seemed to remove the phone from his ear and hold it away from him. In the background, Hackberry could hear voices and echoes inside a large room, probably one with stone or brick walls. "Turn up the volume for Sheriff Holland," the caller said.

Then Hackberry heard a sound that he never wanted to hear again, a cry that burst from the throat and reverberated off every surface in the room and died with a series of sobs and a whimper that the listener could associate only with hopelessness and despair.

"That's Mr. Dowling, Sheriff," the caller said. "As you've probably gathered, he's not having a good morning."

"You abducted Temple Dowling?"

"It's more like he abducted himself. All we had to do was get a little girl to perch her twat on a bar stool, and Mr. Dowling was in the net. Want to talk to Ms. Ling?"

Hackberry could hear his own breath

against the surface of the receiver. "Yes, I would," he said.

"You'd like that?"

"If you want to negotiate, I need to know she's there."

"She was with Civil Air Transport, wasn't she? What they called the Flying Tiger Airline?"

"If that's what she told you."

"She didn't tell me anything. She didn't have to. She has a tattoo of the Flying Tiger emblem on her ass. Have you ever had an opportunity to see it — I mean her ass?"

Hackberry's mouth was dry, his heart hammering, his breath coming hard in his throat. "No matter how this plays out, I'll be seeing you down the track. You know that, don't you?"

"You still think I sound like a peckerwood? I'd like to hear you say that one more time."

Hackberry swallowed, a taste like diesel oil sliding down his throat.

"No?" the voice said. "We'll give you a little time to think over your options. Noie Barnum belongs to us, Sheriff. Want to throw away Ms. Ling's life for an empty-headed government pissant? Do the smart thing."

"Why does he belong to you?"

"Mr. Dowling cost my employer a great deal of money. Barnum is the payback. Tell you what. I'm gonna send you a package. Check it out and we'll talk again. In the meantime, I'm gonna take personal care of Ms. Ling. Don't worry, I won't touch a hair on her head. Promise."

The line went dead.

Anton Ling's captors had placed her in a subterranean room that was cool and damp and smelled of lichen and the river stones out of which it was made. Three ground-level barred windows that resembled slits in a machine-gun bunker gave onto a scene that seemed out of place and time: a sunrise that had the bluish-red color of a bruise, a meandering milky-brown river from which the fields had been irrigated an emerald green, livestock that could have been water buffalo grazing in riparian grasses. But the people tending animals or working in the fields were not Indo-Chinese peasants; they were Mexicans who had probably eaten breakfast in the dark and gone to work with the singleness of purpose that characterized all workers whose aspirations consisted of little more than getting through the day and returning home in the evening without involving themselves in the political considerations of those who owned the land.

The floor was concrete, once covered with a carpet that had molded into a mat of black thread. Against one wall was a wooden bed with a tick mattress on it, and a toilet in the corner with a partition that partially shielded it from view. The bars in the door were sheathed in flaking orange rust, and the stones in the wall had turned black and oily with the seepage of groundwater. Someone had scratched a Christian cross on one stone; on another was a woman's name; on another were the words *Ayúdame, Dios.*

The screaming that had come from another part of the subterranean area had stopped about two hours ago. Briefly, Anton had seen a tall, mustached man in a suit and a soiled white shirt carrying a medical bag. He had studiously avoided looking at her, his shoulders rounded, the back of his head turned to her, his uncut hair hanging over his collar like a tangle of twigs. To someone else, he had said, "I have left you the hypodermics. That is all I will do. I have seen nothing here. I am going back to my bed."

She heard an upstairs door open and feet descending the steps. So far, her captors had not spoken to her without their masks. The man who was approaching her did not wear a mask; he wore elevated shoes, a white sport coat, a monogrammed lavender shirt unbuttoned below the collar, and black slacks. His nose was hooked, the nostrils thick with hair, his cheeks slathered with whiskers, the exposed top of his chest gnarled with tiny bones. He unlocked the cell door with an iron key and pulled it open and came inside the room, wiping the rust off his fingers with a handkerchief. His breath smelled of decay and seemed to reach out and touch her face like wet cobweb. "Frank doesn't like you," he said. "He says you spat on him. He says that's the second time you've done it."

"He tried to take my clothes off."

"He shouldn't have done that. I'll talk to him about it. Sit down." When she didn't respond, he beamed and said, "Please. Don't make everything unpleasant. You remember me?"

"No," she said, sitting down.

"I helped provide the AK-47s you and your friends shipped to Nicaragua."

"I dealt with many undesirables. I suspect you were among them."

"I've always wanted to talk with you on a personal level. You are quite famous. Do you want something to eat?"

"Yes."

"I knew we could be friends."

"You're Josef Sholokoff. You were at my house when your men almost drowned me."

"Maybe."

"You killed Cody Daniels in the cruelest way a man can die."

"The cowboy minister? He was of no importance. Why are you worried about him? You should be thinking about yourself. We're going to put you on the phone with Sheriff Holland." He was still grinning, his eyes so bright and intense and merry that they were impossible to read. "One way or another, you'll get on the phone. Or you will be heard on the phone. You know what I mean, don't you?"

"No," she replied, looking straight ahead.

"You heard the man screaming earlier this morning. He was talking on the phone to Sheriff Holland. He just didn't know it."

"Is he still alive?"

"He might be, if his heart didn't give out. I'll check and see. Do you want to meet him?"

"Where is Krill?"

"These are insignificant people. Why do you keep dwelling on them?"

"I think you're evil. You're not just a man who does evil. You love evil for its own sake. I've known a few like you. Not many, but some."

"With the Khmer Rouge?"

"No, the Khmer Rouge were uneducated peasants who were bombed by B-52s. You're different. I suspect your cruelty is your means to hide your cowardice."

"And you? You didn't rain fire on people who lived in grass huts?"

"I did."

"But *I'm* evil?"

"You don't plan for me to leave here, not alive, at least. Take your lies and your deceit from the room. You're odious in the sight of God and man, Mr. Sholokoff. I suspect your role as a pornographer allows you to feel powerful about women. But in any woman's eyes, you would be looked upon with pity. Your fetid breath and your physical repulsiveness are simply an extension of the blackness in your heart. Any woman who is not of diminished capacity would immediately be aware of that and want to flee your presence, no matter what she might tell you. Ask the people around you and see what their response is."

He was clearly fighting to retain the merry light in his eyes and to keep his grin in place, but his mouth twitched slightly, and his nostrils were dilating. "Do you like my farm?"

"Why should I care one way or another about your farm?" she asked.

"Because it's yours. Your permanent home. You will be among the people, part of the soil, fertilizer for their vegetables," he replied. "What finer fate for a martyr of your stature?"

Preacher Jack Collins didn't like to be pushed. Nor did he like losing control of things or, worse, having control taken from him. Not only had Noie Barnum, ingrate extraordinaire, strolled off from their safe house, he had managed to get himself arrested in a convenience store and put in a county bag that usually housed drunks and check writers and wife beaters. When Noie did not return from his stroll down the highway, Jack had gotten on his cell phone and begun making calls to an informational network that he had created and maintained for two decades, a network that no one would ordinarily associate with a man who dressed in beggar's rags and wandered the desert like a Bedouin. It included hookers from El Paso to Austin, button men from both sides of the border, Murphy artists, street dips and stalls, shylocks, coyotes, second-story creeps, drug mules, corrupt Mexican cops, safecrackers, car boosters, money washers, fences of every stripe, and a morphine-addicted retired librarian in Houston who could probably find Jimmy Hoffa's body if the FBI would take time to retain her.

It didn't take long to discover what had happened. Noie had gotten pinched in the convenience store by the same deputy Preacher Jack had dug up from a premature burial. How about that for ingratitude? Then a snitch just getting out of the bag had spotted Noie in custody and dropped the dime on him with Josef Sholokoff's people. Now several Mexicans were saying that a bunch of guys in camouflage masks had landed a helicopter at the Chinese woman's place, murdered a man in front of a child, and abducted the Chinese woman and a half-breed.

Jack had no doubt who was behind the abduction. Josef Sholokoff wanted Noie Barnum in his possession. The quickest way to him was through the sheriff, and the quickest way to the sheriff was through Anton Ling.

At four A.M. the morning after the abduction, a man who was part albino and part black and who had pink eyes and hairless skin that resembled different shades of white rubber that had been stitched together delivered a new Toyota to Preacher Jack at a café just north of Ojinaga. "There's another registration and another set of plates under the seat. I got you two driver's licenses, too," he said. He put the keys in Jack's hand, his eyes holding steady on Jack's.

"Anyone ever tell you it's rude to stare into somebody's face?" Jack said.

"You're hot."

"You know a time when I wasn't?"

"Not like this. I had a hard time on the driver's licenses. Word is you popped an FBI agent."

"He popped himself."

"A photo guy I use says you're the stink on shit and for me not to come back again."

"You wouldn't try to put the slide on me, would you, Billy?"

"Just telling you like it is."

"You want more money?"

"I was thinking about visiting Baja. Maybe lie on the beach and cool out for a while."

"What do you use for suntan lotion — ninety-weight motor oil?"

"I was speaking metaphorically."

Jack took three hundred dollars from his wallet and folded the bills between his fingers and stuffed them in the man's shirt pocket. "A metaphor means comparing one thing in terms of another without using the words 'like' or 'as.' 'To lie on a beach' is not a metaphor. If I said to you, 'Tell your parents to buy a better quality of condoms,' I would be making an implication, but I would not be speaking metaphorically. Do you understand what I'm saying to you?"

"Grammar was never my strong suit."

"Literary terms have nothing to do with grammar," Jack said. "If you're going to speak your native language, why don't you invest some time in the public library? It's free. In the meantime, don't go around using terms you don't know the meaning of." Jack stuffed the keys to his Trans Am into the man's pocket, on top of the bills. "Drive it to San Antone and park it at the airport. Wear gloves, but don't wipe it down. Leave the keys on the dashboard and the parking stub in the ashtray."

"Somebody will boost it."

"Nobody slips one past you."

"The guy who boosts it will get pinched, and the cops won't know if he's lying to them or not — about where he got it, I mean. You're doing a mind-fuck on them?"

"Don't use that kind of language in my presence," Jack said.

"I'll never figure you out, Preacher."

"Get out of my sight."

An hour later, he drove his new car to within one block of Sheriff Holland's jail and, wearing a hat and round steel-rimmed sunglasses that were as black as welder's goggles, went into a café and ordered a to-go box of scrambled eggs, ham, grits, and toast and a cup of scalding black coffee. He returned to his car and spread his food on the dashboard and ate with a plastic fork and spoon without seasoning of any kind or even seeming to taste it, as though consuming chaff swept up from a granary floor. His windows were down, and the air was cool and smelled of rain, and the storm clouds above the hills were so thick and swollen that he could not tell when the sun broke the horizon. In moments like these, Jack felt a strange sense of peace, as though the travels of the sun and moon had been set into abeyance, as though time had stopped and the denouement of his life, one that he secretly feared, had been postponed indefinitely.

Jack picked up his coffee. It was still so hot, the steam rose into his hat brim and scorched his forehead. But his gaze, which was fastened on the jail, never wavered, nor did his mouth twitch when he drank the cup to the bottom.

The electric light was burning in the sheriff's office. When the front door opened, Jack saw the sheriff walk to the silver pole by the sidewalk and clip the American flag to the chain and raise it flapping in the wind. At the same moment, Jack's cell phone vibrated on the seat. The call was from the morphine-addicted reference librarian in Houston.

"I may have found your Russian," she said. "He owns a place down in Mexico, one with a helipad on it. It's a horse breeding farm. A French magazine did an article on it about five years back."

"Can you find out if he's there?"

"I'll work on it. I found three game farms he owns in Texas and a place in Phoenix. You want me to check them out, too?"

"No, concentrate on Mexico."

"I found something else. Sholokoff's name came up a couple of times with a guy by the name of Temple Dowling. You know him?"

"Dowling was running whores with Sholokoff."

"I did a search on Dowling and found the name of a security service he uses. I hacked into it and discovered Dowling just went missing in Santa Fe. You think there's a connection?"

Jack stared at the front of the jail and at the flag ballooning and popping against the charcoal-blue darkness of the sky. "You there, Preacher?" she asked.

"Yeah, Sholokoff's people probably grabbed him. No one else would have motivation."

"You doing all this to get the Chinese

woman back?"

"What difference does it make?"

"Because there's this story I don't believe. About these Thai prostitutes who were murdered. They had heroin balloons in their stomachs. Sholokoff was using them as hookers and mules at the same time. Some people say you did the hit. At some place called Chapala Crossing. But I never believed that."

Jack could hear the wind blowing in the street, the traffic light at the intersection swinging on its support cables, the tin roof on a mechanic's shed swelling against the joists.

"You're serious about your work, but you'd never hurt a woman," she said. "That's what I told them. That's right, isn't it, Preacher?"

He closed the cell phone in his palm, his hand shaking, his throat as dry and thick as rust.

Krill had never given much thought to the mercenaries he had known. To him, they existed in a separate world, one in which men did not serve a cause or even fight out of necessity. They were simply uniformed employees without depth or ideology, with no desire to know either the enemies they were paid to kill or the civilians they were paid to defend or the countrymen like Krill they were paid to fight alongside.

When Krill thought about them at all, it

was in terms of their physicality and their access to North American goods and to fine weapons of international manufacture. Mercenaries were almost always barbered and clean. When they sweated, they smelled of deodorant rather than the glands. They were inoculated against all the diseases of the third world. Their bodies were hard, their stomachs flat, their shoulders and arms of the kind that could carry ninety pounds of supplies and weapons and take the shock of a parachute opening, sometimes crashing through a jungle canopy in the dark, jolting inside their harnesses with enough force to break the back of a cow.

He mostly thought of them in terms of what they were not. They were not haunted by the specters that trailed behind Krill everywhere he went. They did not fear their sleep or need to drink themselves into a stupor when the light went out of the sky and the wind was filled with the sounds of people crying in a village while their huts burned and belts of cached ammunition began popping in the heat. The mercenaries opened their tinned food with a tiny can opener they called a P-38, their eyes fixed on the task with the quiet intensity of a watchmaker at his craft. The deeds they had just committed, no more than a kilometer away, had already disappeared from their lives. Why should it be otherwise? They were not moralists; they were advisers and oversight personnel and not makers of policy. They came and went, as shadows did. Empires fell apart and died and new nations were born. A footprint in a jungle was as transient as the life span of an insect. The porous stone altars of the Mayans still contained the blood of the innocents who had been sacrificed by pagan priests centuries ago. What were the lives of a few more Indians? Krill believed this was how the mercenaries thought when they thought at all. In truth, he had never really cared about these men one way or another. Not until now.

His cell had a domed ceiling and seemed to bloom with a cool, fecund odor that was like water in the bottom of a dark well or mouse droppings inside a cave that dripped with moisture. There was another odor, too, one that was like mushrooms someone had trodden upon in a forest that never saw sunlight. It was like the smell in the disinterred bodies of his children. It was an odor that only a grave produced.

Krill propped his arms against the bars on the door and watched the mercenary the others called Frank. "You took off your mask," Krill said.

"We're all family here," Frank said.

"You're a nice-looking guy, man. Why are you a hump for a man like the Russian?"

"Sometime we'll have a beer and I'll fill you in."

"I don't have illusions about my situation. But I think you do," Krill said.

Frank grinned. He was wearing a yellow T-shirt scissored off just below the nipples and a pair of black cargo trousers with big snap pockets stitched on the thighs. He had the clean, chiseled features and freshly scrubbed look of a 1930s leading man. "Just out of curiosity, what were you doing with the zip?" he asked. "Don't give me that seeking-forgiveness crap, either."

"What does 'zip' mean?"

"As in 'zipper-head.' I'm talking about the Chinese broad."

"She can absolve sins."

"Did you know your ancestors never invented the wheel?"

"Before the Spaniards came, there were no draft animals. Why would my ancestors want a wheel when they had no animals to hitch it to? They did not spend their time on non-utile pursuits."

"You said I'm operating under some illusions."

"When you killed Negrito, you freed his spirit. You don't know it yet, but you got some serious problems, man."

"You're inside a prison cell and I'm outside of it. But I'm in trouble? You got to clue me in here. I'm fascinated by Indian mumbo jumbo."

"Negrito wanted to be me, to live inside

my skin. The way an assassin wants to become his victim. But he was too loyal to hurt his friend. So you did it for him and let his spirit leave his body and go inside mine. Now, no matter what you do to me, Negrito is going to be waiting for you. That is very bad for you, man. You haven't figured that out yet, but you will."

"Can your friend's spirit rise out of concrete? Because you're gonna be part of the foundation in Josef's new barn."

"*Me cago en tu puta madre.* Or are you already standing in line for that?"

"What did you say?"

" 'I defecate in your mother's womb.' That was Negrito's favorite expression. See, I told you, Negrito is on the loose."

"See my friend there, carrying that bucket out? Know what's in the bucket?"

"The waste your mother usually makes you carry out?"

"Take another guess."

A thick-bodied man, stripped to the waist, with a buzz haircut, was walking up the cellar stairs, a bucket swinging from his left hand. The muscles in his back looked like oiled rope. In the yellow glow of the bare bulb that hung above the steps, Krill could see string-like tendrils of blood on the man's skin.

"The item in that bucket was donated by one of our other guests," Frank said. "Those two guys you whacked and mutilated at

Josef's place were friends of mine. Keep shooting off your mouth, greaseball. I'll make sure you're a donor, too."

At nine A.M. of the same day, an independent taxi operator parked his vehicle in front of Hackberry's office and came inside with a package under his arm. The package was wrapped in twine and thick brown paper. "Got a delivery for you from the airport, Sheriff," he said.

"Who's it from?" Hackberry asked, looking up from his desk.

"I don't know. There's nothing written on it except your name. I got a call telling me to pick it up at the ticket counter and to keep the fifty dollars in the envelope tucked under the twine."

"Where's the envelope?"

"In the trash. I didn't think it was important. What, you reckon it's a bomb or something?"

"Leave it there."

"It's cold. Maybe it's some food."

After the taxi driver had gone, Hackberry went into the outer office. "Pam, tell Felix to go to the airport and see what he can find out about a package that was left for me at the ticket counter. Then come into my office, please."

He pulled on a pair of latex gloves and removed a pocketknife from his desk drawer and opened the long blade on it. He placed the flat of his hand on the wrapping paper. He could feel the coldness in the box through his glove.

"Put on a vest and a face shield, Hack," Pam said.

"Step back," he replied, and cut the twine. He inserted his fingers under the paper and peeled it away in sections from the top of a corrugated cardboard box.

"Hack, call the FBI," Pam said.

He pulled back a strip of tape holding the flaps on the box's top in place and folded the flaps back against the sides. He looked down at a carefully packed layer of Ziploc bags containing dry ice. One of the bags had broken open, and the ice had slid down deeper into the box and was vaporizing against a round, compacted lump of matter wrapped inside a sheet of clear plastic. There were whorls of color pressed against the plastic that made him think of an uncured ham that had been freezer-burned in a meat locker.

"What is it?" Pam said, staring at the blankness of his expression.

He stepped back from the box, his hands at his sides. He shook his head. She stepped closer and looked down into the box. "Oh, boy," she said.

"Yeah," he said.

"It was flown here?"

He nodded and cleared his throat. "Get the key to Barnum's cell," he said.

They went up the stairs together, Hackberry holding the box, Pam walking in front of him. She turned the key in the cell door and pulled it open. Noie Barnum was lying on his bunk, reading a magazine. He put the magazine on the floor but didn't get up.

"Come in and close the door behind you," Hackberry said to Pam.

"Something going on?" Barnum said.

"Yeah, sit up," Hackberry said. "See this?"

"Yeah, a box."

"Look inside it."

"What for?"

Hackberry set the box on the foot of the bunk and picked up the magazine from the floor. He rolled it into a cone and slapped Barnum across the head. Then he slapped him a second time and a third. "I want to tear you up, Mr. Barnum. I don't mean that figuratively. I want to throw you down those stairs. That's how I feel about you."

Barnum's eyes were filming, his face blotched. "You don't have the right to treat me like this."

"Look inside that box."

"Somebody's head is in there?" Barnum said, his expression defiant, his eyes lifted to Hackberry's.

Hackberry hit him again, this time tearing the cover loose from the magazine. Barnum lifted his hand to protect himself, then looked down into the box. The blood drained from his face. "Oh God," he said.

"Tell me what you see."

"It's a hand and a foot."

"Are they male or female?"

"Sir?"

"Answer the question."

"There's hair on the ankle. It must be a man's."

"Look at the hand."

"What about it?"

"Look closer. There's a ring on it. Look at it."

"I'm not responsible for this."

"That's a University of Texas class ring. The hand and the ring belong to Temple Dowling. The people who did this to him will probably start on Anton Ling next. Right now I'd like to rip you apart. Instead of doing that, I'm going to ask you a couple of questions, and you're going to answer them. Got that?"

"Yes, sir."

"Where were you and Jack Collins hiding?"

"Just like you said earlier, right south of the border. But Jack's gone by now."

"Gone where?"

"That's anybody's guess. You see him and then he's gone. He's standing in one place, then in another, without seeming to move. I've never known anybody like him."

"You're just catching on to the fact that

there's something a little unusual about him?"

"I don't know where Jack is. I don't know where Miss Anton is, either. I feel awful about what's happened. My sister died in the Towers. I wanted to get even with the people who killed her. I didn't want any of these other things to happen."

Hackberry let out his breath and felt the heat rise out of his chest like ash off a dead fire. "I want you out of here," he said.

"Say again?"

"You heard me. Hit the road."

"I don't get it."

"You don't have to. You just got eighty-sixed from my jail. It's a first. Burn a candle the next time you're in church."

"Maybe I don't want to leave."

"Son, you'd better get a lot of gone between you and this jailhouse," Pam said.

"Well, you're gonna see me again," Barnum said.

Pam raised her eyebrows threateningly.

"Yes, ma'am, I'm gone," he said.

Downstairs, ten minutes later, Pam said, "Hack, what in the hell are you doing?"

"Fixing to call the FBI," he replied.

But it wasn't for the reasons she thought.

CHAPTER TWENTY-SIX

Pam was still staring at him when he got off the phone. "You told the feds about Dowling's mutilation but not about Barnum?"

"That's right," he replied.

"Why does Barnum get a pass?"

"Because if the feds get him into custody, they'll probably lose interest in Anton Ling. Second, Barnum isn't a bad kid and, in my opinion, deserves another chance."

"You have a funny way of looking at the world, Hack."

"My father used to say, 'The name of the game is five-card draw. You never have to play the hand you're dealt.' He believed everything we see around us now was once part of the Atlantic Ocean, with mermaids sitting up on the rocks, and that one day I would see the mermaids return."

"We'd better get some breakfast, *kemo sabe.*"

"I told you that's what Rie called me, didn't I?"

"Yeah, I'm sorry, I forgot," she said.

"Don't say you're sorry. You didn't know Rie. She'd like for you to call me that. She'd like you."

She looked at him in a strange way, her mouth slightly parted, her face suddenly vulnerable, but he did not see it. Maydeen had just come out of the dispatcher's cage, her anger palpable. "He's on the line, Hack," she said.

"Who is *he?*"

"He just told me, 'Put the sheriff on the line, woman.' "

"Collins?"

"I say we hang up on him. Don't let him jerk you around like this, Hack."

"No, I think this is the call we've been waiting on," Hackberry said.

Jack Collins was sitting at a small table under a canvas tarp propped on poles next to an airplane hangar, a corked green bottle of seltzer and a glass and a saucer of salted lime slices by his hand. A clutch of banana plants grew tightly against the hangar wall, beads of moisture the size of BBs sliding down the leaves. The wind was hot, the canvas riffling above his head, the desert lidded from horizon to horizon with a layer of solid blue-black clouds that seemed to force the heat and humidity radiating from the desert floor back into the earth. The clouds crackled with

645

electricity but offered no real promise of rain or even a moment of relief from the grit and alkali in the wind and the smell of salt and decomposition that whirled with the dust devils out of the streambeds. Jack decided there was nothing wrong with Mexico that a half-dozen hydrogen bombs and a lot of topsoil couldn't cure.

Jack's pilot and two hired killers, the cousins Eladio and Jaime, were waiting for him by the two-engine Beechcraft on the airstrip. The pilot was on retainer, at Jack's beck and call on a twenty-four-hour basis. Eladio and Jaime were available for any activity that put money in their pockets, night or day; if there were any lines they would not cross, any deeds they would not perform, including a drive-by for La Familia Michoacána on a teenage birthday party in Juárez, Jack had not seen it. Their greatest problem, in his view, was the impaired thought processes that seemed to live behind the indolence in their faces. The inside of Jaime's head could only be described as a tangled web of cruelty that was linked somehow to his stupidity and sullen nature. The more intelligent of the two, Eladio, thought that his transparent childlike deceit and attempts at manipulation were signs of sophistication. During a rare loss of restraint with the two cousins, Jack had asked Eladio if his mother had been impregnated by a bowling pin.

Eladio had responded, "You are a man of knowledge, Señor Jack. But you must not misjudge simple men. We think and feel deeply about our mothers. They are the center of our lives."

"Then why do you say *chinga tu madre* to each other at every opportunity?" Jack had said.

"I am not equipped to discuss abstractions with a man of your intelligence," Eladio had said. "But my mother is eighty and still tells stories of her mother, who was a concubine of Pancho Villa and one of those who helped hide his severed head in the Van Horn Mountains. That is the level of respect we have for the women in our family."

Jack had made a mental note about the level of stability in his employees.

At this particular moment, he was irritated with the weather, the clouds of black flies buzzing over a calf's carcass in a nearby streambed, and the fact that the two cousins seemed incapable of doing anything right except killing people. The man who owned the airstrip and the hangar and the improvised café outside it had installed a jukebox just inside the hangar door, one loaded with gangsta-rap recordings that blasted through the speakers so loudly that the side of the tin hangar shook. Jack had told Eladio and Jaime to talk with the jukebox's owner, but either the owner had ignored the warning or they had not bothered. So while he was trying to make notes in preparation for his conversation with the sheriff, his eardrums were being assailed by a level of electronic percussion that was like having a studded snow tire driven over his head.

Jack capped his pen, stuck it between the pages of his notebook, and went inside the hangar, where the owner was cleaning the concrete pad with a push broom. "Can I help you, *señor?*" he said.

Jack pointed to his ear, indicating he couldn't hear.

"You got a problem with your ear?" the owner shouted.

Jack pulled the plug on the jukebox, cut the electric cord in two with his pocketknife, and set the plug on top of the casing. "No, I'm fine now. Thanks," he said.

Then he sat down at his table under the canvas flap and drank a glass of seltzer and chewed on a lime slice, staring into space, each eye like a glass orb with a dead insect frozen inside it. He dialed his cell phone with his thumb and lifted the phone to his ear and waited, his body heat increasing inside his clothes, his pulse quickening. Why would his metabolism react to calling the sheriff? It could be anything, he told himself. Why dwell on it? Maybe it was because he had finally found a worthy opponent.

Or maybe it was something else.

What?

Don't think about it, he told himself.

Why not? I'm supposed to be afraid of my own thoughts? he asked himself.

Maybe Holland is the father you never had. Maybe you want him to like you.

Like hell I do.

You could have taken him off the board a couple of times. Why didn't you do it, Jackie Boy?

The situation was one-sided. There's no honor in that. Don't call me that name.

There was honor in the shooting of the nine Thai women?

I don't want to talk about that. It's over. I did my penance in the desert.

He thought he heard the hysterical laughter of a woman, someone who always hung just on the edge of his vision, ridiculing him, waiting for him to slip up, her smile as cruel as an open cut in living tissue.

When the female deputy answered, Jack said, "Put the sheriff on the line, woman."

Whatever she said in response never registered. Instead, he heard the voice of the woman who lived in his dreams and his unconscious and his idle daytime moments and his futile attempts at joy. He heard her incessant, piercing laughter, louder and louder, and he knew that eventually, he would once again resort to the release that never failed him, an eruption of gunfire that reverberated through his hands and arms like a jackhammer and made his teeth rattle and cleansed his thoughts and deadened his ears to all sound, both outside and inside his head.

"What do you need, Mr. Collins?" the sheriff's voice said.

"I know where the Asian woman is. I can take you there," he replied.

"Where might that be?"

"Down in Mexico, way to heck and gone by car, not so far by air."

"She's with Sholokoff?"

"She and Temple Dowling and the 'breed known as Krill. How's Noie doing?"

"I don't know. I kicked him loose."

"You did what?"

"Last time I saw him, he was walking toward the city-limits sign, whistling a song."

"The feds aren't going to be happy with you."

"I'll try to live with it. Where can we meet, Mr. Collins?"

"You ever lie?"

"No."

"Not ever?"

"You heard me the first time," Hackberry said.

"I'm trusting you. I don't do that with most people."

"Do whatever you want, sir. But don't expect me to feel flattered."

"I'll give you some coordinates and see you

no later than four hours from now. I suppose you'll bring the female deputy with you?"

"Count on it. Why are you doing this, Mr. Collins?"

"Sholokoff shouldn't have taken the Asian woman. She's not a player."

"There's another reason."

"Sholokoff tried to have me capped. I owe him one."

"There's another reason."

"When you find out what it is, tell me so we'll both know. Don't bring anybody besides the female deputy and your pilot. A couple of my men will pick you up. If you violate any aspect of our arrangement, the deal is off and you won't hear from me again. The Asian woman's fate will be on your conscience."

"If you try to harm me or my deputy, I'm going to cool you out on the spot. I'm like you, Jack — over-the-hill and out of place and time, with not a lot to lose."

"Then keep your damn word, and we'll get along just fine."

Jack clicked off his cell phone. Unbelievably, the jukebox sprang to life and began blaring rap music out the door. He remembered that the cord he'd cut had both a female and a male plug and was detachable from the box. The owner of the hangar had probably replaced it and decided to prove he could be as assertive and unpleasant as an imperious gringo from Texas who thought he could come to Mexico and wipe his ass on the place.

Jack went to the plane and removed his guitar case and set it on top of the table. The wind was blowing harder, the heat and dust swirling under the canopy as Jack unfastened the top of the case and inserted plugs in his ears and removed his Thompson and snapped a thirty-round box magazine into the bottom of the receiver and went inside the hangar. The owner took one look at him and dropped his push broom and began running for the back door. Jack raised the Thompson's barrel and squeezed the trigger, ripping apart the jukebox, scattering plastic shards and electronic components all over the concrete pad, stitching the tin wall with holes the size of nickels.

"*Señor,* what the fuck you doin'?" Eladio said behind him.

Jack still had the plugs stoppered in his ears and could not hear him. The only sound he heard was his mother's laughter — maniacal, forever taunting, a paean of ridicule aimed at a driven man who would never escape the black box in which a little boy had been locked.

Krill did not know a great deal about the complexities of politics. A man owned land or he did not own land. Either he was allowed to keep the product of his labor or he was not allowed to keep it. The abstractions of ideology seemed the stuff that fools and radicals and drunkards argued about in late-hour bars because they had nothing else to occupy their time. Though Krill did not understand the abstruse terms of social science or economics, he understood jails. He had learned about them in El Salvador and Nicaragua, and he knew how you survived or didn't survive inside them. Men in confinement all behaved and thought in a predictable fashion. And so did their warders.

Krill had a very strong suspicion that his captors did not understand how jails worked. The gringo Frank was a good example of what American convicts called a "fish." He had not only baited a prisoner but had informed the prisoner of his ultimate fate, which in this case was death and burial in concrete, telling the prisoner in effect that he had nothing to lose. Frank had made another mistake. He had not bothered to note that when Krill was placed in the cell, he was wearing running shoes, not pull-on boots.

Krill had slept three hours on the floor, his head cushioned on a piece of burlap he had found in the corner. As the early glow of morning appeared through the window on the far side of the cellar, a man came down the stairs carrying two bowls filled with rice and beans. He was a strange-looking man, with dirty-blond hair and a duckbilled upper lip and eyes that were set too far apart and skin that had the grainy texture of pig hide. He took one bowl to the cell where Krill believed La Magdalena was being held, then squatted in front of Krill's cell and pushed the second bowl through the gap between the concrete floor and the bottom of the door.

"I need something to eat with," Krill said.

"This isn't a hotel," the man said.

"We cannot eat our food with our fingers."

"Eat out of the bowl. Just tip it up and you can eat."

"*Hombre,* we are not animals. You must give us utensils to eat."

"I'll see what I can find," the man said.

"Bring me a spoon. I cannot eat rice with a fork. Bring us water, too."

"Want anything else?"

"Yes, to use a real toilet, one that flushes with water. Using a chemical toilet is unsanitary and degrading."

When the man had gone upstairs, Krill lowered his voice and said, "Magdalena, can you hear me?"

"Yes," the woman said.

"Did they hurt you?"

"No."

"Where is Dowling?"

"I think he's dead."

"Did they mutilate him?"

"Yes, very badly."

"Listen to me. I must say this in a hurry. I

654

have killed many men. I have also killed a Jesuit priest. I tortured and murdered a DEA informant. I need your absolution for these sins and others that are too many to name."

"I don't have that power. Only God does. If you're sorry for what you did and you renounce your violent ways, your sins are forgiven. God doesn't forgive incrementally or partially. He forgives absolutely, Antonio. That's what 'absolution' means. God makes all things new."

"You remembered my name."

"Of course. Why wouldn't I?"

"Because everyone calls me Krill."

"It's a name you earned in war. You shouldn't go by that name anymore."

"Maybe I'll stop using it later, Magdalena. But right now I got to get us out of here. We need a fork from the man who brought us our bowls."

"Why?"

"There are only two ways we're going to get out of here. I have to open the lock on my door or get a man in my cell. We need a fork."

"I heard you ask for a spoon."

"This man is stubborn and slow in the head. He will do the opposite of what he is asked."

The upstairs door opened, and the man with the duckbilled mouth came down the stairs. There were two dull metallic objects in his right hand. "I got you what you wanted," he said. "Put your bowls outside the door when you're finished."

Krill stuck his hand through the bars and curved his palm around the utensil the man gave him. *A spoon,* he thought bitterly.

"Disappointed? I was jailing when I was sixteen," the man said. "Better eat up. You got a rough day ahead of you."

The single-engine department plane dropped down over a ridge and followed a milky-brown river that had spread out onto the floodplain and was dotted with sandy islands that had willow trees on them. Above the plane, Hackberry could see the long blue-black layer of clouds that seemed to extend like curds of industrial smoke from the Big Bend all the way across northern Mexico. Down below, the willow trees stiffened in the wind, the surface of the river wrinkling in jagged V-shaped lines. On the southern horizon, the cloud layer seemed to end and looked like strips of torn black cotton churning against a band of perfectly blue sky.

The wings of the plane yawed suddenly, the airframe shuddering. "We're fine," the pilot said above the engine noise. He was a crop duster named Toad Fowler who worked on and off for the sheriff's department. "Those are just updrafts."

Nonetheless, he kept tapping the glass on

his instruments.

"What's the problem?" Hackberry asked.

"The oil pressure is a little low," the pilot said. "We're okay. We'll be there in ten minutes."

"How low?" Hackberry said.

"It's probably not a line, just a leaky gasket," the pilot said. "I'll check everything out after we get down. Hang on. We might bounce around a little bit."

"You didn't check everything out before we left?" Hackberry asked.

"It's an old plane. What do you want? Shit happens," the pilot said.

When the plane dipped down toward the river, Hackberry felt Pam place her hand on top of his shoulder, her breath coming hard against the back of his neck.

"We're okay," Hackberry said.

"How do you know?" she asked.

"Toad just told me."

"Tell him I'm going to shoot him after we land."

Down below, Hackberry could see great squares of both cultivated and pasture land and bare hills that looked molded out of white clay that had hardened and cracked. The pilot made a wide turn, the wings buffeting, and came in low over the river, the islands sweeping by, then Hackberry saw a feeder lot and hog farm whose holding pens were churned a chocolate color and buildings with tin roofs and houses constructed of cinder block and then a short pale green landing strip that had been recently mowed out of a field, a red wind sock straining against its tether at the far end. They landed hard, rainwater splashing under the tires. A flatbed truck with two men lounging near it was parked by the side of the strip.

"You ever see them before?" Pam said.

"No," Hackberry replied. "You okay?"

She didn't reply until Toad had cut the engine and gotten out of the plane and lit a cigarette by the wing. "I'm backing your play, Hack, but the idea of getting involved with Jack Collins makes my stomach churn," she said.

"I wouldn't blame you if you stayed with Toad. I can handle it by myself."

"That's not going to happen," she said.

"I have to get Miss Anton back, Pam. If I don't, I'll never rest."

"We're making a deal with the devil, and you know it."

"That's the breaks."

"You mean after this is over, you're going to let that bastard slide?"

"Jack Collins isn't planning to leave Mexico," he said.

Her eyes went back and forth. "How do you know that?"

"Collins brought us here as his executioners," he said.

"Or maybe he plans on being ours," she said.

Hackberry and Pam pulled a duffel bag and a backpack off the plane and walked toward the flatbed truck. The Mexicans standing next to it introduced themselves as Eladio and Jaime. They were unshaved and wore slouch-brim straw hats and unpressed long-sleeve cotton shirts buttoned at the wrists. Their eyes wandered over Pam's body without seeming to see her, the laziness in their expressions as much mask as indicator of their thoughts.

"Where's Collins?" Hackberry said.

"He ain't here," Jaime said.

"That's why I asked you where he is," Hackberry said.

"We'll take you where he's at," Jaime said. "You two can ride in front with Eladio. I'll ride in back."

"Where are we going?" Pam asked.

"You'll know when we get there, *chica*," Jaime said.

"Call me that again and see what happens," she said.

"We are sorry. We do not mean to offend," Eladio said. "Can we look in your canvas bag and your pack? It would be good if we can look at your cell phones, too."

"Why would you want to do that?" Pam said.

"Among friends, there is no need of GPS

locators," Eladio said. "It is good to have things of that nature out of our discussions about the liberation of your friend. That is the only reason I raise this question."

"Look all you want," Hackberry said.

"Thank you," Eladio said. "What fine guns you have in your bag. What is in this metal box?"

"Cookies and fruitcake," Hackberry said.

"You carry such items with you when you go on a serious mission?" Eladio said.

"I have a sugar deficiency. I also thought you might like some. Take them if you like," Hackberry said.

"That is very kind of you," Eladio said. "I have children who will love these."

"When do we see Preacher?" Hackberry asked.

"Very soon. He looks forward to seeing you with great anticipation," Eladio said.

"You come all the way down here 'cause of *la china?*" Jaime said.

"You could say that," Hackberry replied.

"She must be some broad, *hombre,*" Jaime said. "It's true what they say about Chinese women?"

"Do not speak further," Eladio said, raising his finger to his cousin's lips.

"It's just a question. I do not need to be censored," Jaime said. "These are gringos in our country. We do not suppress ourselves to please gringos in our own country."

"It's time for us to see Mr. Collins," Hackberry said.

He and Pam rode in the cab while Eladio drove and Jaime sat on the flatbed. They proceeded in a southerly direction down dirt roads through irrigated farmland for almost an hour. The colors and configuration and flora in the land were like none that Hack could remember. Wild grapefruit and hibiscus and pink camellias and palm trees with long, slender trunks grew in the turn rows. The soil was loamy and tinted a reddish-brown, as though it had been mixed with rust, but the hills were white and bare and gray-backed, like sea creatures that had died and fossilized. The topography made Hack think of imaginative paintings of ancient Egypt that depicted an era when the earth was still recovering from the Flood and deserts bloomed and gatherers filled date baskets with their hands. Why would a man like Josef Sholokoff locate himself in such a place? To re-create the introduction of the serpent into Eden?

No, nothing so grandiose, Hackberry thought. For Sholokoff, Mexico was probably nothing more than a good tax dodge.

The truck rolled down a long embanked road made of crushed stone, the rocks *ting*ing steadily under the fenders, the wind stream warm and sultry, the sky lidded with clouds that emitted no sunlight. Ahead, at a crossroads, Hackberry could see a small, paintless wood-frame store with a single gas pump in front and a screened side porch. Behind the store, the terrain seemed to stretch away endlessly, glazed with salt, cracked and sunken in places, as though a lake had once covered the area but had drained through a hole in its center. Eladio parked the truck and cut the engine. "Señor Collins awaits you on the porch," he said. "Do not take your guns inside. That would cause alarm for the owner of the store. Also, it is a very serious offense to bring guns into Mexico."

"That's like saying it's a serious offense to bring insanity into a lunatic asylum," Pam said.

"I am not educated and do not understand the comparisons you make, *señorita,*" Eladio said.

Hackberry looked through the back window of the cab. "Your cousin is eating the cookies you were going to give your children," he said.

"Jaime, what are you doin', man?" Eladio yelled out the window.

Jaime replaced the tin lid on the container and wiped the crumbs off his fingers. Pam and Hackberry got out of the cab and followed Eladio to the screen door on the store's side porch. She glanced over her shoulder at Jaime, who had remained on the truck bed. "I don't guess these guys are students of Homer," she said.

"Shut up," Hackberry said under his breath. He opened the screen door and stepped inside, removing his Stetson hat. Inside the gloom, against the back wall, he saw a man eating refried beans and strips of steak and sliced peppers from a tin plate with a fork. The man wore a blocked hat and a seersucker coat and a gray dress shirt with no buttons on the collar and trousers that were tucked into the tops of his boots. A guitar case was propped on its side against the wall behind him. For Hackberry, Jack Collins was like a figure out of a dream, not quite flesh and blood, vaporous in its dimensions, waiting like an incubus to attach itself to the fear in its victim, in the way a leech attaches itself to living tissue in order to survive.

"Have a good flight?" Collins said.

"Not really," Hackberry said.

"Sit down. You, too, Deputy Tibbs."

"I think I'll stand. You don't mind, do you?" Pam said.

"I owe you an apology," Collins said, chewing while he spoke.

"For trying to kill me?" she said.

"If y'all had your way, you would have split me open and salted my innards and tacked me to a fence post. I figure what I did was just fair play."

"We didn't come here to talk past history, Mr. Collins. How far are we from our target?" Hackberry said.

Collins pushed two chairs out from the table with his boot. He was wearing a holstered thumb-buster revolver, the bluing rubbed bare around the cylinder, the cartridge loops stuffed with copper-jacketed .45 rounds. "Sit down. Have a Pepsi. The beans and meat aren't bad. We go in at sunset. Once inside that compound, we don't negotiate."

"Listen to me, Collins. You don't make the rules. I do," Hackberry said. "We're down here for one reason only, and that's to save the life of an innocent woman. We don't turn people into wallpaper. If you want to settle a personal score with Sholokoff, you find another time and place to do it."

Collins motioned at the waiter, then looked up at Hackberry. "I bought a big bottle of Pepsi and had him put it in the icebox for y'all. Now sit down and take your nose out of the air. You, too, Deputy Tibbs." He placed his fork on his plate and removed a folded piece of paper from inside his coat. "I've drawn a diagram of the compound and the entrances to it. Are y'all going to sit down or not?"

Pam Tibbs pulled back a chair and sat down, her eyes on his.

"You want to tell me something?" he asked.

"I'd like to park one in your brisket, you arrogant white trash," she replied.

Collins looked across the table at Hackberry. "I'm not going to have this, Sheriff."

"Show us the entrances to the compound," Hackberry said.

"No, you need to correct the mouth on this woman."

The waiter brought a tall plastic bottle of Pepsi and two glasses, then went away.

"We came a long way, Jack," Hackberry said. "You've done a lot of harm to a lot of people, some of them friends of ours. Don't expect too much of us."

"You say I've done harm? Right now the Asian woman and the fellow named Krill are learning what harm is all about. Josef Sholokoff doesn't know Noie is on the street. He thinks he's still in your jail, and he's mad as hell and sweating Ms. Ling and the half-breed because of it."

"You've got someone inside?" Hackberry said.

"What do you think?" Collins asked. "They started in on Krill about four hours ago. If I know Josef, he'll take a special interest in the woman. Why do you think he crucified Cody Daniels and set fire to his church with him hanging on the cross?"

"You tell me."

"It wasn't for money. It wasn't for sheer meanness, either."

Hackberry remained silent.

"Josef was born with the brain of a rodent and the face of a ferret, and he blames God for the pitiful little toothpick that he is,"

Collins said. "For formally educated people, neither of y'all seems real bright, Mr. Holland. But I guess overestimating the intelligence of my fellow man has always been my greatest character defect." He pushed the diagram toward Hackberry and resumed eating, his fork scraping in the grease at the bottom of the plate, his eyes as empty as glass.

CHAPTER TWENTY-SEVEN

They had beaten Krill in his cell and hung him from a rafter in the center of the cellar, where the Asian woman could see him hanging, and then had beaten him again. When they dropped him to the floor, his wrists roped together behind him, he had begun to slip in and out of consciousness and into a place where his children were waiting for him. They were standing outside a traveling carnival, their cheeks smeared with Popsicle juice, the carved wooden horses of a merry-go-round spinning behind them, the music of the calliope rising into the evening sky.

Frank or the man standing next to Frank poured water from a canteen on Krill's face. Josef Sholokoff was sitting on a chair two feet away, one knee folded over the other, smoking a perfumed cigarette that was gold-tipped and wrapped with lavender paper. "Noie Barnum remained for weeks in your custody, but you never made him draw the design of the drone? You're a businessman who kidnaps and sells valuable people, but you never try to extract information from them? You think I'm a stupid man, Mr. Krill?"

"My name is Antonio."

"You came to see the woman for religious reasons? You didn't know she helped transport arms to your country? It's just coincidence that we found you at her house while you were on a spiritual mission? You are a very entertaining man, I think."

"My women have always told me that."

"You worked for the Americans in your country?"

"Of course. Everyone does."

"But you planned to help Al Qaeda?"

"An American helicopter killed my children. But I know now that I am responsible for their deaths, not others."

"Oh, I see. Because you have discovered you are powerless against the killers of your children, you blame yourself and, in so doing, become a saint. So, in our way, we are helping you with your saintliness?"

"You taunt an uneducated man whose hands are bound after you have tortured him?" the Asian woman said from her cell. "You are a very small man, Mr. Sholokoff."

"Frank, take care of that," Sholokoff said.

"Sir?" Frank said.

"Ms. Ling. Take care of her."

"The only way to shut her up is to pour concrete in her mouth," Frank said.

"Then do it," Sholokoff said.

"Sir, we need to finish with the greaser one way or another," Frank said.

"All I get from you are admonitions but never results. In the last forty-eight hours, we have had in our possession a defense contractor, a notorious kidnapper and coyote, and an ex–CIA operative who flew with Air America. We get nothing out of any of them. Are you successful only with a worthless man like Cody Daniels? You certainly seemed to rise to the occasion when you turned him into a living passion play. I wonder about you, Frank."

"That was your doing, sir," Frank said. He was standing behind Sholokoff, wearing tight leather gloves like a race-car driver might wear, his flat stomach exposed by his scissored-off T-shirt.

Sholokoff turned in his chair. "You need to explain yourself, Frank."

"We shouldn't have been wasting our time on the minister. It wasn't me that had the hard-on about him. That's all I was saying."

Sholokoff puffed on his cigarette, his eyes warm and shiny, exhaling the smoke from his nostrils. He put out the cigarette under his foot, then picked up the butt and handed it to one of his men to dispose of. "Frank, tell me this. Why is it that Sheriff Holland is not responding to our calls? Even after we sent part of Temple Dowling to his office. Why is a man like Holland, a personal friend of Ms. Ling, seemingly detached from her fate?"

"I don't know, sir," Frank said.

"Could it be that he no longer has Noie Barnum in his possession? Or that he's closer to us now than he was this morning?"

"You mean he's coming here?" Frank said.

"Put Antonio back in his cell. I have to use the bathroom," Sholokoff said. "While I'm gone, I want you to devise something special for Ms. Ling. I also don't want to have to correct you again. Do you understand me, Frank?"

"Loud and clear, Mr. S.," Frank said.

"*Señor,* you got a minute for me?" Krill said from the floor, staring through the legs of the men who surrounded him.

"You want me to be your friend now, Antonio? To take you out of all this unhappiness?" Sholokoff said.

"Yes, sir. I am very tired of it."

"I'm glad to hear that."

"I don't want to be here when the next bad thing happens."

"With Ms. Ling?"

"No, with you and your friends, *señor.*"

"I think you have become delusional, my Hispanic friend."

"You didn't see what Negrito just did. Negrito was living inside my skin, but he just left my body and went up on the ceiling. Now he's standing right behind you. You are in deep shit, *señor.*"

"Who's Negrito?" Sholokoff asked Frank.

"The guy who's gonna fuck you with a garden rake," Krill said. Then he began laughing on the floor, his long hair hanging in a sweaty web over his face.

Sholokoff seemed more bemused than offended and went upstairs to use the bathroom. Two men picked Krill up by his arms and carried him to his cell and threw him inside. "Hey, Frank," one of them said. "There're scratches around the keyhole."

"What?" Frank said.

"His food bowl is here, but there's no utensil. The guy must have been using a fork on the lock."

"Somebody gave the greaser a fork?"

"Frank, I gave him a spoon," said the man who had brought Krill his food.

"Then where is it?"

"I don't know, man."

"We should tell Mr. Sholokoff," said the man who had discovered the scratches.

"Shut up. Both you guys shut up," Frank said. He stepped inside the cell and kicked Krill in the base of the spine. "Where's the spoon, greaseball?"

"That hurts, boss. It makes my mind go blank," Krill said. "Somebody gave me a spoon? I must have lost it. I am very sorry."

"Frank," one of the other men whispered.

"What?"

"Mr. Sholokoff just flushed the toilet."

Jack Collins had led the way in a Ford Explorer through a winding series of low-topped white hills on which no grass or trees or even scrub brush grew. The road through the hills was narrow and rock-strewn and dusty, the wind as hot as a blowtorch, smelling of creosote and alkali and dry stone under the layer of blue-black clouds that gave no rain.

He had seen white hills like these only one other time in his life, when he was marching with a column of marines in the same kind of dust and heat through terrain that was more like Central Africa than the Korean peninsula. The marines wore utilities that were stiff with salt, the armpits dark with sweat, the backs of their necks tanned and oily and glistening under the rims of their steel pots, their boots gray with dust. In the midst of it all, the ambulances and six-bys and tanks and towed field pieces kept grinding endlessly up the road, the dust from their wheels blowing back into the faces of the men. Ahead, Hackberry could see the white hills that made him think of giant wind-scrubbed, calcified slugs on which no vegetation grew and whose sides were sometimes pocked with caves in which the Japanese prior to World War II had installed railroad tracks and mobile howitzers.

That was the day Hackberry had an

epiphany about death that had always remained with him and that he called upon
whenever he was afraid. He had reached a
point of exhaustion and dehydration that had
taken him past the edges of endurance into
personal surrender, a calm letting go of his
fatigue and the blisters inside his boots and
the sweat crawling down his sides and the
fear that at any moment he would hear the
popping of small-arms fire in the hills. When
the column fell out, he looked at the red haze
of dust floating across the sun and on the
hills and on a long flat plateau dotted with
freshly turned earth that resembled anthills,
and he wondered why any of it should be of
any concern to him or his comrades or even
to the nations that warred over it. In a short
span of time, nothing that happened here
would be of any significance to anyone.
Ultimately, every cloak rolled in blood would
be used as fuel for flames, and the sun would
continue to shine and the rain to fall upon
both the just and the unjust, and this piece of
worthless land would remain exactly what it
was, a worthless piece of land of no importance to anyone except those who lost their
lives because of it.

Just as he had experienced these thoughts,
someone had shouted, "Incoming!" and
Hackberry had heard first one, then two, then
three artillery rounds arching out of the sky,
like a train engine screeching down a track

and then exploding, striking the earth in such rapid succession that he'd had no time to react. From where he was sitting on top of a ditch, he saw the barrage intensify and march across the plateau, blowing geysers of dirt and buried pots of kimchi into the air.

The North Koreans were laying waste to a field filled with buried earthen jars of pickled cabbage. Hackberry continued to stare at the rain of destruction on the most ignoble of targets, bemused as much by the madness of his fellow man's obsession as by the bizarre nature of the event. When clouds of pulverized dirt blew into his face, he never blinked. Nor did he blink when a piece of artillery shell spun toward him like a heliograph, its twisted steel surfaces flashing with light, whipping past his ear with a whirring sound like that of a tiny propeller. He felt neither fear nor self-recrimination at his recklessness, and he did not know why, since he did not consider himself either brave or exceptional.

His lack of fear and his whimsical attitude toward his own death stayed with him all the way to the Chosin Reservoir and his imprisonment in No Name Valley, and up until the present, he was not sure why his fear had temporarily disappeared or why it had returned. With time and age, he had come to think of mortality as the price of admission to the ballpark; but why had this road in Mexico taken him back to Korea? Was he finally about to step through the door into the place we all fear? Would his legs and his mettle be up to that dry-throated, heart-pounding, blood-draining moment that no words can adequately describe? Or would his courage fail him, as it had when he dropped a litter with a wounded marine on it and ran from a Chinese enlisted man who stood on a pile of frozen sandbags and sprayed Hackberry's ditch with a burp gun and shot him three times through the calves and left him with years of guilt and self-abasement that he came to accept as a natural way of life?

The flatbed truck followed the Explorer between the hills, then emerged into a green valley where a paved road lined with eucalyptus trees led due south through meadowland and cornfields and farmhouses that were built of stone or stucco or both. Finally, the Explorer turned off the road and crossed a cattle guard and passed a burned-out house and pulled into a two-story barn that was filled with wind and the sounds of rattling tin in the roof.

Jack Collins cut his engine and got out of the Explorer and pulled his guitar case after him, then shut the driver's door. "The sun will dip behind that mountain yonder in about four hours. If you want, you can rest up," he said.

"What is this place?" Hackberry asked.

"It used to belong to a friend of mine. At

least it did until the army burned him out."

"You've spent time around here before?"

"Now and then."

"Working for Sholokoff?"

"I did some contract stuff for him. I work for myself. I never 'worked' for Josef Sholokoff."

"Why the wait?" Hackberry asked. Through a side window, he could see Eladio urinating inside a grove of citrus trees.

"You want to attack a houseful of armed men in daylight?"

"I don't know if Ms. Ling can afford to write off the next four hours."

"She hit me with a piñata stick, but I'm risking my life to save hers," Collins said. "I don't think she's got any kick coming. Maybe Sholokoff will take some of the starch out of her."

Hackberry kept his face turned away so Collins would not see the emotion he was trying to suppress. Through the window, Hackberry saw Eladio turn his back to the barn and zip his fly, then remove a cell phone from his pants pocket. "What's your plan?" Hackberry said.

"I've arranged to have the cellar door and the French doors left unlocked on the patio. Three of us go through the French doors, and two go straight down the steps into the cellar. In the confusion, we'll pop two or three of them before they'll know what's happening. The others will cut bait."

"How do you know that?"

"They're for hire. They go whichever way the wind vane turns. How do you think revolutions get won? You get the religious fanatics and idealists on your side, people with no monetary interest. What kind of weapons did you bring?"

"An AR15, a cut-down twelve, a Beretta nine-millimeter, and our revolvers."

"Y'all didn't end up with any of that Homeland Security money?"

"Worry about your own ordnance, Mr. Collins. How far is Sholokoff's place?" Hackberry said, his gaze wandering out the window, where Eladio was walking back toward the front of the barn.

"Three miles, more or less," Collins said.

"We go in now."

"Impetuosity might be your undoing, Mr. Holland."

"It's Sheriff Holland to you."

"Not here it isn't. The only title that counts down here is the one you pay for."

"Is there any reason one of your men would be using his cell phone while he's hosing down a lime tree?"

Collins's eyes sharpened, but they did not leave Hackberry's face nor glance in the direction of Eladio, who had just walked through the barn's entrance.

"You saw that?" Collins said.

"Ms. Ling's life is hanging in the balance. Why would I try to throw you a slider?"

Collins's mouth flexed, exposing his teeth, his eyes staring at the straw scattered on the dirt floor of the barn. "You're sure about what you saw?" he said.

Hackberry didn't reply.

"All right," Collins said, his eyelids fluttering. "We go in now. Later, I'll clean up the problem you just mentioned. How about the woman?"

"You mean my chief deputy?"

"Yeah, that's what I just said. Can she take the heat in the kitchen?"

"You're really a test of Christian charity, Jack."

"Don't patronize me. I won't abide it."

"When this is over —" Hackberry began.

"You'll what?"

"Find out a way to get you into a clinical study. I think you'll be invaluable to researchers everywhere. We've always wondered where the gene pool got screwed up. Some think it's because the Neanderthal gene got mixed in with the Homo sapiens's, but no one is sure. Your DNA may contain the answer."

Collins's eyes were lifted to Hackberry's as Hackberry spoke. "Once inside, you'll see what the wrath of God is all about. Don't stand in its way or you'll feel it, too," he said. "You listening to me, boy?"

"Count your blessings, you piece of shit,"

Hackberry said.

Krill's plan to get one of his warders into the cell had not worked, and now he was being forced to witness the acts they were perpetrating upon the body of the Asian woman called La Magdalena. He had not been able to pick the lock with the shaft of the spoon, so he had deliberately scratched the metal around the keyhole, hoping the scratches would be detected and a man would enter the cell in order to search for the spoon. But none of them, particularly Frank, had so far been willing to admit to Josef Sholokoff the nature of their blunder, so Krill stood at the bars, staring impotently at the silhouette of La Magdalena, who had been strung from a rafter by her wrists, the soles of her feet barely touching the floor.

"I was mistaken about you, Señor Sholokoff," Krill said. "I thought I had been captured by the kind of mercenaries I knew in my homeland. But this is not so. As Negrito said, you are all *cobardes.* A nest of cowards. You smoke your purple cigarette with the gold tip and blow smoke through your nostrils like a dragon would, but you are a small, wasted goat of a man, I suspect one that has a very small penis and cojones the size of smoked oysters. Do you torture the woman because she rejected you? I have a feeling that may well be the case. A man like you was never intended to touch a woman of quality. Look at her, then look at yourself. She is beautiful and pure, but the people who smuggle your dope and know you say your whores call you a human tampon. These are not my words but Negrito's. He has a terrible fate designed for the *comunista* with the perfumed cigarette. That is what Negrito calls you, Señor Goat Man."

Five men stood in a circle around the woman. Two of them had taken off their shirts; they both had hair on their backs and large hands and jugheads and ears, the light from the bare bulb over the stairs yellow on their shoulders. Sholokoff stood directly in front of the woman, seemingly oblivious to Krill's taunting, sucking on his cigarette, blowing the smoke on the ash so the tip glowed a bright orange in the gloom.

"Noie Barnum made sketches of the drone," Krill said. "I have them hidden in Durango. I can take you to them."

"You missed the bus, greaseball," Frank said.

"Don't abuse the woman further, Señor Sholokoff," Krill said. "I am the one you want. I am the one who can increase your riches."

"How'd you like a can of Drano poured down your throat?" Frank said.

Through the ground-level window on the far side of the cellar, Krill could see a dirt road winding through the fields and rain starting to fall on a line of white hills and a flatbed truck and another vehicle coming down the road toward the compound, a rooster tail of dust rising behind each, the electricity in the clouds flicking like snakes' tongues, forked and sharp, without sound.

"Señor Sholokoff, your employees have been screwing you behind your back, conspiring against you in order to hide their incompetence," Krill said.

"What's he saying?" Sholokoff said to Frank.

"Mike let the half-breed have a spoon to eat with and didn't get it back," Frank said. "The guy was probably working on the lock with it."

"Where is the spoon now?" Sholokoff said, lowering his cigarette from his mouth.

"I don't know, sir. He isn't going anywhere," Frank said.

"You've decided that, have you?"

"It's not a big deal, sir. I'm taking care of it."

"Not only do you make decisions for me, you also decide whether or not I should know about them?"

Krill could see the rain sweeping across the fields in a gray line, dimming the hills in the background, the flatbed and an SUV behind it turning off the road into an unfenced pasture, the drivers circling behind a pecan orchard.

"You hear something?" Mike said.

"No," Frank said.

"I thought I heard a car," Mike said.

"It's thundering in the hills," Frank said.

"Señor Sholokoff, listen to me when I tell you I have the plans for the drone," Krill said. "I can be a very valuable employee to you. Your men are worthless. Look at them. They cannot think. They hide like children from their responsibilities. I retract my insults, *señor.* They were said in hot blood. We are both businessmen and need to behave as such, without rancor, without pissants like these to obstruct us."

"You shut the fuck up," Frank said.

"No, it's you who needs to be silent, Frank," Sholokoff said, glancing over his shoulder at the ground-level window. "I heard a car or truck. Look out the window, Craig."

One of the men standing closest to the far wall rose on his tiptoes to see outside. "There's a flatbed truck out by the pecan trees," he said. "It's probably some of your field hands."

"They're not supposed to be there," Sholokoff said.

"It's some peons, sir. I can see one of them," Craig said.

"Mike, you get the spoon back from the man in the cell," Sholokoff said. "The rest of you come upstairs with me."

"Sir, the woman is about to break," Frank said. "I got everything under control. I'll check around outside if you want, but don't ease up now."

"You received a phone call earlier. Who was that from?"

"A gal I met in the cantina," Frank replied. "I told her not to call while I was working."

"A girl from the cantina? You are always thinking about your appetites, Frank. Do you never think about the man who took you off a porn set and made a soldier out of you? Do you have no gratitude for the life I've given you — the women, the power, the money?"

"Sir, I got on the cantina gal's case. I want to prove myself to you. Leave me with the Chinese broad. Trust me, you'll have everything you need when you come back downstairs."

"You have a great problem, Frank. You have never been able to hide your lean and hungry look," Sholokoff said. "That's because a black heart has no loyalty. You can only think in terms of your own needs. I do not believe your story about the girl in the cantina. Have you done something you shouldn't? Do you want to confess to La Magdalena?"

"Why do you mock me, sir? I've done everything you wanted, including hanging up that cowboy preacher on a cross." Frank's features sharpened with resentment, his cheeks sinking and pooling with shadow. "I'm surprised you didn't have us throw dice for his clothes."

One of the men on the first floor opened the door that gave onto the stairwell. "Mr. Sholokoff, there's a truck and an SUV out by them trees," he called down the stairs. "The maid hauled freight like somebody stuck a cattle prod up her ass. I sent Toy Boy out."

Hackberry and Pam Tibbs and Jack Collins and Eladio and Jaime fanned out in the pecan trees as soon as they had exited their vehicles. The rain was blowing in a fine mist against a barn that stood between them, dimming out Sholokoff's compound. Hackberry held the cut-down twelve-gauge with one hand, the barrel resting against his shoulder, and studied the main house through his binoculars. Pam was to his right, carrying the AR15 with her left forearm partially wrapped in the sling, a thirty-round magazine inserted in the frame. She had strung two pairs of handcuffs through the back of her cartridge belt and had stuffed a twenty-round magazine in the back pocket of her jeans.

The house was massive, the walls two feet thick, built of stucco that had been painted a mauve color, the flower beds bordered with bricks and packed with soil that was as dark as wet coffee grounds, the yellow and red hibiscus and climbing roses and Hong Kong orchids trembling with rain that dripped off the roof.

The position was bad; the angle of approach was bad; and there was too much light in the sky.

The back door opened, and an overweight Mexican woman came into the yard and walked toward a hogpen with a heavy bucket in her hand. Then she looked once over her shoulder and dropped the bucket, full of slops, onto the grass and ran past the barn into a cornfield.

"I think Jack's inside contact just blew Dodge," Hackberry said.

"Hack, this sucks," Pam said.

"There's nothing for it. We believe in what we're doing," he replied. "Those guys inside don't."

"You and I stay together. I don't want any one of these bastards behind me," she said. "They're planning to kill us. I know it."

Before Hackberry could answer, the back door opened a second time, and one of the biggest men he had ever seen came into the yard. His long-sleeve shirt looked like it was filled with concrete; his neck looked as stiff and hard as a fireplug; his hands were the size of skillets. But his face didn't match the rest of him. It was too small for his head, as though it had been painted in miniature on his skin, his hair cut like a little boy's. A MAC-10 hung from his right hand.

The man looked at the slop bucket on the

grass and walked toward the barn, looking neither to the right or left, entering the open front doors and walking steadily toward the open rear doors that gave onto the pecan orchard.

Before he emerged from the barn, Pam Tibbs moved quickly out of the trees, throwing the AR15 to her shoulder, aiming it at the center of the large man's face. "Drop your weapon," she said. "If you don't, I will kill you where you stand. Do it now. No, it's not up for discussion. Do not have the thoughts you've having. Drop the weapon. No, don't look at the others. Look at me and only me, and tell me I won't kill you. I'm the only person on the planet preventing you from going straight to hell in the next five seconds. The first round will be in the mouth, the second one between your eyes. You will not know what hit you. Indicate what you want me to do."

The man with the miniaturized face stared woodenly at her, his skin slick with rain, his chest rising and falling, the blood draining from his cheeks, mist blowing in his face. Pam closed her left eye and lifted her right elbow, her finger tightening inside the trigger guard. "Good-bye," she said.

"I was just checking the yard. I got no beef with y'all," the man said, letting the MAC-10 fall to the barn's dirt floor.

"Thattaboy. Now on your face. Come on,

handsome, do it. You're making the smart choice," she said.

As soon as he was on the ground, she handed her rifle to Hackberry and stripped a pair of handcuffs from the back of her belt and hooked up the man's wrists, snicking the ratchets into the locking mechanisms. When she straightened up, she was breathing hard, her cheeks pooled with color. "They must know we're here. What now?"

"We go through the cellar door. Let Collins and the Mexicans handle the upstairs," Hackberry said.

She took the assault rifle from Hackberry's hands and wet her lips. She looked over her shoulder to see where Collins and the two Mexicans were. Collins was talking to the Mexicans, all three of their heads bent together. Her breath was still coming short in her chest. "Hack, don't let those guys get behind us. Listen to me on this," she said.

"We're going to be all right."

"Saying it doesn't make it true."

"The way you took that guy down was beautiful. You're my champ, kid."

"Yeah, and this whole deal still sucks, and you'd better not call me kid again," she said.

Not only had the two visual screens inside Jack's head gone on autopilot and red alert, they had also gone out of control. On one screen, Jack had watched the female deputy disarm, take down, and cuff a giant of a man without breaking a sweat, patronizing him while she did it. *That* was more than impressive. Six like her could probably wipe out the Taliban, he thought. In fact, he felt a stirring in his loins that made him uncomfortable, not unlike a wind blowing on a dead fire and fanning to life a couple of hot coals hiding among the ashes. *Rid yourself of impure thoughts,* he told himself. *Do not be beguiled by a painted mouth at a time like this.* In spite of his self-admonition, he could not completely take his eyes off the female deputy.

Conversely, on the other screen were images that continued to disturb and anger him, namely Eladio and Jaime trading glances whenever they thought he wasn't looking, both of them as transparent as errant children, both of them armed with Uzis.

"Through the kitchen, boss?" Eladio said.

"No, we're going in through the patio," Jack said.

"The kitchen is wide-open, boss," Eladio said. "The big man with a child's face left it open."

"No, the French doors take us into the dining room, then down the stairs to the cellar," Jack said. "You two will go ahead of me."

"That's not your usual method, Señor Jack," Eladio said. "You are always our leader. No weapon does damage like your Thompson loaded with a full drum. It is magnificent to behold."

"We're involved in a military action here. We're splitting our forces and catching our enemy in a pincer movement," Jack said. "You know what that is, don't you?"

"No, what is it?" Eladio asked.

"The Germans learned it from Stonewall Jackson. They put their panzers on their flanks, just like Jackson put Jeb Stuart's cavalry on his. You boys are family. You think Stonewall Jackson wouldn't take care of his boys?"

"What is this about Germans and rock walls? This sounds like bullshit," Jaime said.

"Come on, boys, let's have some fun. While the sheriff and his deputy draw everybody into the cellar, we're going to put hair on the walls."

"The gringos are not to be trusted, Señor Jack," Eladio said. "The old one dotes on his *puta*. She has a foul mouth and looks at us with contempt. When they get what they want, they will dispose of us."

"The sheriff is a straight shooter. But that's also his great weakness," Jack said.

"He shoots straight? Shooting straight doesn't have nozzing to do with this discussion. You speak in nozzing but riddles," Jaime said.

" 'Nozzing'? Son, you obviously have a speech defect," Jack said. "When we get back to the States, I'm going to take you to a speech therapist, and we'll cure this problem once and for all. In the meantime, Eladio, could I see your cell phone?"

"What you want it for, boss?"

"To make sure we have service here. It's always good to be prepared," Jack replied.

CHAPTER TWENTY-EIGHT

Through the bars in his cell, Krill could see the rain blowing on the fields and the side of the house, and the hills that looked like giant white caterpillars disappearing inside it. Mike stood in the middle of the room next to the Asian woman, who was still suspended from a rafter. Mike was opening and closing his hands, his wide-set eyes turned upward at the sound of feet overhead.

"I am sorry I caused you this trouble, *hombre*," Krill said. "I have been a soldier in the service of others, just as you are. We take orders from little men who never have to kill or die in battle themselves."

"You talk too much," Mike said.

"Give the woman some water. She's done nothing to deserve what has been done to her."

Mike's attention was fixed on the sound of boots moving back and forth on the floor upstairs, and he could not be distracted. His blond hair was long and oiled and hung in strings over the tops of his ears. His eyes were so widely spaced, they looked as though they had been removed from his face and stitched back in the wrong place. He was a man to whom the fates had not been kind, Krill thought.

"Give the woman some water, and I'll give you back the spoon," Krill said. "Then Frank will not be able to use you as his scapegoat any longer."

"Where is it?" Mike asked.

"In the chemical toilet. Where else?"

"Get it out."

"You have to give the woman some water."

Mike walked toward the bars. "You're going to pay a big price if I have to come inside that cell."

"I am not putting my hand in a toilet for you. I am sorry, *señor*."

"Where are your shoes?"

"They hurt my feet. I took them off."

"Get back against the wall."

"What for, *señor*? I am not a threat to you."

Mike stepped closer to the bars. "Get back against the wall, turn around, and lean on it. I'm coming in." With a flick of his right hand, he whipped a telescopic steel baton to its full length.

"*Señor*, you're not going to use that on me, are you?" Krill said.

"Get back against the wall!"

The woman, still hanging by her arms,

lifted her head from her chest and parted her lips. "Give me some water," she said.

Mike looked over his shoulder at her. "Be quiet," he said.

"I need some water," she said.

"You did this to yourself, lady. I tried to be nice to y'all, and this is what I got. Now close your mouth." Mike turned back to Krill. "You move your ass to the back of the cell. Spread your legs and lean on your hands. Don't tell me you don't know the drill."

"Please give me water," the woman said.

Mike turned around again, his hand gripped tightly on the foam-wrapped handle of the expandable baton. "I've had it with you, lady. You open your mouth one more —"

From the back of his waistband, Krill pulled loose the shoestrings that he had removed from his running shoes and braided into a garrote. He flipped the garrote over Mike's head and jerked it tight around his throat and squeezed Mike's head between the bars, pulling backward with all his weight, the garrote sinking deep into the neck, closing the windpipe and carotid artery and shutting off the flow of blood to the brain. Mike tried to work his nails under the garrote while veins bloomed all over his neck, not unlike cracks in pottery. Krill pulled tighter as Mike slipped down the bars to the floor. Krill grabbed Mike by the back of his shirt so he would not roll away from the cell once he was on the floor.

Krill got down on his knees and reached through the bars and slipped his fingers into the dead man's shirt pockets but found nothing. With two hands, he turned him over so that the dead man faced the cell, his eyes half-lidded as though he had been shaken from a deep sleep. Krill got his hand into the man's left pocket and found a folding single-bladed knife and a wad of Mexican currency and a penlight and a betting receipt from a racetrack. In the other pocket was a three-inch iron key.

Krill was trembling as he rose to his feet and extended his arm through the bars and inverted the key and inserted it into the lock. The key was an old one, and he twisted it slowly so as not to break it off inside the mechanism. He felt the tumblers turn and click into place and the tongue of the lock recede into the door and scrape free of the jamb. He shoved the door open, pushing aside Mike's body.

"Hold on, Magdalena," Krill said. "You are a great woman, a master of distraction, the greatest woman I have ever known. I will get you down right now. I never could have done this without you. You were magnificent."

"Don't talk," she said, her lips caked, her voice hoarse. "His right ankle. You must hurry."

"What about his ankle?"

The color was gone from her face. "He has a gun," she said. "They're moving around upstairs. Hurry."

"No, we get you down first," Krill said. He fitted his left arm around her waist and lifted her weight against him, then sawed through the pieces of clothesline that held her wrists to the rafter. When she fell against him, her cheek and hair touched his face, and he thought he smelled an odor like seawater on her skin.

"The holster is Velcro-strapped to his right ankle," she said. "Take the pistol from the holster and give it to me."

"You are a woman of peace, Magdalena," he said. "You have no business with guns."

"Don't talk in an unctuous and foolish manner," she replied. "A shadow just went past the window. Please do not waste time talking. The men upstairs will show us no mercy."

Krill pulled up the right pant leg of the dead man and removed an Airweight .38 from the black holster strapped to his ankle. The woman took it from Krill's hand just as he heard an upstairs door crash open and glass breaking and a burst of machine-gun fire ripping through walls and doors.

"You have to live for your children, Antonio," the woman said. "You have to tell others what happened to them. From this point, you live among the children of light. You become one with them. Do you understand me?"

"I think I do," Krill said.

"No, say it."

"I understand, Magdalena. And I will keep my word and do as you have said," he replied.

Jack Collins pushed Eladio and Jaime ahead of him, through the patio door and into the dining room, both of them resisting and looking back at him anxiously. "Get to it, the pair of you," Jack said. "You look back at me again, you'll discover another side to my nature. You kill everything that moves on this floor."

"We are campesinos, Señor Jack," Eladio said. "We do not know tactics. We do not even know what we are doing here. What is the profit in rescuing a Chinese woman who teaches superstition to our people?"

Jack stiff-armed him between the shoulder blades, pushing him forward through the dining room, knocking over a heavy antique chair, breaking the crystal ware on a serving table. The first of Sholokoff's men to come out of the hallway was bare-chested, his shoulders and lats stippled with body hair, an automatic in his left hand. He raised the automatic straight out in front of him, his face averted, as though staring into a cold wind and a magic wand could protect him from its influence. At the same time, Eladio shouted out, "Not me, *hombre!* Do not shoot. I am not one of them! This is a great mistake."

Jack fired on Sholokoff's man, a burst of no more than seven or eight rounds that blew away the man's fingers from his grip on the automatic and stitched his chest and destroyed his jaw.

Eladio stared in horror at the man crashed against the wall and fell to the floor. Then he stared at Jack, his eyes seeming to search in space for the right words to use. "I froze. You saved my life, Señor Jack. We must prepare to attack the others," he said. "They're hiding back in the hallway. I can hear them."

"Your fear got the best of you, Eladio," Jack said. "This isn't like gunning down a bunch of teenagers at a birthday party, is it?"

"Yes, I was very afraid. I was speaking insane words."

"I wouldn't say that. You always knew how to cover your bets."

"Let us now go forward, Señor Jack. Tell me what you want me to do."

"Just rest easy a second," Jack said. With one hand holding the Thompson and the other holding Eladio's cell phone, Jack pressed the redial number with his thumb. In the back of the house, a cell phone rang.

"You would think your bud would have enough sense to silence his phone," Jack said. "That's the trouble with treacherous people.

Most of them cain't think their way out of a paper sack. Your man in there sold out Sholokoff, just like you sold out me."

"I don't understand," Eladio said.

"Your bud in there didn't tell Sholokoff we were coming. Otherwise, Sholokoff would have set up an ambush. Oh, here's your phone back."

Jack tossed the cell phone to Eladio. When Eladio raised his free hand to catch it, Jack lowered the barrel of the Thompson and fired directly into Eladio's chest, the shell casings bouncing off the furniture and rolling across the hardwood floor.

"Señor Collins, I do not know what is happening here," Jaime said. "Why are you killing my cousin? Why are you turning your gun on your own people? We came here to fight your enemies."

"You're not my people, son," Jack said. "Turn around and walk into the hallway."

"No, I cannot do that."

"Why is that, Jaime? You don't trust your compadres in there?"

"These are not my friends. You are a deranged man. You've killed Eladio. You speak craziness all the time, and now your craziness has killed my cousin."

"Pick up the cell phone and hit redial again. I want you to give somebody a message."

"What message? That you're killing your own people?"

"I want to tell Josef Sholokoff I'm just getting started. Can you do that for me, Jaime?"

"No, I will not do this. I didn't have nozzing to do with Eladio's transactions. I don't know nobody in there. I am not responsible for what Eladio may have done."

" 'Nozzing' again," Jack said. "I changed my mind about taking you to a speech therapist, Jaime. There's no cure for certain kinds of stupidity. It's kind of like laminitis in a horse. Instead of the hoof curling up, your kind of stupidity shrinks the brain into a walnut. We put horses down, don't we?"

Jaime was breathing through his mouth, staring at the muzzle of the Thompson, his nose crinkling, as though he had no place to put the fear and tension coursing through his body.

"You still have your Uzi," Jack said.

"I want to go back home."

"That's what everybody wants, Jaime. Even if home is just a place they made up in their minds. You know what home is? It's a black hole in the ground where somebody shovels dirt in your face."

Jaime swallowed. "Like Eladio, I took money from the gringo to betray you. My family lives in Monterrey. Get word to them that I am buried someplace and that my spirit will not wander, even if this is not true."

Jack sighed and gazed out the window at the rain sweeping across the fields and the wind troweling green and gold swaths through the corn. "Damn if you guys don't always make it hard. Leave the piece," he said.

"You will let me go? You will not harm me when my back is turned?" Jaime said.

"Did I ever lie to you?"

"I will never tell anybody what has happened here. I will always praise your name when I hear it mentioned."

"Time to haul freight, Jaime. I got my hands full. If I see you on the street somewhere, keep on going."

"I do not know what that means."

"It means some people are hopeless. Come on, there's the door, pilgrim," Jack said, and made a snicking sound in his cheek.

Jaime went out the French doors into the rain and crossed the patio and began running through the backyard, his head bent low. He ran past the slop bucket the maid had dropped on the lawn, past the barn and the cornfield, his clothes darkening in the rain, and was almost to the pecan orchard before he looked back at the house. His face was white and round and small inside the grayness of the afternoon. Jack watched all this from the window, simultaneously looking at the empty hallway, listening to the creaking of the house and the drumming of the rain, waiting to hear the whisper of voices or the sound of footsteps moving across the hardwood floors or perhaps a door slamming or an order being shouted. All he heard were the sounds of the wind and rain.

Jaime, maybe you're a whole lot luckier than I thought, he said to himself.

That was when someone from a back window zeroed in on Jaime with what sounded like a fifty-caliber sniper's rifle and squeezed off a single round and sent him crashing headlong into a tree trunk, dead before his knees struck the earth.

Hackberry had led the way from the barn and across the yard, the rain wilting his hat, driving as hard as ice crystals into his face. He could no longer see the patio and could barely make out the stairs that led down to the cellar door. When he reached the lee of the house, his clothes were wrapped around his body like wet Kleenex. Then he heard the first burst of machine-gun fire. He dropped down inside the stairwell and pulled Pam Tibbs after him.

He wiped the water off the dial of his watch. "That idiot went in early," he said.

"I told you he has his own agenda," she said.

He couldn't argue with her. Trying to put himself inside the thoughts of a man like Jack Collins had been insane. Collins had a Mixmaster in his head instead of a brain.

The door on the cellar was made of metal and had no windows. Hackberry placed his hand on the knob and twisted slowly. The knob rotated less than a quarter of an inch and then locked solid. "So much for Collins's intel," he said.

"Was that the Thompson firing?"

"Yeah, there's no mistaking it." He pressed his ear against the metal door but could hear nothing inside. He propped the cut-down Remington pump against the side of the stairwell and took out his Swiss Army knife and opened the long blade and worked it into the doorjamb, hoping to get it over the tongue of the lock. He heard a second burst from the Thompson.

"Sholokoff's people aren't firing back," Pam said.

"They've pulled back into the house. They're going to make Collins come after them," Hackberry said.

"I think something else is going on. I think he might be shooting his own people."

"Because I told him I saw Eladio making a phone call?"

"That or maybe he found the GPS locator we hid under the cookies and fruitcake and blamed them. It doesn't take much to set him off. He stubs a toe, and somebody has to die for it."

Hackberry pushed on the handle of the knife and felt the blade break off in the jamb. "Darn it," he said under his breath. Just then he heard a solitary shot from what sounded like a high-powered rifle. He picked up his shotgun and went to the top of the steps and looked out into the rain. He could see the cornstalks thrashing in the wind and the gray barn against the pecan orchard and lightning striking in the hills, but he could see nothing of Jack Collins or Eladio and Jaime. Why would the shooter of the high-powered rifle fire only one round? The submachine-gun fire had sounded like it was coming from within the house. Why would someone be using a sniper rifle at close quarters against men armed with automatic weapons?

Unless one of the men with an automatic weapon had bailed and started running and someone had tried to pot him from a door or window?

It was foolish to waste more time trying to figure out the madness of Jack Collins. "Pam, any element of surprise is gone," he said. "So this is the way we're going to do it. I'm going in first. Anybody who's not a friendly dies on the spot. Temple Dowling is probably already dead. The only two friendlies we know about are the hostages, Anton Ling and Krill. The servants are probably gone. That means everybody else is fair game. If I go down, don't worry about me. You blow up their shit, and we'll worry about me later. You got all that?"

"Stop playing the hero. You kick open the door and I go in first," she said. "You're bigger than I am, and you can shoot over and around me. I can't do that with you. I can't even see around you."

"You always argue, no matter what the issue is, no matter what I say, you always argue," he said. "I've never seen anything like it. You're unrelenting. It's like having a conversation with the side of an aircraft carrier."

She wasn't listening. She had tied a blue kerchief around her forehead to keep her hair and the rain out of her eyes. Her white cowboy shirt was drenched and split in back, her jeans and boots splattered with mud, and her eyes were charged with light, the way they became when she was either angry or hurt. He knew that in this instance, neither of those emotions was the cause of the intensity in her eyes. She moistened her lips.

"If we don't get out of this one, it's been a great ride," she said.

"It wasn't just a great ride, kiddo. You're a gift, Pam, the kind a fortunate man receives only once or twice in a life span. But you've got to make it out of here, you understand? I've been on borrowed time since the Chosin Reservoir, and at this point in my life, I don't want somebody else paying my tab. I'm going in first, and you're going to cover my back. If I go down, you stand on my dead body and waste every one of these guys, then pop Collins, no matter what he says or does.

But you get back home to tell the story. You got it?"

"What am I supposed to say? You're pig-headed," she replied. "If we weren't in this spot, I'd shoot you myself."

"You and Rie will always remain the best people I ever knew," he replied. "And both of you became a permanent part of my life. How many guys can have that kind of luck?"

He held his shotgun with one hand and the railing attached to the brick side wall of the stairwell with the other. Then he raised his right leg and drove the bottom of his boot into the metal door. The reverberation shook the lock and the jamb and the knob, but the door held fast. He raised his foot and smashed his boot into the door again, then again and again, each time bending the lock's tongue inside the jamb, until the door flew back on its hinges.

He heard the Thompson begin firing again and empty casings bouncing on the hardwood floors and feet running down a hallway. Then he was inside the cellar, inside the damp-smelling coolness that was not unlike a tomb's, inside the reek of sweat that had dried on the bodies of people who had been tortured, inside the dirty glow of a yellow lightbulb that shone on the faces of Anton Ling and Krill, which seemed as wizened as prunes, as though they had already entered a realm from which no one returned.

The first man to come down the stairs from the hallway may or may not have been armed. Hackberry could remember no details about him other than he was not wearing a shirt, that his head was shaved and his mouth was ringed with whiskers, that there was blood splatter on his chest and arms, that his boots sounded like they had lugs on them as they struck the wood stairs, that his cargo pants were buttoned under his navel, that his mouth dropped open and his face seemed to turn into a bowl of pudding when Hackberry pulled the trigger on the twelve-gauge and watched him buckle over as though he had swallowed a piece of angle iron.

The man who had been first down the cellar stairs had not suffered in vain. As he clutched himself and stumbled and fell down the stairs, three more men followed, shooting over their comrade's head, filling the cellar with a deafening roar of gunfire that echoed off the walls, the ejected casings shuddering in the electric light, the ricochets sparking off the stone walls and the bars and iron plating of the cells.

Hackberry worked the pump on his twelve-gauge and got another shell into the chamber and fired a second time at the top of the stairs. He saw the lightbulb hanging from the ceiling explode and buckshot cut a pattern across the wooden door that opened onto the hallway, but his adversaries were already into the cellar, firing blindly, breaking the glass in the far window, hitting the body of a man who lay on the floor by one of the cells, driving him and Pam Tibbs back toward the outside stairwell.

"Hack! The guy behind the post!" Pam shouted. Then she began firing the semiauto AR15 into a dark corner of the cellar, pulling the trigger as fast as she could, ignoring a bullet crease on her cheek and a blood-flecked rip in her shirt at the top of her shoulder.

Hackberry felt a blow strike him just above the hip, hard, a pain that punched through tissue and spread deep into the bone the way a dull headache might. He pressed his palm against the wound and saw blood well through his fingers, then something vital inside him seemed to fold in upon itself and melt into gelatin and cause him to lose balance and topple sideways toward a pile of cardboard boxes. All the while Pam kept firing, advancing toward the dark place in the corner, positioning herself between the shooter and Hackberry, shouting, "Suck on this, you motherfucker! How does it feel? Did you like that? Take it, take it, take it!"

Hackberry could not see the man she was shooting at. When Hackberry fell into the boxes, he saw Anton Ling and Krill and the silhouettes of two men who had made it to the bottom of the stairs without being hit.

Mostly, he saw the cellar turning sideways and the cardboard boxes coming up to meet him and his shotgun falling from his grasp as the boxes collapsed on top of him, all of this inside a roar of sound that was like a locomotive engine blowing apart, like an artillery barrage marching across a frozen rice paddy south of the Yalu River.

The shooting stopped as quickly as it had begun. The air was filled with smoke and lint and dust and tiny pieces of fiberboard. In the light from the hallway door, he could see two of Sholokoff's men standing in the drift of smoke, one with a revolver, the other with a semiautomatic carbine that was fitted with a skeleton stock. He realized that Pam Tibbs was down, somewhere behind several crates of wine bottles that were broken and draining onto the floor. He could not see either Krill or Anton Ling. He found his shotgun among the cardboard boxes and propped the butt against the floor and used it to raise himself to one knee, his side and back on fire.

He saw the silhouette of a small man go across the doorway at the head of the stairs. "Frank?" a voice with a Russian accent said. "What's happening down there?"

"We nailed the sheriff and his deputy," Frank said. "I've got everything under control."

"Are they dead?" the man with the Russian accent said.

708

"I'm not sure, sir."

"Then *be* sure. Kill them. I want to see their heads."

"You want to see their —"

"I want you to bring me their heads," the man with the Russian accent said.

"Where's Collins, sir?" Frank asked.

"Somewhere in the house. You finish down there and come around behind him. This is your opportunity to redeem yourself. Do not disappoint me, Frank."

Frank raised the carbine with the wire stock to his shoulder and began firing at random all over the cellar, the bullets notching the stone walls, whanging off the cell doors, splintering the cases of wine that were bleeding pools of burgundy on the floor. With one knee for support, Hackberry raised the twelve-gauge and fired at the two men who stood at the bottom of the stairs. Most of the pattern struck a wood post, and the rest of the load flattened harmlessly against a wall behind the stairs.

Hackberry tried to work the pump and hold the shotgun with one hand, but instead of ejecting the spent shell, the mechanism jammed, and the spent shell was crimped sideways between the bolt and the chamber. In the gloom, he saw Pam sitting flatly on her buttocks behind a stack of rubber tires, her legs stretched out straight in front of her. There was a bullet wound in her back and what appeared to be an exit wound in the top of her left arm. She was trying to free her .357 from her holster, but her hand kept fluttering on the grips and the leather strap fastened at the base of the hammer.

"Throw out your piece, Sheriff Holland," Frank said. "I'll talk with Mr. Sholokoff. He's a businessman. This doesn't have to end badly. Our common enemy up there is that smelly son of a bitch Jack Collins. Why take his weight?"

Hackberry's side was throbbing, his face breaking with sweat. He could hear glass crunching under the boots of Sholokoff's men as they began working their way carefully toward the pile of tires behind which Pam Tibbs had taken cover.

"Think about it, Sheriff," Frank said. "The people you're trying to rescue down here are killers. They murdered a guy who tried to treat them in a kindly way. Yeah, that's right. Mike was his name. He was a good guy. He's lying dead on the floor now, with shoestrings wrapped around his throat. How about it, Sheriff? How many guys get a second chance like this?"

Frank had grown cavalier about Krill and the Asian woman. When Anton Ling gathered herself up from the floor with the Airweight .38 five-round Smith & Wesson in her hand, Frank's expression seemed amused, taking her inventory, his eyes sliding over her blood-streaked shift, the bruises on her face and arms and shoulders, the gash in her lower lip.

"I had a Chinese bitch of my own once," Frank said. "Play your cards right and I might keep you around."

Her first shot hit him an inch above the groin; the second one entered his mouth and exited an inch above the neatly etched hairline on the back of his neck.

His friend dropped his semiautomatic to the floor and lifted his hands in the air just before Anton Ling shot him in the heart.

Upstairs, the Thompson began firing again without letup, the rounds thudding into walls all over the house, the casings dancing on the floors, as though Jack Collins had declared war on all things that were level or square or plumb or that possessed any degree of geometric integrity.

Chapter Twenty-Nine

Nobody could say Preacher Jack Collins wasn't a fan of Woody Guthrie. "*Adiós* to you Juan, *adiós* Rosalito, *adiós mi amigo* Jesus and Maria," he sang above the roar of the Thompson as he burned the entire ammo drum, hosing down the house from one end to the other, the barrel so hot that it scalded his hands when he reloaded.

He hunted down Sholokoff's men in closets, crawl spaces, and behind and under the furniture and kitchen counters, blowing them apart as they cowered or tried to break and run.

These were the dreaded transplants from Russia and Brighton Beach or their surrogates in Phoenix? What a laugh.

Jack was having a fine time. He even enjoyed the rain blowing through the broken windows. It filled the house with a soft mist and the wet smell of grass and cornstalks and freshly plowed fields. The smell reminded him of rural Oklahoma during a summer rain, when the rivers and buttes were red and the plains green. His mother took him once to an Easter-egg roll behind a church where she had decided to get reborn. For whatever reason, Jack thought, it sure didn't take. In fact, he'd always had the feeling that his mother had seduced the preacher.

No matter. When Jack's Thompson was deconstructing the environment and people around him, he was no longer troubled by thoughts of his mother's cruelty and the strange form of catatonic trance that seemed to take control of her metabolism and cause her to slip from one personality into another. Well, she got hers when she took a fall off the rocks on the property that eventually became his. It was an accident, of course. More or less. Yes, "accident" was a good word for it, he thought. Even though he had been in his late thirties when it happened, the details had never quite come together for him. How had the chain of events started? She had tried to grab his hand, right? Yes, he was sure about that, although he was a little hazy on what caused her to trip and start slipping backward off the ledge. But he definitely remembered her reaching out, her fingers clutching at his shirt, then at his wrist, then at the ends of his fingers. So he was not really a player in any of it, just a witness. Maybe that was her way of airbrushing herself out of his life. One second she was there; a second later, she was receding into the ground, growing smaller and smaller as she fell, looking back at him as if she had just spread herself out on a mattress for a brief nap.

When anybody got up the nerve to ask Jack how his mother had died, he always gave the same reply: "As she had lived. On her back. All the way down."

Jack loved crime novels and film noir but could never understand the film critics' laudatory attitude toward James Cagney's portrayal of Cody Jarrett in *White Heat.* Would a mainline con like Jarrett crawl into his mother's lap? Yuck, Jack thought. The image made his phallus shrivel up and want to hide. And how about that last scene, when Jarrett stands on the huge propane tank outside a refinery, shouting at the sky? Here's a guy about to be burned to a crisp, and what does he say? "Made it, Ma! Top of the world!"

What a douchebag. Didn't Cagney know better? The real Jarrett would have had his mother stuffed and used as a hat rack or doorstop.

Jack stood in the middle of the kitchen and gazed at the house's interior and the level of destruction he had visited upon it. No one could accuse him of leaving the wounded on the field. Everyone he had shot was not only dead but dead several times over. He turned in a circle, the Thompson cradled across his chest, a tongue of smoke curling out of the barrel. The rain and wind were cool blowing on his skin through the shattered windows. On the lawn, he could see the slop bucket the maid had dropped when she was high-balling for the cornfield. Where oh where was little Josef?

"Can you hear me, little fellow?" Jack called out. "Let's fix a cup of tea and have a chat. Did you ever read *And Quiet Flows the Don?* It was written by a guy named Sholokoff. Are y'all related?"

There was no reply from the devastated interior of the house. Jack felt a terrible thirst but did not want to set down the Thompson to pour himself a glass of water. "It's pretty quiet downstairs, Josef. I have a feeling Frank lost out to Sheriff Holland and his deputy. What do you think?"

In the silence, he walked across the linoleum, bits of glass and china crackling under the soles of his cowboy boots. "I checked the upstairs and the attic, but you weren't there. That means you've got yourself scrunched under the floor or up a chimney. I cain't think of any other possibility. Unless you've already hauled ass. No, I would have seen you. Tell me, do y'all have a volunteer fire department in these parts?"

Jack lifted the Thompson to a vertical position and gazed at the ceiling and then out the window. He went through a mudroom onto the back porch and opened the screen door and looked up at the window in the attic area and at a roof below the window. The roof was peaked, and Jack could not see on the far side of it. However, if anyone ran from the house, he would not find cover except in the barn, the cornfield, or the pecan orchard, where the flatbed truck and Jack's Ford Explorer were parked.

"Josef, I think you might have outsmarted me," Jack said to the wind. He walked to the hallway door that opened onto the cellar stairs. "You down there, Mr. Holland?"

"What do you want, Collins?" the sheriff's voice replied.

"You sound like you might have sprung a leak."

"We've got several dead people down here. You can join them in case you're having any bright ideas," the sheriff said.

"You never give me any credit, Sheriff. What have I done to you that's so bad?"

"Tried to kill me and my chief deputy?" the sheriff said.

"Y'all dealt the play on that one. Regardless, I think I squared the deal when I dug up that young fellow Bevins from his grave out in the desert."

"You're talking too much, Collins. That's the sign of either a guilty or a frightened man."

"It's *Mr.* Collins. What does it take for you to use formal address? In the civilized world, men do not refer to one another by their last names. Is that totally lost on you, Sheriff? If it is, I've sorely misjudged you. I'm coming down."

"We need medical help, Mr. Collins."

"Every one of the locals is on a pad for Sholokoff. They'd have you and your friends in a wood chipper by sunset."

Jack stepped into the doorway, silhouetting against the hallway light, then began walking down the stairs, his eyes trying to adjust to the gloom. His left hand was on the stair rail, his right holding the Thompson at an upward angle. Then he saw the Asian woman and the man named Krill and the sheriff and his chief deputy. "Looks like y'all got shot up proper," he said.

The sheriff had stood up but was bracing himself against a wood post, the heel of his hand pressed into his side. "Where's Sholokoff?" he asked.

Jack didn't answer. He crossed the cellar and scraped back the metal door to the outside stairwell and walked up the concrete steps into the rain and gazed at the yard and the barn and the pecan orchard and the cornfield, then at the roof that traversed the area under the attic window. He stepped back into the cellar, rainwater running off the brim of his hat.

"You planning on taking me out, Mr. Holland?" he said.

"Could be."

"But you won't."

"I wouldn't be so sure about that."

"You won't gun me unless I give you cause."

"What brought you to that conclusion?" the sheriff said.

"Your father was a history professor and a congressman. You were born with the burden of gentility, Sheriff: You either obey the restraints that are imposed on a gentleman or you accept the role of a hypocrite. The great gift of being born white trash is that no matter what you do, it's always a step up."

"You're referring to yourself, Mr. Collins?"

"I'd wager I have more education than anybody in this room, but I never spent a complete year in a schoolhouse. What do you think about that?"

"I don't," the sheriff replied.

Jack ignored the slight and glanced out the cellar window at the yard and the barn and the pecan orchard. Then he took a bottle of burgundy from a shattered crate and broke the neck off against the wall. The glass was black and thick and had a red wax seal on the label. He poured from the bottom of the broken bottle into his mouth, as though using a cup, not touching the sharp edges. "You want one?" he asked.

"I don't drink," the sheriff said.

"You ought to start. In my opinion, it'd be an improvement. Who popped the two guys by the stairs?"

"I did," the Asian woman said. She was sitting on a wood chair, the Airweight .38 in her lap, strands of her hair hanging straight down in her face. "You have something to say about it?"

"You decide you're not a pacifist anymore?"

"You murdered nine innocent girls, Mr. Collins," she replied. "I don't think you have the right to look down your nose at me or anybody else."

"If you ask me, your true colors are out, Ms. Ling. You're a self-hating feminist who tries to infect others with her poison. I've been entirely too generous in my estimation and treatment of your gender. The serpent didn't make Adam eat the apple. Your progenitor did. You're the seed of our undoing, and I won't put up with any more of your insolence."

"I warned you once before about addressing me in that fashion," she said.

"Mr. Collins?" the sheriff said softly.

"Enough of you, Sheriff," Jack said, his eyes burning into the woman's face, his hand flexing on the pistol grip of the Thompson.

"Ease up on the batter," the sheriff said.

"I said you stay out of this."

"We all fought the good fight, didn't we?" the sheriff said. "I appreciate the help you gave us. I appreciate your saving the life of my deputy R. C. Bevins. No one here should judge you, sir."

"You should have stayed in politics."

"I *am* in politics. I hold an elective office. How about it, partner?" the sheriff said. "A time comes when you have to lay down your sword and shield."

Jack could feel the fingers of his right hand tightening on the pistol grip and the Thompson's trigger. The rain was sliding down the cellar window and swirling through the door that opened onto the outside stairwell. Inside the steady drumming of the rain and the coldness seeping into his back, he realized the mistake he had just made and the price he would pay for his anger and pride.

He had forgotten about the chief deputy, the one called Pam Tibbs. In spite of her wounds, she had eased her .357 Magnum from her holster and stepped behind him and pointed the muzzle into a spot one inch above his hairline. He heard her cock the hammer into place.

"Put your weapon on the floor," she said.

"What if I don't?" he said.

"I'll cut all your motors," she replied.

"Do as she asks, Jack," the sheriff said.

"He already has," Pam said, ripping the Thompson from Jack's grasp with her bad arm. A surge of pain twisted her mouth out of shape, and she let the Thompson clatter to the floor.

"Y'all don't know who your friends are,"

Jack said. "I'm fixing to torch the place and fry Josef's bacon. He's hiding up there on the roof someplace. If it hadn't been for me, your heads would be on a pike."

"You're done. Get out," Pam said.

Jack turned and looked at her numbly. "Do *what?*" he said.

"Be gone. Into the darkness, where you belong," she said.

He continued to stare at her and at the smear of blood on her cheek and at the wounds in her arm that had painted her shirtsleeve red and at the steady rise and fall of her breasts and at the loathing in her eyes.

"I he'ped y'all," he said. "I made up for —"

"For what?" Pam said.

"The past. All of it. I ate out of Dumpsters and bathed with ash and sand. I wore the rags I pulled off a scarecrow."

"Lose your revolver and turn out all your pockets," she said.

"Why?"

"I collect car keys," she replied.

"That's all you have to say, you fat bitch?" he said.

She pulled his revolver from its holster and slung it into the pile of empty cartons. "Don't go near any uncapped tubes of roach paste," she said.

Hackberry and Pam watched Jack Collins walk into the rain, glancing back at them like an errant child being driven from the school yard. "Where to now, boss?" Pam said.

"We blow Dodge and head for the plane," he replied. "I have a first-aid kit in my duffel. How are you doing?"

"I think the bullet that exited my shoulder didn't hit any bone. Anyway, it's numb now. Hack, you don't look good."

"I never do."

"Is the round still in you?"

"No."

"How can you tell?"

"I can't. But it's time to go home."

"I think you're bleeding inside. Maybe we ought to wait it out. R.C. must have a fix on us. He and Felix and the others might be coming any minute."

"I think the Mexicans found the GPS," Hackberry said.

"Why?"

"Because Collins has contempt for the Mexicans. He never would have relied solely on them. Had they not found a GPS, he would have searched us and our gear himself."

"Look," she said, pointing into the rain.

Hackberry realized he was about to witness one of those moments when evil reveals itself for what it is — insane in its fury and self-hatred and its animus at whatever reminds it of itself. In this instance, the medieval morality play had a cast of only two characters:

Josef Sholokoff running through the rain for the safety of the barn or the cornfield or the pecan orchard, and Preacher Jack Collins in pursuit, driven from the light by his fellow man.

The two of them came together in the yard, sheets of rain sweeping across them at they struck and clawed at each other. Then Jack Collins picked up a stone and swung it hard into Sholokoff's head. When Sholokoff fell backward and got up and tried to run toward the cornfield, Collins hit him twice more in the back of the head, then dragged him, fighting, past the slop bucket that still lay on the grass. In the roll of thunder that sounded like cannons firing in diminishing sequence, Hackberry watched Collins strike Sholokoff again and again with the stone, then lift him up and throw him over the top slat of the hogpen.

The squealing and snuffing sounds of the hogs in the pen were instantaneous.

"Holy God," Pam said.

"They may not have been fed in days," Hackberry said. "Let's get everybody together. I'm going to carry the Thompson. It's not a good idea for Krill to have access to any weapons. He still has a capital charge hanging over him in Texas."

"What do you want to do with him?"

"That's up to him. If he wants to take off, let him go."

"You don't want to hook him up?"

"We'll probably never see Noie Barnum again — the guy who started all this. Why lay all our grief on this poor bastard?"

"Look at me."

"What's wrong?"

"Your eyes are out of focus."

"No, I see fine."

"Your face is white, Hack. You can hardly stand up. Grab hold of my arm."

"I'm right as rain," he replied, the horizon shifting sideways.

The four of them walked out into the storm, the soaked countryside trembling whitely each time a tree of lightning printed itself against the clouds. The hogs had all moved into a corner of the lot in a half circle and were snuffing loudly, their heads down, their hooves churning in the liquescence around them, the bristles of their snouts coated with their work. Hackberry held his forearm tightly against the hole in his side and tried to keep his eyes on the horizon and put one foot after another, because the gyroscope inside him was starting to sway from side to side and was about to topple over.

He had learned to march in the infantry and sometimes even to sleep while he did. It was easy. You kept your eyes half-lidded and swung your legs from the hip and never struggled against the weight of your pack or your weapons. You just got in step and dozed and let the momentum of the column carry you forward, and somehow you knew, out there on the edge of your vision, there was always one to count cadence. *You had a good home when you left, you're right. Jody was there when you left, you're right. Sound off, one, two, three-four! You're right, you're right, you're right! Reep! Reep! Reep! Sound off! One, two, three-four!*

It was a breeze.

"Hack, hold on to me. Please," Pam said.

"Miss Anton is walking barefoot. You don't think I can cut it?" he replied.

"I should have popped him," she said.

He didn't know what she meant. They had entered the barn and should have been grateful for the warmth and dryness it offered them. Then he saw the firelight flickering in the midst of the pecan orchard. He set down the Thompson and the shotgun and walked to the open doors and stared at the flames swirling up from the interior of the Ford Explorer and the cab of the flatbed truck.

So this was both the reality and the legacy of Jack Collins, Hackberry thought. He wasn't the light bearer who fell like a shooting star from the heavens. He was the canker in the rose, the worm that flies through the howling storm, a vain and petty and mean-spirited man who left a dirty smudge on all that he touched. He had no power of his own;

he was assigned it by others whose personal fears were so great, they would abandon all they believed in and surrender themselves to a self-manufactured caricature who had hijacked their religion.

But Hackberry knew that if there was any lesson or wisdom in his thoughts, he would not be able to pass it on. The only wisdom an old man learns in this world is that his life experience is ultimately his sole possession. It is also the measure of his worth as a human being, the sum of his offering to whatever hand created him, and the ticket he carries with him into eternity. But if a man tries to put all the lessons he has learned on a road map for others, he might as well dip his pen into invisible ink.

They walked miles in the rain, into the hills and through ravines and across flooded creek beds, the sky growing blacker and blacker. Pam stumbled and dropped the AR15. Krill picked it up and then pulled the shotgun from Hackberry's hand and placed both weapons across his shoulders, draping one hand on the barrels and the other on the stocks, his head hanging forward.

"Give them back," Hackberry said.

"I am all right, *señor,*" Krill said. "I would not harm you. You are very good people. I like you very much."

"You're wanted for a capital crime," Hackberry said.

"I know. But that has nothing to do with us. This is Mexico," Krill said. "It is a place where everything is crazy. I told that to La Magdalena when I cut her down from the beam in the cellar. I told her she smelled like seawater. I told her she was probably a Chinese mermaid and didn't know it. She thought that was very funny."

"Say that again?" Hackberry asked.

"I'm very tired. We must go on," Krill said.

That was what they did. On and on, through rocks and brambles and thorns and deadfalls and cactus and dry washes and tree branches that lashed back into their faces and cut their skin like whips. The sky was as black as oil smoke, the explosions of lightning deafening inside the canyons. But when the four of them ascended a trail that led to a bare knoll, a peculiar event happened. They found themselves in front of two telegraph poles that had no wires attached to the crosspieces; to the west of the knoll was an infinite plain that seemed to extend beyond the edge of the storm into a band of blue sky on the earth's rim. The wind was bitter and filled with grit, the telegraph poles trembling in the holes where they were sunk, a twisted piece of metal roof bouncing and clanging across the knoll's surface. Krill stood at the top of the knoll, his arms hanging over the rifle and shotgun stretched across his shoulders.

"It's stopped raining," he said. "Look, you can see it blowing like crystal behind us and out on the plain and down in the canyon, but here there is no rain. *Qué bueno.* I think I will stay right here."

"Come with us," Anton said.

"No, this is my place. I am content here," he replied. "Good-bye to you, Chinese mermaid. And thank you, Sheriff Holland and Señorita Pam. All of you are very nice."

So this is how it ends, Hackberry thought. A man under a capital sentence stands impaled in a grandiose fashion against a blackened sky, ignoring the fact that he has become a human lightning rod, while two women and another man gaze up at him, all of them stenciled like figures on a triptych, all of them caught in roles they did not choose for themselves.

Maybe the mermaids have not made it to Texas yet, but give them time, and in the meanwhile blessed be God for all dappled things, wherever they occur, Hackberry said to himself, his eyes fixed on the band of blue light in the west.

ABOUT THE AUTHOR

James Lee Burke was born in Houston, Texas, in 1936 and grew up on the Texas-Louisiana Gulf Coast. He attended Southwestern Louisiana Institute and later received a BA and an MA in English from the University of Missouri in 1958 and 1960, respectively. Over the years, he worked as a landman for the Sinclair Oil Company, pipe liner, land surveyor, newspaper reporter, college English professor, social worker on skid row in Los Angeles, clerk for the Louisiana Employment Service, and instructor in the U.S. Job Corps. He and his wife, Pearl, met in graduate school and have been married fifty-one years; they have four children.

Burke's work has twice been awarded an Edgar for Best Crime Novel of the Year; in 2009 the Mystery Writers of America named him a Grand Master. He has also been a recipient of Bread Loaf and Guggenheim fellowships and an NEA grant. Three of his novels (*Heaven's Prisoners*, *Two for Texas*, and

In the Electric Mist with Confederate Dead) have been made into motion pictures. His short stories have been published in *The Atlantic Monthly, New Stories from the South, Best American Short Stories, Antioch Review, Southern Review,* and *The Kenyon Review.* His novel *The Lost Get-Back Boogie* was rejected 111 times over a period of nine years and, upon its publication by Louisiana State University Press in 1986, was nominated for a Pulitzer Prize.

He and Pearl live in Missoula, Montana.